The Echo Watch

Steve Rzasa

The Interstice Universe

Remains
Mirages
Shivers

The Echo Watch

Airfoil: Origins
Airfoil: Drake City

Mercury on Staff
Mercury First Up

Mercury on Guard
Mercury for Hire
Mercury at Risk
Mercury is Hot
Mercury out Cold
Mercury off Course
Mercury with Style

Become the Past
Tangents

Interstice Undone
(with J.J. Johnson & Jason Joyner)

A Bad Guy

Acknowledgments

I've long been fascinated by the idea of doppelgängers. Comic books, movies, television shows—whenever the topic arises, I watch with interest. Part of the intrigue is watching an actor play their same character with a vastly different personality or in an alternate life circumstance.

That's where Dominic Zein came from.

Simple, really. I was overwhelmed with activities and couldn't figure out how I would juggle them. Wouldn't it be nice to have another me to do those things, so I could relax and spend time with my family, freed from some of life's pressures?

Of course, the story's only interesting if that arrangement becomes a deal with the Devil.

Fyodor Dostoyevsky's *The Double* is a great, taut thriller that provided inspiration for *The Echo Watch*. I highly recommend it as a creepy read.

Special thanks go to Mark Bentley and Howard Ohr, as my primary readers. Becky Dean did a tremendous job singling out character motivations and course-correcting Dominic. My boys, Ben and Nate, were invaluable as early reviewers, because if they don't like a story, I might as well scrap it.

For all my family and friends, well, just be glad you're stuck with me and not my evil twin.

CHAPTER ONE

Every time I walk down Main Street, I see double.

The buildings here share parentage. They have the same red brick, same stone cornices, same number of tall windows. Every wrought iron railing and brass address plate on the south is duplicated on the north.

Clients like Mrs. Dockery couldn't care less.

"You said a slate roof was a perfect fit." Her voice isn't softened when filtered through my phone's tiny speaker. She's just as strident as if she were walking beside me. A tiny dog yips rapid fire in the background. I swear it'd provide more pleasant conversation than its owner.

"Mrs. Dockery, I assure you, the slate will match."

"No, the color's all wrong! There's too much blue in the shingles."

"They're green. Moss green. Each shingle is laced with the color, mixed with gray."

"But they're blue, I'm telling you. I have the sample right in front of me."

I massage my forehead. They're moss green. I opened the package myself and dropped it by Mrs. Dockery's house the same day. She wasn't home. I should have waited for her, because had I done so, we could have avoided this headache-inducing conversation. "Ma'am, if they're not the color you want—"

"We need to change the color. I won't have blue on my house. You know how I feel about blue, Mr. Zein—it's depressing."

If all my clients were as rabid in their opposition to a single color, I'd never get any projects finished. I stow my complaint behind my lips and calculate my fee from this job. Yes, well worth the aggravation. "All right, why don't you stop by the office—"

"I'm much too busy. Come to the house Tuesday afternoon."

It's Monday night. My watch says 6:30. "I can't do that. What about next week?"

"Only if it's Wednesday of next week. I have Garden Club and then my grandchildren are coming to visit. Wednesday is the earliest."

How is it a retired widow has less free time than I do? "All right, next Wednesday. Three o'clock?"

"Three twelve. I'll expect a new color palette."

"We can take the shingle sample outside and see how it appears in natural light, Mrs. Dockery. That should clear up any misunderstanding."

My phone beeps. She's gone. "Have a nice evening," I mutter.

Wonderful lady. Wonderful like a chipped tooth. I switch to the calendar app. 3:12, next Wednesday. Better program it with a handful of reminders. It will take 20 minutes to get out to her subdivision of ranchettes, and there's no way I'm going to be late.

Warm light washes over me. The amber glow is a welcome reprieve from the cold blues of early evening. Rampart's downtown is lined with pale yellow-white globes for streetlights. They top slender chrome-sheathed poles. Way too modern a look to mix with the century-old twinned business block. But the effect is pleasant enough.

Pedestrian traffic mingles all around me. It's so thick a press that, if not for the gold windows, I'd have walked right past the Caerphilly Pub and Grill.

I push open a thick oak door. Sound envelops me—thumping music and rumbling talk. I smell burgers, and steaks, and salt. Shoes squeak on checkered white and black tile. There's a long bar of polished wood to the left, lined with a brass rail. The woman working it must be in her mid-20s, maybe five years younger than me. She's tall, has sparkling blue eyes and long blonde hair tied in a complex braid. She sees me and sends a smile.

I can't blame her. My reflection sums up my appearance nicely—thick black hair combed so every strand is accounted for, golden brown skin, eyes as dark as the bar's wood, black jacket, blue Oxford unbuttoned at the collar, gray slacks. If not for the band of platinum on my ring finger, I'd be ordering a drink and angling for the bartender's phone number in the next ten seconds. Jessica would object, I'm sure. Instead I smile back, adding a mini salute.

Jess should be meeting me tonight, but she can't. Mirror situation of last week, when I had to bail last minute on her evening out. Too many plans to review. She's got a pile of tests to grade.

All this stuff between us makes for missed opportunities.

I find an empty two-top in the back, near the windows and the hall to the restrooms. I drop my messenger bag beside the seat and slump into the chair. The furnishings in here are wooden with black metal supports. Passersby are muted replicants of themselves hustling silently by the window.

"Get you something?" A young Latino man with a shaved head materializes, pad and pen poised.

"Beer. Alaskan Amber."

"Got it. Be right back."

I set my phone at the edge of the table. Something pricks my awareness—the sensation of a person staring at me. First thought is the bartender, but there's no way she can see this table from the front. Too many support beams and booths block the line of sight.

I glance out the window and stare at myself.

It's the same face, the same shirt, same jacket I admired in the entry glass as I came in. The difference is in the subtle smirk. He winks.

I don't wink. Ever.

A trio of women sweep by, laughing, and he's gone. I'm gone.

"Here you go sir."

The beer bottle drops into place at the center of the table. "Thanks." I'm still staring out the window.

Weird. Talk about a funny afterimage. I've blinked away the glow from a camera's flash before. Was this the same principle?

I pluck at the fabric of my left pants leg. It takes me a full minute to realize I've engaged in the habit before I can put a stop to it. Annoying.

"Hey. You see somebody we know?" The chair opposite me groans. Metal legs scrape wood planks. Curtis Marin sits down, his knees thumping the underside of the table. He's sitting twice as far back as me. Everything about the man is outsized—big head, big nose, big beard, big mouth. Like an oak tree with a grin. And stuffed into a massive, expensive suit.

Curt waves his hand in front of me. The other cradles a tall glass of an amber ale. His beard is a thick red and draws even more attention to his head being shiny as a cue ball. You know how they claim you can see mischievousness in a person's eyes? Curt's is advertised on big neon signs. "You saw someone hot."

"No. No, I don't think so."

"Yeah? Liar. You can't keep them for yourself. You're married. Chained."

"I'm supposed to share with my single buddy?"

"Of course! Friends share things."

"You won't let me borrow the Jeep this weekend."

"You do *not* touch Sheryl."

"I was going to take Jess up to the mountains."

"No."

"It's a Jeep, Curt, not your girlfriend."

"No."

"This is why you're single, you know that."

He shakes his head. "No. I'm single because I have exacting standards."

"You do realize there's a finite supply of supermodels on Earth and a very small percentage of them live in Colorado, right?"

"Shut up, Z."

"Seriously, this guy … He looked like me. The guy standing out there was wearing the same clothes."

"Same haircut, too?"

"Yeah."

Curt nods, his expression grave. "That's because it was your reflection."

"Not what I meant."

"Pretty sure you defined 'reflection' right there, Z."

"Humor me, all right? The guy winked at me."

"Naturally. Even you think you're hot."

I roll my eyes. Doesn't stop Curt from laughing so hard I'm afraid he'll shoot beer out his nostrils like water from a fire hose. No kidding, I've been on the receiving end before. "Forget it."

"Hey, sorry, but you're cracking under the strain if you think your reflection's making faces at you."

"Even more reason for me to take time off."

"Exactly."

"In your Jeep."

"Yes—wait, no. No way."

The image lasts well into our conversation. I lose track of Curtis's tales of pursuit—blonde or brunette, Latina or Asian. My brain's too full of tomorrow. Appointments, deadlines, calls, emails. I'll try to make a list. It won't get done.

My phone buzzes. Work email. Great, the Vitalis want a breakfast nook in place of the kitchen island and French doors I spent the last couple days shoehorning into their renovation. They'd like the redesign tomorrow.

"Changes to the plan?"

I nod.

"Which one?"

"Vitali kitchen."

Curt gags. "Shut the thing off."

"Not possible. I'm second in line at the firm, Curt. When clients say jump, I'm the one who answers how far and over what obstacle."

"I figured. That's how you got here." He targets me with the glowing rectangle of his phone. Yes, that's me on the cover of the *Rampart Post*. The headline trumpets, **He's Home: Local Architect Dominic Zein Attributes Success to Immigrant Roots.**

I scowl. Not quite what I said. My parents being Lebanese didn't make me a skilled architect. Hard work and late hours got me where I am. Though I am thankful my family moved here, it happened long before I was a hint.

"Ah, you'll handle it. Always do." Curt gulps the last of his beer. The belch rattles our glass tabletop. The women at the table next to us glare with the intensity of lasers. Guess Curtis isn't in pursuit mode tonight. "Tell you what: Take Sheryl."

"Serious?"

"I can tell when a man's in need—need of four-wheeled awesomeness."

"Three nights."

"One."

"Three."

"Two."

"Three."

"Th … Shoot. Fine, three." His knee bumps the underside of the table. A saltshaker topples. White grains scatter over the edge. "But if you so much as drive near a pigeon, you'll be in my driveway scrubbing his aerial bombardment off by hand."

I chuckle. "Good luck with that."

My phone's notification light pulses. E-mail. Again. It has to be the Vitalis.

"You gonna get that?"

"Well … I should."

"Go for it, Z. I won't judge."

I type furiously in response to the Vitalis. <I can see you in the office first thing tomorrow, 8 a.m.>

Wait. I swipe up the calendar app. No, I'm supposed to meet with Dr. Huang and review the initial sketch I did for their dentist office. Delete that sentence. <I can see you in the office at 9:30. Please bring any additional changes you need. Remember each change pushes the timeline for completion farther down the road.>

Send. The last sentence makes me shake my head.

"Problem?"

"These clients. They won't remember half of what I tell them, even if it's stored in their Inbox. I'll be lucky if they show up on time."

"You need a less stressful job. Join me, my son."

"When you say 'me' I hear 'the dark side,' Curt."

He laughs, the sound deep from his belly. "I'm an engineer. You know, the guy who tells you your awe-inspiring design dreamed up in a feverish afternoon of sketching and CAD play won't amount to a house of cards because it violates gravity. Far as you're concerned, I am the dark side."

"Yeah, because you spoil all the fun of imagination with your pesky reality-based physics."

"You wound me, sir. Walls collapsing in on your rich clients would be way more fun than safety."

"Killjoy."

It's good for us to laugh again. My sides ache, a welcome discomfort.

Our waiter comes back. We get a second round—beer for Curt, a hard cider for me. The latter has a sharp, crisp flavor to it.

I glance at the window again. Just me, reflected in semi-transparency. None of the other bodies beyond the smoky glass bear any resemblance. They're in conversation with each other or caressing their phones as the glow provides illusory warmth against the fall chill.

Curt's right. I'm cracking. Unlike him, all jokes aside, I don't see the out. My job means money. Money means the mortgage gets paid, the car's not repossessed, Jess and I have the wherewithal to do the things we want—when we have time to do them, that is.

"You want to stop by Bentley's Thursday night? I've got some folks lined up for pool. We could do that thing where we hustle them out of their beer money. Good times."

My mind cycles through the to-do list. "Jess is working that evening. She's got a historical program for the museum. I've got to get dinner ready. Plus, there's the restaurant remodel. Tyson and I are tossing around preliminary concepts. If we can settle on one, I might have time to—"

Curt's sigh is long and deep, like a steam train's exhale. "Forget it. Stop by if you can. I don't want you getting behind."

"Sorry."

"Don't apologize. Lock things down. You've got to trim your schedule. You pile on all this junk and, yeah, you get great work done, but what's it costing you?" Curt swirls the contents of his beer bottle. "Decades from now you'll wind up like my dad. Retired, and not a single friend lined up, because he's left them all in the dust."

The words make sense. For Curt, they're a downright epiphany. Doesn't make them simpler for me to swallow. "Easy for you to say. No church council on Tuesday nights, no meetings before the planning commission, no late hours pushing for the perfect drawing for your clients."

"Don't be a jerk. I know you don't like it. Doesn't mean it isn't true."

I blow out a breath. "Yeah, probably. You're right."

"I am." Curt sets down his bottle and digs for his wallet.

"Save it. I'll get this one." Mine's already out, debit card tapping the table.

"One of these days I'll be faster on the draw." Curt holds up his hands as if in surrender.

I chuckle. "Why bother? You really want to spend more money?"

"Touché."

"Don't strain your brain."

I wind between tables. Conversations overlap, creating a pleasant rumble beneath the music pulsing overhead. The bartender laughs at something a pair of men in sharp suits have just said, while passing two glasses of red wine to women in blue jeans and sparkly blouses. She's the same blonde who smiled at me when I came in. She's new here—Cami? I spot the nametag right before we make contact.

"Oh, hey." Her voice stays soft and yet manages to cut through the press of sound around us. "Ready to start another tab? I can have Hector bring you guys another round."

"No, we're good." I slide my card across the polished wood. "Need to settle up for myself and my cheap friend."

Her smile freezes. She's a mannequin. "Okay, um, you're already clear."

My turn to blink. "I don't think so. I don't have a receipt." At least, I don't think I do. A quick investigation of my phone confirms it: no email. No paper in my pocket, either. Am I that stressed, that I don't recall talking with a pretty young woman? Because if I am, my issues are worse than originally forecast.

She laughs, but I can hear the edge. It's the laugh of someone being polite to humor someone else they wish would go away. Maybe she thinks I'm attempting to be cute. "You just paid. Thirty-seven fifty, plus seven for the tip."

"When?"

"Like two minutes ago."

"You're not messing with me."

"About getting a decent tip? No way. You stood right there and gave me your card. Asked me how I liked my job. You leaned on the bar just like that."

I'm leaning on my right arm, elbow down, forearm cocked up. My thumb and finger rub together.

She giggles. "Same."

I do it when I'm thinking. A glance around the crowded room reveals nothing but other faces, most of them people I don't recognize. Curt is invisible from the bar, as is the entire section of tables where we sat.

"So, yeah." Cami shrugs. "Thanks for the nice tip." She hustles to the other end of the bar, where and guy and his wife are sharing a plate of nachos smothered in cheese and chicken.

One of the businessmen sitting next to me snorts. "Wow. That was smooth. Does playing crazy work for you?"

I fake a grin. "Hey, worth a shot."

"It would have worked better if you hadn't just walked out the door like she said. What'd you do, circle around to the alley entrance? That's creepy."

They laugh and ignore me in favor of resuming their political debate. But it doesn't solve my problem. The bill's paid. I'm not out $44.50. This should be a good thing.

I left? And came back?

There he is again. Passing by the window. Same shirt, same coat, same gait.

Me.

I slip between clusters of drinkers and push out the front door. The evening air's so cold it snaps warmth from my face. Music fades. The traffic's roar replaces the rhythm, echoing off buildings. Footsteps of passersby might as well be an army's boots.

There. Half a block up.

I walk quickly, unsure why I'm unable to make myself run. This should be an easy choice. It's identity theft, right? But the weirdest kind. It's like those jokes you see on Facebook, about wishing someone would steal your data so they pay off your student loans. For a moment, he vanishes. Then I glimpse a short, black haircut. The head twists. His profile stands out in a frozen second—aquiline nose, narrow cheekbones, eyes as brown as chocolate.

And he's gone.

I reach the corner. My breath comes out in feathers. The chill seeps through my shirt. I've left my jacket inside.

There are people and cars up and down Federal Street. Many customers are seated at tables lining the restaurants and bars to my left, where stainless steel fire stands fill the roles of their ancestors. The diners laugh, joke, and refuse to surrender to autumn. All kinds of faces shine—white, brown, and every shade between.

None are mine.

I rub my forehead. This is insane. Cami the bartender must have made a mistake. I'll leave an extra tip at the bar. Just in case. I don't want her getting in trouble for a bizarre Good Samaritan's actions.

Curt cranes his neck as I approach our table. "Where've you been? You need GPS to find your chair?"

"No. Saw somebody I thought I knew."

"Gotcha. Old friend?"

I knock back the last of my cider. "I was wrong. It was just a trick of the imagination."

Curt's right. I need a break worse than I thought.

CHAPTER TWO

Next morning. 5:30.

I'm staring at the ceiling and the spectral shadow of the fan. Everything else has the sickly green glow of our alarm clock.

Music seeps under the door. Jess's exercise soundtrack has a great beat to it, befitting a cardio workout. She's got the volume low enough I hear it as a faint murmur, soothing me back to sleep.

I don't remember much of my dreams. Running to the car, running along the roofline of the house, jumping off Palisade Cliffs. My heart races faster than I can drive. I burst back awake with sweat drenching me.

My phone hums. The buzzer jackhammers the table. My reminders always wake sooner than I do.

Everything's a blur until I shower. No coffee for me. My heart doesn't respond well to caffeine. I find myself unable to focus. So, I take a long soak until the steam obscures the mirror.

There's a triple knock at the door. I don't bother to answer, and two seconds later Jess barges in. Even if she wasn't the only other person in the house, I'd know it was her—the squeak of her tennis shoes on the loose tile at the bathroom threshold, the musical laugh as she shakes, the curtains, the shape of her silhouette through its transparency. All are as familiar as my breathing.

"You're up early again."

"The phone won't let me sleep."

The curtain whips aside. Jess has long black hair tied back in a ponytail and olive skin with golden undertones. Her eyes are a pale hazel. I've heard them described as icy, but there's nothing but warmth behind them when they're directed my way. She's wearing a set of neon pink and black leggings, and a black tank top with yellow side panels.

First thing she does is giggle. Then she gooses me.

I spray the shower nozzle back, eliciting a shout. "You're gonna make me late."

"Late only by your own standards. Nobody else is at your office at 7."

"Office hours are for people who slack off." I dry off and toss the towel at its bar. Missed. Second try goes the same.

"Mr. Lack of Coordination." Jess slings the towel into place. "Do you want to go out and get dinner when you get back?"

"No, don't wait for me. I'll help get the stew ready for the crock-pot this morning, before I head out."

"I've got it." Jess wipes water off my chin. Kisses me. "Are we ready for the weekend? Is Curt amenable?"

"Cabin's reserved. Plus, we're getting shared custody of Sheryl for the duration."

"Wow. Did you bribe him?"

"I just said he's gorgeous."

Jess snorts. "Did you get the spot?"

"Our favorite."

"Under the aspens."

Despite the steam clouds getting sucked up by the ceiling vent, and the condensation I sweep off the mirror, I can feel the cold snap of mountain air as distinctly as if we were already there. The feel gets blown away by the rushing agenda of emails, meetings, and plans. There's no way I'll meet my handful of deadlines by Friday night unless I cram.

"Don't forget to pick up Sammy from the vet. He's probably going to be off after the surgery."

"Right. Don't suppose we're going to get our neighbor to pay the bill."

"I didn't ask."

"You didn't?" I pull on my shorts and a pair of gray slacks. "C'mon, Jess, her mutt tried to chew the head off Sammy."

"Mrs. Cortez lives alone. She couldn't have pulled them apart while they were fighting."

"Never should have been out of its house. The dog snaps at us every time we walk to the car or take out the trash."

"Well, Sammy was poking his head through the fence gap—which you said you'd fix."

"Still her fault."

Jess folds her arms. "I'm not going to have this argument again."

I lather up and run the razor down my cheeks. "No need to argue when I'm right."

"Dominic, don't be a jerk. I know that's difficult for you."

"It's only one thing I need you to do …"

"You could have taken care of it just as easily."

"Right. I'll squeeze in an argument with our semi-senile Brazilian neighbor, who prefers broken Portuguese, right before the team meeting, or maybe in-between client visits. I'm never going to move up in the firm at this rate."

It's petty, and I know it, but the words escape regardless. Jess's expression turns to stone. Her lips are pressed tight. I can hear her breathing through her nose. Couldn't be a clearer warning to back off if I'd triggered our home security alarm. Best to shut up and keep shaving, hoping for zero cuts.

"Let me know when you're done," she snipes. "I'll take my shower. Maybe I'll even have time to go chat with Mrs. Cortez later, since I don't have anything better to do today—like the IEP meeting with a parent who never wants to show up, or the review of the unnecessary curriculum change the history department's pushing."

And there's the slammed door. My hand slips. Gives me a prick and a spot of red, glaring like a stop light against the shaving cream. Great. Better get the toilet tissue on it now, so the flow's staunched by the time I have to leave.

It will give us more time to cool down.

We conduct breakfast in silence broken only by the clatter of silverware. Jess's omelet is almost enough to seduce me into apologizing. But my bacon's stellar, too. It's a truce.

I'm out the door at 6:45. Jess waits for me there, wearing a blue robe. Her hair still smells of shampoo. She's got another three quarters of an hour before she has to depart. The scents of the shower snap me back to our argument.

"Sorry," we say in chorus.

I rub her back and kiss her on the lips. "It's okay. I'll call Mrs. Cortez, see if we can hash it out over the phone."

"If you can't, maybe you can duck out from work for a half hour and we can visit with her after I get home. I should be done after 5."

Technically our office closes then, but the odds of me leaving when the door gets locked are slim to none. "Sure. We can try it. I'll drop Sammy at home when I take lunch." Only if I drive at hyper speed.

"Thanks. I love you."

"Love you, too." We kiss again.

The BMW's already running. It's a silver beauty, engine purring with contentment I'd ascribe to a cat, if I ever owned one. Which I've never, because I'm allergic. I toss my laptop bag on the passenger seat, atop scattered papers—junk mail. A quick double-tap of buttons pumps music through the speakers, from the 90s station.

Our neighborhood sits atop Pinnacle, a huge plateau bordering the south side of Rampart. There's a couple hundred houses up here, none of them older than a decade, all of them boasting of prosperity with multiple floors and garages. I follow the winding road past the wood and concrete steeple of the Fort Garman Historical site, dropping down the sharp decline of Fort Street into the city.

Dualpoint Architecture is in its heart, where Fort forms a triangle with Main and Federal. It's a slant-roofed building, twin peaks sloping toward the riverbanks a mile away, with wood beams and stonework stacked in tasteful balance. Mirrored glass on both sides reflects the velvet blue of the vanishing night and the pink-orange mix of the oncoming dawn. Not too modern, not too rustic. It's the perfect advertisement of our design skills.

My office is in the southwest corner, bound on two sides by windows and a third by frosted glass bordering on the hallway. I can see the tiny blinking lights of my desk phone and computer monitor as I pull into the parking lot. Only two other cars in attendance—a blue Camaro and a white Lexus SUV. Instantly my stomach twists. Garrett Kaminsky, the senior architect and one of our two owners, is here. So is Tyson Jacobs.

Wonderful.

The building's quiet as I enter my office. It breathes like a sleeping giant, the ventilation rustling broad green leaves on the coffee bean plant Jess gave me when I got promoted. I don't drink the stuff, as I said, but the greenery is soothing.

Tyson hates the thing. Which is a problem, with him being my superior. If everything were right with the world, I'd already be part-owner, and we'd at least be equals.

I push aside thoughts of career advancement and dive into the Vitalis' plans. Out go the French doors and the island. I save a backup copy with yesterday's date on the file, on the off chance they change their minds yet again. That way I don't have to reinvent the wheel.

The breakfast nook presents a problem. Putting it in the same location will require blowing out a wall, especially if they want seating for six. But if I skip chairs, go for an L-shaped bench around the wall—that fits. New problem? The windows will be far smaller. And they've been adamant about admitting more light.

I tap a steady beat on the side of the mouse as the cursor floats over the icons. Wait … what's the roofline like in this corner? If it has the proper angle, maybe they'd be okay with—

"Knock, knock."

There he is. Tyson Jacobs leans on the doorjamb. He swirls a coffee mug, emblazoned with the black letters "Get Back to Work." A few drops spatter onto my carpet. It's a dark fabric, so it won't show, but it's irritating regardless. Tyson doesn't seem to notice, nor is he bothered by the potential for the same stains to appear on his shirt, which is pale blue with white collar and cuffs. He's got deep brown skin. His beard and mustache could have been trimmed with a laser. When he grins, his teeth are perfectly straight and brilliant.

He doesn't grin.

"Busy, Tyson." I set about extending the windows. Here's hoping they'll both fit and please the Vitalis. "Client wants these changes today. I'm meeting them at 9:30."

"You got time to do that, with Dr. Huang coming up in less than an hour?"

I flick a glance at my Smartwatch. 7:15. "I do, if you'll let me attend to these alterations."

"If you get backlogged, there's no shame in handing off your work. Especially if you can't handle it."

He would like that. Tyson is the other owner, though Kaminsky is majority. Tyson angles for the best clients and the biggest jobs, which is his right, of course. If he had his way, Dr. Huang's office reno would have been his from Day One.

He can't quite stand it that Huang requested me.

"No thanks, Tyson. I think I've got it." I lean back in the chair. He's obviously not going to let me get my work done until whatever's percolating pours out. "What can I do for you? Run out of clients?"

Tyson snorts. "Please. Got enough on my plate with the First Northwestern Bank expansion. Plus, you owe me sketches on the Brunkhorst restaurant."

I slide a manila folder across the desk without taking my eyes from the Vitalis' open designs. "Right here."

"Good. We're on to review these Thursday, right?"

"Any chance we can do it Friday morning?"

"Nope. I got a brunch."

"That sounds like fun."

"It is when it's members of the planning commission." He grins. "Seems there's talk about ratcheting down the architectural standards in one of the downtown districts, which would make it more of a pain for us and our clients. My job is to spend some of our cash to convince them otherwise—you know, by chatting over mimosas."

"Keeps you busy."

"Billable hours are through the roof."

"If that's the case, you're doing an awful lot of standing around. Is your client paying for you to bother me?"

"I don't know who you think you are, taking up these jobs left and right so there's fewer for the rest of us."

"Is there a problem with the quality of my work?"

"You're bound to slip up, Dominic. You do that, no amount of the old man's doting is gonna cover it. Sloppiness makes us all look bad."

My fingers, interlaced on my desk, tighten together. "I resent the implication that I'm getting sloppy. Again, if there's a problem with the quality of my work, address it directly. Quit dancing around your complaints."

"You've got nerve."

"What I've got is a job to do."

Tyson shakes his head. "Fine, hotshot, check your email. You're so good at all this it shouldn't take you more than a couple days to get it done."

Get … what? I minimize the screen and pull up my email account. The inbox awaits with sixteen new messages. The most recent is from Tyson Jacobs, AIA.

"If it ever gets too rough working in Rampart, Zein, I'm sure they could use architects like you in Lebanon."

I glare at Tyson, but he's already gone from the door, footsteps receding down the hallway. There's one for today's scorecard. What are the odds he'll strike out by lunch? Decent.

Back to the email. The message is terse, but as I read it, I'm less concerned with the construction than the content. Procyon Foundation wants to build a new set of facilities on the east side of the city, toward the river. They apparently approached Dualpoint and Tyson snatched up the job, and now he's requesting that I be added to his team. He's already got Anna Syler, one of our other staff, lined up. My lip twists. There's no way I'm going to have time for this, and I'm all set to reply with an emphatic "No" when I notice Tyson's carbon-copied Kaminsky.

So, the boss already knows.

I let out a groan. Leave it to Tyson. He's going to push me into this project and pawn off as much of the drafting as he can. Ideas are his strong suit. Grunt work, not so much.

There's still time to cut him off, however, if I can change Kaminsky's mind.

I plow through the changes to the Vitali kitchen. It's hardly a polished product, but as I print out a draft, I decide it's far from sloppy. There's still a half hour before I have to meet with Dr. Huang.

My watch blinks. It's a text from Jess. <Sorry about this morning. I love you!>

Yes, it was a rough start to the day. We can sort out the mess later. <Love you too. We'll make it up this weekend.>

As I'm walking down the hall to Kaminsky's office, her reply comes back as a simple emoji.

< ;) >

Garret Kaminsky's door is propped open. His doorstop is a shoe-sized lump of volcanic rock, its surface shimmering green and violet with the lamps overhead. I rap my knuckles on the frosted glass.

"Come on in, Dominic. I figured I'd see you first thing." Garret Kaminsky peers over thin, gold frames of thick glasses. He's got one of those Roman noses that remind me of a gargoyle's but married to his craggy features it's a good look. Bushy white eyebrows rise up in greeting. His hair's mostly gray, slicked to one side and parted so straight he must have used an architect's scale. He's wearing bright red suspenders today, coupled with a yellow bowtie. "Have a seat."

I sink into the chair opposite his desk, and immediately wish I had started with hot chocolate, or perhaps something stronger. It must be a trap for unsuspecting clients who think they're going to push their way over on a soft old man. The cushions draw me in, readying me for a nap.

"Procyon?"

I nod. "Just got Tyson's email."

"And?"

"There's a lot on my plate right now."

Kaminsky chuckles. "Which one?"

"You knew I was busy already."

"Yes, I did."

"Tyson's fully capable of handling this on his own. Adding me to the mix will create too much friction."

"Yes, I know. But I also know Tyson runs the risk of pushing the client away if he comes on too strong at the first meeting. That's why I want you in the seat next to him. You've got a better personal touch with the clients, always have."

My chest puffs up at that praise, but not enough to dissuade me from getting out of this mess.

"That said, I wouldn't give you the Procyon job solo, either. Your designs are commendable, Dominic, but you're not quite up to Tyson's snuff. You play it too safe, most times."

"Safe? What about the Welton? The hotel looks like a spaceship."

"And you earned every second of the fame from that one. But most of your work is clean, precise, and … safe." Kaminsky holds up a hand, as if he's forestalling an attack I haven't launched. "Don't argue. Your skill's always been good, and you've gotten better in the seven years you've worked here. But you and Tyson are two entirely different sides of this firm. That's why I'm putting you both on

Procyon. Yes, I know Tyson can get arrogant and lazy, but he's one of the best I've got."

"One of the best."

Kaminsky smiles. "Fishing for compliments? You just got one."

"Thought I'd try my luck for two in one day." I smile back.

"Don't let your ego explode." Kaminsky flips through the stack of papers on his desk. The upside-down label reads, "Procyon," set in thick black type next to a four-pointed white star bordered by twin black parallelograms on the right. There's several bulleted lists in there, along with photographs of very futuristic structures, ones I assume belong to the Procyon headquarters. "Tyson's arranged a meeting with the honchos for this project on Saturday, 10 a.m. We'll have it right here, in the atrium conference room."

I'm nodding along like a good employee until the word "Saturday" stings my awareness. "Ah, Mr. Kaminsky, I'm out of town this weekend."

"Oh? I didn't think I cleared that."

"You did. I have the e-mail response." Because I'm not stupid enough to hinge a romantic weekend away on my boss's memory, which at times resembles a sieve.

Kaminsky rubs the bridge of his nose with two fingers, eyes pinched shut. "Hmm. Well, get me the receipt for whatever reservations you have to cancel. I'll reimburse it. Not really fair for you to lose money on your time off when I've got to chain you up."

"I'm not worried about losing money. My wife and I have planned this for a long time."

"Ah, that's what you're worried about losing. Quality time." He makes quotation marks in the air around the latter phrase. "Not much to be done about that. She'll understand."

Jess will understand? He didn't see the look I got this morning. "I can't just back out of this. Forget the money. If I don't—"

"The rest of that sentence should end with 'Show up for the meeting, I'll regret it,'" Kaminsky cuts in. "Consider this, Dominic: Everybody around here is up to their elbows in work. You know why? Because there are too few people on staff. Why? Because, ironically, the market's still depressed enough we don't have the same amount of jobs streaming in that we used to—and the ones we do get, are not as extravagant, so we can't afford to keep a bigger staff on payroll. Bottom line: I need all hands on deck for the Procyon job, and that includes your hands. Clear?"

I wince. Clear. That's Kaminsky-speak for, "Conversation over. Back to work." "Yes, it is."

"Good." He goes back to his papers. "Get me your receipts, like I said. And tell your wife I said I'm sorry."

As if that will placate Jess.

The meeting with Dr. Huang goes smoothly. He gushes about the office design, offering a few suggestions for minor alterations, but overall, he walks away happy. Which is good, because I only half pay attention to what he says. I'm still steamed about the weekend project.

A hundred schemes circle each other in my mind. There has to be some way to get out of the Procyon work, at least for the initial meeting. Why not let Tyson take all the credit on this one? He wants it. The only reason I'm on the team is so he has more time for glad-handing, and so Kaminsky can keep him on a tight leash.

Which also means Kaminsky can keep *me* on a tight leash.

"Thanks again for all your efforts, Dominic." Dr. Huang holds out his hand.

I blink. We're standing on the curb outside the café. A paper cup steams in my grasp. The laptop bag bats gently against my jacket in the brisk morning breeze. I shake hands with him. "You're welcome, Lee. I'll have Anna contact you for the color matching. We'll get the interior squared away."

"Appreciate that. Monday will do fine. Have a good weekend."

I glower at his backside as he heads for his Mercedes.

The BMW is parked around the corner. I hit the fob but realize I've left it unlocked, again. Well, in this part of downtown theft isn't as big a problem as one might suspect. Federal between Second and Third is packed with the newest stores, the trendiest boutiques, and the most upscale restaurants. I'm hard-pressed to find a car older than 5 years on either side of the street.

In my gloom, I pop open the driver's side door and slide into the seat. It's still warm from my drive over, a welcome comfort from the cold outside. My breath fogs the windshield. I shut the door and start the engine.

"Let's stay put for a while."

I shout in alarm. My hand goes for the knife tucked into my belt. It's a nice, compact model with a serrated blade, made for easy use, but even as I tug on the handle, he grabs my wrist. The shape of those brown fingers is immediately recognizable.

They're mine.

I'm staring at me.

He's wearing a blue wool jacket and a Rampart Sentinels baseball cap, complete with the stylized frontier soldier standing behind a silver stone wall. Nothing like my black coat. But the slacks, the shined shoes—they're identical.

More importantly, so are the eyes. They're the same ones that connected with me last night, and the same ones I saw in the mirror this morning as I shaved.

My eyes.

"You don't look so hot."

There's no mistaking the voice, but my mind can't sort out what my senses are telling it. "Who are you?"

He lets go of my wrist and offers his hand to shake. "Dominic Zein. Let's go for a drive."

CHAPTER THREE

I keep my eyes on the road and focus on Rampart's downtown. The clean lines of the newest office towers and the shining glass of its renovated storefronts soothe my jangled nerves.

It's better than giving the gibbering panic in my mind a focus.

He—I—whoever this imposter is, just sits in the passenger seat as calmly as if we were old friends out on a sightseeing tour. "It's quite the town. Can't say I know much about it, other than there's a lot of people wanting to move here from elsewhere. Featured by *True West* as one of the Top Ten Trendiest Cities, wasn't it?"

"I can dial 9-1-1 and have you arrested in about two minutes," I snap.

"Yes, and that would be funny, wouldn't it?" He shakes his head. "What are you going to tell the responding officers? More importantly, who would they arrest?"

Hearing him speak with my voice is the part that churns my stomach. Everyone's voice sounds different when they're recorded, because the sound's traveling only through air, and not through muscle and bone of their head. People say it all the time, though. "Is that what I really sound like?" To everyone else, it is.

This man looks and sounds just like me. The way he drums his right thumb on the door panel, the cut of his sideburns—they're all familiar.

"What do you want?"

"Me?"

"Yes. I assume this is an elaborate identity theft. Wouldn't it be easier to swipe my bank PIN, or my email password?"

He laughs. Do I really sound so … annoying? "Yes, it would be. No, this isn't theft, and it isn't a hallucination, just in case you're wondering."

I'd entertained the thought, briefly.

"Take us somewhere private, why don't you. Holloway Park."

It's a quick drive across the Van River, where the city gives way to sprawling suburban neighborhoods. Beyond their clusters are giant wheeled irrigation systems, the center pivot kind, just starting to add green to their fields in the early spring. Holloway Park is a broad crescent fenced by pines and oaks. Winding paved paths cut deep into the planned woods.

I park us far away from the smattering of other vehicles and keep the engine running. Really tempted to take another try at the knife— but if he's me, and dressed like me, how do I know he doesn't have one? "Okay, explain. You can't possibly be me—Dominic Zein, I mean. There's only one of everyone."

"Not in this case. It shouldn't be that preposterous. A French photographer took pictures of more than 200 people and their doppelgängers. The very word comes from the German for 'double goer,' and it's been part of the world's mythology for centuries."

"Yes, but … you're not just someone who looks kind of like me." I tap the side of my nose. "That scar, from chicken pox …"

"Been there for a long time."

"How do I know you haven't had it put there?"

"Surgery?" He laughs again. "What would be the point? Dominic, I want to help you, not hurt you."

"I don't understand." And I don't want to. My appointment with the Vitalis looms. There's plenty of work to be done, not only to prep this new Procyon job, but also to figure out how to get my weekend freed up.

"I've had a blessed life," he says. "One that's left me endowed with a great deal of finances and an abundance of free time. None of that, sadly, fulfilled me."

He reaches into his pocket, and I go for the knife, ready to stab and shove him out of the car, make an escape, do whatever it takes to end this increasing lunacy. But he raises an eyebrow, in that same way I do when someone says or does something idiotic. The mirror expression is enough to freeze me. "Just my phone."

I hold the knife, my other hand welded to the steering wheel.

He sighs. "As I said, my life was unfulfilled. What good did having all that money, all that time, do if I had no one with whom to share it? I was aimless—until I saw this." He powers up the screen.

It's another image of me, the same one Curt showed off last night. The same magazine article with the same headline burns a bright rectangle.

"That's how I knew you were out there. That's when I knew what I could do."

"And what was that?"

He gestures at the back seat. For the first time since I got into the car, I realize all my customary pile of papers are dumped there. "Look at all that. You're under a mountain of work. I read the article, saw how many jobs you've done in recent years. And judging by the way you're storming around town, barely paying attention to your clients, it isn't getting better."

"I am not ignoring my clients!"

"Didn't say that, but come on, you can't deny you gave poor Dr. Huang the short shrift. I saw you two. He did all the talking, and you nodded so much I thought your head would fall off."

"This is insane. So, you're stalking me, and I'm not supposed to be worried?"

"It isn't stalking, Dominic, it's research. That's what I'm trying to tell you. That's why I'm here." He taps his phone on the dashboard. "I'm here to offer my services."

"Your services."

"Of course. Haven't you wished there was another of you to get more done? Who hasn't, really? Everyone is drowning under too much work, too many obligations, too many things they have to do when they should have said no from the beginning. Well, I can ease your burden. I can catch up on backlogged designs when you need to go to a meeting. I can cover a client phone call while you go home to have dinner with your wife."

The memory of my conversation with Kaminsky slams me full force. "How do you know about my wife?"

He rolls his eyes. "Don't be naïve. There's a passing reference in the article, and you put far too much personal information on Facebook. She's pretty, by the way."

"Get out."

"Why? You don't believe me? What can I say to convince you? You need personal background details?"

I shake my head. "There's nothing you can say. Anything can be looked up on the Internet—my parents' names, hometown, graduation dates."

"Blood type, A-positive."

"Someone could have—"

"Don't argue. You're being purposely stubborn, because you do believe I am you, and there's nothing you can do about it."

My brain slams against a mental wall. "If you were me, tell me a favorite memory about Father."

He snorts. "That arrogant prick? The only favorite memory you could possibly have is that he's absent from your life."

I stare at him.

"Of course, I imagine having the pool table underneath your place setting at dinner was a comforting memory."

He could have heard about Father being aloof when I was a child, I suppose, but that, coupled with the dining room table—he seems so certain.

"See? I do know you—because I *am* you. You've seen me sitting here doing all the things you do, and you're still in denial. That's how you work. That's how *I* work." He sighs, and the sound is unnervingly familiar. How many times have I done it when Sammy's ripped up a magazine? "Dominic, I don't want anything to go wrong with your life. Just give me a chance. All it will take is one time to convince you, one instance of taking your place and giving you a breath of freedom you couldn't catch."

I stare at my hands, one clasped to the wheel and the other holding my knife—except the blade lies flat against my pants leg. What was I thinking? Was I going to stab a man who looks just like me? A man who, yes, has been spying on me, but who hasn't done anything wrong? All he's done is …

Last night comes flooding back, sharp as a flashlight through my fog. "Caerphilly. You were there, outside the bar and … you were the one who paid the tab."

He nods.

"I can't believe it. No wonder she thought I was insane."

"Can you blame her?" He grins. "It was a pretty good test, and it went off without a hitch. I don't suppose that will be enough to convince you."

"It just convinces me I owe you more than thirty dollars."

He laughs. "This is rough for you, I get that. Tell you what." He opens the door. Cold air billows in. "I've sent you my contact info. Take what time you need. When you're ready, and trust me, you will be, get in touch. We'll set up a couple of tests, so I prove to you my worth."

He shuts the door and walks off. Is he planning on taking a hike all the way back across the river? No, there's a sedan parked on the other side of the lot. It pulls out from behind a dark blue SUV, and he gets in the passenger side.

I tuck the knife away and scramble for my phone. The indicator light trembles, and I can't figure out what's wrong with the thing, until I realize it's my hands shaking. I suck in a long, shuddering breath. Easy. No one got hurt. He didn't do anything wrong.

Right. Except for impersonating me in public and hiding in my car.

I pull up my email. There it is.

From "Nick."

My thumb hovers over the Delete button. One push, it's gone to Trash, and I'm back on my way to work. But the weekend problem looms like a storm cloud. Procyon Foundation. Tyson.

Jess.

I rub my forehead. Rather than deleting the email, I punch the phone number listed in its body. It's added to my contacts, under "Nick."

Maybe. Just … maybe.

I'd better get going. The Vitalis will scream if I'm late.

I shouldn't have bothered worrying. They're the ones who show up fifteen minutes past the agreed upon time. And, of course, the re-design came from her, not him, it turns out.

Which means I get to stand there and smile while they rant at each other.

"A breakfast nook? Are you serious?" Gary Vitali is short, with thinning black hair and a thick mustache. He's shaped like a barrel, and currently so incensed his neck is beet red. "We got a dining room. And the island would take care of seating in the kitchen."

Francine Vitali glares down at her husband as if she's considering stepping over his corpse en route to her goal. She's an inch taller than me, mostly slim, and the beneficiary of surgical enhancement in more ways than one. The black pants and tight silver shirt she's wearing are perfect for a nightclub, but terribly out of place in their dated living room. Everything, from the wallpaper—wallpaper? I just vomited in my mouth—to thick red carpet, screams early 1990s. "I want a breakfast nook. I need a place to have my coffee without hearing your snoring through the walls."

Gary snorts.

"Yeah, like that." She smiles at me, a slow curl of the lips that makes me uneasy to think about standing here next to her husband. "It looks perfect, Dominic. I knew you'd get it right!"

Not going to make eye contact with Gary, that's for sure. "Thanks. Is there anything else you both need?"

"I need you to get rid of the breakfast nook," Gary mutters. "The island and those goofy doors are enough."

"They're French doors!" Francine snaps. "They're classy."

"Then why don't you want to keep them?"

"Because I want the breakfast nook!"

I clear my throat. "Tell you what. Let me leave you with both of these." My folder has two printouts in them. I place both on the coffee table. "Here's your options. Let me know which works better for you."

Francine leans forward—too far forward, with that shirt on. "What do you like best, Dominic?"

I glance sidelong at Gary. He just grinds his teeth.

"I think that's a decision best left to you two, as my clients." I rise and gather up my folder. "Either way, Dualpoint will get the designs finalized and work with the contractor you've chosen."

"Thanks, kid. We'll call you." Gary's got the front door propped open.

And that's my cue.

"'Bye!" Francine calls.

I drive off, glad to leave them behind. Nick's offer echoes in my head. It would have been nice to skip *that* mess. Between the two of them sniping, I could have dropped the papers on the floor and run off to my next task—but of course, that's bad form when dealing with clients. They need hands held, and egos soothed.

Sure would be a change to let someone else do the soothing.

My phone rings. It makes my heart jump. Nick?

Nope. Jess. "Hey, hon."

"Hey yourself. The vet called. Sammy's all set."

"Okay, yeah, I should have time to get him around lunch. Unless you've got a break coming up …"

Jess sighs. "Not likely. My so-called 'break' is full of planning I didn't get to do while I was taking a boy to the principal's office."

A headache, already in bloom since this morning, blossoms full. "I can handle it. I'll text you after I drop him at home."

"You're my hero. How's work so far?"

"So-so. Clients are interesting."

"That bad?"

That gets a chuckle. "Probably."

"Well, go look online at the photos of the cabin. That'll boost your mood."

The headache only intensifies. There's no point telling her yet. If I'm going to fix the problem, it's better to keep it quiet—at least until I can talk to her in person. I'm not dumb enough to ruin my wife's weekend over the phone. "Will do. See you later."

She blows a kiss into the receiver and hangs up.

I slap the phone down on the passenger seat. Great. Just great.

Still fuming, I pull into Dualpoint's parking lot and make a straight line for Tyson's office. It's at the opposite end of the hall. He's hunched over his keyboard, both monitors filled with concept designs. A raft of drawings is spread across the desk.

"Your turn?" Tyson keeps typing, without looking up from his screen.

"This weekend meeting."

"With Procyon? Bingo."

"No bingo. I'm taking Jess up to Estes Park."

"Ah, no, you're helping me schmooze the Procyon people, because that's what I told Kaminsky you were doing."

"You can handle the meeting without me."

He scowls. "Of course I can handle it. That's why I'm part-owner, and you're the hired hand. But you need to be there so the clients can be impressed by our wonder boy. You're the poster for Dualpoint, Dominic, as much as it grates on me."

"And here I thought I was just good at picking up your slack."

The typing stops. Tyson turns in his chair, and levels a finger at me as if it could shoot a bullet through my chest. "There's no slack. There's only the things I don't want to do, that I can pawn off on you because your work's passable. The answer is no."

"Tyson, don't be an idiot," I snap. "I can plow through Procyon's proposal this week, get some notes and sketches thrown together, and have enough of a packet to add to your stuff that it'll guarantee they'll sign with us. There's no need for you guys to have me at the table, let alone on call from Friday through Sunday."

"Did you hear what I just said? Are you really that privileged the word doesn't translate? N. O. No." Tyson pulls a thick packet of papers from underneath the drawings. "Procyon" is stamped across the cover sheet in bold blue, slanted letters. Their foundation's symbol, a stylized star, is embossed beneath. "Study this front to back."

I take it with all the enthusiasm of picking up a dead rodent. "You sent me this."

"Yes, as a PDF attachment, but I figure you'll do better actually reading it if it's handed to you. Besides, it'll look nice atop that collection of trash you got in your front seat."

I skim a few pages. Most of it is corporate BS, but there's some designs and there's the same bulleted list and photos Kaminsky had on his desk. "I'll get you everything you need by Friday morning."

I'm halfway out the door when he barks, "You'll be there Saturday, or you'll be job-hunting."

That halts me with one hand on the frame. A cold, heavy sensation sits in the pit of my stomach. He's never threatened dismissal before. Not even at his angriest. Yet when I face him again, Tyson isn't glaring at me. He doesn't show any emotion, just a cold, blank expression. "Kaminsky won't let that happen."

"You sure about that? Call my bluff." Tyson returns to whatever he's typing. "Be there at quarter to ten, so we can review our game plan with Anna. I don't want any slip-ups. Make sure you're at your perky immigrant best, Dominic, or you'll be teaching finger painting to preschoolers."

He must be really done, because even though I linger there for a few seconds, my pulse accelerating, he ignores me as thoroughly as the mess on his desk. My fingers grip the door and, for a moment, my imagination flashes me through slamming it shut with such force the glass shatters.

That would go over well.

Instead I storm back to my office and plow through the work I need to get done. I search up every building Procyon's done, sweep across each page of that stupid printout, and mark off every point of interest I can use to make the presentation a hit. It does nothing to cool my ire, which builds until my pen rips a gash across an entire sheet of Procyon's futuristic buildings.

I spin my chair around and stare out the window. The view is filled with Rampart's skyline. How many of those structures bear my imprint? How many were dreamed up from my imagination? I count five, at least, with many more below the horizon.

No way Tyson's going to push me out.

But I can't let the weekend go unavenged. Jess will be heartbroken.

My phone sits on the windowsill. I snatch it from the edge, hit the Contacts list.

Nick's number is the most recent addition.

It's crazy. No way. But I'm desperate—desperate to keep up my pace, without driving myself over the edge because of stress.

What's that saying about cake and eating it?

I dial.

"That was quick."

"If we're going to try this, I set up the test," I say.

"Name the time and place."

I exhale. "Meet me at the post office."

CHAPTER FOUR

I meet Nick—me, as he claims to be—at the Boswell Building down the block from the post office. It's a steel and glass office tower, positioned at a 45-degree angle to the street. The whole of the post office is reflected perfectly, a pale sandstone building sprawled across the far end of the block. The American flag flaps in the breeze.

"You call me, and I'll pick up, so I can keep the phone on during the entire transaction." Nick still wears the ball cap, though up close and outside the parked BMW I can make out more details of his face. There's a few wrinkles at the corners of his mouth I don't recognize, and a couple extra gray hairs—or am I merely forgetting? With the two of us reflected on the Boswell's windows, there's four Dominic Zeins in conversation.

"So I can listen in? All right." I glance at the fluttering flag.

"Second thoughts?"

"Why do you ask?"

"Your left pant leg. A bad habit, but I can't break it, either."

He's right. My forefinger and thumb on my left hand tug at the material along the seam. I glare at him and stuff both hands into my pockets.

Nick chuckles. "There's no pressure, Dominic. Call it off, if you like. We can always try somewhere else, on another day. But when you called, I gathered by the sound of your voice it was an urgent matter."

"That's putting it mildly."

"Work or home?"

"Both, and the conflict between them."

"Ah. That's never good." He smiles. "I envy you. Never been married. Always been a single fellow and had decent enough luck with the ladies to avoid loneliness. Marriage, though …well, it's always been an unreachable goal."

The conversation isn't easing my nerves about the weekend meeting and cabin trip, which both approach with each passing second. "Let's get this done. If you can pull a fast one in the post office, I'll be willing to take it a step further."

"I don't see it as a potential problem. That lovely bartender thought us similar enough."

"Okay, fine, but Margie Cho has handed me my mail since we moved to Rampart."

"Seven years."

I raise an eyebrow.

"Come on, Dominic, this tactic of acting surprised every time I comment on your biography is taxing. I've studied up. The Internet is a great place. Plus, it helps I've conducted a few quiet test runs prior to the Caerphilly."

The thought sends a trickle of sweat down my shirt. "You've been … me? Elsewhere? With someone else? You didn't have my permission!"

"Relax. I ordered tea and hot chocolate a few places I'd seen you at. Half-Full, for one. The kid there knew what I wanted before I had two words out of my mouth."

I rub my forehead. Pressure builds in my temple. "You can't just pretend to be me like that."

"I realize that, but I had to try it myself. Don't strain your brain."

The words root me to the pavement. It's the same thing I said to Curt last night—the same phrase I needle him with when I've one-upped him, especially at pool. "How'd you know that?"

"Know what?"

"Strain your brain."

He gives me a raised eyebrow that indicates I'm the crazy one. "I say it all the time. In fact, I should probably cut back, because people give me dirty looks—but not like the one you're doing."

"No. No, I'd keep that one."

"See? Another indicator this was preordained." He gestures at the post office. "Shall we?"

"Fine. But I'm going to stand somewhere I can see you." Right now, we're between the building and several tables clustered behind a burnished metal fence with wood posts. Akaiyama, a sushi bar, takes up half the Boswell's bottom floor. They're only open for dinner this early in the week, so the umbrellas are furled, shielding us from the passers-by behind a forest of red and white stripes. "Give me the hat."

"Fair enough." He hands me the ball cap, which I press to my head. I doff my jacket and swap with him. The sleeves and torso fit as well as any piece of clothing I own.

Nick gives me a pair of sunglasses from his pocket, dense black shades. I put them on. The quasi-spy disguise seems ridiculous. On the other hand, Nick appears just as I did in the bathroom mirror this morning. Somewhere between our first meeting and this one, he's found a shirt that matches mine.

"Not together," he says. "Give me time to get to the steps, then cross over and follow me."

I nod. He heads up the street. Does he walk like I do? I can't tell if his gait approaches mine. He does swing his right hand, with the left tucked in his pocket.

I realize I'm standing the same way.

My phone buzzes. I duck between a rare gap in traffic, making my way up the opposite sidewalk. The phone buzzes again, insistent.

Nick mounts the stairs.

I pick up the call and dig around for earbuds. I've got a Bluetooth one, for when music strikes my fancy during long, silent hours after closing. It rests snug in my ear. Distant, echoing footsteps filter through.

I follow his path up the steps.

There's a double vestibule of glass framed in brass. Post office boxes wrap in and around walls, in an M shape. Footsteps rap on marble floors. I find a long shelf full of government pamphlets, scattered around a blank space usually reserved for tax forms. There haven't been physical copies from the IRS for a couple of years now.

A few local organizations, such as the library, have their newsletters stacked on one corner. I page through one, making sure I'm turned at enough of an angle to see down to the main counters.

Margie Cho looks up at everyone who drops off letters and packages except for children. She's perpetually beaming, which marks her as an oddity among her postal employees. There isn't a single smile on a pallid or dark face in the building. My heart thuds as Nick waits his turn in line. For me, this would be a cinch—I have a standing arrangement with Margie to hold any packages addressed to me. In return I drop off drawings for a deck she and her retired husband have fiddled with off and on for four summers.

She'll never fall for him.

Nick steps to the counter, and smiles—not a grin, but a polite curl of the lips.

Eerie.

"Hello, Dominic." Margie's smile broadens. Her voice is tinny through the Bluetooth earpiece. "Running early today?"

"You know how it gets." Nick points to the clock above her. "Time's not stopping for anyone, is it? Got to grab the mail and drop off some sketches for another client."

Sketches. My eyes widen. He doesn't have any sketches for her today. If Margie's put off by that …

"So where are my latest ideas? Gal can't stand here all day for her health."

"Yeah, well, I'm empty today." Nick leans on the counter. "Can I take a raincheck?"

She shakes her head. "And still get your mail? You are demanding, aren't you?"

"That is why I'm great." Nick flashes a grin at her.

I wince. That's not how I'd do it. I've begged off before, but not so showy, not so …

"Oh, all right. I suppose—but only if you bring me two next week."

"Two, definitely. But three if you're lucky." He winks.

Margie chuckles all the way back to the mailroom. I can't see her retrieve my mail, but the whole time she's gone, Nick taps out something on his phone. Whatever it is, it's verbose—his fingers fly so fast he has to have typed a paragraph. He only breaks concentration when Margie returns with a handful of magazines and a stack of envelopes. Nick takes them, flips through the topmost. "Ack. Bills."

"Nobody likes those. I'll see you next week."

"Yes, yes, you will, my dear. Farewell."

She's still laughing as he saunters out of the mailroom. It's all I can do not to trip him as he goes by. Yes, he managed. Barely. He could have blown it.

So what? Why did that frustrate me? If he had, I could have told him to get lost. Then I'd be back to my problem of Procyon versus the weekend with my wife. That was a situation I wanted desperately to resolve.

Yet watching me be me, and not have it actually *be* me …

Nick waits for me back at the car. He's already opened the mail, and scowls at the contents of the bill. "You're paying that much for your Internet service? Seems like a rip-off."

"Hey." I snatch it from him. "It's a federal offense to read somebody else's mail."

"Only if it is someone else's."

"Stop that!" I grab his collar and pull him in close. "What was that in there? You weren't being me! Margie was—"

"Completely fooled." Nick breaks from my grip. He smooths his collar, seemingly unruffled by my irritation. "Look, I've proved my point, twice now. First a stranger, then someone who knows you as an acquaintance."

I lean against the BMW. My head's spinning. What am I doing here? What am I even trying to prove?

Nick folds his arms. There's a glint of something on his right wrist—an armband. Not a fitness tracker, like many of my colleagues wear, but decorative. It's a silver metal that shimmers with streaks of violet and green depending upon how the sun hits it. Reminds me of a mussel shell held aloft at the beach. It's wide, too, probably two inches. But who am I to begrudge a wealthy man's accoutrements? "Why did you even call me? If you're playing around, I'm not going to wait. I do have better things to do, Dominic, but I'm putting all those on hold so I can help you."

I run my hands through my hair. Breathe. It's all under control.

"Okay, I'm going to take off. You obviously need some time." Nick thumps his fist on the car window. "Are there any further questions?"

"No. You did what you said you could do." A woman walking by, deep in conversation on her cell phone, glances at us. She doesn't seem perturbed by our proximity. None of the people strolling the sidewalk at lunchtime do.

Lunchtime.

The vet.

I whip off the ballcap and hand Nick the sunglasses. "My coat."

He doffs it, swaps for the blue jacket, smiling the entire time. "Forget something?"

"Wouldn't be the first time." I slide into the driver's side. "Wait … do you need a ride?"

He waves me off. "Get going. I'll catch lunch somewhere."

I roar off from the curb. Nick's visible in the rear-view mirror. He waits on the street corner, one hand in his jacket pocket, the other's tapping away on his phone. An SUV pulls up. The same navy-blue model from our meeting in the park. All I can see is the city skyline reflecting across the windshield. Must be nice to have a personal driver.

Of course, my doubts whisper deep in my head, *you could have something like that if you take him up on his offer.*

The young man working the front desk at the veterinary office frowns through a beard that's far too big for someone so thin. "Did you get our text reminder?"

"Yes, and I was already on my way. Is Sammy ready?"

Wordlessly, he goes into a side room and emerges with a big Black Lab dragging him along by the leash. Sammy slams into me, not content with me rubbing his head and behind the ears. He's got to plant his paws on my chest and lick my face.

He whines in the backseat until I wind a window partway for him. Only when he can stick his head out at passing traffic does he enter a happy, slobbering trance.

I drop him at home, pausing just long enough to zip through the kitchen and grab a half-sandwich from the refrigerator. Salami and cheese on rye. It's cold, sure, but that and a bag of chips are going to have to suffice. The aroma of the stew Jess tossed in the crock pot tortures me the whole way out to the car and back down into Rampart proper.

Traffic's so badly backed up on Federal I eat my lunch and answer two emails before I steer into Dualpoint's parking lot. Tyson's there, twirling his keys. My stomach turns. Doesn't he have anything better to do?

"I'm listening," he says as soon as I clear the car door.

"To ... what?"

"To whatever you're going to offer me to make the whole weekend problem go away." He brushes something off the end of his sleeve. "Like, say, taking over the entire Brunkhorst project plus another one I've got on the back burner."

"You're kidding. I'm swamped as it is."

"Me too. Difference is, I ain't married and I don't have a woman who expects a nice weekend away."

"I'm not taking on any of your work, Tyson. Forget it. You'll get your Procyon stuff on time."

"I'd let you off the hook if you made it worthwhile."

There we go. I glance at his shining watch, his name brand shoes. Rumors abounded about his taking payoffs for various and sundry things. He'd never approached me outright before. Part of me is flattered. The other part of me wants to run him over. "I've got work to do."

"Yeah, I guess so. Enjoy lunch!"

Great. My burden's increased to the point our part-owner thinks it's a good idea to solicit me for a bribe.

I fantasize about going to Kaminsky with my concerns, but where would that get me? No closer to part-owner myself, that's certain. Never mind. Better to keep this conflict between me and Tyson and keep the boss happy. Which means not only do I have to appease Tyson, but I have to pretend like we have a decent working relationship in front of the man who can determine the fate of my career.

I shake my head.

The rest of the afternoon is a blur, with projects and sketches and phone calls mingling into a never-ending stream. Five o'clock looms on the horizon like a mushroom cloud. Why, I don't know. It isn't as if any of us besides the front desk staff are leaving on time.

My phone buzzes, right in the middle of composing my first draft of a design concept for the Procyon building. The image of a broad, sweeping building with a sharp, curving wall blinks out of my mind.

It's Nick. <Ran into your buddy Tyson.>

All thoughts slam to a halt. <What did you say? Tell me it was nothing.> My fingers pound on the keys.

<He made a puzzled comment about my jacket and wondered why you were back out of the office. Thought you were swamped. I told him I needed a break.>

I moan. <You're going to get me fired.>

<Not at all. He started blabbing about expecting you to pay him for getting out of whatever meeting is coming up this weekend. I told him not to worry, because I'd taken care of it.>

The words burn up out of the phone screen. This is insane. I should be on the phone to the cops.

Like he said, though … Who's going to believe me? More importantly, the imposter could turn around and say I was the fraud. <Shut up. Shut up and stay hidden, or whatever it is you do when you're not me.>

<Relax. It's done. I'll be at your meeting. You've got three days to get me up to speed.>

<No, Nick.>

No response.

<This isn't going to work!>

Still nothing.

I slap the phone on the desk. This is turning into a complete mess.

And yet … he did well pretending to be me at the post office. He also, apparently, pulled one over on Tyson. That's not an easy task. The man can dig through any nonsense, and as I'd experienced, isn't easily swayed.

I push the worries aside, making room only for the whisper that says, *Maybe. It could work. Give it a try.*

What's to lose?

I'd have a much happier wife, that's for sure.

It's been dark for hours by the time I get home.

The cold wind gives way to warm smells of slow-cooked brisket and vegetables that have stewed in the sauce. Sammy barks twice, tail wagging, circling me like a fighter plane escorting a heavy-laden bomber. My back aches and my eyes burn.

"Where've you been hiding all day?" Jess greets me with a kiss. It banishes the last vestiges of cold from my face.

I catch a hint of wine on her breath. "What, no glass?"

"It's on the counter, right next to mine." She winks. "Hint: It's the less-full one."

Her phone's out on the granite countertop of the island. Pop music trickles out. A fresh loaf of bread awaits cutting under the cabinets next to the fridge. Beyond the kitchen, the dining room table is set. Neighborhood lights twinkle against a black sky, over the shadowy outline of our backyard fence. Sliding doors open onto a deck, its contents covered against winter's onslaughts.

"I'll get Sammy his food." My laptop bag goes on the counter. Sammy escorts me to the pantry for a can of his favorite. The label says it contains salmon but it sure doesn't smell like the stuff I've had downtown.

"Thanks." Jess takes a sip of wine, then reaches for a knife. "How was work?"

"Oh, you know. Work." My phone buzzes. It's tucked in my bag, not my pocket, but the sound is unmistakable, an angry bee trapped in the pouch. Still makes my leg vibrate. Ghost of the familiar.

"Come on, you know the drill—name one interesting thing."

I snag the full glass of wine and toss back more than one's supposed to sip. Sammy whimpers. He pushes his nose against the drawer nearest the pantry, then scrapes it with his paw. "I know where the can opener is. Maybe I should train you to use it."

He barks, tongue lolling. No sooner does the can pop open than he's seated on his haunches at his bowl, erect as a soldier on guard duty.

"Avoiding the question." Jess's knife saws through bread.

"No, just thinking." Thinking about my doppelgänger, the one who's successfully impersonated me a handful of times in a couple days, as a spoon scrapes out the last of Sammy's so-called "salmon" dinner. "We've got a big new client, some private foundation called Procyon. I'm supposed to have the first meeting with them."

"Oh, that's good. Solo?"

"No."

Something about the way I say the word triggers her concern, because she pauses sawing bread to look over her shoulder. "With Tyson?"

I nod.

"Well that sucks." She raises her wine glass in salute. "I'd say it isn't as bad as arguing with a second-grade girl who's barricaded herself in the stall of a restroom about why she can't throw her assignments when they don't turn out right, but you might have me beat."

"Tyson's a smart guy. Probably smarter than her." The wine's dry, but I prefer that. My phone goes off again. Speak of the devil …

"It's going to explode if you don't answer," Jess teases.

"Funny girl." I take her hand and kiss the knuckles but reach around her for the phone. It isn't a call, though, or a text. Just a reminder.

I have to be somewhere in half an hour.

"You've got to be kidding." I rub my forehead. "Stewardship committee, for church."

"Oh." Jess checks the calendar on the fridge. The white squares are filled with notes written in flowing blue cursive, a constant stream of events cataloging our lives. She keeps them with such fervor I wonder if she's ever even opened the calendar app on her phone. "Yes, it's right there. Seven o'clock, St. Lucius."

Today's fatigue batters at the sides of my head. "Okay. I'd better get a plate and get shoveling."

"Don't worry about it." She says that, yet the words don't sound like what they spell. "Go ahead and spoon it out for us. I'll get the bread to the table."

We start eating, in a semi-comfortable silence. Sammy licks his bowl clean and lies down by the edge of the dining room. There's no fence but he stays at the boundary. He knows he might get something. Waiting for the scraps to be thrown by a generous hand.

That sets me to fuming about the situation with Tyson. Why should I continually bow down to him, when I'm every bit as talented?

I get tired of waiting for my scraps.

"Hey. When the meeting's over, let's watch a movie." Jess smiles. "We can pull up something on Netflix. Something fun, silly, relaxing."

I can't stifle a grin. "We're behind on the one with the British people who look at houses all day and never wind up buying one."

Jess snorts. "Oh, come on, you know that drives me crazy. They never make a decision! And no one says what they do after! It's the complete opposite of an American show!"

The lamplight makes her hair gleam, her eyes glow. It catches on the lines of her blouse and the curve of her neck.

And here I am, fifteen minutes from going to a meeting with a bunch of old men worried about how we're going to pay for a Sunday school classroom. It's my responsibility. I should walk away. But that would be admitting failure. That would be giving up. There's people who depend on me to get things done.

There's also my wife.

"You mind if I make a quick call? It won't take long."

"Not supposed to do phones at the table."

"True, but if I do, we can make movie night start earlier."

"Ooh, a negotiator." She taps her fork on the plate. "Okay. Permission granted."

My turn to chuckle. "Give me one second."

Away from the table, in the dark quiet of the living room, I dial Nick's number.

"Evening. What's the decision?"

"I have a meeting tonight. I want you to go in my place."

"Hmm. No worries if I read something meant only for your eyes?"

"It's my church's Stewardship committee. Nothing complex. Just sit there and nod. When Harold Kana complains about whether or not the offerings this month will be enough, tell him not to worry. We've made plenty before. This season's always slow."

"Check. Easy enough to remember. Anything else?"

"I'll text you a link to the committee's page on the St. Lucius

Maron Church website. It'll help you learn their faces."

"Good. I can keep the page open on my phone. I take it the meeting's soon."

"Seven."

"Okay, I'll be there. Don't fret, Dominic. It'll be fine. I'll report in tomorrow morning. You enjoy your evening at home. Stay calm."

"Thanks."

"Thank you."

He hangs up. Immediately there's a lightness to my chest. Hadn't even noticed the weight, until it lifted. I didn't have to go anywhere. Work could stay away this night.

Jess is nudging her food around the plate. She doesn't see me come back in, not at first. Her fork scrapes porcelain. She stares at the meal, as if seeing through the table. It isn't until I step into the dining room that she looks up, her expression brightening like the sun dawning.

"New plan: Take my time with dinner and we'll fire up a full movie tonight." I salute her with the wine glass.

"Really?" She smiles. "What about your meeting?"

I take a long sip. Part of me is still anxious about the coming proceedings. Can't fathom what kind of mess I'll be in if Nick makes a misstep. Then again, how bad could it be? Don't we all have days in which our co-workers, friends, even family note a marked change in personality? Such a change can be attributed to any number of things, from a bad night's sleep to frustration over personal goals to even indigestion.

Whatever concerns I have are buried under an avalanche of exhaustion. Forget that. "Turns out I didn't have to go. That leaves us the evening together."

An hour later, with Jess curled up next to me in the dark on the living room couch, I immerse myself in a slow, soothing love story. Second glass of wine warms my insides. Jess's hand warms my chest.

"Are we all set for this weekend?" she asks.

I picture Nick's smiling face—my face.

"Yes, should be ready to go," I say.

CHAPTER FIVE

The Vitalis are the first voicemail of the day on my phone, before I can even get to the office. They've requested a third option for their kitchen, because apparently it requires too much brainpower to decide between the original design and the new breakfast nook.

"If we don't come up with something else, she's gonna rip my head off," Gary grumbles through the tiny speaker. "And if I'm dead, I can't very well pay you."

Francine snaps something at him in the background. I roll my eyes. It is a good thing these two are keeping current on their bills, or else I'd recommend to Kaminsky we tell them perhaps they need a different architectural firm—not that they'd have an easy time finding one. All the others in Rampart are as neck deep as us.

"We'll need to look at those on Friday, so we'll stop by the office." He hangs up.

"No time, no call back instructions." I shove the phone aside and pull up the kitchen designs. A couple swift clicks of the mouse empty the frame within those walls. Round Three.

My intercom beeps. "Yeah?"

"Hey Dominic, you have a second?" Anna Syler. She handles interior decorating for the firm. "I wanted to talk with you about Dr. Huang's remodel. If you're not busy."

"Not busy? Wait, is there such a thing?"

She snickers.

"Sure, drop on by."

Anna's office is just off the front entry, next to a work room arranged with all kinds of samples—carpet, paint swatches, marble chips, and the like. She shows up at my door carrying a large tablet and stylus. She's tall as me, with long brown hair and longer legs. The floral skirt and purple blouse are in sharp contrast to her eyes, blue as sapphires.

She sits opposite me and tilts her head. "Something's wrong."

"Obvious, is it?"

"You're glowering more than usual."

"Vitalis."

She winces. "Sorry."

"Yeah, well, occupational hazard. What've you got?"

"Four color schemes for Dr. Huang." She swipes at the tablet, spins it on the table for me to view. "They're all based on his previous paint and decorating schemes. I figure he should find at least two of them appealing. We can always take elements from the other two for his redesign."

I scroll through the four options. "Some of these colors—they don't look like anything I've seen in his office. But they're nice. I think he'll enjoy them."

"He should. These—" She highlights a few of them. "Are from his home."

"His home? What'd you do, wait outside with a paparazzo's camera?"

"No …"

"Wait, I have it. You mailed him a gift with a spy camera implanted. Now it's on his coffee table."

She laughs. "No! Tax records. There's plenty of photographs of the exterior at the Rampart city assessor's webpage. When you download them and zoom in close enough, you can see inside and ..." Her eyes widen.

I can't help laughing. "That pretty much defines espionage."

"Oh, stop. You know what I'm saying. Anyway, if we can sign off on these, I'll run them by Kaminsky and get them to Dr. Huang by lunch."

"Sounds perfect. I'm going with Option Two. Option Three's the runner up."

"That's what I was thinking, only in reverse."

"Close enough."

We let it go quiet for a while. Anna smooths a wrinkle on her skirt. "You have plans for the weekend?"

"Do I ...? Yes. Jess and I are renting a cabin at Estes Park. Just a couple days, be back on Sunday evening."

"Skipping church?"

"Just this once should be allowed. I'm there all the time." With the exception of last night. The sensation still has me giddy. Yet, there's no communication from Nick. I've fended off the urge to text him three times. Even now I have a hard time smiling at Anna and not punching the contact number on my phone.

"Curtis asked if I'd like to join you all for pool Thursday night." She rests her tablet on her lap. "I think he's assumed I'm an easy mark."

"Don't tell me you're a pool shark."

"Not a shark, really, but I've won plenty of games. You?"

"My father has a pool table that doubles as a dining room table. I'm serious, you remove the tablecloth, two wooden panels, and a bundled-up blanket—Presto. Instant billiards ..."

Hmm. Nick knew about that. Was it possible I'd let it slip to more people than I remembered? Or had I brought the story up to Anna because it was fresh in my memory from that first traumatic meeting with my double?

"Wow. Here I thought my roommates in college were serious

about the game. They never used one as furniture, as far as I know."

Thursday. I told Curtis I couldn't show up. But with Nick stepping in … "Maybe I'll see you there."

"Maybe so. That'd be fun, to have someone on my team."

"There's no sense in letting the engineers win."

She presses her hand to her throat. "Terrible!"

My phone vibrates. Ah, perfect.

Anna rises. "You'd better get that. I'll see you later. Want me to message when Kaminsky's available?"

"Sure. Let me know. I'll back you up when he argues about the 'ugly modern color scheme' you've picked."

Anna wields the tablet like a weapon. "Hey, now, he's bad but he's not that bad. See you later."

"Later." I watch her go, mind churning with possibilities about pool night. The phone's continued buzzing kills those fantasies. "Hello."

"Good morning." It's Nick. Strange hearing my voice talking to me. "Thought you'd like an update."

"Nobody's complained, yet, so I assumed you were successful."

"Completely. I'll send you an email with a more detailed summary but suffice it to say you're credited with keeping a cool head when certain committee members lost theirs."

"I kind of wondered. Did Harold give you any trouble?"

"He griped about how much you all were spending on the outreach program to the food pantries in the Tannery district. I let him have his spiel then sighed and rolled my eyes."

Mine, meanwhile, got as big as dinner plates. "You … what?"

"I mentioned he might have failed in his Christian duty. After all, didn't Christ say whatever we do for the least of these we also do for him?"

"Wow. I would have paid money do see the look on his face. You're sure he didn't have a stroke?"

Nick laughs. "Oh, no, he's just fine, but I'm lucky to have my skin still attached after he flayed me alive. Give him some time. He'll calm, once he figures out I'm—we're right."

"What'd everyone else do?"

"Pretty sure they were trying not to laugh."

"Okay. So … other than that, it went well?"

"Of course. You'll see it all in my summary. Anything else I can do for you?"

"Not at the moment. I do want to get together to go over the Procyon packet. I'll forward you a copy."

"Surprised you're not worried about my discretion in such a matter."

I stare at my screen. He has a point. Here I am, willing to share a confidential client document with someone I barely know—and yet, he shows he is me. The way he handled Harold Kana? It's how I've always wanted to react. It's what I'd always wanted to say to that sanctimonious, arrogant old man. Here, in Nick, I have the chance to say those things, to do those things, without consequence.

Sounds perfect.

"I can trust you, can't I?"

"I will treat your life like it was mine, because what matters most is helping you achieve what you want. You and I are tied together. I won't sever that connection."

"Appreciate that. I'll check in later."

"Good luck."

It isn't five minutes before an email shows up, no name attached to it, rather just a collection of numbers and letters. The subject heading is "Stewardship." Not until I open the message do I breathe easily. Nick's as good as his word. The summary is two pages long. He must have compiled it long before our conversation. It lays out the major points discussed during the meeting, with quotes from some of the committee members.

Those quotes convince me of the summary's veracity. Harold Kana's comments are spot on—they bleed sarcasm through the screen. The others are accurate, too, demonstrating Nick's observations of the committee members' habits, right down to fiddling with wedding rings and repeated phrases.

However this Nick, this other me, earned his money that's parlayed into so much free time, I'm willing to bet it was in communications. The man can take notes with the best of journalists.

I hit "Reply" and attach the Procyon documents.

I've just finished the response when my phone buzzes again. The number isn't familiar. "Hello?"

"Dominic. I hope I am not bothering you."

The warm, accented voice is unmistakable. The Rev. Olin Hamra is our pastor at St. Lucius. "Good morning, Father. How are you?"

"Well. I am most pleased I was able to decipher this device on only the fourth try."

"Ah. New phone?"

"Yes. One of my younger colleagues encouraged me to, in his words, join the 21st Century. Thankfully I have managed to avoid making any grievous errors." He takes a breath. "Dominic, I wonder if I may impose on you to join me for a discussion this afternoon."

The bubble of my ego inflated by Nick's conversation pops. The meeting. Nick must have left something out, or not mentioned something I'll soon find out in my email correspondence. Either that, or he just wants to talk about my—rather, Nick's treatment of Harold Kana. "Anything the matter?"

"No, I simply wish to talk about the Stewardship committee. There were questions raised last night that bear further scrutiny. I must say, it was refreshing to see a certain individual humbled—not that I advocate infighting, but often our egos must be lovingly reproved by those with whom we serve.

I bite back a laugh. Leave it to Father Hamra to express admiration without saying straight off. "Well, sure. I can squeeze in something at lunch. Is 12:30 okay?"

"That would be fine. Please join me in the sanctuary."

Church is fifteen minutes away in lunchtime traffic. But there's no getting around it. As tempting as it is to have Nick sit in, I won't put him face to face with my pastor.

Besides, he needs to study up on Procyon.

"I've got some materials to drop off and then I'll see you."

"Most excellent. Have a pleasant morning."

"You too."

I tap the phone against the desk as my mind whirs along like my computer when it's desperately trying to load AutoCAD. Better finish the Vitalis new concept so I can run it by them before meeting with Father Hamra. While I am concerned for the eternal state of my soul, not getting my head bit off by clients is a more pressing and immediate matter.

The best I can come up with on short notice is a long, broad kitchen with an extended counter and windows that wrap in an L. There isn't time for embellishment, just basic overhead view floorplan and a quick 3-D render. I print both and dash for the car.

Getting to the Vitalis by 12:15 requires some creative maneuvering, both in terms of speed—I know where the police like to set up speed traps on Wednesdays—and navigation. Turn down Gampetro Street, across to Vallarta, hang a right on West Jonas. Puts me in the right neighborhood without much traffic hassle.

There's so few cars along the route, in fact, that it's easy to notice an SUV following me.

Navy blue. Nick's ride.

I scowl. It's bad enough Tyson feels the need to ride herd on me. I don't need my double, a man who so far has proven very helpful and nothing but altruistic, making sure I do my job right.

The visit with the Vitalis is mercifully short, in large part because of Gary's absence. Francine's eyes go wide at the design. She's near enough her perfume is potent enough, I'm sure, to drop a would-be robber into unconsciousness. "It's beautiful! Wait until Gary sees this. Dominic, I don't know how you do it, but I'm ready for the contractors to start knocking down walls!"

I smile and give a short bow. "My pleasure, ma'am."

"No need to 'ma'am.'" She holds the papers close to her chest. "Have you had lunch yet? Want to join me for a glass of wine?"

No way. "Unfortunately, I've got an appointment right after this one, so I'll have to decline. Very much appreciate the offer."

"Some other time then."

Again, not a chance.

I wait until two blocks later to pull over to the curb, abruptly. The SUV behind me does the same thing, pausing by a stand of new aspens planted along a bright white sidewalk. No one gets out.

The walk's short, made shorter by my irritation propelling me a long at speed-walk velocity. Nick has the window rolled down by the time I arrive. He's smiling. When is he not? That gaudy bracelet of his nearly blinds me. "Fancy meeting you here."

"I think the word you're looking for is 'stalking,' Nick. Why are you following me?"

"So I can become familiar with some of your clients and their neighborhoods."

"It's creepy."

"No, it's shrewd. I get to know where these people live, what their tastes are, I can better serve them when I'm filling in for you. Case in point." He waves his phone. My email's centered in the frame. "This Procyon stuff. Fascinating. I've got some great ideas already."

"Well, quit tailing me. I'm meeting with Father Hamra over at church. I don't think you need to spy on me there."

"Good point. Already been to it." He lowers his sunshades. "He's a nice guy. I respect the way he handled the meeting—offering advice, little to no interference. I've known worse. Fine, we'll go around to some of the other buildings you've done. I heard you're doing work on Dr. Huang's dentist office and one of the restaurants, right? This would be far easier if I got your client list."

"We'll talk about that later. Focus on Procyon." We. I lean in, angling for a look at the driver. He's a big white guy, hair buzzed to a thin carpet of blond, graying above the temples. He too has his eyes concealed behind dark sunglasses. "Not going to introduce me to your buddy?"

"He's my driver, not my buddy." Nick thumps his fist on the windowsill. "See you around."

The SUV drives off. I'm left standing on the curb, watching it blend into the rest of the emerging traffic.

St. Lucius Maron Church is on the western edge of Rampart, down by the Van River. Out here, among the single-story bungalows and the outcroppings of huge two-story, six-bedroom, four-bathroom McMansions, it stays low in defiance of the landscape. It has a short barn shape, with sloping sides to the roof and wings jutting to either side—one a school and attendant offices, the other a fellowship hall. The church brings to mind a miniature Gothic cathedral, albeit stripped of the sharpest edges. Eggshell white mingles with sandstone.

Father Hamra waits in the back pew. He's a short man, with curly black hair peppered with gray, and a mustache black as coal against sandy brown skin. The traditional priest's uniform of black highlighted with a white collar fits snug to a stocky, yet not portly, frame. He smiles over his shoulder when he looks up from reading. "Ah, Dominic. Welcome."

"Father." We shake hands. His grip is strong, far improved from the shell of a man I knew up until last year. There's still a pale band where his wedding ring once resided. "What's on your mind? You said you wanted to talk about the meeting."

"Yes. Please, sit." The pew creaks under our weight. "I spent a great deal of time this morning on the telephone with Harold."

"I hope Mr. Kana wasn't offended by my statements."

"Not unduly. You know Harold—his heart is broken, so he lashes out at others in an effort to fill the void of his son's rejection."

I blink. Of all the things that stuck in my mind when I thought of the man, that was not one of them. "I didn't. Is he …?"

"Living in Denver, with a young man very dear to him." Father Hamra folds his hands on the closed Bible sitting upon his lap. "It is a sad thing, to see father and son torn apart from each other. They are both frequently in my prayers."

I nod. Not much to say to that.

"Unfortunately, Harold does not yet see the error of his ways where his intractable attitude on the Stewardship committee is concerned. I had hoped to broach the matter with him slowly, as we had discussed after last month's meeting." He raises one bushy eyebrow at me, the body's version of semaphore.

"Sorry." We had indeed discussed it. The memory flashes through my head as clearly as scenes from the movie Jess and I watched last night. Did I recall any of the talk when I told Nick to take my place at the meeting? Of course not. It was buried deep in the piles of other things I must remember. "It was … the man got under my skin one too many times. He's being stingy with our blessings, something we should share with the community at large. Someone had to put their foot down."

"I agree. The manner in which it is done, however, makes the difference."

"Of course. Again, I am sorry."

"Do not worry yourself. Harold will calm down and so will you. I for one am glad to see it out in the open, rather than concealed behind tight smiles."

"Amen to that."

Father Hamra nods. He's watching me with great care, as if I'm a bird that will startle. "Now, is there anything you wish to discuss?"

"Me?" I shift in my seat, uncomfortably aware of my phone pressing against my leg. "Not that I know of."

"You seemed—more composed at last night's meeting and yet, more restless than I have seen. You were alive."

"I've hardly been dead."

"None of us are dead who believe." He tilts his head to the side. "But you were also unwilling, I noticed, to let the normal circular arguments of certain committee members dominate the meeting. If anything, you took command."

That's hardly how Nick put it in his summary, but yes, he did steer a few conversations in ways I approved. "I think … I just got tired of things being the way they always were. Something had to change, so I took a risk." True enough. This is skating perilously close to lying to my pastor.

He nods, and his gaze wanders to the front of the sanctuary. The crucifix is illuminated in a golden circle. Christ, with his eyes closed, his wounds bloody, his body beaten, hangs from a mahogany cross. "Risks often carry great reward, provided they are undertaken for the noblest purpose."

We don't need to get into a conversation about purposes.

His attention returns to me. The smile appears. "If you wish to talk further, Dominic, I can certainly listen."

That's it? I was expecting a 20-minute lecture. Though Father Hamra's homilies have been of a different sort. "No, but …" There is one thing pricking the back of my mind. "Are you familiar with the term doppelgänger?"

He gives me that same look. "German, isn't it? It means double walker. Someone who bears a quite uncanny resemblance to another."

"Yes."

"Well, I once knew a woman who found another who could have been a twin sister while on an overseas flight." He shakes his head, smiling. "The other woman had lived in Israel her whole life and no one in this woman's immediate family had any relations there for generations, as far as she knew. I saw the photographs—quite astonishing."

I nod. "Okay, I understand that, but … I mean, could there ever be a person who is truly the same as us? A duplicate, I should say, not just someone who looks the same. And I realize people have found others who share very similar tastes …"

Father Hamra pokes my chest with an index finger. "No matter the untruths surrounding us, there is only one you, because every soul is unique. Everyone is knit in the womb—following the same pattern, yes, but with the master's individually tailored tastes. It is the greatest beauty of this world. Even when those souls are taken from us, we remember their individuality."

I glance at that bare ring finger. "Of course. Thank you, Father."

"You are most welcome. Will we see you this Sunday?"

Nick can't be me. Yet … there's so many ways in which he's a perfect fit for my life, at least for the drudgery that keeps me from enjoying the good parts. No matter what Father Hamra says, I'm unwilling to forgo this chance. "Jess and I will be out of town on a vacation, just a short trip to recharge."

He smiles, and there's a wistful quality to it. "I wish you both a blessed time together. Some things—and people—are worth the time away from the rest of the world."

They are.

And with Nick's help, I can be in the world and apart from it at the same time.

CHAPTER SIX

One thing keeps nagging me. How good or poor are Nick's abilities as an architect?

So far, he's been able to pass as me in situations that don't require a great deal of skilled knowledge. Personal interactions, yes, but when it comes to my design work, well, they're as much a part of me as the way I snore if I don't sleep on my right side, or the way I pluck at my pants when anxious.

The thought bothers me all through the evening, so much so that most of my conversations with Jess are a smear across my memory. Even as I plow through the Vitalis' redesign—number three, recall—there's an urgency behind me that takes a while for me to identify.

Finally, I call Nick. "You've got to prove to me you can actually do what I do."

He snorts. "Really? You think I can't mimic your drawings? You'd be right. Mine are different, but they're just as good."

"Forgive me if I don't take that assertion on faith."

"Oh, I know, you need proof. Can't blame you. What kind of guardian angel would I be if I couldn't perform this particular miracle for you? Tell you what: Come by my apartment. We can't very well meet in your office, Dominic, and being in public together poses bigger problems. It's been risky enough."

Fair point. It's near noon on Thursday and by now I'm neck deep in Procyon preparations, so it's easy to make the transition. I transfer the necessary files onto my laptop, gather printouts into a folder, and head out.

He's renting a place just off downtown, in the 600 block behind Federal. I didn't even realize there were apartments above the stores there—not ones anyone would want to rent, that is, and certainly not someone who has a personal driver for his brand-new SUV. I don't spend much time around the back-alley liquor shops, and the ones with misspelled neon sticker signs advertising cheap electronic goods.

Nick's big, blond driver meets me at the top of a slanted stairwell. The tile underfoot is chipped. A couple more break as I walk the hall. Faded wallpaper curls back, revealing mold embedded in plaster.

"Afternoon," I say.

He stares back at me.

"Which one's Nick's place?"

He points at a thick, wooden door with a reinforced metal frame. Doesn't take his gaze from me for a second. He's dressed in a dark blue polo shirt, gray windbreaker, and jeans. Sunglasses are hooked through his collar. Can't find a wrinkle on him. He could easily be slathered in bronze and made into one of those sculptures on Monument Avenue.

I open the door, which is unlocked. I was half expecting it to be barricaded, or at least have a dozen chains and deadbolts. But no, just one big locking mechanism that appears solid enough to repel a police battering ram.

"Come on it," Nick calls. "I hope he didn't bite."

The space is a far cry from the rundown neighborhood over which it watches. It's a broad, open floor plan loft. I walk through an immaculate kitchen, full of shining steel appliances and glistening stone countertops. I count three reflections of myself staring back, goggle-eyed. Beyond that is a sprawling living room, sparsely furnished with a couch and two chairs, plus a wooden coffee table covered with papers. All three are black with metal frames. There's two doors to the left—bedroom and bathroom? Sweeping beams overhead are gorgeous. They're stained a darker shade than the floorboards and reveal square nail heads. Iron fittings, exposed brick walls, there's even a half-scrubbed remnant of pop brand logo.

"I didn't have the heart to clean it all off." Nick's standing by tall, narrow windows, a long row that looks out on a sprawling view of Rampart. The sky seems darker than when I saw it outside; the windows could be UV-tinted, I suppose. A modest flat screen television hangs on the wall in the middle.

Nick has two bottles of pop, one already opened and partially drained. "Thirsty?"

"Always." His fingers have traced imprints in the condensation. I take the proffered bottle. The first sip is rewardingly frigid. Funny, even though it's a cold morning out there, I'll take chilled pop without hesitation.

"Got the Procyon materials?" Nick gestures at the coffee table. "I've set out a few ideas of my own."

Those papers? I'd missed them because I'm distracted by the wood grain of the floorboards. There's a pale circle, big enough for me to sit down in with legs extended, that appears to be fading. "Sorry, materials?"

"Come on, Dominic, you've only had one sip," he teases. "Can't be buzzed already."

"Right." I sit, but glance over my shoulder. The pale circle's gone and with it, the smell that lingered—Smoke? Could be a woodstove. They're not supposed to be allowed in downtown buildings, but someone nearby could have one. Didn't see any stacks on this building, though …

Nick snaps his fingers. "You're out of it this afternoon, aren't you?"

"Yes, I guess. The Vitali project …"

He scowls. "I don't know how you put up with those people."

"How close were you following me the other day?"

"Not close enough to hear anything, so I dropped in this morning."

I sputter pop. It sprays onto the pages spread on his table.

"If you don't like my work, just say so." His tone is much drier than the drawings.

I wipe my mouth with the back of my hand. "You can't just drop in on my clients! Geez. Fine, I'll get you the list if you'll stay off them until I say so."

"Well, that was my mistake." He smiles. "That Francine, though, she must think you're quite the guy. I thought she was going to offer me a tour of the more private rooms of the house, if you catch my drift."

I groan. "Don't tell me you did anything stupid."

"I wouldn't dream of it—the telling or the doing. Don't strain your brain. I told her I needed to take another look at the kitchen, made some notes, and got out of there before she could grab hold of my rear end."

I chuckle at that. "Smooth escape."

"I like to think so."

"So what've you got …" My words fail as I finally focus on the Procyon sketches he has set before us. They're inspired. No other way to put it. One of the concepts is a huge tower with a curved, indented form that makes me think of a broad blade of glass, albeit one made of gleaming blue windows. It bears a sharp resemblance to the building I'd dreamed up, the one with the sweeping wall—the one I'm banking on as the primary to dazzle the Procyon reps on Saturday.

There's another, a domed structure that's less thorough. It's more of a quick sketch, with half-erased lines. "Where did you get this one?"

"The dome?" He shrugs. "It popped into my head when I was looking at the requirements for their space. Something that will fit, but isn't too ostentatious, don't you think?"

I'm speechless. My hands fumble with the laptop computer's lid until I can crack it open, the screen flashing on. There's four concepts stashed in an open folder, none of them more than basic brainstorms, with the exception of the sail building. One of those … "Look." I swivel the computer.

It's a domed office, with three buildings joined in triangular arrangement, sloped sides, greenery and parking spaces tossed in for scale.

The only difference between mine and Nick's is the tilt of the walls and the placement of the shrubbery.

He shakes his head and takes a long draw on his drink. "That is pretty amazing. You see what I mean? We were destined to do this."

As stunned as I am by the similarities—forget that, the sheer *exactness* of our designs—I recoil at the word. "Destiny's not a thing I'd trust in. Destiny didn't get me where I am today. My grandparents leaving a place where their families died and me working harder than anyone else put me in that office."

"I have no doubt of that. Call it preordination."

I keep my thoughts to myself, leafing through his drawings instead. Destiny? No. My grandparents are good people, who were in a terrible situation, and they took the steps necessary to change the rules of the game. They left Lebanon, waited patiently to earn their citizenship, worked whatever jobs needed to build a good life for their children. One of them, the youngest son, became my father. How could I do anything else to honor them? I am not about to roll over and give up, not with the likes of Tyson Jacobs wanting to toss me back on the next flight to the Middle East. What did he know of my life? I was born here just like he was.

"Let me state it this way." Apparently, Nick's not about to leave me in quiet contemplation. "I'm putting my all into this, Dominic— to be a gift to you, when you need it most. You've given up a lot to get to your station in life."

"It's been a busy few years—"

"Don't prevaricate. I know how you feel. All those hours hunched in the sickly glow of your computer monitor, churning out page after page of drawings, these buildings that other people get to enjoy, people who don't value the strain it caused to finish them. Those buildings all come to life, and yes, it's satisfying to see them rise into place on the skyline, but honestly, is it worth the time lost you could have spent with friends? With your wife?"

I gaze at the fizzing liquid in the bottom of the bottle. "There are days I … resent it. All of it. Yes, I won't argue that." There's a tremendous freedom to saying it. The words tumble free. Resent! I've never spoken the regret to anyone, not even Curt, or Jess.

Nick nods, his expression somber. "I understand, really. That was me years ago. It's the burden I can take up for you. I'm thankful you've given me the chance. Together, we can do great things for this city, for you name, while keeping your loved ones close to you."

"You're selling hard, Nick."

"Only because I want a satisfied customer." He chuckles. "It doesn't hurt to let you know how I feel—how *we* feel. It isn't all that different."

"Never met anyone who's dug so close to the truth of my life." And there is no shaking the oddity of sitting across from myself. "Of course, for this to work, you are right—I'll get you my client list. And you can keep doing whatever it is you're doing with your clothes."

He plucks at the Oxford shirt. It's similar style and color to ones I have. "I'd thought of that. You send me some pictures of what's in your closet, brand names and the like. We'll get it sorted out. But as it stands, I'm nailing it."

I shake my head, chuckling. It sounds eerily similar to his laugh. "Just don't get cocky."

We settle on the domed offices for our Procyon presentation—his presentation?—with my sail building and his tower as the two backups. Nick promises to merge our twin designs, clean them up, and have them to me later in the day. Good deal. That way I'll have something to show Tyson on Friday.

With Nick stashed in his loft, brain churning for the Procyon project, I'm free to catch up on my other clients. Dr. Huang's office requires another meeting with the dentist, this time with Anna by my side. Between the two of us we get his go-ahead on the interior, thanks to Anna's covert reconnaissance of his color preferences. She winks at me, and I return a subtle thumbs-up.

By the time 3:45 rolls around, I realize something's odd about my office. The last emails are answered, files put away, and clients' nerves soothed. I even managed to put an envelope in the mail to Mrs. Dockery, who has eluded my to-do list for a few days. The goal is to satisfy her fussing with side-by-side comparisons of the shingles. She won't be lulled until I show up with sample in hand, but it should keep her from calling for a while.

So … 3:45, and I can take a break. It's as rare as a solar eclipse.

I phone Jess. "Hey."

"Hi. What's up? Is everything okay? Sammy's good?"

"No emergencies."

Some of the tension bleeds from her voice. "Oh. Okay."

"I wanted to see if you were available to get tea."

I count to five in the space it takes for her to respond. "Is it April Fools Day already?"

We both laugh. "Seriously, Jess. I've got some time before my appointment with the Brunkhorst people. You busy?"

"Yeah, papers to grade, lesson plans for tomorrow." A pen taps softly in the background. There's country music crooning, from her computer speakers, I don't doubt "But that doesn't mean I can't make time for us to relax. Sure, let's go over to The Shattered Mug. You're treating."

"Sounds perfect. See you."

"Love you, Dominic."

"Love you, too."

I lean back in the chair, stretch my arms and—what the heck—put my feet on the desk, ankles crossed. I cannot recollect the last time I could do this. It makes me want to pause time and sink into the seat, eternally frozen.

"Zein? You look comfortable. What's going on?"

Tyson frowns at me from the door. He's got his sleeves rolled up, and his tie's been discarded.

"Nothing, Tyson."

"That's what it looks like."

"I'm caught up. Don't be too jealous."

"Of what? You thinking you can slack off because magic dirt makes you the same as me? You've got no idea what it means to work to the top, Zein."

My fingers tighten behind my head. Let him think that when I bypass him, and Kaminsky makes me a part-owner. An equal among the three of us. I won't let him bait me. Not today, not in this moment. "What do you want, Tyson? Besides reminding me you're a charming xenophobe, that is."

"Procyon."

The images Nick and I have concocted flit through my mind as fast as a barn swallow on the wing for insects. "Going well. I'll have one main concept and two backups for the presentation Saturday. You?"

A muscle twitches in his jaw. "I'm ready."

Come on. He couldn't be more anxious if he were standing outside the conference room in only his underwear. "Glad to hear we're on the same page."

"We'll be on that page when you give me your designs."

"What, so you can put your name on them?"

"Don't insult me. I've got my own, but since I'm the lead on this, I'll do the presenting.

I scoop up my phone and car keys. "Perhaps we'll discuss this later. I've got tea with my wife and then Brunkhorst at five. Excuse me."

Tyson doesn't make way. We stand face to face. I'm not much for fights—generally, I defuse them verbally. But if there's been anyone who's needed a good punch, it's this man. "You're late. I'll take over your spiel. See if the client would be happier dealing with me solo."

"That's not how it works."

"It is if and when I say so." Tyson smirks, but he steps into the hall, arms spread in a flourish so as to allow me passage. "Have fun out there not being part owner, Zein."

Enough. Enjoy your free time. It's rare.

Yet, if Nick's carrying more of the load, why not take advantage of it more often? He called it destiny, or divine will. Whatever confluence of events put us together, it doesn't matter. I slip on my shades and gun the BMW into traffic. He's helping me take control of my life.

The Shattered Mug is a bustling café on the corner of Juniper and Federal, housed in a gray stone three-story tucked between two banks. There's a handful of college students slouched over tables, faces zombified by tablet screens, earbuds sealing off sounds of the business professionals' rumbling conversations. The place is full of a heady aroma—coffee, sugar, cinnamon, and hints of caramel.

I beat Jess there, securing a table by the window. Makes it easier to people watch, which is nearly as much fun as perusing the local architecture. I have most of the latter memorized, anyway. People, though, are ever-changing.

Today, especially, I notice the men and women hurrying along. They're all checking phones. They're tapping texts or jabbering calls. I smile, let the sun warm me and get rid of the outdoor chill. Not me, not here.

The window seat also allows a great view of Jess as she walks up. I could watch in slow motion, rewinding over and over. She's got on a pale-yellow blouse, made blazing bright against her toffee skin, and tight blue jeans. Black hair blows free over her shoulders.

Reminds me of how Anna had her hair loose today.

The thought knocks me clean off track. Where did that come from? No sooner do I play innocent with myself than I confess. Come on, Dominic. I can't deny Anna's attractive—and by that, I mean a beautiful woman. And I've been spending a lot of time with her. It's the nature of the job. Puts us in close contact.

My memory foists the wink and the thumbs-up as Exhibit A. Why do I feel like I'm on trial? It's a good warning. I'll tread more carefully.

Jess grins. She can't help it. "You look nice."

"Thanks." I pull out her chair, kiss her on the cheek—except she turns and intercepts me with her lips. Much better. Any musings of Anna dissipate.

"How was your day?"

"Oh, not bad. Busy like usual, but I found some creative ways to lighten the weight." Here's hoping Nick is working just as hard as I think he is. Judging from his output to date, I don't have any reason to worry. "You?"

"Nothing terribly exciting. I did have to chastise a young man for lewd comments about his fellow female classmates." Jess grins. "I used my soft voice."

I feign a shiver. "It's a wonder he's still alive. Did he incinerate on the spot once he realized you were angry enough to destroy him?"

"No, sadly not. A quick trip to the assistant principal's office helped rein him in."

"Nice. You want the pumpkin spice?"

"What else would I drink this time of year?" Jess's phone beeps. She checks the screen. "Oh. I had to leave myself a reminder about that."

"About pumpkin spice?"

"No. Mrs. Cortez."

I rub my forehead. Yes, we both forgot about talking to her. "I don't suppose she's sent us a check for veterinary expenses."

"No. I don't suppose you talked to her."

"Nope."

Jess bites her lip. "Okay, we should do that tonight."

"Not really looking forward to having that argument. You know how she gets …" I stare at the window. My reflection is identically thoughtful. "Never mind. I'll take care of it."

Jess watches me, as if I'm planning to bolt. "Really? You'll just … talk to her?"

"Sure. This afternoon, before I come home." And yes, I'm fully aware of my final appointment of the day, but the details of a rapidly formulating plan spin in my brain. "Don't worry about it. This way you can get caught up with your lesson plans and it will be all fixed by the time you get home."

She reaches for my hand. "Thanks, Dominic. It means a lot."

I wink at her. "Anything for you."

Up in line for our drinks, I start pounding out a text message. <Got a quick job for you.>

Nick's right on it. <Shoot.>

<Mrs. Cortez. Elderly neighbor. Her dog bit ours when ours went through fence gap. Sammy's bills are her responsibility.>

<Okay. What do you want?>

That gives me pause. I glance back at Jess, who's eyeballing the passers-by. We'll have fun comparing notes on the state of humankind. <Talk to her and get her to do something about it. She owes us $200.>

<Ouch. Consider it done.>

I exhale. Good. One less thing I have to do—and in this case, having the bill covered means $200 that could be better spent on something other than stitches for Sammy. Like, say, a fancy dinner in downtown Denver this weekend.

Jess accepts the steaming cup with closed eyes. She inhales deeply. "Mm, my hero. This was a great idea."

"My pleasure." I raise my cup in salute. Steaming mint tea warms my cheeks. "Here's to time for ourselves, as of tomorrow afternoon."

"I'll drink to that." She sips. "Did you remember I've got the historical program this evening?"

Ah, yes. "Not really, but I figured there was something. I'm on deck for the lamb *kibbeh*."

"Your *teta*'s recipe? Perfect."

"I am an expert at it."

"Were you going to work while I'm gone?"

"I was …" Another idea. "But Curt has his pool gathering at Bentley's. I think I'll swing by and see if we can't give the engineers a run for their money."

"That sounds like fun. Tell him thanks again for letting us take Sheryl to the cabin."

"I won't kiss him, if that's what you're insinuating."

She laughs. We go on like this for the next half hour. There's no one else clamoring for my attention, and I can't help thinking I could get used to this life.

It's past six when I get home, headlights illuminating Jess's red Hyundai compact car in the driveway. Lights are on in the kitchen. Sammy's shadow goes tearing through the living room. The air's crisp and clear. Stars pinprick the blue velvet overhead.

Funny. No word from Nick about how the conversation with Mrs. Cortez went. I shrug. I'll take no news as good news.

"Mr. Zein?" Mrs. Cortez hurries toward me down her walk. She's so short I think she could saddle Sammy and ride him into the sunset. Her hair is bound in a gray and silver bun, and her long green coat is wrapped as tight as a snowsuit. She waves a slip of paper like a surrender flag. "Here you go, please, take."

"Take?" Her hand stops fluttering long enough for me to accept the paper. It's a check, all right, and shaky handwriting has filled it in for $200.

"Please. I am so sorry. It won't happen again. Vero was bad, he won't bite Sammy again." She crams the sentences in, rapid fire. Her eyes are so wide the whites are unmistakable, even in the darkness. Hands grip the top of her jacket shut.

Hands that are trembling.

"Thank you, Mrs. Cortez, we appreciate it. I promise I'll get the fence fixed up. Sammy shouldn't have stuck his head through."

"No, no, it was our fault. My fault. You were right. Not a good neighbor." She shakes her head so fast I'm certain it will fall off.

This isn't right. I reach for her shoulder. "Is everything all right?"

Mrs. Cortez backs away, eyes even wider, if that's possible. "No, please, we are okay now. Good night!"

She's back inside before I can blink. The click of her deadbolt is faintly audible.

I frown at the check, then look up again at her house. She watches me through parted curtains, but must see me there, because she whips them shut. Two more sets of curtains close, though lights are clearly glowing around the edges.

"Dominic?" Jess is framed in a rectangle of golden light. Sammy's paws scratch at the front step, as he struggles to run up for a greeting, but Jess has him by the collar. "I heard you pull up."

"Oh, yes. I'm fine." I wave the check. "Mrs. Cortez came through."

"Great! Come show me while you get dinner ready."

"Sure, in a second."

The door shuts. Sammy whimpers behind it.

I head up the walk, sparing a last glimpse at Mrs. Cortez's house. Whatever Nick said to her, it certainly did the trick.

It also frightened her.

CHAPTER SEVEN

Bentley's is a 70-year-old bar in the Tannery district, adjacent to downtown. This eastern section of Rampart isn't the cleanest part of the city, nor is it crime-ridden. It's tired, perhaps, six by eight blocks of exhausted urban structures and overworked people. Odds are if you live here you work two jobs, and that may or may not be enough to make ends meet.

Tannery abuts downtown Rampart, separated by a single block of newly refurbished apartment buildings along Polk Avenue. Bentley's, then, acts as neutral territory, a place where the people who spend the workday dressed in clean shirts and ties mingle with those who are likely to wear grease and blue jeans. Usually, such mingling means opposite sides of the room.

Curt's head snaps around when I walk into the room. He's got a pool cue in one hand and a bottle of beer in the other. "Guys, somebody must've cracked me on the head, because I'm hallucinating," he says. "Dominic Zein is not working tonight!"

A ragged cheer goes up from his cohorts, all of them engineers from various firms. Mostly men, with a few women, they outnumber architects in the room two to one. I wave at a couple of colleagues from Plan Out, one of the newer companies across town. We've got a friendly enough competition going. They're chatting with Anna, who's sitting cross-legged on one of the stools at the bar, in a black skirt and pale blue buttoned-down shirt. She winks at me.

Before I can salute back, Curt has his arm wrapped around me. "Hey, Z, glad you could make it, but what'd you do? Quit?"

I chuckle. "You're hysterical. How about you get me a bottle first and a pool cue second, so I can show your band of jokers the proper way to play this game?"

"Yeah, okay." Curt raises his voice. "I think the architects are wanting this to turn into a full-blown challenge!"

Catcalls follow. "Let's see it, Zein!" one of the engineers dares.

I shrug. "Waiting on my weapon of choice."

While Curt's gone for a bottle of beer, I get a text from Nick. <Hope you got your check okay.>

<I did. What did you say to Mrs. Cortez?> Her fearful expression won't be leaving me soon.

<Nothing out of the ordinary. Firm reminder of who was at fault and the legal ramifications of us not squaring things away amicably.>

<You threatened to call the cops on her?>

<Didn't take long to figure out who was living at her house. What're the odds that nephew of hers doesn't have proper documentation? Gotta say, Dominic, it's a shame if ICE gets a phone call.>

I stare at the phone. Cold. That's just—cold.

But he didn't actually call Immigration. He just forcefully insinuated. And our vet bills get paid, and Mrs. Cortez keeps her dog on a tighter leash. All is well.

That doesn't do enough to banish the sickening sensation.

<I'll have the last Procyon notes emailed tonight.>

<No worries. I'll read them tomorrow morning.>

<Ah. Out tonight?>

<Bentley's. Pool with friends.>

<Enjoy it.>

It's a strange thing, talking to yourself, but I come away from the exchange with a bold fire in my gut, like I could tackle anything.

"Here." Curt hands me a bottle and clinks his against mine. "As for the cue, Z, you go pick your own. That way you can't claim it's jinxed."

"Now why would I do such a thing?"

"Um, because you have twice before, and you think it's funny to rag on this poor soul." He clutches his hands to his chest. "Besides, if you make me do it, I'll renege on the Sheryl deal."

I cough on my beer. "Bad idea. Then you have to face my sweet Jess."

Curt winces. "Never mind on that. Just get the cue and play!"

He's generous enough to let me break, which I chalk up to his arrogance. Like I said, we're outnumbered by double, so he must feel cocky tonight. But he should know by now it's always a bad idea, because I can almost always knock the first ball into one of the corner pockets.

Like the seven ball that goes spinning out of sight.

At first it seems we architects are going down in flames, with the four of us missing more shots than we make. But then Anna joins, and that all changes. She sinks one from the far side of the table, and after Curt fails to get the same one, nonetheless.

The game ends with us winning by two shots.

Curt shakes his head. "I'm at a loss for words."

I mime blowing chalk off the end of my cue. "How about embarrassing, mortifying, humiliating—"

He punches me in the shoulder, but he's still grinning. "You're a pain, I'll give you that. Why don't you come sit next to me and watch me find outstanding ladies with whom I can converse?"

"Wow. You're just full of it, aren't you?"

"If by it you mean amazingness, then, yeah." Curt guides me to an empty stool and orders up another couple of beers. He pays—the consequence of being on the losing team.

"You guys all set for the wild weekend?

"I'd hardly call it wild. Just a couple nights in the cabin."

"Nice. And … your bosses are good with this?"

"I'm all set to be away from work, if that's what you mean."

"Huh. Thought they kept you on a way shorter leash."

I shrug. There's no way to explain to Curt how I've managed to slip said leash. He thought I was cracking up from strain that first night in Caerphilly, when I'd first spotted Nick. Chalked it up to seeing my reflection. Couldn't blame him, however, because the same theory had occurred to me.

Until I knew better.

"Whatever your new plan, Z, I'm proud of you becoming a big boy and telling work where to get off." He salutes me with the bottle. "But I'm going to put money on you taking your laptop up to the cabin and playing with your drawings while Jess is sashaying around in her lingerie."

My turn to hit him. He winces and rubs his shoulder. "I'm not that brain dead. No, work is covered. No plans, no projects, only us two."

"What a good husband." Curt rolls his eyes. "Do me a favor—don't put Sheryl over a cliff. She has this thing about collisions."

"I'll do my best not to drive like a nervous teen."

"If you drive like that, we're all in trouble." Anna slides onto the stool next to mine. She's got an empty glass of something that smells sweet. "Curt, does that bottle feel nice and cold up against it?"

He frowns. "Against what?"

"Your burn from losing."

I snort and manage not to spray beer all over the bar. Curt stares at her a moment before bursting out in laughter. Yes, it's a bad joke, but I can't fault her timing.

"What gives inviting these rude folks to my function?" Curt starts to rise. "Let's switch seats, I'll do some investigating of her true motives."

"Don't strain your brain." It slips out without my forethought, immediately summoning a mental picture of Nick diligently completing my project preparation. I wait around for feelings of guilt. None show up. "Anna isn't your type."

"Too beardy," she says solemnly.

"Yeah, right." Curt snickers.

"So, you and Tyson all set for Procyon on Saturday?" Anna's leaning forward on the bar. "I'm looking forward to hearing about it next week."

"We'll do fine, as long as we don't kill each other," I say. "Especially in front of the clients."

"Kaminsky would frown on that."

"Yeah, as in fire you both," Curt points out.

"Not Tyson. I doubt part-owners get fired."

"Oh, cheer up." Anna rests her hand on my arm. It stays there for longer than a quick, reassuring pat. "They wouldn't be able to get half the work done that they do with you gone."

I flash my winningest smile. "Thanks."

"Okay, kids." Curt pulls on my shirt collar, and I grab the edge of the bar in time to prevent toppling backward. "Let's fire up another game."

"Good!" Anna pokes him in the chest, pressing close to me as she does. Whatever perfume she's got on tugs at my senses. "I could use another win. Don't wait around, boys."

Curt watches her walk to the tables. I'm busy dabbing a napkin to the spilled beer on my shirt. "Man, you had better be careful."

"Yes, I could have had the entire bottle on my front. Thanks for that."

"No, her. She have a boyfriend?"

"Possibly. I don't recall."

"Recall fast, because she's into you, and you're not exactly playing Mr. Happily Married tonight." There's a severe crease on his forehead.

"Are you lecturing me on proper workplace behavior?" I wave the bottle. "Because this isn't work."

"And you're dancing way too close to the fire, Z. Trust me. I've got way more experience with this sort of thing than you do."

"You aren't even married, Curt."

"Yeah, no, but I've been dating one girl and developed an … inordinate interest in the other. It turns out bad. Like, Sheryl getting keyed bad." There's no joshing to his tone. "Watch yourself, okay? For Jess."

There's a surge of irritation inside, like a bubbling pot that boils over its sides. Tyson's riding me to be a good company man, and now Curt wants me to play nice? And yes, I know Curt's right, Anna's not my wife, and I shouldn't be hanging out here if I'm … I'm what, exactly? Anger mingles with embarrassment. "You know what? I'm going for a walk. Start the game without me. Maybe with one fewer person you guys will stand half a chance."

I storm out the door, letting it close out the loud music and Curt's frustrated call. Great. One night out to be myself, and I get lectured by my lecherous buddy on how not to flirt with a co-worker.

At the same time, as I walk toward my car, I can't suppress the voice whispering, *He's right. What were you thinking?*

"Just leave me alone," I mutter. "I need a break!"

Right then, glass shatters.

A car alarm explodes. I know the sound like my footsteps. It's the BMW. Someone's trying to steal my car?

My impulse should be to call 9-1-1, and I do get my phone out, but my legs carry me toward the crime in progress. I'm not about to let anyone take what's mine.

But when I get there, down the block and around the corner from Bentley's, I see someone else is already acting on the same sentiment.

Three men are fighting one. There's a tall, thickset white guy with a thick brown beard and a ratty black T-shirt worn over brown long sleeves, plus another, paler guy who is far shorter and bulging against a tan jacket. The third one is a black man in camouflaged pants and a forest green muscle shirt that shows off his tattoos, wearing a red knit hat.

Their opponent has already put the bearded guy through a vacant storefront window. He's climbing to his feet, blood streaking his face.

What are they even doing around? My car door is propped open, the interior lights ablaze, and there's some of my papers spilled on the ground. No one but me seems interested in them, because they get trod upon.

The black guy takes a couple of swings but the opponent—I can't see his face for the gray hooded sweatshirt concealing him—steps around them as if they were imagined. He strikes with his right hand, and I catch a gleam in the distant lamplight.

There's a bright flash, and the black guy cries out, his voice ragged with pain. He's on the ground, clutching his chest. His clothing smolders like a spent cigarette.

The shorter man has a gun. He shoots, the sounds like incredibly loud firecrackers.

I'm expecting the foolhardy but competent defender to flop on the ground, mortally wounded. Instead, flashes of light explode around his hand, the same hand he used to strike down both the black guy and the bearded assailant who's clambering out of the shattered window.

The shorter guy stares at his opponent, then his gun, as if trying figure out why the rules have changed. Then he must regain his bearings, because he aims for another fusillade.

His hesitation has given the guy in the hooded sweatshirt time to close the distance. He grabs the top of the pistol, wrenches the shorter guy's grip aside. A glowing strip of light around his right wrist intensifies, from red up through yellow to white. The attacker shouts, and it's unclear why, until the gun drops to the pavement. It's heated up like a coal.

The hooded man drops the now unarmed thug with a flurry of blows that put him against the nearest wall, capped off with a brutal elbow hit to his head.

The black guy gets up, and runs down the street, abandoning his companions. He doesn't get far before blue and red lights appear around the corner.

Of course. The hooded man pulls a phone from his pocket, the screen already ignited. He must have called the police at first sight of the three would-be carjackers.

The man who'd gone through the window has made it onto the sidewalk. He staggers at the hooded man, but falters, misses a sloppy punch, and goes facedown into a puddle. The back of his jacket is dark with blood, in long streaks where he must have gotten sliced up by the window glass.

And the hooded defender? He's gone down an alley, across the street.

People spill out from the restaurants and bars, including Bentley's. The street, formerly empty except for parked cars, is suddenly full of shouting and murmurs. The police, six men total, start cordoning crowds.

"Z!" Curt hurries up. There's a sheen of perspiration on his face, and he reeks of both beer and cigarette smoke. I realize I probably do, too. Anna's right behind him.

"You should probably go back inside," I tell them.

"Are you kidding? I heard gunshots! Thought you got yourself mugged."

Anna stands next to me. Her perfume cuts through the stale smoke. "Are you hurt?"

"No, of course not, I never got anywhere near the … whatever it was." What was it? Some Good Samaritan keeping my car safe? It's an odd thing to protect. "Some guys were breaking into the Bimmer, and, well, all three of them got smacked around by … I don't know who."

"Everybody back it up." The police officer, a tall, young man with a sharp nose and thick blond mustache, urges us back. He wears mirrored shades, despite it being past 8 in winter. "Keep away from the scene, please."

"Officer, my name's Dominic Zein. That's my car over there. Can I show you my ID?"

The cop glances over his shoulder. His name plate flashes silver under the streetlights, and I spy "Ambrose" in black type. "Hang on." He triggers the radio mounted to his shoulder. "Got a guy here claims he's the registered owner of the vehicle."

Curt pats my shoulder. His hand shakes. Anna touches my palm. I don't move from her reach.

"Yeah, Ten-Four." Ambrose sniffs. "Okay, come with me."

The thirty feet around my car look like a war zone. There's blood smeared on the sidewalk, glistening crimson streaks mingled with rain puddles. Shattered glass crunches underfoot. The police have the black guy in cuffs, pressed up against a squad car. He's muttering and shaking his head. The bearded one is cuffed, too, but the cops are taking a bit more care with him, as they staunch the flow of blood from myriad wounds. One snaps into his radio for an ambulance.

The short guy is a bit more hysterical than his companions. His eyes are stretched open. "My gun! It got hot, man! Thought it was gonna peel my skin off! I could smell it burning, man!"

"Yeah, guns you shoot will get hot," Officer Ambrose mutters. "Genius work, here."

"Says he got a look at the attacker's face, Sarge."

"Sure he did." Sarge? Yes, Ambrose does have three blue chevrons on his shoulder. "Bet he put up a heroic fight against some nut after these three got interrupted in their auto theft."

"No, man! I saw him! He had this thing on his arm, and it glowed! Made Carl's shirt fry! He was—" The guy stops struggling against the other two officers, finally letting them get his wrists bound. "You."

It's my turn to put on a bewildered face. "Me, what?"

"You! You were him! You got that face!"

Ambrose frowns, but this time at me. "Sir, I'm going to have to ask your whereabouts."

"I was in Bentley's." Suddenly I'm preoccupied with the position of Ambrose's hands on his belt, which are very close to his holstered pistol. Also, I'm grateful my last run-in with law enforcement was a speeding ticket two years ago. "With friends. There's a bunch still here. We were playing pool and I went out for a walk."

"Into the middle of a fight?"

"No, like I said." I point behind him. "That's my car."

Mistake. As soon as my arm goes out, Ambrose's hand slips to the butt of his gun. "Easy. Keep your hands where I can see them."

"Sorry."

"It was you! I seen you! You made my gun almost melt, man!" Short guy starts pulling against the two cops attending him.

"Cruz, Henson, get him out of here and shut him up!" Ambrose snaps. "Sir, I'm going to have to corroborate your story—"

"Hey!" Curt and Anna break from the crowd. "What's wrong?"

"Folks, didn't I say something about staying back?" Ambrose glares at them—or he must be, because I still can't see his eyes behind those infuriating sunglasses. "We've got an ambulance and a couple more units coming, so I'd be happy to detain all of you in the back seat if you can't listen."

"Okay, but—" Curt gestures at me. "We were with him. In the bar."

"Both of us," Anna says. "He's been with us the whole night, until he walked out."

"That's when I saw the fight. I heard the glass break when whoever that guy is got pushed into it," I add.

Ambrose takes in the full view of blood and glass. "More like thrown."

"Him! It's him!" The short guy's reedy voice carries through the commotion.

"Zip it!" One of the officers slams the door shut. He glances back at us. "Sorry, Sarge, guy's high. Not sure on what but he's half out of his brain."

"Great. That'll make for getting a fun statement." Ambrose sniffs. "Okay, you three, stay here. I'm gonna have Henson take statements. Mr. …."

"Zein."

"Right. Don't worry about what that nut says. People nowadays, they see one guy who looks like he's from the Middle East, they think everybody's the same guy named Abdullah or something. Probably can't even tell the black guy he's working with from a dozen others. Drug-addled and stupid punks." Ambrose frowns. "But you do look familiar. Didn't I read about you somewhere?"

My cheeks flame. That article again. "Yes, sir. It was in the *Rampart Post*."

"Check." Ambrose snaps his fingers. "That's where it was. Okay, Mr. Zein, just hang on and we'll get everything cleared up. Don't worry about your car. Let us take some prints, square away evidence, and you can go through it, see what's missing or damaged."

"Thank you, Sergeant."

"No problem." Ambrose moves off, barking orders to his officers. He was correct—two more squad cars and an ambulance have arrived. The three men get bundled up and driven away.

"We'll wait here with you," Curt says.

My phone buzzes, jolting me from my stupor. Heart pounding, I tell him, "Sure. Just, uh, let me text Jess and let her know what's going on."

Anna's hand leaves mine. It was there the whole time, wasn't it? If Curt noticed, he didn't say a word. Good thing, too. My brain's such a mess right now I couldn't be sure of my reaction.

I take a couple steps away, off the curb, into the empty space between two cars. My phone screen glows up at me.

The text isn't from Jess. It's Nick.

<You're welcome.>

CHAPTER EIGHT

Friday morning, Jess is already packed. She must have finished last night, before I got back from Bentley's.

Other than wrinkling her nose at the smell I brought home, she isn't worried much by the BMW break-in. Of course, I have altered the account of the night's events. The three men getting pummeled remains. The part about Nick breaking it up, I omit.

"Nothing was missing?" She pulls a tray of *manakish* from the oven. I can't stand the smell, but it's been one of her favorites from childhood, so I get sliced tomatoes and mint from the refrigerator.

"No, and my papers weren't badly ruined."

"I won't say I told you so, but, if you hadn't left all your stuff in the car …"

"That sounds an awful lot like I told you so."

"At least the police have it all sorted out."

Yes, except for the part about an avenging passer-by who looks like me. Fortunately they consider the testimony of stoned thieves invalid, but I'm not nearly as relaxed.

My phone's silent on the corner of the table. No lights, no notifications, which is perturbing because Nick didn't respond back to inquiries after he texted me last night. Hasn't responded this morning, either.

"Dominic?"

"Hmm? Yes, they do have it under control. Insurance should cover the damage, but other than the door, there's nothing broken." Meanwhile I'm wondering whether I should have followed my impulse to drive over to Nick's in the middle of the night. It didn't occur to me until after I got home, past 11. But how to explain to Jess? Paranoia would only serve to tip her off.

With breakfast out of the way, we continue our conversations, getting ready for our afternoon departure to Estes Park. The reservations are confirmed. I pack my clothes. Jess will drop me by Curt's place this morning so I can pick up Sheryl, leaving the BMW to recuperate in the garage over the weekend.

"You didn't say much about the rest of your evening."

For good reason. The memory of Anna's hand pressed against mine still sends lightning through my body. That alone frustrates me. The whole goal was to spend more time with Jess and lighten my workload. What good does replacing myself for specific times do if I'm going to squander it. "It was Curt and the other guys, so, not much to report. Fortunately I didn't have to drive anyone else home. We hung around long enough everyone had sobered up before they got behind the wheel. Also, we beat them. Twice."

"Pool sharks." She laughs. "Make sure you tell Anna thanks."

That stops me in the middle of looping my tie. "What?"

"Because you won." Jess makes a motion with her hands. "And … you don't owe Curt any money, yes?"

"Oh. Right." I flash her a smile. "That is one of my life goals."

She kisses me. "You seem out of sorts. Worried about the meeting today?"

The run-up to Procyon. Tyson and I are supposed to finalize our plan of attack. Compared with what I witnessed last night; I think I'll be fine. "Should go just fine. Provided I don't vault the table and strangle Tyson with his tie."

Jess rolls her eyes, but there's a hint of a smile on her lips.

Curt's condo is on the river, on the west end of Rampart. Ten units are lined up shoulder to shoulder, facing out to the suburbs and farmland to the north. Peaked roofs, fake stone, pale siding, lots of tall windows—they're a regular collection of chalets. Not any of our work. Plan Out created them.

Curt's waiting for us, garage door yawning. Sheryl's parked on the concrete slab. Water beads where he hasn't finished wiping the Jeep down and runs in rivulets down the driveway seams. It's—well, Curt would say "She's"—a silver and matte black 2015 Jeep Wrangler, two-door, hard top. The sides reflect the Van River and Jess's car as we pull up to the curb.

"See you at four." I lean on the window and kiss Jess good-bye.

"Can't wait." Her smile is coy. "You won't need to honk at the front of the school. I'll wait outside."

"Ah, just standing around for any man to sweep you off your feet? I should be jealous."

"You should be on time."

Curt whistles as the Hyundai disappears down the street. "Kinda envious, my friend."

I pat Sheryl's fender. "You should be."

"Hey, hands off." He snaps at my knuckles with a rag, then proceeds to buff the spot I just touched. "You do whatever you want with Sheryl—ugh, within reason, okay? No playtime in the back seat."

"Curt, don't strain your brain. We'll keep her tidy."

"You'd better." He tugs at his beard. "Come to think of it, I should charge a deposit."

"No."

"Why not?"

"Because you're my friend, and wouldn't do anything so crude, especially in light of us architects smearing you engineers across the pool tables with back-to-back victories."

He winces. "Have to poke that wound. Okay, she's all yours."

"Thanks."

Curt hands me the keys, but when I grab them, he doesn't let go.

His expression is suddenly somber. "Take the time to focus on what's important, Z."

"I will." I frown. "Such as …?"

"Your wife."

My gut twists. "If this is about Anna, let's find a new topic."

"No, let's not. Watch yourself around her."

"I am. Notice I went home without her."

"Don't mouth off. I'm serious."

"Curt, if you're so worried, why don't you pursue her? Take her mind off me."

"She's not into me, Z. She's into you. So I'm telling you again, as a pro in these situations, unless you're prepared to cause some major damage, be careful."

He's right, of course, but it's the whole thing of the man most cavalier with male-female relationships lecturing me on fidelity that makes it hard to digest. "Okay, I will. You've made a good point."

"Wait." Curt clasps both my shoulders. He lets the keys remain in my custody. "Does this mean I'm right, and you're wrong?"

"Maybe." I grin. "Just maybe. That's all you get."

"Eh, I'll take it. You kids have fun this weekend. Don't stay out too late. Drink responsibly. Oh, and make sure to go to bed early." He exaggerates a wink.

"I'm going to drive off and pretend like you didn't say that."

"Later, Z."

I'd forgotten what fun it is to drive the Jeep. It rumbles down the streets, letting me tower above the traffic—the sedans and compacts, at least. There's plenty of pickups and SUVs vying for attention.

A block from Dualpoint Nick finally calls.

"Morning. Got your texts."

"Good thing. Tell me that wasn't you who beat those guys."

"You mean the scum trying to steal your car? Yes, it was, and before you ask, I regret only that I didn't put all three of them in the hospital. Missed my goal."

"You can't do that!"

"Do what? Protect my property? Now you're nuts."

"It's my car, Nick."

"Ah, but if we're doing this swap properly, we're sharing, aren't we?"

"Yes, I get that. Hence the texts of my wardrobe, as bizarre as that seems."

"So, don't worry about it. The cops think of you as an upstanding citizen, no doubt. They're not going to take the word of those three over you. Not with witnesses to back you up. Shall we get down to business?"

"Hang on a second. What were those flashes? Something sparked off your wristband, and I swore that attacker's shots—"

"He was wasted. Never came near me. I had a taser that must have carried a little too much voltage for their tastes. Anything else, Mr. Detective?"

I blow out a breath. He gets no response from me as I park the Jeep in my regular spot. Tyson's here. So's Anna. "Fine. Don't do anything else like that."

"I promise to keep my vigilantism to a minimum."

"Let's focus on reality."

"Fine by me. Your meeting today."

"It's the prep for tomorrow's."

"Shall I put in an appearance?"

My mouth flaps open and shut, without sound. The automatic response would be "No," but now that I ponder it, what better way to make sure there's no trouble with Saturday? Not that I'm worried. Much. "Okay. The meeting's at 9. Pick up the BMW at the house. I left the garage door unlocked, and the keys are on the seat."

"That's trusting. What did Jess say?"

The way he says her name so familiar needles me. "Didn't say anything to her. She doesn't need to know about this. Not yet."

"Sound policy. All right, I'll text you when I'm on my way. Same gambit as the post office?"

"That will work."

He hangs up. I tap the phone to my mouth.

This could be a very bad idea. But I'm ready for the change.

Our conference room is an airy space. Sunlight filters in through slanted windows, so much so we had a layer of dust on the light fixtures. One long table, glass with steel legs, is centered on a slate gray carpet. There's a phone unit in the middle.

Tyson has his Procyon materials laid out in four piles, precise as a military convoy. I want to jostle each one, until they're a mess. He doesn't look up as I get into my chair. "You're late."

"Hardly. You didn't set a time for this meeting. How can I possibly be late?"

"I meant getting to work, Zein."

It's 8:01. "I'll be sure to mark myself down as tardy. What's it to be, the rack or impalement?"

Tyson glares up from his paperwork. Dark circles under his eyes give him the appearance of someone who's been in a brawl, but his immaculate hands indicate otherwise. I catch a whiff of something sour. Alcohol? A pang of sympathy cuts through the walls erected against his taunts. The man has deeper problems than backtalk from me.

"Tell you what, when Kaminsky gets in, let me do the talking, and you sit there and smile," Tyson mutters. "Look pretty, like your newspaper photo."

And the sympathy vanishes.

"Morning, gentlemen." Kaminsky ushers in a cloud of cologne, and the scent of leather, the latter courtesy of the battered valise he sets on a third end of the table. Anna's right behind him, carrying her tablet and a thick binder. Post-It notes feather one side. She's got options for internal colors already.

"Morning." I have my laptop up and running, but I keep the screen facing away from everyone. I'll be the obedient employee and let Tyson start off.

It will make it more satisfying when it comes to my turn.

"Procyon Foundation." Tyson stands. He unfolds a huge sheet in the middle of the table. Anna slides the teleconference phone out of the way. The page features a seven-story building, made of three towers joined by enclosed walkways. Each one is white, with gleaming glass reflecting an idyllic bay. "This is their headquarters in San Camillo. It's a thirty-year-old design, so obviously some of the choices made are dated—"

Kaminsky clears his throat. He pats his valise. "Vintage doesn't mean dated, Tyson."

"Of course not." Tyson's cheeks darken, but he doesn't break stride. "Their flagship building has influenced their other offices—Seattle, Houston, Miami, Chicago, Drake City."

He slides a sheet of paper atop the giant image, one for each name as he says them. He isn't exaggerating. The styles vary by region. The Miami structure has the same color scheme as San Camillo's, right down to tint of the glass, while the Chicago building is a dark, narrow high-rise. But they don't exceed seven stories, and each one is made of a cluster of three towers joined by similar enclosed walkways. A few have enclosed courtyards, while Drake City's and Houston's have parking in the center, due no doubt to their locations in their respective cities' downtown.

"Should be a simple enough theme to replicate," Tyson says.

"Is that what you and Dominic have decided?" Kaminsky peers over his glasses at the drawings. He slides the largest—and thus the entire pile—toward him with the eraser end of his pencil.

I cover my hand with my mouth, as if I'm deep in thought, to restrain any cutting response. If Tyson had bothered to seek my input, I'd likely agree with him that we should follow Procyon's pattern. But he didn't, and here we sit, two partners with designs neither one of us has seen.

"We've got, uh, similar outlooks." Tyson matches my gaze. There's a warning there, either *Help me pull this one off the edge!* Or *Stay shut up and let me handle this.*

I'll err on the side of Option A. "We have our own takes on the design. Tyson and I agreed it was better to create them independently, then bring them to this meeting and see what we could synthesize out of the individual sketches."

Kaminsky flicks his gaze to each of us in turn. There's a smile lurking on his lips, but he doesn't give it full reign. "I'm glad to hear you're cooperating."

Tyson goes first. I must say, his plan for a seven-story, triple tower that looks like three mountain peaks is daring. They're too severe for my taste, but then again, so is the architect himself.

"This is the best of the batch I came up with." Tyson thumps a fist on one of his immaculate piles. "I can have the rest ready for the client, too."

"I appreciate that, but this is striking." Kaminsky holds the image up to the light. "Reminds me of their Chicago building, but with a Western touch that sets it apart from something that otherwise would sit on the shores of Lake Michigan."

"Thanks." Tyson smiles and leans back in his chair. "What about you, Zein?"

It's as if I didn't come up with a plausible excuse for our lack of partnership a few seconds ago and saved him from a scolding by our mutual boss. One of the many hazards of working with Tyson. Fine by me, if this is how he wants the game to progress. "Two possibilities." I spin the laptop around.

The images are set up in a slide show format, so that the domed structure appears first, then, after 10 seconds, fades into the sail structure.

"I do like those," Kaminsky mutters. "A lot."

"The domed one has a similar feel to their San Camillo head-quarters." Anna opens her binder, pulls out a couple of sheets of colors. "This is what they use on the various floors. I've been emailing back and forth with one of their reps this week, so I can get a better look at their palette—well, except for the seventh floor. They gave me the run around on the specifics for that one."

"Corporate secrets and other nonsense." Kaminsky sets Tyson's design aside and gestures. "Dominic, can you bring up each of those in turn, please?"

"Sure. I've got prints, too." I pass the pages around. Anna's expression lights up at the sail structure, with its three sweeping edges.

Tyson's fingers crumple the edge of the sheet before he sets it aside.

"These are good," Kaminsky says. "And by good, I mean both of them. I think these will easily pass muster with the Procyon representatives. Anna?"

"I'll have options for both by lunch." Anna smiles. "Then I can review them with each of you in turn."

"Sounds like a plan." Tyson's tone is stiff. "What else do we need to be ready for Saturday? I assume Dominic and I are still on point for that meeting."

A not-so-subtle dig that I'm not getting out of our first chat with the client just so I can get out of town for the weekend. I smirk but keep my head down. Tyson won't be disappointed, but neither will I.

"Oh, I wouldn't have it any other way." Kaminsky holds up our drawings, side by side. "These tell me I was right putting you two on the same team."

"Okay then. Let's figure out our plan of action."

"I'm amenable to Tyson taking the lead," I say, absent any sarcasm. Why would I not? With Nick filling in, it makes sense for me—him— to keep a low profile.

Tyson fumbles with the dome drawing as he hands it back to me. Probably trying to asses what's prompted sudden camaraderie.

Not camaraderie, Tyson. Self-preservation.

My phone buzzes. Nick. <Outside, when you're ready.>

Panic jolts me. I give everyone at the table a smile. "Sorry, got a call. Problem with Sammy. Mind if I take it outside?"

Kaminsky chuckles. "If it keeps us from hearing your dog bark over the phone, by all means."

Anna rolls her eyes, but nods in agreement. They bought it.

Doesn't make me feel better about lying to them.

Or for this subtle swap.

Nick's leaning against the Jeep when I get outside. My mind rebels against the sight of myself. His shirt, pants, and shoes are identical to mine. Yet, something about his stance is … off. There's too much cockiness to his lean, and his expression is a billboard for disdain.

"Nice rig." He raps his knuckles on the gas cap.

Good thing Curt isn't here. He'd keel over. "That's Curt's truck."

"Your friend, yes? The one with the beard."

"Nice to know your stalking continues."

"Please. I watch your Facebook feed." Nick waggles his phone.

"Get off Sheryl, will you? Everyone knows I'd never lean against her—or even touch another part besides the door handles, unless I had a rag ready to wipe off the prints."

"Sheryl." He makes a face and eases off the Jeep as if it were suddenly radioactive. "He names his vehicles?"

"He discovered Sheryl Crow when we were in college. Call it a state of perpetual lust."

Nick just shrugs, as if the mention of such a celebrity singer elicits little feeling from him. Maybe he's never seen a picture of her—she's gorgeous. "All good things to know. Are we ready?"

"The materials are on the table." I fit the Bluetooth to my ear.

Nick dials in and grins. "Good luck."

"Thanks. But I think I should wish you the luck."

"Oh, you'll need to refrain from overreacting. I doubt you're calm while you're on the sidelines and I'm in the game. But I won't need any."

I steer the BMW out of the parking lot. Nick slips in the back door of our building, disappearing from the rearview.

My fingers drum on the wheel. This is crazy. I could get fired. Or arrested. But there's a madness that's pushing me down the road, around the next corner, and onto the block behind Dualpoint. I can argue this is all for Jess, so we have a happier life together, with more time spent absent from meetings and client emails and redesigns. But the more I focus, the more I admit that's a half-truth.

It's all about me.

I want the time off. I want to enjoy my life, rather than slaving until I'm worn out, left with nothing but high blood pressure and a divorce.

There's no way I am going to end up like my father.

Mother couldn't handle his ambition. Certainly, he did well by both of us—supporting his wife and child, just like his parents did, and their parents before them, only he neglected the most important part of the equation.

His family.

I park between a pair of sedans. There's no resentment. Sorrow crushes my chest. Father did what he thought was the best for us. But it drove a wedge through our home, to the point he started staying late at the office, progressing to his getting an apartment of his own. He's remarried now. Mother lives with her sister.

I have to temper the same ambition with the resolution that I cannot, I will not, wind up like him.

Sound crackles through the earpiece. Nick's voice filters through, slightly broken by static, but intelligible. "Sorry about that. Dog issues. You know how the neighbor can be."

Kaminsky's chuckle booms. "I think that goes without saying. Did she ever claim responsibility for your dog's injuries?"

"She certainly did. Paid for the bill. I was very impressed she chose to do the right thing."

Murmurs of approval from Anna and Kaminsky give me the chills. Mrs. Cortez's frightened face fills my memory—her face, and the way she ran back to her house. Nick may have come on too strong in order to solve the situation.

Yes, but the bill is paid, and along the same train of thought, three men who thought they could steal my car learned otherwise. Perhaps Nick is overeager. Yet, if I can't find a solution through straightforward channels, how can I blame someone else for doing so on my behalf?

"About Saturday's line up." Tyson's voice is taut, even through the phone call. "You're okay with me being in charge?"

Nick doesn't say anything for a moment. "Well, Tyson, I mean what I say, and if I say you're the man in the lead, then that is what will happen. Talk to me about your approach for Procyon. I'm sure we can dazzle them with our combined work. Whatever you need."

There's a series of sputtering coughs—Anna, who sounds like she's choking on her water. I can't blame her. It's all I can do to stifle a laugh of my own. Fortunately the call is muted on my end.

"Okay. Sounds good. Let's start off with how we want things set up for their arrival. I'm thinking we have our designs run through a projector, right up on the wall." Tyson's chair squeaks. His voice fades some; he must be walking the room. "And when they come in, you be ready with the handouts. I'll greet them at the door."

"There'll be a copy of each one for them, no problem," Nick says.

Just like that, the fear, the anxiety, the strain, they all flee. I slap both hands against the steering wheel. Wish Curt were here—we could skip over to Caerphilly for a beer in celebration.

Instead I wait until the meeting wraps up. There's plenty of notes, written in my hand and Nick's, when we quickly swap vehicles in the parking lot.

"You did great!" I slap his shoulder. If I were any more fired up, we'd have just won a soccer match.

Nick laughs. "Easy, Dominic. We'll see how it goes Saturday—but rest assured, you'll have both your job and a happy client waiting when you get back."

I swing over to Rampart Valley High School. Jess is waiting out front. She waves good-bye to a gaggle of teachers, some of whom slink back indoors toward whatever mounds of paperwork await.

"Finally." She lets out a ragged breath the instant the Jeep's passenger door slams shut. "Quick! Before somebody sees me and remembers I still work here!"

I chuckle and take the Bypass loop around the east side of Rampart. Fifteen minutes later, we're on the interstate, with the city disappearing behind a long, slanted butte. The last of its green-hedged suburbs vanish among rolling brown hills.

"Thank you so much for keeping this date," she says. "I'd hoped for a long time you'd be free enough so we wouldn't have to cancel."

Rampart's gone. A weekend without the chains of responsibility is ahead. "Yes, me too."

CHAPTER NINE

Saturday morning, I awake in a pleasant haze.

My eyes refuse to open fully. Golden light filters in between the curtains. The bedroom is chilly enough I know the stove needs to be lit.

Jess rolls over, curled up against me. Her hair and T-shirt are as rumpled as the thick quilt keeping the cold morning air at bay. Her arm lies across my chest.

Wood creaks somewhere in the cabin. Outside, chickadees bound up and down a stand of pines, flashes of black and white glimpsed against blue sky through narrow gap of glass on the other side of the room. Otherwise, no sound. No cars. No phones.

I glance at my duffel bag, drooping over the edge of a caned chair. My phone is in there, buried among clothing, but it's turned off. Completely powered down.

Just like me.

I'd promised myself—and Jess—this much. I would not be available to anyone or anything this weekend. Only time I'll turn it on will be when Rampart's skyline appears on the horizon when we roll back into town Sunday. She'd done the same.

I ease out of bed. The floor is shockingly frigid after the warmth of two bodies mingled. I drag on a T-shirt and dig up a pair of wool

97

socks.

"Mm? Where're you going?" Jess's eyes are slits.

"Read for a bit. Tea?"

"Please. Bring me a cup?"

I bend over and kiss her nose. "Sadly, you'll have to join me on the porch to claim that reward."

She snorts and rolls over. Her hand slaps around in search of the quilt's edge, jerks it up around her shoulders. "Too cold."

"Give the stove time."

The cabin's a simple affair—small bedroom and bathroom in the back, living room and kitchenette out front. Boards bend and creak underfoot. The interspersed rugs have loose threads, assembled of riotous shades that make me wonder if the weaver was colorblind. Anna would cut them to shreds, then burn the scraps.

Hmm. Best leave that thought aside.

Stove lit, fire dancing atop the logs, I take a steaming mug out onto the porch. There's no one else visible from here. The only signs of civilization are Sheryl, whose windshield is covered in a sheet of frost, and the power line arcing down between the pines. A rutted road winds a quarter mile to a wider dirt road. There's a dozen more cabins spread throughout this mountainside tract, but they're distant enough for everyone to have the desired privacy. Before long a tendril of smoke rises above the treetops, smearing as the breeze carries it east. Someone else is awake.

I grab a tattered paperback from inside the living room and lean back in a lopsided rocking chair. The cushion's freezing, but it doesn't matter. I plant my heels on the railing and breathe in freedom.

This is the sensation I desire every time we grace the pews of St. Lucius—which, admittedly, is not often enough. No committee meetings, no gossip, no infighting. Simply, peace.

I delve into the novel, putting aside even those worries. Surely Father Hamra won't begrudge a man escape, no matter how temporary. He may, though, take issue with how I've done it.

It's so tranquil that, at first, I assume the ticking noise is something hitting Sheryl's frame. In fact I'm halfway from the chair—Lord preserve our safety if Curt finds a scratch—when I realize it's my watch. That earns a chuckle, until I see what time it is.

9:55.

A jolt banishes the last of my morning fuzziness. The Procyon Foundation client meeting starts in five minutes. I should be there, with a raft of plans ready to wow the client—at least, as much as I can wow them with Tyson holding the leash and making me jump hoops. But I'm not there. I'm three hours away.

Nick is my substitute.

Reciting a psalm, broken and misspoken, helps soothe the anxiety. When it doesn't disappear, I bolster faith with facts. Nick did great in the run-up meeting yesterday. He's proven he can fool my co-workers, though there's a pang of guilt when I realize what that means. I've lied to all of them—Mr. Kaminsky, Anna, and yes, even Tyson.

But it had to be this way. What's better, to fudge a few things at work for a while, or to turn my back on my wife and my private life in favor of career? Besides, it isn't as if I'm missing any work, or doing a subpar job. Nick's designs are fantastic. His work is equal in quality, and his creativity shares my spark. He can be me.

There's nothing to do but sit back and drink in this tea, this book, and this perfect morning. Whatever the result from today's meeting, I can't change it. I've made my decision. The consequences can wait until I return.

Footsteps. Jess is in the kitchen, pouring her own mug. She's pulled on her favorite shirt, the soft, long-sleeved pink one with white elephants stenciled all over, atop the T-shirt. The flannel pajama pants are a nice touch. Jess waves at me through the window.

I wave back. What had I been thinking? Pouring hours away at work, right down the drain, like my life would somehow magically replenish when they're spent. Prancing around the offices like I owned them, toying with the affections of a single woman while I moaned about how little time my wife and I had to spend together. It was about time control returned to my hands, whether by my doing or, in this case, the generosity of a stranger.

A stranger who wasn't that strange after all.

Yet, I can't help pondering his endgame. He's awfully giving of his time and talents. That's a good thing, for me. However, some of his choices have been less than restrained. Purposely needling Tyson, for example, and intimidating Mrs. Cortez, not even mentioning coming to the defense of my helpless car. How did he even know how to fight like that, anyway? Martial arts training, taken to the extreme?

I flip to the next page. Whatever Nick is doing, I'll have to be more careful. He hasn't gone against any of my wishes, and he's done all the tasks required, but he can't just be allowed to run about pretending to be me. Someone's bound to notice.

Trying to explain what's really going on threatens me with a headache.

"Did you hear about the fight downtown?" Jess slides a rocking chair near me, the legs scraping on the deck. She sits cross-legged.

Speaking of Nick … "Of course. I reported it." I sip the tea. Mint wafts over my face.

"No, not the men who tried to steal the car. I'm talking about in the back alleys. I guess there was an electronics store and a crew were stealing everything they could get their hands on. Someone interrupted it, badly beat the robbers."

Tea dribbles down my chin. "No. When was this?"

"Yesterday, I think." She frowns, thinking back. "Very early in the morning. The police said they didn't know whether it was the same guy who stopped the car thieves, or a related group—maybe a rival gang."

"So, someone else stole the electronics."

"No. Nothing was taken."

"Huh. That's interesting." And disconcerting. "What street?"

"Somewhere behind Federal. I don't remember the address." She grins. "If I had my phone, I'd Google it for you."

"You'd be breaking our agreed-upon restrictions."

"What fun are rules if you can't occasionally break them?"

What fun, indeed. I'm willing to place money on the theft occurring in the 600 block. A first-floor electronics store, behind Federal—and the would-be thieves are stomped? Nick. Has to be.

Part of me is quietly furious, sitting there reading and drinking tea and chatting with Jess. How could he endanger my identity by gallivanting around the city, getting into fistfights or Taser assaults? All it would take is for the police to grab him if he fails to slip away, and there'd be a very long, complex, and confusing explanation required.

Yet, the other part of me admires what he's doing. I'd never admit it openly, but in this day and age, where so few men take matters into their own hands—physically, that is—the idea of a vigilante is stirring. Imagine. Why wait around for criminals to commit their offenses and get arrested in the aftermath, if at all? What if you could interrupt the process? Catch them red-handed, as it were. Not that I am advocating being judge and jury, just preemptive law enforcement.

I let the fantasy slide away. Whatever Nick does in his free time is none of my concern, so long as he lives my life the way I want him to.

We take a pair of mountain bikes into town, following trails around hills. There's no snow yet, and the skies are dazzling blue. Jess scoots ahead around a corner, laughing, and when she slows for a deep rut, I take advantage and speed by.

Our impromptu race ends on the edge of downtown. By then we're sweating enough that we doff our jackets and slug down a half bottle of water each. People pack the streets, carrying bags full of whatever trinkets they've decided were worth buying.

Jess finds a clothing store first thing. "You might want to take a walk." She rests her head on my shoulder. "I know how exhausting it is to watch me being gorgeous."

I roll my eyes, chuckling as I do. "Of course. Don't let me miss anything especially jaw-dropping."

"If I find a hot sweatshirt, I'll message you a pic."

"Hey, we were supposed to leave out phones at the cabin."

"I did." She pokes me in the side. "'Bye."

She'll be in there a good hour, no doubt striking up a conversation with the clerks. I opt for the general store a block over. It's only a few years old, but it has that vibe of a run-down, vintage establishment that survived the town's nascence.

A glint of metal catches my eye. Knives. There's a whole row of Swiss Army models, from simple blades up to the ones as thick as a paper towel tube. Some are used. One in particular has a variety of tools yet is slim enough that carrying it around in my pocket wouldn't be too onerous. I've wanted a new knife for years. This one, worn down as the logo is, reminds me of Father's. For all his faults, he was always prepared to tackle any project—on the rare occasions he was home—convinced his knife would solve the problem at hand.

The clerk is a college-age girl. She takes my cash and delivers the change, counting it out without having to read the register's digits. Impressive. As she dumps the coins into my outstretched hand, she smiles, her eyes squinting as if in concentration. "Weird."

"I don't usually get described that way."

Her cheeks go red. "Sorry, not, um, the way you look, sir, but … it's kinda déjà vu. Like I've given you change back before."

My insides seize. The half-smile stays welded to my face. "Yes, it's always a strange sensation, isn't it?"

"Yeah." She shakes her head. "Anyway, have a nice day."

"You too."

First thing I do is slide the sunglasses back on. I want to run back to the bike and put my helmet on to complete the disguise. It never occurred to me Nick would have spent time somewhere else nearby Rampart before stepping into my life. It's ridiculous, of course. Colorado is a big state, but not so big as to avoid running into someone with whom your double may have already interacted.

There's a newspaper rack out front, for the *Estes Park Trail-Gazette*. Without my phone to keep me connected to the outside world, a newspaper should suffice to sate the urge. Besides, I'm fascinated by the local feel to small publications. I can picture Jess rolling her eyes as I add this one to my collection. Our last road trip, we stopped in four Utah towns. I brought back a newspaper from each one.

It's the usual litany of local goings-on, small crimes with a few majors sprinkled in, along with garden club announcements and retirement features. National news is no surprise—this country despises that one, the president promises to take swift action, fleets and armies rearrange, people are starving or thriving. I skim through for the Colorado focus.

A photo gives me pause. It's small, a mere thumbnail under the headline **Body Found in Abandoned Home.** Some homeless man died, alone and bereft. I shake my head. Reading the details of his lonesome life fills me with grief, as these kind always do. Even as fractured as my family has been, the idea of spending one's last days without any companionship, mired in poverty, is tragic. I cannot imagine his hopelessness.

Apparently, the police are still seeking a cause of death, though they indicate its natural causes. Something about the photo, however, prompts a second look. Perhaps it's the man's eyes. Where did they get the picture, anyway? Ah, criminal record. Minor infractions, such as—

Wait.

I step farther onto the sidewalk, where I'm out of the building's shadow. Sunlight shines across the photo. I tip the paper at a different angle. The man's face is haggard, gaunt, and bearded, but the eyes— the brow. They're familiar.

Perhaps … I cover the lower half of his face with my hand, obscuring everything from the nose down.

It *is* him.

Nick's bodyguard.

He's far from clean-cut and appears to have missed too many

meals, but the eyes, the nose, the general shape of his upper face—they're the same.

I read the article line for line, not scanning, but digesting every word, looking for some hint. There. A name. Eric Christopher Talbot, age 38, ex-Army, long history of substance abuse and petty theft. Parents were Russian émigrés in the 1970s. Served with distinction in Operation Enduring Freedom.

Certainly wouldn't surprise me if the real bodyguard—Eric, I suppose—has a similar skill set. I can see him standing outside Nick's apartment, with that stance that shouts military or police training.

This begs a troubling question. I fold the newspaper under my arm and start for the clothing store at which I left Jess. Grappling with the appearance of one's doppelgänger is one thing. But to have another at the same time? And serving as the driver-slash-muscle for said doppelgänger?

Again, I don't know what I'd tell the police. Sure, I may have found someone who looks just like your dead homeless veteran, but he's the personal driver for the rich man who has offered to take my place at onerous work and home tasks? No. Not an option. Not unless I want to be given a wellness break from work—one that accompanies a pink slip and a recommendation for hire at somewhere else.

The sooner I check in with Nick, the better.

And I think I have further questions for Father Hamra.

Sunday morning, we stay in late again. By the time we head out to lunch, I'm equal parts well-rested and exhausted.

Jess is oddly quiet as we begin the drive back to Rampart. She watches the hills and homes undulating outside the window. I've got the radio turned up, to my favorite satellite station, the rock beat thumping off Sheryl's door panels.

"Hey." I place my hand on hers, resting as it is on her leg. "Are you okay?"

"Hmm?" She's got her chin propped on her hand. She gives me

a sideways look, accompanied by that smile—same one that makes me, well, stupid and brave at the same time. "Yes. Nothing's wrong."

"You must be pretty deep in thought, though, if you can't muster the enthusiasm to whine about my music choices."

"That doesn't mean they've improved."

I laugh. "See? More like it. Seriously, Jess …"

"Have you thought about having kids?"

Yikes. It's a good thing Father taught me to drive with steady hands on the wheel. A pickup rushes by in the left lane just then, rattling the Jeep with its diesel exhaust, but Sheryl doesn't so much as swerve. "Ah, not since we last talked about it."

"For three months, nothing?"

"All right, it has crossed my mind." On a few occasions. And when I see little boys with black hair and dusky skin. "But I haven't changed my opinion. We're swamped. Adding a child to the mix now …"

"Yes, I understand, but if not now, when?" Jess sighs. "You're thirty, Dominic, and I'm only a few years younger. Some of my friends already have a couple of kids and manage quite nicely."

"There's also people our age who aren't even married."

"Also noted. That shouldn't affect our decisions."

"Shouldn't it?"

She frowns. "Are you afraid of something?"

"Me? Afraid? Jess, I spend most of my working hours talking to strangers about my daydreams that get transformed into buildings. If I were afraid …"

"Don't change the subject."

"I'm not. I'm not afraid of having children. What I am is worried that we can't be parents—that the life we'll give them would be comfortable, but absent love."

"Even if I stayed home for a while? Maybe a few years, while they were youngest."

A distinct image of a mound of bills, unpaid, flashes through my mind. "Then what? I work harder and longer to cover expenses, even with cutbacks in our family budget, and I'm never around."

My tone's become too snappish; I go silent.

Jess touches my hand. "Dominic, you won't become your father. And we can get by with less."

"I know." I give her a smile and squeeze her hand back.

What bothers me though, is the revelation to myself that I don't want to get by with less. I want to succeed. I want to show everyone I can do everything and anything.

Fine, then. Nick remains a necessary part of the equation.
We swing by Rampart High, where Jess's car has been parked for the weekend. Our caravan's next stop is Curt's condo. He's gone somewhere, on his motorcycle, but I leave Sheryl in the driveway. Then, just because I am a kind and thoughtful friend, I plant a sprawling handprint on the driver's side window.

The BMW is in our driveway, as if it never left. I give it a once-over. Nick deserves credit; my stack of papers is right where I left it, with a folder on top. The Post-It on the cover reads, *Summary from yesterday. All good!*

And it must be, because my email is full of effusive messages from Kaminsky and Anna, plus a cooler but equally appreciative note from a woman named Loredana Lark, a corporate representative for Procyon. Apparently, she is a fan of the dome design.

Not a word from Tyson. That could be good or bad, depending upon the circumstances.

Sammy is whiny when he greets us inside. He won't leave my side the whole time we're unpacking, so much so I have to take five and give him some serious love to calm him.

Jess comes in and bumps her bag against the door. Sammy barks at the loud noise. "Hey, easy, boy, easy," I murmur.

"He's jumpy," Jess says. "Ally noted it."

She's got an invoice in her hand. It's from the middle-aged woman who takes care of Sammy when we're out of town, along with a half-dozen other dogs. Small business, but reliable. She got Sammy Friday morning and dropped him back just before we arrived, which is not optimal but, in her defense, she had a busy couple of days.

"Can I see?" Her note does say Sammy became very agitated when he got home, running about sniffing everything with frantic intensity, but calmed enough she felt it was safe to leave him. No mention, though, of the BMW being gone, or of Nick, which would have been a more pressing concern than Sammy missing his human parents. "Well, I wouldn't worry. Probably he's skittish after the whole thing with Mrs. Cortez's dog."

"Probably. I'll go check the messages."

Sammy whines and licks my face, paws propped on my chest. "Hey, come on." I scratch him behind his ears, which reduces him to a tongue-lolling, sappy-faced ball of fur. "Let me finish, and we'll go toss the ball around, all right?"

At "ball" he barks, and bolts from the room. The aforementioned toy squeaks, off in the laundry room. Yes, he's ready to play.

"Dominic? Come here."

Jess is by the answering machine, because we do maintain a landline. I don't want everyone to have my cell phone number. Last thing I need is a sales call coming through in the middle of a client conference. "What is it?"

"A message, for you." She chews her lip. "It's a Sergeant Ambrose."

"Ah. He was the officer who's investigating the car break-in." I punch the replay button.

"Mr. Zein, Sergeant Ambrose, Rampart PD. I wonder if I could come by the office tomorrow. Already talked to your co-workers about the vandalism and wanted to see if you had anything to add. I tried to locate you today but couldn't. I understand you all had a meeting yesterday prior to Mr. Jacobs' car taking a swim. Anyhoo, give me a call at this number and we'll set up a time. Appreciate your cooperation."

A swim? Tyson's car?

"That's strange." Jess has her cell out. She's tapping a search. Go, Google. Suddenly she puts her hand to her mouth, and I can't tell if she's laughing or crying. As soon as I see the headline, I know it's the former.

Joyride Lands Architect's Ride at Bottom of the Van.

There's Tyson's SUV, indeed. It's hard to make out in the photo, but then again, I've never seen it submerged in the Van River.

"Wow." Jess wipes a tear. She must mistake my expression for chastisement. "Oh, come on, Dominic, you hate the man. You're not going to grump at me for laughing at his expense, are you?"

"Not at all. I'm just too shocked to laugh now." I manage a grin. "But I will, once the reality sets in."

And once I have a talk with the guy who did this.

CHAPTER TEN

onday morning. Jess is off early for a staff meeting. We kiss at the door. She's subdued. "Are you working late tonight?"

"Probably. There's a lot on my plate." I hold her hands. "Are we good?"

"Sure." Her smile's wan compared to the start of the weekend.

"Thinking about the children question?"

"So much for not being obvious."

"Let's give it some time to consider. I'm not wholly opposed. Besides, who wouldn't want a smaller version of handsome me running around the house?"

She snickers. "How did you know that was my motivation?"

Her departure give me time to review the email from Nick. He's submitted a lengthy recap of Saturday's meeting, but the salient points are bulleted: Procyon likes the dome design; Tyson's designs were completely ignored; Procyon's Loredana Lark wants a follow-up meeting with Tyson and me; Tyson is mad.

The last point makes me chuckle. Naturally he is. Why would the week start without Tyson wanting my head on a plate that's already full?

Of course, it doesn't help matters his truck took a dive under the

Van River.

There's time enough to swing by Nick's apartment, which I opt to do rather than stopping at the office. His email is detailed enough to get me by for the day, but I'm not going to chance missing some fact that may be helpful.

Besides, there's a curious situation I need to satisfy.

Caution tape is slashed across the windows to the electronic stores. A cluster of people are working inside. None appear to be police.

My phone buzzes. Nick. <Park in the alley.>

There's nothing back there but empty dumpsters and bits of trash blown about by the wind. Dust stings my face. The back stairs are just as worn down as the front. This time, Nick's driver stands in the hall, facing the opposite direction. His stance is identical to that of my first visit.

I picture him with a scraggly beard, sporting a weeklong hangover, and can see the resemblance to the dead Eric Talbot.

"Morning."

He speaks. That's an improvement. "Good morning," I say.

"Nick's inside." His tones are precise.

"Thanks."

Nick is already dressed for his day, in the same black slacks, brown shoes, and pale-blue shirt as me. He grins, caught in the midst of straightening a dark green tie with silver stripes. "There he is. How was your weekend?"

"We had a great time. Good food, good rest, good reading, mountain biking, and hiking ..."

"Time well spent with Jess."

"That it was."

"Anything else?"

I keep my silence. "As a matter of fact, we talked about children."

"Or the lack thereof in your life."

"Something like that."

"I see. All good to know. What's your opinion?"

"Not sure how we can handle having a kid, both financially and …otherwise." I'm also unclear why this has all spilled forth. Perhaps, talking to Nick is like talking to myself. We all do it—those conversations in our minds with the other us, only I'm gifted with a flesh and blood manifestation. "My father wasn't the best, or most present."

"Mine was … distant. I understand. Jess should, too." He nods. "Ready for the return?"

"Yes. I wanted to see if you'd left anything out."

"From my report? Dominic, I'm hurt. The only thing I could be guilty of is downplaying how irritated Tyson was."

"Did you show him up?"

"No, I let him take point, and he tripped himself up. Cracked a couple of jokes about Procyon finally finding the best city in which to build. Didn't get a smile."

I wince. Tyson hates it when people don't respond to him with anything but a "Yes, sir" or a happy handshake. "Let me guess. They liked you better."

"What isn't to like?" Nick winks, and it's brimming with confidence. Is that what Anna sees, when I do it?

Speaking of which … "How was everyone else?"

"Anna's gorgeous."

"That isn't what I asked."

"Oh, I know. Just stating what you may have missed."

"Don't get any ideas."

"Why? She's single, and so am I."

"Yes, but *I* am not."

"You've been in her company quite a bit, though. Who would notice if I spent more time around her?" Nick picks up a bag from the couch. It's the same brand as mine, though sporting less wear and tear.

"Curt would."

"Valid point. I thought I'd drop in on the Vitalis today, then catch up with Dr. Huang."

"Good idea, but first—Tyson's car."

Nick nods, his face a pleasant mask. "Shame, isn't it? I understand the police are looking at a bunch of kids who have been doing the same—stealing rides, leaving them odd places after some joyriding. It's been in the *Post* for a couple months now."

"Come on, Nick. Was it you?"

"Are you seriously asking me if I stole a car and crashed it in a river?" Nick sighs. "No, Dominic. That isn't my style."

"Yours is more street fighting."

He snorts. "You mean downstairs? The Xians have had enough hardship. They didn't need some street scum stealing their livelihood. I took care of it."

"Like my car thieves."

"I don't appreciate your tone. Where is the gratitude? Between you and the Xians, I've put a stop to two crimes." He holds up his fingers in V formation. "And then you accuse me of an outright crime of my own."

"Maybe I overstepped. You say you didn't dump Tyson's car. What about Eric?"

Nick's face freezes in a smile. "I'm sorry, who?"

"Eric. Eric Talbot."

The smile vanishes. "I think you've got the wrong name for my assistant, who has an alibi. He's been watching me."

"Eric Talbot is a man who died in Estes Park. A homeless veteran." I cross my arms. "One who looks a lot like your bodyguard."

"It isn't as if people of similar appearance are rare. Too bad they didn't have the chance to help each other out by now."

"So, what's your guy's name?"

"Chris."

"Chris …?"

"Chris. He prefers to be discreet. In his line of work, his personal life is a liability." Nick spreads his arm wide. "Hate to pull this card on you, but we both need to get to work—unless you're not done with the interrogation."

I run a hand through my hair. "All right. Anything else you need for the week?"

"Your email password."

"Are you joking?"

"How else am I going to communicate with your clients?" He holds up his hands to forestall the argument I'm about to make. "Reset it when we're done."

"When are we done?"

"Whenever you say so, Dominic." He dons a pair of sunglasses and opens the door. "Shall we get going?"

He's right, of course. I can't very well have my clients receiving emails from somebody who isn't me, and someone who is, about the same jobs. So I give him the password.

But I keep a close eye on my Sent box.

By the time I get to Dualpoint, Kaminsky is there, and Anna, plus several staff—but no sign of Tyson. None of the cars are new, either, so I know he hasn't come in a replacement ride, yet.

Kaminsky is at my door before my bag hits the table. "Dominic."

"Good morning. How was—" I choke back "your weekend" from the end of the question, because from his perspective, I was with him most of Saturday. "Your day off?"

"Sunday's hardly a day of rest for me," he says. "Bonnie has a great honey-do list around the house. I keep telling her I'm not retired yet, but she says it's better to get all the grunt work done *before* I hand myself the gold watch. That way we've got more time to take the RV and visit the grandkids."

"Sounds like a great plan." Grandkids. The sooner Jess and I have children, the more time we'll have to spend with ours. Better put that thought process back in its box and open up the one in my mind labeled "Procyon." It's less confounding this early in the morning. "So, what's next?"

"What's next is you and Tyson continuing your excellent work with the Procyon project. Though it seems they'll be mostly talking with you."

"I'm sure Tyson and I will have plenty of opportunities for collaboration. He is the lead, after all."

"For now." Kaminsky leans on my desk. "You and I both know he wasn't at his best. Frankly, his arrogance gets in the way—that's why I wanted you on this project. And we've seen now that I was right. From here on out, expand your role. If Tyson sounds like he's going to once again put his foot in his mouth, be there to have something intelligent come out of yours."

I nod. "Of course."

"Good." Kaminsky smiles. "This one's important, Dominic. Procyon will elevate us to the national playing field. Don't let it slip from our grip."

"You can count on me."

Staring at the space where he stood, I realize that's only a half-truth.

The back door slams. I don't need to see him to know it's Tyson, but I can't resist. I grab a folder of Procyon materials and head for the hall.

He's typing on his phone, sunglasses tucked into his shirt pocket. His lips move with a muttered conversation.

"Morning, Tyson."

There's a dull anger in his eyes when he looks up.

"Any luck?"

"On what?"

"Finding out who dumped your car."

He scowls. "Not talking to the cops at the moment. They've got suspects, or so they tell me. No, this is the insurance company. You'd think I lit my own truck on fire with a Molotov cocktail and posted it on YouTube for as helpful as they've been. It's underwater!"

"If you need any help with anything …"

"Like you helped me Saturday? By kissing up to Procyon?"

"I didn't kiss up to anyone. I did my job."

"You sure did. Made me look like an idiot."

"I doubt you needed help with that."

He advances on me, phone squeezed in his hand, and for not the first time I consider I need to watch my mouth when talking back to Tyson. "This doesn't change anything. You may be Kaminsky's favorite for this project, but it's mine. Get in my way again, and you'll be collating printed pages. You got it?"

His finger's poked in the center of my chest. Slowly, without taking my eyes from him, I shove it away. "I understand. And you need to understand I will do my job to the best of my abilities, no matter what—or whom—impedes progress."

Tyson storms to his office and slams the door shut.

Right. Well, that could have gone better. Rather than dwelling on it, I dive into the Monday morning stack of work. Nick's got the Vitalis under control, and with access to my emails, he can review most of the conversation. I dash off a quick message to him about Dr. Huang's project, and start up a new file for the Procyon building.

Barely a half hour's gone by when my phone goes off—my desk phone, this time. I grab the receiver. "Yes?"

"Dominic, you've got a Sergeant Ambrose on Line 2." Cassandra, our front desk assistant, shoots the words out rapid-fire. Another line rings in the background.

Already? He is on my call-back list. But I guess it won't wait. "Thanks, Cassie."

"All yours."

I clear my throat, and take a swig of tea, before punching the button. "Good morning, Sergeant, this is Dominic Zein."

"Mr. Zein. I wanted to visit with you."

"Of course. About what happened to Tyson's car, wasn't it? That's a shame." Takes considerable effort to put actual regret behind the sentence. "When would you like to meet?"

"Eight thirty."

As in, 15 minutes from now. "I can't very well decline, Sergeant, so come on over."

"Thanks."

"Can I ask what specifically is on your mind?"

"Nothing much. I couldn't reach you this weekend, and I have to interview all the Procyon staff about their whereabouts on Sunday."

Panic jolts through me. Sunday I was in Estes Park, before returning home with Jess. Except as far as everyone else was concerned, I was in Rampart, because Nick was playacting me. "Sure. Sure thing. I'll see you then."

He hangs up.

I grab my cell phone before I've placed the receiver down. Got to get ahold of Nick.

<Where were you Sunday? Need alibi. Police coming to talk. Hurry!>

Nothing back within a couple minutes. I can't sit around worrying, so it's back to the drawings. They proceed slowly, and I have to make several revisions, because it is apparently difficult to focus on a brand new, high-paying project when police interrogation looms.

<Eight-fifteen,> he texts back.

<Don't strain your brain. You were at church, then lunch on your own. Top Mile Fitness from 2 to 4. Worked in the office until late.>

My mouth drops. Church? <You went to my church? How did you explain to people about Jess not being there?>

<Said she was run down from school, needed rest. Father Hamra was very understanding. Didn't stick around for small talk.>

I sag against the cushions. It's a good thing I didn't tell anyone about our trip this weekend …

Oh no. My meeting with Father Hamra. I talked to him about the Stewardship committee, and he asked if he would see us in church. My fingers mash the touchpad. <He knew we were going away!!!>

<And I told him we had to cancel. Because of Jess. Will you relax? I have it handled.>

My heart's racing. And, at the top of the phone's screen, time is ticking. Sergeant Ambrose will be here soon. <The gym. I haven't been in ages. How'd you get in?>

<Told them I'd misplaced the card. Nice kid at the desk. He took my ID and let me in. So, I need your gym card to get a copy.>

<You can't forge it!>

<It isn't rocket science, Dominic. Now, when the police ask where you were, go through the list and don't turn into a babbling idiot.>

Quite the pep talk. I swipe back on the phone for the itinerary, then scribble it on a Post-It. I put my phone away and read the note, over and over, until I can say it to my reflection in the screen with as much honesty as I can muster.

Neat trick, considering it's a lie.

Three minutes later, Cassie buzzes my desk again. "Got Sergeant Ambrose in the lobby for you."

Isn't that perfect. He's early. "Thank you. Send him back, please."

Ambrose knocks on the door frame, but I'm already up out of my seat. He's in full uniform, wearing the same mirrored sunglasses. Indoors. "Mr. Zein."

"Dominic, please." We shake hands. I'm certain he could lift Tyson's truck out of the Van River with his grip, but I match it well enough. There's enough of a leftover imprint I consider returning to the gym, as my doppelgänger did. "Have a seat."

He has a small notepad with a ratty leather cover, and a pencil missing its eraser. I can't see what he's written but it doesn't matter. The scrawl appears as indecipherable as Arabic script, which I never bothered learning from Grandfather. "We've narrowed down a timeframe for the theft of Mr. Jacobs' car going missing. Seems it was dropped in the Van around one thirty Sunday."

"That's very specific."

"Handy when there's a traffic camera four blocks from the river."

I steady my hands by folding them in my lap. "So, you have the culprit on video."

"Nope. Just a shadow in the driver's seat. Tinted windows make it hard to see anything more specific." Ambrose brushes the bottom of his mustache. "Where were you?"

"At that time? Probably at the gym. Top Mile Fitness."

"Did you swipe your card?"

I grin sheepishly. "Forgot it. I hadn't been there in a long while, but the staff were kind enough to take my ID instead. I'll have to dig through my desk at home."

"That's nice of them." The pencil scratches on the pad without him looking up. "And the rest of the day?"

I outline the rest of Nick's itinerary, praying he's got proof for all those places. "You can check with the church or the gym. Someone can corroborate my appearances there."

"Probably not necessary, but we'll see. We're treating this as a crime of opportunity, but do you know anyone with a grudge against Mr. Jacobs?"

I sincerely hope I'm not blushing, what with my face burning. "None I'm aware of."

"No workplace drama?"

"Other than typical rivalry for clients?"

"I'm a fan of honesty, Mr. Zein."

"Well, I'm sure my co-workers can tell you Tyson and I do not get along. We work together well, in terms of combining efforts on projects, but we're civil."

"Not going to be getting a beer with him anytime soon, though."

"We've all got colleagues like that, Sergeant. Even you, if I had to guess."

He chuckles. "You know it. Okay, so, any angry exes?"

"Don't believe he's ever been married."

"Girlfriends? Flings?"

I shrug.

"Right." More notes. I'm a pair of tiny reflections in his sunglasses, which he's still wearing. If the goal is to induce discomfort, he's successful. "It's possible the perpetrators cased the area before taking the truck. You happen to notice anyone strange hanging around your building lately?"

"Aside from the occasional homeless, no." And my exact duplicate.

"Bummer you guys don't have any exterior security cameras."

"Or interior. Mr. Kaminsky is a staunch advocate of privacy, for his employees and our clients."

"Libertarian type."

"You'd have to ask him."

More pencil scratching. "Let me ask you something else—or tell you, I guess. We had a robbery downtown, Saturday night. Some guys knocked over an electronics store. Or they tried to, I should say."

"Oh?" If he's referencing what I think he is, I'd rather not mention I was in the vicinity a couple hours ago.

"Yeah. Funny thing. Some private citizen with way more energy than common sense put the smackdown on them. Real bad—we had to haul a couple to the hospital, still cuffed. Best part is? They claimed the crowbars they used to bash in windows heated up like lava. Molten." Ambrose shifts in his chair. Sunlight glints from his glasses, leaving spots before my eyes. "Their assailant was hooded, and in a ski mask, but one of them swears we're dealing with a Middle Eastern guy. Just like in your almost car theft."

"I don't understand where you're going with this, Sergeant."

"Nowhere, maybe. Like I said, we're dealing with non-rocket scientists." He removes the sunglasses. I've never seen blue eyes so intense, shards of the frozen Van River stalking me. He could be a bird of prey diving for fish. "But this is twice now I have crimes stopped, in progress, by a supposedly Middle Eastern guy. You're Middle Eastern …"

"Surely not the only one," I interject. "St. Lucian's, for one, is home to many."

"And you were at one of the scenes."

"This sounds dangerously like profiling."

"Nope. Observation." He smirks. "Could be a different guy. Lots of those in Rampart, Colorado, or so you say. What, Syrian? Like the refugees?"

It's probably a criminal offense to hit a police officer, so I decline. "Lebanese."

"Right. It's in your article. You know what's not in that fluff piece?" He leans his elbows on the desk. Aftershave wafts across. "Where you were on Saturday night."

"In bed."

He nods.

"Unless you have any further questions, Sergeant, I have clients' work that needs attending." I return to my keyboard, praying he'll take the hint. Sweat soaks my shirt. Police questioning is nothing I studied in college.

"Fine for now." He rises and dons the glasses. It takes all my composure to not breathe a sigh of relief when he shields his eyes. Feels like the hunt is over. "Tell you what. You stick to doodling, I'll stick to keeping criminals in handcuffs."

"I'm no vigilante."

"Neither am I. Let's keep it that way." Ambrose rubs his mustache as he leaves.

As soon as his footsteps fade, and I hear Cassie bid him a good morning, my fingers slam the keyboard. What is Nick thinking? He's jeopardizing our arrangement with his insane hero complex.

I reach for my phone. No. He's with the Vitalis right now. But we have to formulate a new plan. One that does not involve me being questioned by the police.

Forget it. I call him anyway. No answer. Straight to voicemail. "Nick, it's Dominic. Call me as soon as you can. Your evening activities are causing headaches."

I hang up. Tap the phone against my lips. Before I realize it, I'm tugging at my pants leg with my hand. Stop it.

There's a text. Jess. <Mrs. Cortez just called. Sounded upset. She wanted to know if we'd seen Eddie.>

I frown. Her dog? The same one who bit Sammy? <Probably left her gate again.>

<Can you check on her on your lunch break?>

I should send Nick. But he's busy, and with the lighter workload, I could make the trip. <Okay, will do.>

<Thanks. You're a lamb.> She attaches the image of puckered lips.

Here's hoping I'm not wasting my time. I dive back into the Procyon work, eyes shifting occasionally to the phone.

Nick doesn't call.

CHAPTER ELEVEN

The sky's thick with clouds, not letting a hint of blue through. The forecast is for snow in a day or two, no more than a dusting. The wind has bite to it.

Sammy paws at the back door as I wander the yard. There's no indication Mrs. Cortez's dog was here. I follow Sammy's tracks, via ruts he's worn in a couple of corners, but nothing else. The gap in the fence is propped shut with another board, my makeshift fix until I can get to the hardware store.

Wherever Eddie's gone, it isn't onto my property.

I don't see him beyond the fence, either. Undeveloped land sprawls in a brown swath for a few miles southwest of our neighborhood, interrupted by dingy green scrub brush. I wait for signs of movement. Eddie's a black Lab, so he should be simple to spot.

That proves as useless as inspecting the yard. I don't see him up or down our street, either.

A flicker of movement from Mrs. Cortez's house catches my eye. She's peering from the front door, which is cracked open enough to let her see out the screen door.

"Mrs. Cortez?" I do my best client smile and walk slowly. Here's hoping she has gotten over whatever scare Nick delivered. "I didn't see Eddie anywhere nearby."

"Thank you for looking." She's quieter. Her hands stay pressed against the door's edge. She doesn't come outside.

"Did you call Animal Control?"

"No, not yet. They aren't very nice. They complain about Eddie getting loose."

Then perhaps you should keep your gate shut. I nod, instead of voicing my frustration. "Well, if I see him, I'll call you first, all right?"

"Yes, thank you. I just don't want him to bother anyone. Especially my neighbors."

She shuts the door. I'm left staring for a moment, wondering where the dumb mutt could have gone too. Probably he's stationed outside someone else's fence, barking into their yard and harassing their dog. Of course, I don't hear any barking.

My route back to the BMW takes me over a smear on the curb. I hadn't noticed it before, as it was concealed by the garbage cans. Looks like motor oil, maybe grease. Stands out stark against the white concrete. I kneel for closer inspection.

It's red. Thick and dark, nearly brown, but a crimson shade. Blood?

I shake my head. Who knows what Mrs. Cortez had in the trash? Hopefully Eddie hadn't gotten his jaws on a local cat. If so, I'd have to reevaluate my promise to not call Animal Control if I found the dog.

There's time enough for a couple loops around our subdivision. No luck. A stray cat goes hurtling across the road, but other than that, everyone's animals seem to be fenced properly.

Enough of this. I still need to eat, and I'd better swing by the post office for more stamps.

There's a considerable line in the lobby, and I wait as patiently as I can—which is to say, checking my email for updates from Nick. One comes across just as I'm about to put the phone away.

<The Vitalis are good to go. Nice solution for their conflict, by the way. I made some modifications, attached. Want me to forward them to Kaminsky? Also, I should make arrangements to talk with

your charming Anna about Dr. Huang's office. Stop by the apartment if you have the chance and haven't eaten already.>

I open the PDF. He did good work, streamlining the rough designs. <Looks great. I'll be there ASAP. Yes, go ahead and send the Vitali project to Kaminsky. As for Anna, leave that for me.>

Margie Cho clears her throat. She's smirking at me. "Can't stay away?"

"No, I'm plenty awake." I return the smile. "Sorry, busy. I need a book of stamps."

"Sure thing. Appreciate the latest rendition. We're going to get the permits this spring."

"Good, good." I realize fully what she just said. "Did you say away or awake?"

"Away. I don't have any mail for you."

"Empty today?"

She hands me the stamps and takes my debit card. "No, because you were just in here a half hour ago. Far perkier, too."

Nick. Now he's randomly picking up my mail? He hasn't said a thing. "Everybody can be forgetful, once in a while."

"Don't I know." She tilts her head as she hands me my card back, accompanied by a receipt. "You take care."

"Thanks."

Sergeant Ambrose's conversation is fresh on my mind as I leave the post office and head downtown. Nick wants to meet and have lunch? Fine.

But we're going to test our boundaries.

I pull up in the alley behind Nick's apartment building. Chris is out there, heaving a pair of garbage bags into the Dumpster. He gives a nod, then lets me in. Follows me every step of the way.

Nick is hunched over a laptop, frowning at the screen. There's a new smell in the kitchen—spices, mustard, deli meats. A pair of sandwiches hunker together, with bottles of pop propped between.

"Where's my mail?"

He snorts. "Subtle. It's on the table."

Just a pair of advertisements, a clothing catalog Jess likes, and a political flyer. I wave them in his face. "This wasn't part of our arrangement."

"Do we really need to do this now?"

I push the lid of the laptop down. "Yes."

Nick sighs. He sets the computer aside and crosses his legs. "By all means, lecture."

"Sergeant Ambrose had a lot of questions for me."

"I'm sure he did."

"He also warned me to stay away from this part of town in the evenings, so that I wouldn't be tempted to engage in vigilantism."

"Ah, he's taking an interest in my handiwork."

I raised my hands to the ceiling and walked off. My steps take me across the same pale circle in the floor, and once again, it fades from view as I passed, its color matching the rest of the boards.

"Say what you're thinking."

"I'd rather not. Father taught me to mind my words when I'm angry."

"Angry? About what?" Nick rises from the chair. He gets one of the pops and takes a swig. "About how successful this venture has been to date? If so, I suggest you need counseling. Thanks to me, you've caught the eye of one of your firm's biggest clients. Your rival is none too pleased about it, which makes him more liable to foul up. He's vulnerable. Now is your chance to press the advantage."

"By doing what?"

"Don't be dense. Curry favor with Kaminsky. Make Tyson look bad." Nick makes a face. "It shouldn't be too difficult, given the mishaps he's facing."

"Which are your fault."

"Funny, I don't see you running to the police and claiming you know who it was who dunked Tyson's car in the river."

"Only because they'd never believe me." I point a finger at him.

"But if you step out of line again—"

"You'll do what? You'll turn me in." Nick opens his sandwich. "Don't be absurd. It's more than just our appearances, Dominic. When they compare our fingerprints, they will match. If they take a DNA swab, they'll find it's the same as yours. Nothing about me will point to anyone else but you."

He pulls his wallet from his pocket and flips it open. The driver's license is secured behind a plastic window. It's mine. Every detail—height, weight, address, hair and eye color, even the untidy signature scrawl—is identical. Nick went to great lengths to duplicate it, as evidence by the smudges all over that add authenticity by making it seem worn.

My guts roil. A headache builds. "You told me we would stop this whenever I was ready."

"I did, and that still holds true." He takes a bite from his sandwich and leans against the counter. "But you're not ready. Why would you be? I've only just begun to streamline your life. Think of your weekend. You can have more of those. Your career, your wife, your friend—all can take equal precedence, without loss of time."

"Until you get bored, or feel you've accomplished whatever it is you wanted to accomplish."

"As I said, I am here as a blessing to you. Don't squander it." He pats the remaining sandwich. "Come on, let's eat."

"Not hungry." Here's hoping he doesn't notice my stomach growling. It isn't all nerves unsettling me. Lunchtime is passing far too quickly.

"Whatever you want, Dominic. Let me give you some advice: Enjoy this. It won't last forever, and when I'm gone, you'll be even more thankful." He grins. "Of course, by then, you'll be kneeling on my doorstep like a jilted lover begging for my return."

"Don't flatter yourself. I got alone fine for years before you appeared."

"There's the operative word. 'Fine.' Why be fine when you can thrive?" He waves his hand in front of his face, as if shooing an errant fly. "You know what, I'm done with these pep talks. Take your mail, and for pity's sake, be grateful!"

"I am. I'm only asking you refrain from drawing further attention to yourself—to the both of us—if this partnership is going to continue. You messing up my life will not help me succeed."

Nick's expression turns somber. He puts down his lunch and stands right in front of me. Hands—my hands—rest on my shoulders. "The last thing I would want is to hurt you. We're one and the same. Whatever I do in your shoes, be it damaging or beneficial, has the same effect on me. Don't worry. I won't let anything happen to you."

For all the absurdity of what he's saying, my heart squeezes. The timbre of his voice, that stern look coupled with a caring touch—it could be my father, reborn decades younger. How many times did I rely on such an assurance? Even when he was mostly absent from my life, he kept this promises, and I admired the man for never backing down.

Almost as much as I fumed at his failures.

There's a message on my cell phone from Jess when I get back in the car. <Any luck?>

<None>, I type back. <Unless Animal Control nabbed Eddie.>

<Can you check in with them? Stop by?>

Check in? I start the engine, letting it rumble the floorboards. She has to be joking. <This is the same dog that bit Sammy. Do we really need to send out a search party?>

Nothing comes back after a while. My lips twist. Jess is a fast texter. Anything more than a couple seconds in the middle of a conversation means I've goofed.

I don't have time for this. I really don't. If she has a soft spot for that mutt, she can handle it.

I squeal tires pulling onto the street from the alley. A horn honks. Delivery van nearly sideswipes me. Whether he wasn't paying attention, or I was distracted, I don't care. Nick's motives should be reassuring. And I should be happy. Who wouldn't want to have another self taking care of the busy stuff, freeing up time to spend with friends, with one's wife?

Same wife with whom I was arguing.

The phone's screen lights up. <She's our neighbor. You could be a little more compassionate. She already paid the bill.>

I let it sit until I get back to Dualpoint's parking lot. There's a silver Lexus sedan parked right next to my spot. Don't recognize it. Nor do I know any clients with California plates, though the Procyon people, now that I consider it, hail from San Camillo.

<If you're worried about Eddie, go check.>

Seconds tick by. Probably I shouldn't have worded it like that.

<Fine. I'll go look. But we need to talk about this. I'll be home after 5.>

I blow out a breath. And I'm sure that will be a delightful conversation.

It isn't until I get to my office that I realize there's another notification on my phone. Cassie texted. Seems there's a visitor.

She's seated at my desk when I come in.

"Can I help you?" Cassie will get an earful about this. No one's supposed to be in our offices when we're out. Too many confidential items about—contracts, designs, and the like.

But the only work on my desk is the Procyon project, pages sprawled drunkenly over the edges, free of their folders. At least, they were. The woman stops in the midst of arranging them. "There's no need to be distraught, Mr. Zein. I'm well aware of the need for client confidentiality."

It's cliché to say time slows when she stands and turns around, but so help me, it does. She's tall, fit, with flowing red hair that dangles in sweeps over her shoulders. Eyes as blue as the sky over Estes Park meet mine. Red lips purse in a smile. Freckles are scattered across the bridge of her nose and tops of her cheeks. She wears a white blouse with a slate gray jacket and skirt, cool, clean colors that highlight her natural radiance.

The Procyon ID badge on her jacket takes away some of the worry but introduces a new one. Black letters read "Loredana Lark, Operations." This is the woman who was present at Saturday's meeting. The one with whom Nick dealt.

The one who likes the designs I didn't present.

"Pleasure to see you again, Ms. Lark." I offer my hand.

Her grip is cool and measured. "Likewise. I hope I haven't intruded."

That accent—British, though muted. "Not at all. I'm running full throttle today, but what's new there?" I wait until she sits, then take my place on the opposite side of the desk.

"Indeed. I can commiserate. There's many a time I've wished to have my workload reduced."

"I think everyone can understand that desire. Kind of wish for more hours in the day." I smile.

"Or another me to achieve all those things, since one can hardly add a single hour to one's life."

My hand nearly misses the mouse. "Oh, I don't know. That could be a mess. I have enough trouble keeping track of what I have to do, let alone if I had two of me to wrangle."

"Yes, quite, but with the proper preparation, I'm sure it could be achieved." She smooths a wrinkle on her skirt. Her posture is ramrod straight. "Quite the mental exercise, is it not?"

What game is she playing? I'd find witty banter with a beautiful woman as much fun as the next man but coming on the heels of my last visit with Nick, it's—disturbing. Too close. Easy, Dominic. She's a client, making small talk. "I take it you've looked over the preliminary designs."

"Merely skimming. Your vision is aligned with ours. The directors couldn't be more pleased. My purpose here is to make sure the project stays on track."

"I understand. Does the timetable—?"

"The timetable is negotiable."

"That will depend on Tyson's and my workload." And what

Kaminsky decides is commensurate with the amount of money they're paying. Given the price tag, my guess would be fast. "But I'm comfortable saying we can close a final exterior design by the end of the week."

"Admirable. Procyon wants to start construction in the spring."

"Sorry, *this* spring?"

"Yes."

"That's quite the rush."

She doesn't blink very much. Her stare is unnerving, yet entrancing. I'm torn between watching her every move and wanting a pair of Sergeant Ambrose's sunglasses so I can hide my eyes from her gaze. "Whether or not it is out of the norm isn't your concern. Procyon's goal is to have the building complete by next year."

"Surely, you're aware the permitting process itself can drag on for months, depending upon the neighborhood in which you choose to build. And no offense, ma'am, but the zoning rules for downtown Rampart are different than whatever they have in San Camillo."

"It is my job to make certain there are no obstacles to the project," she says, her tones cool. "Am I understanding you correctly, Mr. Zein, that you have a problem with the speed at which this work will progress?"

"Not at all." Not anymore, that is. Nick and I can slam through the design phase, even with Tyson assisting in his cumbersome way. "We're happy to make Procyon our top priority."

"We."

"Mr. Jacobs and I, as well as the whole company."

She nods. "I see."

I gather the pages she's straightened on my desk. "Did you have any specific questions about the process?"

"No. I came primarily to ask if you had any questions of me." She smiles, but there's nothing pleasant about it. "We will be working closely on this project, after all."

"Nothing about the design, no." I turn over a few pages, running through a list in my mind. "The only thing I saw missing is information about your organization's needs."

"I don't follow."

"Usually our firm works with the client to establish their needs for the interior space of a new building—for example, functionality and aesthetics. While we've had great success coming together on the latter, you've provided us with very little in the way of the former. To put it simply, Ms. Lark, we don't know what you want to use the building for."

"Procyon Foundation exists for the betterment of society," Lark says. "Our interests are diversified—supporting research of cutting edge medical and information technologies, provision of affordable housing, job training and employment assistance …"

"Yes, I saw on your listing that you even dabble in archaeology."

"I believe we can best prepare for the future by studying the past. Every event, no matter how minor, influences the course of history. Don't you agree?"

"I do. But none of that answers my question." I spread my hands to indicate my office. "You look around here, and you know what it is I do. Now, besides the basic workspace layouts for your support and clerical staff, you haven't given us any indication of the interior design for the upper floors, especially the seventh."

"That isn't your concern."

My teeth grind. There's always a client like this, one who insists she knows better about the interior layout of spaces than we do. "Ms. Lark, our firm has dozens of years' experience with this kind of office design. If you could give us some indication—"

"There is nothing more you need to know about the seventh floor, other than to give us the room we need to operate."

"At least tell us something about these operations, so we can better accommodate your needs."

She leans forward, hands folded primly on her lap. "My needs, Mr. Zein, are for this building to be complete next year. I need a space for my people to do their work. Whether or not they are pleased with a lovely carpet or a happy arrangement of office spaces is irrelevant. We have provided you with the basic plans for our other buildings around the country and given you guidelines for the new design. More than that is not your worry."

For someone who said she'd be willing to answer my questions, she's awfully insistent to steer us away from this line of conversation. But I'm not a fan of letting potential obstacles wait around until the last moment to be fixed. "Nevertheless, if you could send me a sample layout from these upper floors, I'm sure we could expedite the design process even more than what's been anticipated."

Her eyes narrow. For a moment, there's only the sound of me shuffling papers, as I ignore her and pretend extreme interest in whatever I'm reading. "Very well," she says. "I will see how my superiors feel on the matter."

"Good. Glad to hear it." I give her my best keep-the-client-happy smile.

Unfortunately, that only causes her to stiffen her posture. "One thing, Mr. Zein. A general question about your workload, since you broached the topic. Do you find yourself buried, having such a prestigious firm attracting clients?"

"There are times, yes."

"Yet you're quite relaxed."

I settle into my chair. "I've found better methods to handle the work. Those methods haven't come without their complications, but by and large, it's made an improvement on my quality of life."

"I see."

"I must say, Ms. Lark, I rarely get clients who are so concerned about my personal well-being. Most want the job done, regardless of the toll it takes on their architect."

"No person can do good work when he's pushed beyond his point of balance between productivity and peace." She rises. "I will contact you, one way or the other, about the information you requested."

I mirror her moves and offer my hand again. "Thank you."

She doesn't shake it. "There's a beautiful creature called the orchid mantis. Have you ever seen one? Likely not. It hails from southeast

Asia. Passing insects mistake it for a lovely flower, because of its soft pink and white hues, its gently curving shape. They think they have found something good and pure, something that will nourish them—right up to the moment when the mantis devours them."

The image of Lark transforming into a giant and gorgeous mantis-woman brings me no comfort. Kafka's *Metamorphosis* seems more inviting. I don't have a reply for her.

"Make absolutely certain that you do not fall prey, Mr. Zein, even when you're tempted by the sweetest flower."

She leaves me standing there, gaping at the doorway.

That evening, I manage to get out the door right at 5. You couldn't meet a happier man if you tracked down the guy who'd just won the state lottery.

I even find time for a jaunty salute at Tyson as I waltz past his door. He's hunched over his monitor, oblivious to my presence in any case.

"Zein."

Apparently, not. "Yes?"

"You've got those ground floor elevations?"

"First one's in your box. I thought you'd have critiqued it by now."

"Haven't had the time." He scowls at me. "Something you've had a lot of, lately."

I shrug. "Found a good groove and completing a lot of my work ahead of schedule."

"Wanna share your secret?"

"Sorry, it's classified."

"Then maybe you'd better take on a couple more jobs."

"Again, sorry, but no. Kaminsky's happy with my workload the way it is." I lean on the doorjamb. "Having trouble?"

He turns back to his project, muttering under his breath.

As nice as it feels, I can't stop thinking about Loredana Lark's warnings. Is she really that paranoid about me digging too deeply into Procyon's plans? And what could she possibly be worried I'd do? I wasn't going to take their layout and post it on Facebook. That's simply bad business.

Of course, she may have meant something entirely different.

Whatever her motives, the conversation reminds me of Nick. My concerns press up against the benefits of his substitutions. What do I really know about him? How do I even find out? The man's never given me a real name, or a surname, same as his bodyguard Chris. His resemblance to the dead veteran is …

Wait. Chris. He took out the trash today. If Nick has receipts, or paperwork, anything bearing his true name, I want to see them.

You could just ask. The thought badgers me as I drive into the alley. There's no sign of Nick's SUV. Upstairs windows are dark.

The Dumpster isn't locked. I shove aside refuse from stores, and restaurants, judging by the gagging stench.

There.

The topmost black bag is heavy, but it's definitely the one Chris brought downstairs. I struggle with the knot, trying to hold my breath against the smell. It's taking too long. More and more cars pass by the end of the alley. Someone's bound to see me.

The Swiss Army knife. I dig it from my pocket and cut a jagged slit down one side.

Fangs flash.

I shout, dropping back onto the ground. The knife clatters on the asphalt. What was that? Is Chris into taxidermy?

Only one way to be sure.

I regain my footing. Carefully, shaking fingers pry the bag open.

It isn't the remains of a wild animal.

It's Mrs. Cortez's dog.

Eddie's head stares up at me from the rip.

CHAPTER TWELVE

I stare at the screen until my eyes burn.

"Are you coming to help?"

"One moment." I click the next link. Nothing. Type in a new search.

"We're going to need a new rule: if you don't help cook, you don't eat." Jess's voice is sing-song, echoing from the kitchen. Sammy barks, in apparent agreement.

Neither sound urges me from my chair. Window after window flashes by, none yielding the information I seek. It doesn't matter how many times I upload a photo of myself—the image match comes back with more of the same. Me. But, actually me, situations in which I've been photographed. Nothing points to Nick.

And I've been at it for a couple hours now, trying every search term I can think of. Nicholas Zein. Nick Zein. It is a long shot, seeing as how he never gave me a last name. Why would I have bothered asking for one? He said he was me. I believed him—believe him, even now, as I troll webpages for accusatory data.

I thought his arrival in my life was a miracle. How could there be another me? We're supposed to be unique.

I blink and see the severed head of Mrs. Cortez's dog bagged in a dumpster behind Federal Avenue.

My heart accelerates. The nightmare image won't abate. I can easily substitute Sammy in the poor animal's place.

Fear melts into anger. The idea that someone would do that …

Bodies the same, but souls, never.

Sammy nuzzles my side. I pet him, grateful for the distraction, and thankful he's unhurt. There's rough patches in his fur where the vet stitched him up after his tussle with Eddie.

I tell myself I'm a different man than Nick, but how did I react when I found out Eddie had bit Sammy? It wasn't with charity. I wanted that mutt dead. Didn't care how. Certainly, I never followed through on it. Simple passion.

But Nick …

The question was, why? The dog never did anything to him. What did he gain from killing it? Or having Chris kill it?

The very idea nauseates me.

"Hey." Jess's hand brushes the back of my neck.

I minimize all the open windows. My fingers envelope hers. "Sorry, I've been busy for a bit."

"Try ever since I got home. And before that, I imagine, given how slumped over you are."

"Am I?"

"You start out a foot taller when you dive into the Internet. Then the slouching takes over."

Can't hide a smile at that. She knows me.

"What's the big project? More on that Procyon company?"

"No, something requiring research beyond what I can do at work. More of a hobby."

"Admiring yourself?"

I spin my chair. She's got an eyebrow raised, and if I hadn't looked, I'd have sworn she was tapping her foot. Whether or not her students find her intimidating when she's in search of an answer seems moot.

"You had a lot of pictures up there. Don't tell me you're thinking about starting a trophy corner in the house, because I'm opposed to it."

"Ah, but what if I add more pictures of you?" I take her hand and kiss it. "Whenever you want to get back to dinner, I'm ready to be your sous chef."

"I don't think you are. Why were you browsing yourself online?"

"Just seeing what my platform produced. You know, whatever it is clients see of me when they look for me. Dualpoint isn't only about the work—it's about us as the faces of our firm. Public image."

Jess holds her gaze for a moment, then rolls her eyes. "You're being weird, do you realize that?"

"No weirder than usual."

"Weird, and forgetful."

I can't think of what I might be forgetting—which, I suppose, is the point. "It's best to save us both the time and tell me what you mean."

"The dog. Eddie? You said you'd check on him."

"I did."

"And?"

"I told you. No sign of him running around." Which is true. My facial muscles freeze in place. I ease into a smile meant to distract her. "And before you dig any deeper, no, I did not call Animal Control."

"Dominic …"

"Let's not get started on this. It's her dog, first of all, and second, when I spoke to her at lunch, she didn't want to contact them. I suspect she's afraid they'll seize Eddie, and given how many times he's been loose, I can't say I'd argue."

"If they take him, she'll be heartbroken."

"Yes, but she'll also be law-abiding."

Sammy pushes between us. He rubs his nose against our hands. His tail swats my leg. The look on his face is plain enough. *Quit fighting, guys,* with a healthy dose of eyebrows rising and lowering to make his point.

"I just thought it'd be better if we could help her out," Jess says.

"You mean if I could help her out."

"Well, yes, it's become easier for you to leave work than it is for me, Dominic. I can't bolt out of class, and my planning time is for exactly that—lesson planning."

"It isn't as if I don't have work to complete, Jess."

"You've been getting through it quicker. What's wrong with using that extra time for our neighbor?"

"Because it's my time." I rub my hand through my hair, surprised at the bitterness. "Year after year spent doing things for everybody else—for work and for church and all my other responsibilities. Finally, I have what I've needed most: time."

She folds her arms. It would have been less subtle for her to don a Kevlar vest. "Time for yourself."

"For me, and for you. Come on. It was great for us to get away over the weekend, wasn't it? Something we'd wanted to do forever, denied because my schedule wouldn't allow it. Now it does allow ..." I'm suddenly stuck for an explanation.

"Allow for what?"

"For us to live! Not just exist, day to day, gathering our money and spending it as fast as it comes in, but to live our lives. To pursue the things we want."

"Your work's always been what you want. Architecture's been yours forever."

"And teaching's been yours. But should they consume our every hour?" I hold her arms. "There needs to be time for us. There needs to be time for our life together."

She nods, but I can tell by the set of her jaw the argument isn't concluded. Merely put on hold. "Okay."

"Shall we?"

"Only if you feed Sammy first," she says as she walks back into the kitchen. "If you think you'll have time to do it."

I shake my head. How is it she can sense when I'm tiptoeing around what I really think? Yes, it's great she and I can be together more, thanks to Nick's replacement efforts.

But she's right. It's the greater availability of my time, of time for me to do what I want, that appeals the most. I'd be a liar to say otherwise.

So apparently, I am a liar.

The next morning, I lie awake listening to Jess's music as she exercises. I should get up and shower, but instead I roll over. My phone's within reach. I know, because its screen refused to provide me answers last night when I awoke twice in the early hours to continue the search. My dreams swirled rabidly, images of Nick and Chris, intense pain, the sensation of my body being torn and patched, like a brick wall knocked over and rebuilt with fresh mortar.

This has to go away. I have work to do. Maybe Nick didn't know what Chris did. But he did know about Tyson's car. And he admitted to vigilantism.

How did that tie into killing off my neighbor's dog? It doesn't make sense.

I'm sickened all over again.

Jess and I small chat through the morning. Twice I come so close to telling her what's going on, I startle myself with the intensity of the need to share this secret. In the end, we kiss each other good-bye, and she smiles as I drive off.

No, I can't tell her. She'd be in denial, and think I was covering something else.

Curt, though … Curt's been my friend for years. Longer even than Jess. He'll probably think I'm nuts.

But he's just crazy enough himself he might not.

I text him to meet me for coffee and tea. His response is immediate: <You got it.>

He's waiting for me at The Shattered Mug by the time I park behind Sheryl—half a car length. No need to earn a chastisement before the day's begun.

The wind's got a cold bite to it, and there's a light dusting of snow everywhere. Most of its already melting from the sidewalks, but the tops of cars are still coated. The warmth of the café embraces me as

I pull up a chair across from him. Whatever Curt has smells sweet.

"Hot chocolate." He blows steam off it.

"With mint."

"Yep."

"That's a far cry from black coffee, Curt."

"Hey, a guy's got to branch out. You never know what new things I'm willing to try."

"Of course." I glance around the room. "So which girl are you stalking?"

"Z, that hurts. It's not stalking."

"I bet Wikipedia and Rampart PD would agree on the definition."

"It is not—" He cuts off as a cute Japanese woman with a purple stripe in her hair stops by our table to take my order. She appears to be our age, maybe a bit younger, and wears a Shattered Mug red apron.

She grins at him as she leaves.

"Great. So much for trying something new." I shake my head.

"You know, you've been goofy enough you don't get to judge."

"What? How?"

"Um, gee, let me think." He tugs at his beard, putting on an exaggerated expression of puzzlement. "Like when we had lunch yesterday and you were going on about how great Anna was, after I just told you to stay away so you don't get burned!"

Lunch? Yesterday? My mind rewinds. Nick's apartment, and our tense conversation therein. He had a sandwich. I took mine with me. Had I even eaten in, in the midst of the rest of Tuesday's blur? "At lunch."

"Yes, Z. Lunch. Meal between breakfast and supper. Unless you're a hobbit, but you don't strike me as the geek type."

"Right." Where in the world had we eaten? Never mind that, what had I eaten? And what had we talked about?

Scratch that. What had Curt and Nick talked about. I rub at my forehead. Nick's persistence is admirable, but if he doesn't take care, he could unnecessarily complicate everything. It could be, though, he's testing for such a complication, to make his portrayal of me more convincing.

"What's going on, man?" Curt asks. "You've been strange ever since Bentley's the other night. That whole mess with your car almost getting stolen, the fight, then you show up for lunch swaggering like a frat boy. That was real fun. Hence my sarcasm." He squints. "Anna. Hang on. You two didn't—"

"No! I told you, there isn't anything between us."

"That isn't what I saw, and sure wasn't what you said."

"Keep your voice down and listen. She's just a work pal. That's it. I've barely spoken with her lately." And that's true. With everything going on, Anna's been the last person on my mind. Which isn't to say I haven't noticed her. That's impossible.

The thoughts make me grimace even as I dismiss them. *Really, Dominic?* And Curt's still peering at me, expecting a reasonable answer. Unfortunate I don't have one for him. "What I said the other day … I wasn't myself."

"No kidding. That was the stupid version."

"That's harsh."

"Call it fact. You going to tell me what's up?"

"It's related to how I've managed to free up my work schedule."

"I'd wondered. All of a sudden, Mr. Pencil-to-the-Paper can come out and play and take off for the weekend. It isn't you, Z. Even more odd considering the rumors I've heard about Dualpoint."

"I wasn't aware of any rumors."

He chuckles. "You wouldn't be. They're the kind floating around outside your walls. Word is your gang is courting a big, rich foundation that wants to build a big facility in Rampart. Same word is, everything got hammered out at a pow-wow this weekend."

"You know I won't say anything about a client until the firm issues a release."

"Relax, no corporate espionage here." Curt gulps his hot chocolate. He gasps. "Wow, okay, that's still blazing."

"If it wasn't, they would have to rebrand it 'lukewarm chocolate.'"

"Shut up." Curt gazes out the window, twisting his mug in circles on the table.

"What's wrong?"

"Nothing."

"Curt, come on."

"Look, I thought maybe you were, I don't know, paying some college kid under the table."

"To …?"

"To do your work. Draft the stuff you didn't have time to complete. AutoCAD until his fingers fell off while you hung out at the bar and took second honeymoons. Any of the above."

I slump against the chair. "And then pass it off as mine? I'd never do that. I can't believe you thought I would …" I wave my hands, as if I can conjure up the rest of the sentence that won't offend my best friend yet adequately expresses my outrage. "Cheat."

"Yeah, okay, but I didn't think you'd cheat on your wife, either."

"I haven't!"

"You're skating awfully close to the edge of thin ice," he mutters.

I drink my tea so he can't see me scowl. What does Nick think he's doing? Hanging around Anna when I've made a promise to minimize our contact and telling my friend the opposite of what I've said. He's got to be more careful. If Curt were to let slip his concerns to Jess …

Of course, I cannot blame it all on Nick. I'm guilty of stoking Curt's ire. This thing with Anna—my actions precipitated Nick's interest in her. She and I flirted long before he showed up. But, no, I would never do anything to hurt Jess.

If I think it enough, surely it will keep me from danger.

Curt raps his knuckles on the table. "Wake up. So what's your excuse?"

"My excuse is … complicated."

"More complicated than hiring a stand-in to do your homework?"

"I don't think you'll believe me."

"Shoot." He shoves aside the mug and interlaces his fingers. Curt could be Sergeant Ambrose prepping for an interrogation.

"How about this: I have a duplicate me who shows up when I'm busy to help juggle my workload."

Curt stares, his face a concrete slab. Then he bursts with laughter. I pray for a mask to conceal me as the other customers' heads pivot. Curt slaps the table so hard hot chocolate sloshes over the rim. I mop it up with a napkin.

"Man, Z." He rubs a tear from the corner of his eye. "I needed that laugh."

"Yes, you did." I smile, though it's the mask I'd wished for, a cover for disappointment. "Told you it was unbelievable."

I'm at my desk an hour before Nick calls.

"What possessed you to have lunch with Curt?" I snap.

"Research, Dominic. He wasn't suspicious."

"He thought I was—you were weird."

"If you're going to get paranoid every time someone thinks I'm you acting 'weird,' this partnership won't work. He was fine. I didn't say much, and frankly, I didn't have to. He filled all the silences."

Well, he noticed that much about Curt. "I have an afternoon meet with Mrs. Dockery."

"She's the one fussing about her siding?"

"Shingles. You've looked over the information."

"I have."

"Meet me a block from her house at 3. She wants me to show up at 3:12."

"You're the boss."

He hangs up. I don't ask about the dog, though the sight of the Dumpster is burned into my brain, or about Eric Talbot. He's already proven stubborn about the latter. And I've tried searching for more information about the deceased veteran. Nothing. Same nothing as when I looked for Nick and his lackey Chris.

"Hey." Anna leans through the door. "Hungry?"

"Hmm? No, not yet."

"I thought we could get lunch. Some sushi take-out. I've got a whole folder of ideas to go with the elevations Tyson showed Kaminsky."

Sushi's tempting. So's the company. Curt's words, accompanied by his frowning visage, flit through my head. "Perhaps we'd better look them over in the conference room. We can keep the business in house."

"Oh. Sure." She frowns. "Is something wrong? You hinted—you said it'd be nice to spend more time together."

"I do enjoy our working relationship. But I want us to keep that the way it is."

"Nothing else."

"No, nothing else." Can I say it with one hundred percent sincerity? I can't answer. All I can do is sit here, hands folded, and think about Jess. Not about Nick working an angle with a woman to whom I'm attracted—and vice versa.

But something else weighs on me. Something Anna just said. "Do you have those elevations? I assume you mean for Procyon."

"Yes. These." She hands me the folder. When I take it, though, she doesn't let go. "Keep our options open."

I don't say anything. She releases the folder anyway. And leaves me with a smile.

The smile fades when I leaf through the papers inside.

Twenty steps later, I slap the packet on Tyson's desk. "Explain this."

He's swiping through images on his phone. Without looking away, he says, "Those would be my elevations."

"Your elevations." The packet crumples in my grip. "These are the ones you asked *me* for."

"Nope. They're mine. I don't appreciate what you're implying, Zein."

"Don't give met that," I snap. "I can open the files on my computer and show you—"

"Show me nothing. They aren't there."

"What?"

"Go check if you don't believe me." He swivels in his chair. "I'll wait. Got a lot of messages to catch up with. But it won't matter. There's nothing there. The files are in the server, under my name, created on my computer."

"You …" I step back. Every word from his mouth feels like what I've imagined a gunshot should be—sharp, throbbing pain. "You accessed my computer."

"I have the administrative passwords. Easy enough." He sneers. "Maybe you didn't think I could do it. That you're the only one skilled enough. But Kaminsky was wrong to let you in on this project. It's mine, starting from right now." His fingers thump the desk. "It should have been mine from the get-go."

"Of all the arrogant, conceited …" I grind my teeth. "Who do you think you are? There's dozens of architects with more talent in their left fingernails that you have in your entire body. The only reason you've made it this far is I've done all the grunt work around here while you take the easy projects!"

He plants both hands, his face inches from mine. "I knew you thought like that. Typical. Don't talk to me about grunt work. Grunt work was my Ma takin' two jobs and me cleaning toilets late on school nights to pay rent. Grunt work is slapping burgers on a griddle while my classmates are partying, so I can sock away every cent to get my degree. You know how hard I've worked to get into this position? I won't let some raghead kid take it away."

"My family has worked just as hard as yours, Tyson, and we've every right to what we've earned."

"Everything you earned could've belonged to someone else better," Tyson growls.

I swipe the folder off the table and stalk to the door. Every argument I can summon is ready to present to Kaminsky, with the folder and my laptop's files as ammunition. Except …

"Yeah, what're you going to do? March into the man's office and tell him I'm a fraud? I've been his loyal employee twice as long as you. Procyon may sing your praises but if you take your files and try to tell Kaminsky I've replaced them …" Tyson shrugs. "That's low. That's the scummy thing a young up-and-comer tells the boss when he's angling to push out the other owner."

He's right. Kaminsky has entrusted a lot of me, lately. But Tyson's reliable. Even though Kaminsky wanted me to make sure the Procyon deal was preserved, he kept Tyson in charge. How much would I risk trying to reveal his treachery? "What do you want?"

"I want you to do what you've been doing best—work. Churn out those Procyon designs, get me the elevations, and I'll add them to my own. Don't fuss about credit. Play nice, and I'll do you a favor."

"I don't want any favors from you."

"Really?" His grin's all malice. "Not even if I agree to keep an anonymous email about your fooling around with Anna from getting to your wife? And Kaminsky? He's an old-fashioned dude, you know, and he's been muttering about how friendly you two are."

Threats won't get me anywhere. Ice floods me. "I would appreciate your discretion."

"I'd appreciate you getting out of my office and back to work."

I stand in the hall, listening to Anna's soft voice discussing an unintelligible topic with Kaminsky. My temples ache.

He can't do this. I haven't done anything wrong.

But that doesn't matter if I can't prove it.

CHAPTER THIRTEEN

Tyson is thorough. He's left me no options.

It doesn't matter how deep I delve into my computer. All my files are backed up in our server and even my laptop syncs to the building's network when I walk through the door. It keeps us from making mistakes—say, if a client needs the latest iteration of a project design, we don't accidentally send them the old file prior to the newest changes.

It also means that all the drawings I've submitted for Procyon's review, to Tyson's folder, bear his name. Even the ones sitting on my laptop's hard drive.

I slap the keyboard. What am I supposed to tell Kaminsky? Yes, I've produced several elevations, but Tyson's stolen them. It isn't even what he wanted me to do, primarily. I'm supposed to keep Tyson from torpedoing the project, by smoothing his rough edges during interactions with the Procyon representatives.

As long as Loredana Lark approves of our work, and doesn't hate Tyson, we're successful in the boss's eyes.

All right. But he doesn't have everything. Because when it comes to formulating designs, yes, most of my work is computed-aided. When I daydream the initial concepts, however, I draw.

The notepad is buried in the bottom of my computer bag. It's twisted, as if it's been in a life-and-death struggle with my computer and lost the violent battle. A couple pages hang loose, torn half from the wire binding. Doesn't matter. I flip through with such urgency I rip some of the casualties clean out.

There. The first-floor elevation, or at least, a partial sketch of it. There's smudges from where the side of my palm smeared pencil, and a yellow stain in the top corner. That'd be mustard.

I scowl and sag against the chair. Really? This is the best evidence I can concoct? Curt will be merciless. Wait until I tell him my grand plans to salvage my job.

Perhaps he's not the one to let in on this problem, though. My phone says it's 2:15. I have to keep my appointment with Mrs. Dockery.

Nick could do this nicely.

Heading out the door, I find Anna on her way down the hall. She's got her coat buttoned, and a bag slung over her shoulder. It bulges with a pair of binders, plus her tablet. She takes one look at the packet tucked under my arm. "Mrs. Dockery?"

"Is my disdain palpable?"

"You look like you have a lot on your mind."

Yes, and she's one of the items on the list. We walk out to our cars in companionable silence, though given our last conversation, the tension is understandable.

I open the door, and stop, hand on the frame. "Anna, I didn't want things to wind up like this. If I've misled you, I apologize."

"It's okay," she says, with the hint of regret and downward glance that informs me it's anything but okay. "You've been—different lately, and I thought it meant something would change. What I'm trying to say is, you and I should be more careful. Things get misunderstood."

"Yes, they do."

She seems about to add more, but instead climbs into her VW Jetta. The diesel engine rumbles as she drives off to her appointment.

I head the opposite way, to Mrs. Dockery's house, regretting everything I've said or done around her to make it that much easier for Nick to up his ante. What was I thinking? She wasn't my wife. Spend enough time with someone, though, and perhaps growing closer is inevitable. The situation was complicated by us being of opposite sexes.

Can't believe Curt was right.

Nick's waiting a block away, at our appointed rendezvous, five minutes before 3. Today, as always, he's dressed the same as me, in the same black jacket zipped up to the neck. He's even found sunglasses that are identical. They sport polarized blue lenses, adequate protection against the bright winter's sun and the glare from scattered snow. So far, he's doing a good job heeding the texts I send first thing in the morning to coordinate our wardrobes.

"You look terrible." He leans against the SUV. Chris's shadow sits still as a statue behind tinted windows. "Rough day?"

"Tyson."

"Ah. Him. What's he up to?"

"Besides stealing my work and labeling it as his own, not much."

Nick's smile twists. "Is that so? What steps have you taken to remedy the threat?"

"I've found pencil sketches I can use when I go to Kaminsky—"

"Forget your boss. You know with whom he'll side. Tyson's been his boy for years. You're still the newcomer, no matter how hard you work or how much of your life you hand over to the firm. What's needed is a taste of his own medicine."

Good. He has something mind. "I'm amenable to suggestions."

"You take back what's yours, Dominic. Don't stand by and let Tyson bulldoze. How did he get his hands on your stuff? I assume by using his administrative access to relabel the files. Well, then, you can't do that, obviously, but what you can do is take the drawings to Procyon yourself."

"Without Tyson."

"Absolutely. Tell Procyon you want to update them. Leave Tyson out of the loop. He'll find out, yes, but by then, you'll have completed your task—to position yourself as the go-to guy and plant seeds of distrust against Tyson."

"I can do that."

Nick smirks. "Is that so? The look on your face, like you're going to vomit, says otherwise. Like it or not, this is a fight. You don't win by standing by politely and playing by the rules when the opponent is set on cheating."

"No, I fully understand. It's a matter of fighting dirty."

"Dirty, clean—the adjectives are irrelevant. What's needed is victory."

"Okay. I'll contact Lark and schedule a—"

"Lark? Don't trust her." Nick frowns. "There's something about her that feels …off."

"What isn't to trust? I've only met her once. She seems competent, if cold."

"Perhaps that's why I think you should stay away from her. We don't know anything about these Procyon people, and if you're going to break out knives against Tyson, I don't want the possibility of her stabbing you sideways when you're facing a frontal attack."

Something about his tone pushes me the wrong way—though to be fair, I feel so tightly wound that anyone's commands will be sufficient to snap me. "Well, I don't know anything about you, either, Nick, and that hasn't stopped me from trusting you."

"Don't strain your brain. I've been honest with you."

"Why is it I can't find any evidence of you?"

"Been researching me online? What's Google got to say?"

"Stop it," I snap. "You know full well you're an enigma, as far as electronic records are concerned. Nothing shows up. It's all me! I can't even find your surname."

"It's Zein." He grins. "You just won't accept this miracle, will you?"

Miracle. That's how I've thought of it. More and more it reminds me of the folk tales of the devil sitting on one's shoulder. Makes me wonder who's the angel on the other perch. "And what about Chris? He and his look-alike—"

"Stop worrying about it. If you want to dig around, be my guest, but you're not going to find anything. Don't question me about Lark, either. I have every right to be cautious, and you'd do well to follow my footsteps." Nick straightens his coat and heads down the block.

"Did he kill Mrs. Cortez's dog?"

He stops. Wind flicks his hair, but Nick doesn't move. When he finally faces me, he's impassive. "What dog?"

"Don't give me that. I saw it. Cut up in the trash bags, tossed in your Dumpster like refuse." Bile rises in my throat. Push through the fear, Dominic. You have questions that need answers. "Come on, Nick, what's going on? Fighting thieves, sliding Tyson's car in the river, the dog—you're making a mess."

"I have no idea about Mrs. Cortez's mutt. What's the issue? Can't you consider it an issue solved? No more injuries to Sammy, no more running amok in your neighborhood. Whether or not Chris was involved … I'll talk to him." Nick keeps walking.

I catch up to him and grab his arm. "He's right there in the truck! Ask him."

Nick yanks his arm free and pokes me in the chest. I gasp. The shock is enough everything goes black for a second, and when I recover, I'm down on one knee. My breath is ragged, white wisps fogging the air. Muscles quiver. It felt like the world's worst static shock.

"I've had enough of your griping," he murmurs. "You asked my advice, and you got it. I don't know about the dog. I will ask Chris. Stay away from Lark. Outmaneuver Tyson. Want me to write it down?"

I shake my head. Words can't form. My heart finally slows.

"Good. Let's go deal with this old lady and be done with it. I've got to talk the Vitalis into signing off on the final design—as if there's ever anything final about dealing with them."

Back at the office, the first thing I do is hit my email for the messages

I've exchanged with Loredana Lark.

Whether or not Nick is paranoid about her is irrelevant to me. I have more vital things to consider—such as, what's happened to the preliminary exchange we had about the empty floors in the new Procyon building. She is hiding something, yes, but every organization is within its rights to keep secrets, especially a foundation with as much cash and capital tied up in its operations nationwide.

I can't find the emails.

They must have been moved into Trash, accidentally. I click open that folder.

Nothing.

My scowl deepens. What, am I losing my mind this morning? Perhaps the whole tasering by Nick was a symptom. Though, it did remind me of watching him take down the car thieves outside Bentley's.

Then, like now, I never actually saw a Taser.

So where are my emails?

They're gone from the Sent folder, too.

This is insane. How envious would Tyson have to be to eliminate emails from my account? He doesn't hold the password to it. Only Kaminsky does, as he does with all of ours. He's the only …

No. I gave Nick the password. He's been using it to communicate with the clients. I scroll through message after message of his dialogue with Dr. Huang, the Vitalis, and the Brunkhorst restaurant people.

But nothing from Lark.

I reach for my phone, thumb poised to dial, but just as quickly discard it on the desk. What good will it do to confront him, yet again? He's so sure about our arrangement's success. His confidence infects me. I want this job to go well, badly, more than I've wanted anything else my entire career. Nick's right—this could make us.

Make *me*.

But it still baffles me. Why would Nick delete our communications? He must be keeping them somewhere, to keep up the appearance that he's me.

My desktop phone beeps. Cassie, in the reception area. "Yes?"

"Got a delivery for you, Dominic. Would you like me to bring it back?"

"Sure thing."

Instead I get Mr. Kaminsky, holding a small brown box. I don't recognize the company on the label, but there's no mistaking it's addressed to me.

Dominic Barnabas Zein.

Must be a misprint. I never use my middle name—Mother loved the tales of St. Peter's loyal fellow preacher, but I still think it sounds redneck. I prefer my middle initial.

"How Procyon coming?" Kaminsky asks. "Their people have done nothing but praise you since Saturday."

"Thank you. We're doing well."

"That Ms. Lark's got a keen mind for all this planning. Had a few good discussions with her, and she's quite confident you'll get the job done."

"Tyson and I, you mean."

Kaminsky chuckles. "That's what I mean, yes, but it isn't what she said. She got frosty when I mentioned his name. I suppose that's what happens when you use Tyson's more, ah, unpolished approach on a woman who's used to calling the shots."

I nod and smile, more pleased than I'll ever let my boss know. What I really want is to drag him into Tyson's office, thundering about the injustice of having my work stolen by a jealous colleague. Instead I accept the box from him, shaking it. Sounds solid.

"You two need to put together a presentation for the rest of the firm," Kaminsky continues. "I'd like a brief update Friday afternoon, no more than 10 minutes. Add on another 20 for questions and follow-up."

"We can do that."

"Good." He raps his knuckles on the edge of my desk. "Dominic, this all turns out well, we're going to have a very long and positive discussion about your presence here. There's a couple young grads

I want to hire on for CAD work, plus a lady who's getting her start in architecture—but to do that, I need your office. Which means, I need to move you up the hall closer to mine. Commensurate to a salary boost, of course."

"Of course. I mean, thank you. That's … excellent." I stand and shake his hand.

"Good. Very good." Kaminsky walks out whistling. *Whistling!*

My grin melts. That won't happen if I don't follow Nick's suggestions. As much as the thought sickens me, I'll have to make an end-run around Tyson.

Fortunately, I have Loredana Lark's cell number.

She proves easy enough to reach. "Mr. Zein. How can I help you?"

Kaminsky was right. Frosty isn't a cold enough adjective. "I'd like to set up a time to discuss the project's progress. Are you available tomorrow?"

"No."

The lack of a counterproposal, or even another sentence, after the answer throws me for a moment. "All right. So, ah, perhaps Friday?"

Seconds blink away on my Smartwatch before her replay cuts across the phone signal. "Mr. Zein, my superiors want me to work with your firm on this project, and I have great hopes you will prove instrumental to its success, but not if you insist on whipsawing."

"I'm sorry, ma'am, I have no idea what you're talking about. I assumed from our discussions we'd formed a decent rapport." This is my polite client speech for, I have no idea why in the world you're angry.

"Do you recall my response to your email yesterday?"

"Yesterday? I'd sent you a second request for detailed information that was missing from the original Procyon proposal, but never received anything …"

The missing emails. The box sitting on my desk looms.

"Mr. Zein."

The address label says NKR Printing Solutions. Office supplies, stationery, …

Business cards.

"Mr. Zein? Are you still there?"

I rip open the box. Shredded brown paper litters the floor. Inside are cream-colored business cards. My stock ran out a couple weeks ago. The reorder ran late. And now it's here with all my information, including Dominic Barnabas Zein in black font next to the Dualpoint logo.

But the email address is wrong.

Instead of dbzein, it's dzein.

"No." I click frantically on the link to our company web, and slash through to the contact page.

There's my face, smiling for the happy clients, with my name and certification, plus contact phone …

The cell number's different. And the email is the one on the cards, dzein.

"Mr. Zein!"

Lark's imperious voice smacks me back to reality. "Yes? What?"

"Are you well? Is something amiss?"

"There may be." But how to explain it. "Did I change my contact information? That is, did I send you—"

"Of course. The message came in from Dualpoint. You updated all your relevant information." Her tone softens to inquisitive. "As a matter of fact, you said you're no longer using this number. Have you changed your mind?"

"No. That is …" I rub my forehead. "Keep this number, for now."

"What of the other?"

"It's still in use, as far as I know." As is an apparently false email account, one which Nick has used to replace my business account. Whatever his issues with Loredana Lark and Procyon Foundation, he's taken his skittishness too far.

"Am I to understand you wish our prior partnership to continue?"

"Yes. Absolutely. When you receive calls on the other phone …"

I wave my free hand around, as if I can pluck the answer out of the recirculated office air and send it through my cell to the listener.

"I shall endeavor to maintain a neutral stance when calls come in on the new number. As for this number, I shall treat it as … authentic." For moment, I think I can hear typing on a keyboard. "Mr. Zein, if there is anything else I can do to keep our communications secure, do not hesitate to ask. And, remember the mantis, please."

"I will."

I press the edge of my phone to my lips. Thoughts chase each other in my head, like Sammy and Eddie snapping across the fence. A poor idea—it brings to mind Eddie's carcass in the Dumpster.

Sergeant Ambrose's business card peeks at me from behind my keyboard. It doesn't help matters that the only policeman with whom I've had an extended conversation is the one eyeballing me for Nick's vigilante attacks.

Speaking of business cards …

I dial the front desk. "Cassie?"

"Yes, Dominic?"

"Those business cards I reordered …"

"I know they were late, but you did call for those last-minute changes. Right before you had me update the contact page on our website."

My jaw flaps shut. "No worries. I, ah, just wanted to let you know they turned out well. Very slick."

"Okay then."

I crumple one of the new cards and shove it in my pocket.

There's no one at Nick's apartment.

He's avoided my texts and calls all day. Not even this new false number—my supposed phone number—leads me to him.

Neither does Chris answer his door.

I back up from the sidewalk, balancing on the curb. It's dusk.

There's no sign of the lights coming on. The SUV isn't parked nearby, nor is it stashed in the alley.

I punch the new number one more time.

"You've reached Dominic Zein. If you're a client in need of immediate assistance, my email address is—"

Again with the phony information. I want to throw the phone against the wall, but that would deprive me of my only lifeline to Jess, Curt, and the others in my life.

Wait. Would Dominic have tried the same trick with those outside my professional circle?

Before I can text Jess or call Curt, headlights blind me. Some fool has turned the wrong way down the street, rolling up to within feet of me and—

Oh. Red and blue lights flash atop the car.

"Mr. Zein." Sergeant Ambrose leans on the door. "Out for a walk? No, not here. Not with your Bimmer parked three cars back, on the other side of the street."

I hold up my hand until he resolves into his normal self, as opposed to the shadowy blob he'd first appeared. "Sergeant. I was looking for a friend."

"In a neighborhood far from your normal stomping grounds? This isn't even the condos at Stone Hall."

Curt's neighborhood? "Have you been following me?"

Ambrose comes around the front of the car, both hands braced on his belt. "Watching, but that doesn't always mean in person. I'm a decent social media navigator. I'm more interested in why you're back here at the scene of a foiled crime, the second one in which the robbers claimed an Arabic man beat them cold."

"As I said, I was looking for a friend, but I must have the wrong address." I make a show of checking my phone. "If you'll excuse me, I'm expected home for dinner soon."

"Listen." Ambrose cuts off my path back to the BMW. The squad car's lights strobe across his sunglasses. "We've had some better luck with Mr. Jacobs' carjacking. Turns out a blond fella was spotted in the vicinity. Met one lately? Tall, thick neck, military build?"

"I've met no one accused of a carjacking." Close to the truth.

He nods but doesn't seem convinced. "Remember what I said about keeping clear of this area of Rampart?"

"I don't think it's in your jurisdiction to dictate where I can go, Sergeant."

"Nope. Just giving a friendly reminder about what's best for public safety." He tips his chin, until icy blue eyes glare in bright slits over the top of his glasses. "And don't think I'm not watching for another screw-up, Mr. Zein. There's something wrong. I don't know what it is. Can't prove anything. Not yet. That'll change."

He's gone, along with his car, leaving me blinking at blobs of light in the dim evening. Wherever Nick is, he'd better quit hiding. We need to get on top of this, soon.

Before it gets worse.

Jess is quiet all the way through dinner. My questions about her day are met with monosyllabic answers, so I switch tactics and fill the silence with the more mundane details of mine. Any mention of Nick tasering me, Tyson threatening me, or Anna—well, Anna and me—are left locked away.

Later, dishes done, and Sammy sent outside for an evening romp, we sit together on the couch. I'm reading *The Economist*, but the way she's flipping through her novel I know something's still amiss. "Jess, what's going on?"

She closes the book. "Stace Carpenter's pregnant."

Ah. "That's great. This makes, what, her and Uly's second?"

"Their daughter's three." She props her arms on her knees and smirks sidelong at me. "I guess this is my not-so-subtle way of broaching the topic again."

"I haven't had much time to consider it."

"What have you had time for? Hanging around?"

"That isn't fair. I've cleaned out my schedule. Been around more.

We've had evenings together, which hasn't happened for a long while."

"Yes, and yet you're still avoiding the question."

Frustration flares. "This is ridiculous. I'm taking great pains to improve our life, and you're complaining that I haven't thought enough about adding a child to the mix—which will undo everything I've spent the past couple weeks working toward."

"It isn't as if she would pop out of my womb tomorrow." Jess stands, arms folded, like a shield against her chest. I sense I'm about to regret my sharp rebuttal. "And there's no need for the attitude, Dominic. This isn't a surprise I've sprung on you."

"No, it isn't, but there's the constant questioning."

"What's wrong about that? We said we wanted a family."

"That was years ago. Things change. People do, too."

"I haven't. I thought you hadn't. Obviously, I was wrong. I understand your worries—you don't want to be a deadbeat father, but I don't stress about that at all. You're responsible, hard-working, caring … all the things I want our children to be."

I shake my head. "This isn't the time. Not now."

The phone rings, insistent. My cell phone's going off, too, buzzing like crazy. I'd say I'm relieved for the interruption, but the two of us need to finish this conversation. Jess sighs. "Fine."

Hmm. The F-word. "Jess, I'm not against the idea of having children. It's just—there's nothing to benefit us or a child right now."

"Nothing? Nothing except the sheer joy of bringing a new life into this world and the love that comes with it. I don't want to wait forever, Dominic—and neither do you. I want to enjoy our children and grandchildren while we're young."

The phones keep at it. "We should probably get it," I say, but Jess is already on her way to the house phone.

I check my cell. It's Curt. <Did you hear!? Everyone's blown away. How'd it happen?>

I hate it when he plays the mysterious pronoun game. <What?>

"Dominic?" Jess's voice tremors. "Please. It's for you."

Her hand's shaking as bad when I take the phone. Tears glisten at the corner of her eyes. My heart stops. All I can think is, *Mother's in the hospital.* "Hello?"

"It's Kaminsky." My boss's voice is gruff, as if he's choking back something overwhelming. As it is, he has to clear his throat twice before continuing. "We've … the police called. Tyson …"

I blink. For a second, I wonder if he means they've caught Chris, arrested him for drowning Tyson's SUV. "What's wrong? What's happened?"

"Tyson's dead."

CHAPTER FOURTEEN

Dualpoint is in chaos.

Faces blur by as I move through the hallway. Hands reach out, murmur words I cannot comprehend. People I rarely see during the workday, colleagues who don't have time to greet each other in the morning, gather in tight knots of hushed conversation.

A voice rises above the rest—Kaminsky. He's shouting at someone, and his answerer uses a mellow, unruffled bass tone in an attempt to soothe him.

"Dominic." Anna's crying. She slings her arms around my neck and sobs into my shoulders. Hot tears soak my shirt.

"It's okay. It's all right." I have no idea what's happened to Tyson, or if anything I'm saying is true. His office is dark. The chair is vacant, but it seems he should step through the back door at any second, wondering why we're all weeping, admonishing us to get down to work.

Anna lifts her head. Her face is inches from mine. I hate seeing her in distress. Like anyone else in my life, I want her to feel … better.

Her nose presses against the side of mine, lips parted, her mouth brushing my cheek.

What has Nick done? Did he already kiss her? She's far too familiar with me, and I haven't done anything to warrant this kind of reaction.

Have I?

There's a sharp intake of breath behind me. The haze surrounding events rips away and time snaps back with startling clarity.

Jess didn't want to stay home, not once she heard about Tyson's death. She insisted on coming to the office. Her way of showing support.

Anna's eyes widen.

I pull from her embrace. My heart batters the inside of my ribs. Desire and anxiety clash.

Jess stands there, her emotions thundering all over her face. There are no tears, only a hard set to her jaw, and a stern gaze I imagine would have her students on their knees begging for mercy.

"Jessica," Anna says. "Th-thank you for coming."

She reaches out to shake hands.

Jess considers the intruding appendage, perhaps wondering if a ruler from my desk would be sharp enough to sever it at the wrist. She looks at me, next, and says, with all the finality of a judge passing sentence, "I'm going to talk to Cassie."

I don't bother trying to explain anything. There will be time enough for the debate later.

Kaminsky's voice rises a notch, making him audible over the murmurs. " ...better explain what you're doing to catch him!"

"Sir, you'd better calm down, or I'm making room in the back of my car." Sergeant Ambrose.

Their voices filter from Kaminsky's office. I push between people, without looking, not turning around when Anna calls my name.

I shoulder the door open. Kaminsky's got his hands on his hips, neck beet red, face sweaty. What there is of his hair is tousled. He's wearing a rumpled flannel shirt and blue jeans with a hole in the left knee. One of his shoes is unlaced. The sight hurts me more than, sadly, knowing Tyson is dead.

If Sergeant Ambrose could turn me into a human piñata with his gaze, he would. The sunglasses are nowhere to be seen. "Mr. Zein. I'm sorry to be the bearer of bad news."

"Tyson ..."

"Shot. Appears to be a robbery. His cash and credit cards were taken, phone, watch. The assailant left everything else. Mr. Jacobs had stopped at Northwestern Bank ATM and was in the middle of a withdrawal."

"They left him to bleed on the sidewalk," Kaminsky snapped. "Animals."

I just stare at them. Tyson's been shot and killed. Murdered. A thought shoots through my head like lightning—*He won't be such a pain anymore*—and I immediately dismiss it, shame burning my guts. The man's dead. Regardless of how he treated me, someone somewhere cared for him. I didn't fully hate him myself. There was no denying the quality of his work, the creativity of his design. Admiration mingled with disgust.

"We appreciate you making the trip to speak with us in person, Sergeant," I say.

He nods, but there's nothing comforting about the way he examines us. "There's going to be a lot of questions in coming days. Figured you folks should get a heads-up."

"I need to talk to my staff." Kaminsky staggers from the office, as if he's been physically assaulted.

I start to follow, but Ambrose cuts me off, repeating our encounter street side below Nick's apartment. "Where were you tonight?"

"At home, with my wife. Ask her yourself, if you like. The office called both our home phone and my cell."

"Which did you use to answer?"

"The home phone. Sergeant, if you have suspicions, I'd prefer you come out and say them."

"Not going to happen. That's my prerogative. Yours is staying out of trouble, and so far, you're doing a poor job."

"I haven't done anything wrong."

"Yeah, but the wrong things happen in your proximity. It's really trying my patience, and I don't have much to spare. I'll be in touch."

He's gone before I can turn the questioning around. And Jess takes his place in the doorway. "I'm ready to leave."

There isn't much I can do here. Why did I bother showing? For support, yes. Kaminsky is a wreck, but he makes his way among our staff, consoling. He's the father of our extended family—a family in which the obnoxious older brother has died.

The analogy breaks down when Anna walks up to him.

Jess and I pass them without a word, even to each other.

The silence holds longer than any I can remember in our marriage. Not even Sammy's insistent greeting can raise either of us from our doldrum.

Jess's phone smacks against the kitchen counter. "Is she why you don't want to have children?"

It's so far afield from what I thought would strike me that I can't formulate an immediate response. "She … Anna? No, she has nothing to do with it. She has nothing to do with anything. We're not—"

"Don't. Don't say it." She's trembling. "How stupid do you think I am? I saw the way she looked at you. The way she clung to you. I'm not going to stand here and let you tell me is was nothing, Dominic, like I'm some naïve teen girl who moons over your every word."

"Anna's a colleague, and I've never done anything inappropriate." Her holding my hand outside Bentley's immediately leaps to mind, as if there's a marquee sign flashing. Fair enough, but we didn't cross any lines.

Nick, on the other hand …

My doppelgänger is hardly a persuasive alibi to offer a hurt spouse.

"I told you I didn't want to hear it."

"Well, you're going to, because I won't stand here and be accused of cheating when I haven't."

"She's looking at you like you're hers!" Jess snaps. "And after our weekend together, all our time spent getting away from work life, talking about … family, that was the last thing I wanted to see!"

"Anna is … confused about what she wants. I'm keeping my distance, and yes, tonight she was vulnerable, but we all are. Tyson's dead, and it wasn't a car wreck or an accidental medicinal overdose, Jess. Someone shot and killed him. We're all torn apart. So, the last thing on our minds should be separation, a wedge between us when we need each other."

"I don't think you do. Need me, that is."

She could have hurt me less with an ice pick through my chest. "That's a nasty thing to say. Of course I need you. We need each other—it's why we're married!"

Jess shakes her head. "You need your work. You need the approval of everyone around you. Me? I'm in that second category."

"Stop talking like that. You're just upset."

"Of course I'm upset! That woman was … she …" Jess holds her hand to her mouth. Tears stream.

I draw her, enveloping her with my arms. Sobs wrack her body. "You don't have anything to worry about. I love you, not her."

She breaks free. "Then you need to show it."

"Ah … that is what I'm doing."

"I don't mean that. You work with her every day. I've trusted you on that for years, but you broke that trust."

"I haven't broken anything, but hypothetically how do you think I should repair it? Worst case scenario, she leaves, or I do."

Jess arches an eyebrow.

Heat floods my face, accompanying a surge of indignation. "You're serious? You want me to quit? No. Absolutely not. You just said I'd poured myself into this job. How can I walk away from it?"

"There's other architectural firms in Rampart and even nearby. Bigger ones."

"Bigger ones? If I wanted one of them, I'd have cut and run years ago! Dualpoint is my best chance for advancement precisely because it is small. I love having clients who know who I am—even the ones who drive me crazy! You can't buy that kind of personal interaction and recommendation in a larger firm. Plus, Dualpoint being small means I can face the possibility of taking the reins down the line."

"You want to own it."

"Of course I do!" Sammy bolts from the outburst. Jess folds her arms and sets her jaw. "Are you kidding? I was all set to wait another decade or more before Kaminsky retires. That, or Tyson fouling up in such a monumental fashion as to open a chance for my buying part ownership. I didn't think my opportunity would come about as fast as it did."

Jess stares at me with such shock that I wonder if a burglar has broken into our house when I wasn't looking. "He's *dead*, Dominic, and you're rubbing your hands together because you can take his job?"

"No. My hands are right here."

"Don't be smart."

"I'll say whatever I'm thinking, Jess, since that's the agenda for this discussion. I've wondered about my job. So what?"

"So what? Have compassion for him and his family. Consider his soul. Did he even go to church?"

"Couldn't tell. I was more worried about the immediate effect of his envy on my career."

"You're being cruel."

"That isn't what I meant." And yet, it is. There's a cold, dark corner in my heart that's smugly pleased Tyson is out of the way. The bulk of my soul is sickened by the very idea—and yet, that foul whisper won't abate.

Here I've been wondering how Nick, whose personality seems much hungrier than mine, could think he and I are one and the same. It seems his actions aren't so unexplainable after all.

Jess snatches up her phone. "I'm going to be late."

"Hang on, we need to settle this."

"It is settled." She sounds weary. "You're staying at your job, and I'm not going to press about starting a family. Why should I? Everything's just fine the way it is."

I'm not dumb enough to follow her upstairs. The door slams

shut. I sag against the refrigerator.

Sammy pokes his head around the corner. He cocks it to the side.

"Don't say a word," I mutter.

The next morning, she doesn't bother coming downstairs before I leave. She's awake. I can hear the footsteps above.

I pause at the door, hand on the knob. There's plenty I could say—about us, about Anna, even about Nick, but I'm too raw from our arguments, from lack of sleep … From Tyson's death.

En route to Dualpoint, I can feel the strain pressing in. I have to get this weight off my chest. Curt doesn't understand. I tried the truth with him and, as expected, he laughed it off.

But I'm not out of options.

Twenty minutes later I stand on the concrete porch of a bungalow tucked behind St. Lucius church. White siding needs a repaint, which is budgeted for this spring. Snow clings to green shingles, making a patchwork pattern. Melt drips from the gutters, spurred by the morning sun.

"Dominic. This is a pleasant surprise." Father Hamra's smile slips when he opens the door to let me in and gets a clear look. "What is it?"

The whole mess spills out, backward—Tyson's death, the argument with Jess, the complexity of my relationship with Anna, conflict over the Procyon project, the police interest. All of it but Nick.

We're at his kitchen table. I pluck at my pants leg before I realize the habit's set in. My other hand grasps a steaming mug of tea like a life preserver.

"I take great joy in shepherding my flock," Hamra says, "But perhaps it is better to tackle one difficulty at a time."

"Sorry."

"There is no need to apologize. This is what sin and the devil conspire to make of our lives."

"A mess?"

He nods. "You love Jessica."

"I do."

"And she loves you. Go to her and apologize. As for this dalliance in your workplace—" Hamra sips his tea. "Well, I need not quote the proverb our Lord gave regarding this matter."

"You'd have me quit. That is the real-world equivalent of cutting off my right hand, isn't it?"

"I am not a fan of dismemberment, and gouging your eye would inhibit your gift as an architect just as badly. No, Dominic, you must be clear with this woman."

"I have. She knows there's nothing."

"But it sounds as if she's hearing two different things from you." More like two different things from two of me.

"The police. I do not understand their interest in you."

The bottom of my stomach drops out, the same sensation as hitting a rough patch of turbulence. I felt the same way before telling Curt … "Father, the other week I asked you about the prospect of a doppelgänger."

"I remember."

I meet his gaze. "I have one."

Nothing changes. There's neither condemnation nor amusement. "Go ahead."

"He is … he's me. I know what you said, about us being created individually, but this man knows all about me. He can be me in situations, work or otherwise, and no one is the wiser. Granted, his personality isn't exactly a match. There are several times he's handled things differently—but I've found some of them to be for the better."

Hamra holds his mug. He searches its surface. "The Stewardship meeting?"

"Yes."

"That was … him, not you?"

I squirm in my chair. A visit to the principal's office would be less awkward. "It was."

"Amazing. And this weekend, when you came without Jessica—

"

"Also him. Jess and I were in Estes Park."

"This is astonishing. Instances of two people who look so similar as to fool others is real enough, but … to find someone who is truly *you* …"

"He found me. And he's been a tremendous help. I've gotten more done in the past week and a half than I'd thought possible. It's left me with more time to spend with Jess and my friends. But …" I blow out a breath. "But I think he's involved in criminal activity. There's been at least two cases in which he's intervened to stop crimes in progress."

"Ah. The question of vigilantism versus law enforcement." Hamra nods. "On the one hand, we have the desire to do good for others, and on the other, we are called to obey authorities."

"He also had Tyson's car dumped in the river."

"The same Tyson who passed?"

"The same."

"And the police?"

"They think I could be a suspect. Why not? Two sets of thieves have pointed out a Middle Eastern man who looks a great deal like me as their assailant."

Hamra considers this, and his silence stretches on for so long I wonder if he's been struck mute by my revelations. "Father?" I ask.

"What is it you want me to say?"

The bluntness takes me aback. "Tell me what to do. I don't have the wisdom to handle the problem."

"God's wisdom is sufficient. It is He who gives you the answers."

"Except when he doesn't. What do I do when he's silent? He lets crime exist and death—" Tyson's face flickers through my mind. "He doesn't stop death."

"None of what you have said is false." He's gazing out the window. Drops of melted snow catch sunlight, turning into miniature prisms that sparkle with reflected rainbows.

There's no sign of the anguish I feel. "How did you do it?" I blurt.

"You lost your wife and child. How did you fix things when everything broke? You lost everything and yet you're sitting here, far more settled than I am, and my problems aren't nearly as terrible as yours were."

Hamra smiles. "You assume I did anything. His hand picked me up. He brought me comfort. I will not deny the heartbreak. Let me be clear: I never understood Job as clearly as my time in the darkness. My soul was sick. I … well, I wanted to die. Often I came close to granting myself that wish."

It's chilling to hear, but I do remember that Father Hamra. For months after they were killed in the car wreck, Hamra was cold, closed off, stiffly going through the motions of Mass. He had never been a cheery fellow, at least not during the brief year Jess and I knew him when we first started attending St. Lucius, but there were rumors he was terribly sick. Sick, as in mentally ill.

Yet, a couple months later, this incarnation of Father Hamra gradually appeared. His smile returned and broadened. I can remember the warm spring wind through open windows in the Sanctuary when I first heard him laugh. Since then his homilies struck home as never before, buttressed as they were by a reborn fervor for Scripture.

If I could have that same hunger, I'd be a happy man.

"You see, Dominic, when all my efforts and reason and emotion failed me, the Lord reminded me—in a whisper, not the thunder I expected—that I was not alone. Even with my family taken to His side, I was loved. I would never be an orphan. My Father stayed by my side." He raises his mug. "As I will stay by yours. Whatever you need to make it through this trying time, ask."

"Thank you." My phone buzzes at me. It's nearly 8, and there's a text from Kaminsky. <See me first thing when you get in.>

Speaking of principal's office … "I have to go, Father, but I appreciate your listening."

"I have been told it is my strength." Hamra rises with me, and we shake hands, he clasping mine with both of his. "This man … this other you. He frightens you, doesn't he?"

How in the world he ascertained this baffles me, and my reflex is to respond with disdain …until I realize he's right. Nick does frighten me. Not that he poses a threat, really, but his complete disregard for consequences to his actions is born of a such a freedom I've never experienced.

What frightens me more is that I want what he has.

"You have already said you think his acquaintance may have aided in committing crimes," Hamra says. "Is it possible he had a hand in Mr. Jacob's murder?"

Another thought I'd denied myself, or at least, kept suppressed. Chris killed that dog, I'm sure of it, and Nick already admitted he'd dropped Tyson's car in the Van River. But outright murder of a man? "He's a doppelgänger, too. His equivalent is a dead homeless veteran found in Estes Park. If they both had military experience—like Nick and I share architectural skill—it is possible. But what can I do about that? The police won't believe me. And if Nick's involved, the last thing I want is to turn him in. We're the same! He claims our DNA and fingerprints and blood match."

"Has he proved it?"

"No. No he hasn't." I'm too sheepish to admit I haven't wanted to try. The satisfaction of having him replace me when things get tough overwhelms rational thought.

"Take what precautions you must. Find proof, one way or the other." Hamra places a hand on my shoulder and makes the sign of the cross with the other. Instinct and habit kick in. I mimic the gesture. Funny how something as simple as moving one's hands in seemingly meaningless motions brings renewed confidence. I feel a fool for not doing it sooner.

"And here." Hamra reaches up to his cupboards. He sets a metal tin on the table.

He peels back the lid and removes a revolver.

It's old. The edges are smoothed, the metal burnished and dark. The grip is wood, it too worn with age. The smell of steel and oil pervades.

Hamra opens the cylinder, spins it. It's loaded with six bullets. He closes it and hands the gun to me, fingers wrapped around the top of the cylinder, thumb across the bottom of the trigger guard, muzzle pointed at the floor.

I stare at him.

"Your soul is preserved through grace," Hamra says, as he guides me to the door, palm pressed to my back. "But if this man is truly a danger, you must protect yourself and others."

I take the gun.

He leaves me standing on the porch. The door locks shut behind me.

CHAPTER FIFTEEN

Silence greets me at the office. The phone at the front desk rings, but no one's there. Lights are on, but no one's around. Not even Cassie.

Kaminsky's alone in his office. He shuffles through a stack of papers, glancing back and forth between them and his monitor. When he looks up, his eyes are rimmed red. He's wearing his formal work attire again, but sans tie, and his sleeves are rolled up. "Dominic. Thanks for coming by."

"It seems I'm the only one. Just your car and mine in the lot."

"That? I let everyone who did show up go home." He shakes his head. "Cassie made it two steps from the front desk before she broke down crying. There's no point forcing people to adjust after a tragedy, not until they're ready. If you need to go home, let me know. It's not coming out of anyone's sick time or vacation."

"Appreciate that." I sit across from him. "What's on your mind?"

"Tyson." He fans out the top pages. "Specifically, his work on Procyon."

"We've both been busy with it."

"That's apparent. What isn't apparent is why some of your drawings have his name on them." He taps one elevation for the Procyon building.

I clear my throat. "There was a … misunderstanding about our allocation of labor."

"Listen. I'm the last one who wants to speak ill of the dead, but I'm also not stupid. I know your work, and I know—knew his. Yours has elegance. His had power. The changes are subtle, but I know where to find them. So, imagine for a second Tyson is still with us and tell us what he's been up to."

"All right. He came to me a couple days ago and told me he was relabeling my work as his. I was to keep producing, with the understanding he'd claim credit for the bulk of it."

Kaminsky glares over his glasses. "If I hadn't found these at his desk, I'd have said you were feeding me baloney to get him in trouble. I can't believe he'd stoop so low. What was he going to gain from it?"

"I think it was more a question of how he could stop me from gaining." My temperature rises. Kaminsky can't be this blind. "Surely you've noticed his antagonism. He's envious of my success and felt threatened by my position with Dualpoint."

"Hmph. He could've always asked me." Kaminsky folds his arms. "No offense to you, Dominic. Your work's brilliant. But I had no intention of replacing Tyson with you. Didn't think you were ready and that isn't saying you're a novice or some rookie. You just needed more time to mature into a greater role here."

"I understand." To an extent. Tyson's antics and adversarial nature had long ago instilled in me the belief I could do a far superior job. At least I would not constantly belittle the staff, or certain members among them. "Tyson did good work. He was the right choice to head the Procyon project."

"He was. But now he's gone. Know what hasn't changed? I still have a major client on the hook who wants a huge building constructed faster than anyone who's walked through my door in 20 years. You've got to step up."

"Sir?"

"Don't play coy. You know as well as Tyson did the importance of Procyon to our future. This puts Dualpoint out there for everyone to judge. What're they going to see? A firm that's taken a hit and retreated to home kitchen renovations and dentist office rebuilds? Or a company of experts ready to tackle every major project that crops up?" Kaminsky holds up my elevation that Tyson relabeled. "This is what I need from you. Can you provide it?"

I hesitate for only a handful of seconds. Of course I can provide it. That's what I've always done. Conceit reminds me finishing Procyon's building with my name—and my name only—listed as the lead architect will lead to great things. Great things could mean, if I planned them right, less time in the office and more time in my life, if I found and hired the right subordinates.

Unreal. Give the heart a moment's daydream and all humility is trod underfoot. That isn't to say it disappears when I push it down. It waits.

"I can, and I will," I say. "Whatever you need from me, you'll get."

"Outstanding. That's what I wanted to hear." He passes me a slip of paper. "The administrative passwords to the server. This should help you undo whatever mess Tyson's left. I'll have to get his email login from Cassie, but you should be good to go."

I hold the slip at eye level. It's the key to right the wrongs done to me.

Too bad it had to come at the expense of Tyson's death.

But wait … "Sir, if you're giving me these, does it mean …?"

Kaminsky smiles. "That's right. Give it a couple weeks, for everything about Tyson's position to settle. Then we'll talk about making you part owner. There's nothing that'd make me happier, son." He holds out his hand.

I shake it. Part of me wishes Father could be here, in this room, to see the moment. The other part of me is glad he's never going to set foot in Dualpoint. "Thank you. Thanks very much."

"Forget it. I mean that. You earned this. Whether or not Tyson …" Kaminsky breaks off. He removes his glasses and rubs his face. "I'm worn out, Dominic. What with the memorial service we've got to plan and Procyon knocking on our doors, my brain's fried."

"Let me worry about Procyon. You can tend to the service and whatever else needs to be done." I stop at the door. "If I'm going to do this, however, I'm going to put my other projects on hold."

"You can, or you can bring in one of the draftsmen on board. I'd go with Ray."

"All right, thanks."

It's an odd thing, to both mourn someone's passing and bask in a promotion. It isn't until I get back to my desk that I realize my phone's buzzing. The sound is strange, more metallic than usual. I grab it from my bag.

The revolver's there.

My heart skips. I hadn't forgotten, but I suppose not looking at it made the fact of its ownership dreamlike. Father Hamra hadn't really given me a weapon. That's insane.

Except, here it is. Missing serial numbers and all.

I frown. I'm no gun expert, but I know what that means. This is a firearm meant for criminal use—or at the very least, one meant to be untraceable.

But the phone …

It's Nick. My guts churn. I'd hoped for Jess. She hasn't contacted me all morning. But I have not made the effort, either. Typical of us. Neither wants to be the first to apologize.

<I saw the news,> Nick's message reads. <Seems like you're about to get busier.>

I misspell a dozen words before Autocorrect can sort out my angry typing. <Where have you been?>

<Doing your work, as per our agreement.>

I take a picture of the box of new business cards and send an attachment over.

<Ah. They arrived faster than I thought.>

<What's the deal with these? I never gave you permission to change my contact information.>

In the lag before his response, I shove the box into my laptop bag. <You've been preoccupied,> he texts. <Work. Jess.>

<We've had a rough patch.>
<Children again?>
<Bad fight. Haven't heard from her this morning.>
<Did you contact her?>
<No. Not yet.> I scowl. What am I doing? Treating him like my friend or writing as if to myself. <You need to reset my contact info.>
<Really. How's that going to go? Cassie will think you're slipping. And suppose she tells Kaminsky. How much more is he going to trust you if you're goofing up things as basic as your contact information?>
He doesn't know I've just had the ownership talk. But he's no fool. <With your vigilantism streak, it's too bad you couldn't stop Tyson's killer.>
<You told me to lay low, remember?>
<Change back the information.>
<No. It's simpler to keep it this way. I'll give you access to the voicemail for the new phone number, if you're so convinced you need it.>
My fingers mash the phone screen so hard they leave concentric rings of rainbows. <Are you crazy? This is my career!>
<This is our career, Dominic. You wanted my help. You have it.>
<That wasn't what we agreed!>
Nothing comes back. Minutes tick by, and I realize he's done with the conversation.

I grab my car keys. I'm supposed to get assistance for Tyson's workload, and Dr. Huang's ready for an update, but there's time for a spin over to downtown and Nick's apartment.

Except, the last time I tried showing up unannounced, he was nowhere to be found. Sergeant Ambrose's appearance also cooled my desire to confront Nick, explain to him how he has to follow my lead.

All right. Think. This can wait. Just push through the day, get the new contact information from Nick, and set up a meeting.

I gather my bag for the appointment with Dr. Huang. The gun's weight slaps against my side. What did Father Hamra know about my situation? He seemed adamant about needing protection.

Remembering how big Chris is, extra caution couldn't hurt.

Dr. Huang is, thankfully, the most cheerful of my clients.

Just me and him, this time. No Anna. She texted me while I was en route. <We've already talked interiors. It's your turn. Let's catch up on it over lunch. Or dinner.>

The idea is tempting, and I'm startled by how fast the image of Anna's face lit by candlelight appears in my mind. Not a good idea. Especially today.

Nick responds to my requests for the new contact passwords after five insistent queries. <Come by this evening. Tell Jess you're meeting Curt. We'll get this all sorted out.>

I scowl. He has a way with arguing around my reasons—not surprising, when one considers he's constructing them with the same mind.

Is he really me?

The thought digs at me through my meeting with Dr. Huang, blurring everything he says, right up through our concluding hand-shake.

Work consumes me the rest of the day, as I plow through Procyon designs. Kaminsky has restored all my drawings and given me Tyson's work. Blending them will take time, but the end result is worth it. I pass them on to Nick—and, in a fit of pique, Loredana Lark. Let him take it as a reminder he's not the one in charge.

A last visit with the Vitalis drains the rest of my patience. They snipe at each other with such vehemence, all I can do is keep a smile sealed in place while the fantasy of running both of them over with my car—repeatedly—plays on a loop in my head.

It doesn't help matters that I dread going home.

The lights are on; Jess is home. Great. It's past six, but since we never talked about when I'd be home, I have no idea whether or not

I'm walking into an ambush.

Doesn't matter. I know where I went wrong. Apologies do not come easy but are necessary. I open the front door. "Hey."

Whatever I expected, be it a sullen gaze or a tearful apology, I get neither. Instead Jess drapes her hands behind my neck and kisses me full on the lips for a very long time. I let the laptop bag drop to the wood floor. Sammy bumps my leg, letting off a single happy bark, but I shove him away with the finesse of a forward passing the soccer ball to his mate.

After what feels like hours but is only a few minutes, we break apart, both gasping as if we'd run a couple miles. "Hi." She smiles coyly.

"Well. Wow." I grin. "And here I thought there would be a knife between my ribs. That's quite the welcome home."

"After lunch, can you blame me?"

My grin freezes in place. Lunch? I ate egg salad and chips at my desk, accompanied by a dusty can of orange soda I found in the back of the employee fridge. This smells like a test. I'm not about to fail. "Yeah, good point."

"Thank you, again. D'Antonio's was lovely."

That's her favorite hole-in-the wall Italian restaurant, a little on Baker Street, in the Merchant District. I was nowhere near there today. She couldn't …

No.

Him.

"When in doubt, go Italian food." I hold her about the waist and brush her hair. She presses against my hand, smiling at me. I smile back, but my brain's a churning mess of bubbling anger that threatens to overflow. "Glad you liked it. I'm sorry about this morning, you know."

"Oh, you don't have to apologize again. I said all I needed to. Such a good listener."

"I have been studying."

She laughs and gives me another quick kiss. She heads for the kitchen. "Want a glass of wine?"

"Sure."

"Merlot or cabernet?"

"Whichever you've got open."

I hear the bottle clink and her shoes clack on the floor. I pick up my bag and set it on the coffee table in the living room, gently, because what I really want to do was bash them through the wood.

Nick took her on a date. My wife.

Traitor.

I double-check my phone. No messages from Jess. Why should there be? There haven't been all day. None from Nick, either. I switch on the data. There's an email, with an attachment.

"I was thinking Mexican tonight. Our enchilada recipe?"

"Sounds good. I'll get chopping the greens." My thumb hovers over the icon for the attachment. Open it. Do it.

I have to know.

My thumb stabs down. A black square appears, dimming the rest of the screen behind it. I wait for the blue wheel to stop spinning.

My heart thuds.

There's a photo of Jess, smiling.

And his face pressed close to hers, also smiling. I can't see much of their surroundings, besides the plates of ravioli and cacciatore poking into the bottom frame of the image. Light pours in from the street through windows behind them. He's wearing the same turquoise shirt I put on this morning.

The message with it, I'd ignored, but now I read: <Just in case she asks to see how the pic turned out. Great restaurant. Better woman. You really ought to get to know her better.>

I throw the phone the length of the room. It bangs off the wall.

"Are you okay?" Footsteps from the kitchen.

I retrieve it just as Jess walks in. There's a crack in the case, but otherwise it's unscathed. "I dropped my phone. Nothing's broken."

She hands me a glass of red wine and toasts with hers. "To a better end of the day than its beginning."

"Hear hear." She doesn't say anything about the phone. It must have landed behind the couch.

I make sure the photo's downloaded and saved before I join her in the kitchen. The tart smell of lemons and limes fill the room. Her knife thunks through them rapid-fire.

"Tell me about your day," she says. "Good?"

I pull lettuce and tomatoes out of the crisper. My slices are vigorous enough one tomato spurts its innards across the cutting board.

"Interesting," I say. "Very interesting."

After dinner and dishes and a second glass of wine, I tell her I'm going to run downtown to see Curt. She tilts her glass in a salute. "Tell the poor boy I miss him but add my gratitude for letting us take his dear Sheryl."

"I'll do that."

She stops me at the door. "Are you okay?"

"Yes. Why?"

"You seem on edge. Is it Tyson?"

"No."

"Okay. What about the phone company? Did they hassle you about changing your cell phone number?"

"My number …" My hand squeezes so hard the car keys leave imprints in my palm.

A minute later, I'm driving down Federal, ignoring the speed limit and other drivers, the latter of which honk their displeasure as I cut off one motorist after another.

Ten minutes late I'm at Nick's apartment. I slam the buzzer button. The door unlocks.

Chris waits outside the loft, frowning at me. He doesn't move aside.

Let him stand there. The revolver's easy enough to reach. But if he has training similar to his dead other, it may not make a difference. "We have an appointment. Should he be pulling back on your leash?"

Chris checks his phone, as uninterested in me as I was in the afternoon's schedule. Whatever he sees must satisfy him, because he nods and opens the door.

"There he is." Nick stands at the window, a bottle of beer in hand. "How did the rest of your day go? I have to say, it was nice getting to chat with Anna this afternoon. That's quite the bright woman you work with. And lovely. Though I think I mentioned that."

"Shut up." I point at him. "You need to stay away from my wife."

"Just proving a point, Dominic." He takes a swig and wipes his mouth with the back of his hand. The armband glints at the end of his sleeve.

"That being what? Showing me how far I can be pushed before I snap?"

"No. Demonstrating my ability to replace you in a given situation. Curt's been convinced. So have your co-workers and your clients. Now, your wife. Not as drop-dead as Anna, mind you, but charming nonetheless."

"Don't do it again."

"You misunderstand. This wasn't a test. This was preparation."

The door shuts behind me. Metal rasps. Chris blocks access, arms folded.

"I'm going to pretend you didn't barge in here like an officer of the law, barking orders at me to cease and desist." Nick's tone is flat and soft. "I'm also going to pretend you're not clenching your fist, as if I've stolen your favorite toy on the playground. We can continue this conversation in a civilized fashion."

"There's nothing to continue until I have your word you'll stay clear of Jess. And I'm going to change the access to the cell phone and email, so you'll stop mucking with them. You'll get messages when I pass them along to you." I step closer. Chris's footsteps echo mine.

Nick doesn't seem perturbed. He smiles as he swirls liquid in the amber bottle. As he closes the distance, that strange circle I'd spotted on the floor seems to ripple, like heat over hot asphalt. It's gone as soon as I notice. Surely it can't be a trick of the sun, not with it being dark outside.

"I will do no such thing," Nick murmurs. "I like being you. In fact, you're here because I want to discuss a new arrangement."

Father Hamra's advice for self-protection filter through my anger and fear.

Chris takes another step.

I yank the gun free of my pocket and aim it at his chest, gripping with both hands. "Back up. Now."

Chris freezes in mid-stride. He's too far to touch me, and he stays put. Whether or not I actually present a threat is beside the point. I haven't shot anything since Curt took me to try his collection of firearms a year ago.

"That is the stupidest thing you've done." Nick holds up his hands, imploring me to be calm, I suppose.

Calm is the last thing on my mind. "No. That was agreeing to work with you. Listen to me: You will stay away from Jess and from Curt."

"Fine," Nick says. "Fine. Put the gun down and we can talk—"

His wrist tilts sharply. Light blinds me, and something slams into my chest with great enough force to render me without breath. A shock like thousands of bees stabs every inch of skin.

When my vision clears, I'm on my hands and knees. My mouth is dry as the foothills without rain. The gun's gone.

Chris has it.

Nick's armband is glowing, seemingly white hot, yet it causes him no discomfort. A shimmering gold aura surrounds it, leaking from under his sleeve. He shakes his head. "This isn't how I wanted tonight to go. But you've forced my hand—pun intended."

"What?" is all I can croak.

"Time for you to leave."

CHAPTER SIXTEEN

Eight ten.

Funny thing, focusing on the time right before I'm certain I'll die.

Chris hauls me to my feet. He uses my shirt collar as leash and lever. The fabric tears across my throat. Metal gouges the side of my head. That oil and steel smell fills the air.

"Chris won't shoot you. I don't want you dead." Nick takes a swig of beer. His armband's glow fades, though a series of odd carvings still pulse with whatever latent energies remain. "Yes, I suppose this is a funny way of showing it. I understand if that comes as only mild reassurance."

"Who … are you?" My throat's raw. You would think I had walked from Denver to Rampart in mid-summer, without a drop of water.

"Dominic Barnabas Zein, grandson of Lebanese refugees to the United States. Architect by training." He grins and shows off his wrist. "Though a far more lucrative and exciting job offer came along."

"You're … into some kind of advanced technology. That's what you used to Taser the car thieves, too."

"Taser is a crude comparison. This is nothing so mundane. I couldn't care less about the inner workings. Results interest me. The what, rather than the how or why. It serves my purposes. Chris, show our friend to a seat. I'm neglecting my duties as host."

The muzzle's pressure lifts, then returns in the form of a glancing blow. My balance skews. I claw the air, seeking a handhold, but Chris shoves me onto a couch. Relocating only mildly improves the smothering sensation of vertigo.

"He's got a rough touch. Sorry about that."

I dab at warm liquid dripping from my temple. Blood. "You say you don't want me dead. That means you want my help."

"That's a broad assumption. I do, after a fashion." Nick sits opposite me. He suddenly grimaces and rests the near-empty beer bottle against the wrist bearing the armband. "Repeated use wears on one."

Staring at the ornament helps right my senses. I can finally focus on Nick, the room around us. "Can't you just take it off?"

"No. I can't." There's a tightness to his voice. He watches me keenly, but never once looks at the armband. "It isn't a weaponized version of a Rolex. There's a complex bonding process involved, nothing as simple as slipping on a leather strap."

Chris stays behind me. I cannot see the gun, but I have no doubt it's trained on my head again. A brief fantasy of leaping over the couch and wresting the gun from him flashes through my imagination, three times, and in each scenario, I wind up either bleeding to death, shot through the head, or charred to a crisp by Nick's strange armband. None of those options appeal to me.

"I never pegged you for a gun owner," Nick says.

"It isn't mine."

"Oh, I know. We would have found it by now."

He waits, legs crossed, arm draped over the back of his couch. I replay the sentence twice before it reaches through my addled brain. "You've been in my house."

"Many a time. How else do you think I was able to keep so abreast of your life's goings on? You sending me photos helped tremendously, but sometimes it was easier to see first-hand. Of course, after the first few visits, Chris recommended surveillance rather than breaking-and-entering, which makes a great deal more sense."

He reaches under a pile of papers on his coffee table. He opens a laptop one-handed. The screensaver resolves into a slew of images, clustered in tiles. Our garage, our kitchen, our dining room, our backyard …

Our bedroom.

Nick clicks on one and it enlarges. Jess is curled up, reading a paperback, on our living room couch. The detail's fine enough I can see her eyes drooping and the faint red residue in the wine glass perched on the end table.

My fingers mangle the edge of the couch. "You've been spying on me."

Nick sighs. "When we started this business, I'd hoped you'd be as intelligent as me. But sometimes you disappoint. Yes, Dominic, I've been spying on you and up to this point it's always been for the purpose of making your life better. Everything I've done has been to that end!"

"The car thieves, I understand. But the break-in downstairs?"

"I felt bad for the store owners."

"Tyson's truck?"

He scoffs. "The man was an arrogant prig. He needed distracting, so Chris took his truck for a joyride to deflect his attention from you."

I shake my head. "But … Mrs. Cortez's dog."

"Again, getting rid of that mutt—your word, not mine—takes pressure off another corner of your life." He grins. "Makes things easier for me, eventually. Though, not as easy as the latest step."

I turn around, slowly, so as not to provoke gunfire from Chris. There isn't the slightest sign of consternation, only a flat, hard stare. "You had Chris kill him."

"What? No!" Nick chuckles. "I did that myself."

Cold sweeps over me. I can't escape. I could end up like Tyson—or the dog. Admitting criminal activities is one thing. To sit here, across from myself and hear confession of murder come from the same mouth I've shaved around, the same one in which I've brushed teeth … "The police will stop you. They'll find the gun, or match the bullets, or something."

"That would be a possibility, if there were any bullets to find." Nick levels his armband at my face. It flares.

I have no idea what he's demonstrating but I also have no desired to be super-Tasered again. I duck, not caring about Chris holding the revolver behind me. I have to get out of here.

The air overhead sizzles. Whatever passes by does so with such heat the side of my face feels sunburnt. A sparking yellow-white orb, looking like a flattened disc, leaves an afterimage.

It spatters against the far wall. Brick chips litter the floor, and a charred gouge appears dead center of the peeling pop brand logo.

Nick nods. "My aim is rusty, but I have not had much call for that function. See, Dominic? The police, I'm sure, are baffled why the 'bullet holes' in Tyson's body have no exit wounds, nor do they have any shards left behind by projectiles. No powder burns at close range, either. There is nothing to tie his death back to me."

"Except my testimony. And if you're not going to kill me, you can't stop me from going straight to them." Can I get past them to the door? My heart's hammering. My thoughts buzz so fast I can't form a plan. There's no way out of here.

"Yes, that will be hysterical when they arrest me. How do you think they'll react when they slap cuffs on the same man who just told them who the culprit was? Two of us and one dead body. Which one of us will they believe?" Nick ticks off points on his fingers. "I have the email and business cards, I have the mail, I even have the keys to your car—well, I do now. Chris?"

The gun prods my neck. "Stand." It's the only the third or so word I've heard him speak—surprisingly soft, with a hint of dejection or sadness. Grandfather sounded the same. "Empty your pockets."

I set everything I have on the coffee table, my hands trembling— wallet, car keys, spare change, cell phone, Swiss Army knife.

"Good start," Nick says. "The jewelry, too."

My watch follows, as does the silver crucifix around my neck. I never pay it attention, but frozen in this moment, I hold it on my fingertips. Father Hamra tried to warn me. There's so much for which I have to atone.

It joins the rest of the pile.

I slip my ring off and add it to the top.

"Good. Chris, let me see that weapon."

Chris hands him the revolver. "No serial number," he murmurs. "Vintage model."

"I figured as much." Nick shakes his head. "All I ask is people follow my instructions, heed my orders. And what do I get? Insubordination. Here I'd hoped he'd be smarter than this. Ah, well."

He hands the revolver to his lackey. Chris brings my laptop bag over, leans it aside the table. My world dumped onto a heap.

"Take a good look, Dominic. This is you. This is what you've made important." His mouth twists. "Papers and messages and trinkets. Meanwhile, your wife's alone, your friend's missing his pal, and the woman for whom you've been pining at work—she's available. These are all situations I'll remedy, in due time. But first, I think it's time you pay up."

"You already have my money."

"Not what I meant. I spent a great deal of energy being you. It's only fair to return the favor."

Nick leaves the room. Once more the fantasy of overpowering Chris enters my mind, but even as it reboots, Chris draws a semiautomatic pistol from behind his back. It must have been tucked in his waistband.

"Put these on." Nick throws a set of clothes onto the table. It's a gray jacket, black shirt, and urban camouflage pants.

"I'm not wearing those. You're going to let me go."

"I appreciate your sense of humor. Chris?"

Chris aims for my chest.

Without further arguing, I strip off my shirt, slacks, and shoes. The replacement clothes fit as well as any pair I've worn, though they seem threadbare in places, as if they're finishing out a long lifespan. "Walking down the street in this getup will not help you take my place. And there's a decent chance Rampart PD's own Sergeant Ambrose is waiting for me."

"Lucky for us both, you won't exactly be strolling out the front door." Nick shakes his head. "You really have no idea what this is all about, do you?"

"How could I? You keep telling me you're me, but you've had such a great life you want to improve mine. Now you're forcing us to switch roles and dressing me up like a …" I raise my arms. Chris' gun barrel bobs as it follows the motion. "I don't even know what."

"It's been a nice change getting out of the old uniform. Wearing your clothes, sleeping in a comfortable apartment, enjoying fine food and—" He grins. "Beautiful company. This is the perfect place in which I can lay low. But to do that, I have to make sure the people looking to detain me have someone else to detain."

Nick steps past me, to the open space on the wood floor. He stops a foot short of the pale circle. I realize the light illusion is back, but as Nick raises the armband, the illusion intensifies. Light swirls across a pulsating bubble that reflects back the windows, the television, the kitchen, even the three of us men. The images skitter and warp, mingling in grotesque disarray. Inside the thin walls of the sphere, a shadow forms—a shadow with no focal point, not grown off anything. It expands into a dark circle inside the walls.

Wind whips around the loft, flapping papers, shaking blinds, sending dust sifting from the rafters. Boards tremble underfoot.

"You're going to take a trip in my stead," Nick says. "The people pursuing me will never be sated until I'm in their custody, but there's no chance I'll let them get anywhere near me. The only thing that will keep them at bay is if they catch me—and that's the favor you're going to return. You'll take my place. Permanently."

Chris grabs my arm, shoves me forward. I stumble on an uneven floorboard and stagger in Nick's direction. As fast as he reacted with the armband earlier, I expect him to blast me before I can get nearer, but he's focused on the strange sphere, eyes glinting with—hunger? Yet, his posture is rigid, restricted, as if he's approaching the formation with the greatest care.

The butt of Father Hamra's revolver juts from his pocket.

My chance.

I grab for the revolver. Chris's hand latches onto my shoulder. I yank the gun free and slam back as hard as I can. My head collides with his jaw. Teeth clatter. There's a grunt. Stale breath makes me gag.

Nick shouts something, but whatever command it is gets lost behind the shattering gunshot. My ears ring and the back of my head aches from the impact with Chris's face. I swing the revolver around, desperate for a shot—

A fist smashes into my ear. Does not do anything for my hearing.

I squeeze the trigger.

There's another explosion, this one muted by my already damaged senses. This time Chris shouts. More blows rain down, but I'm not letting go of the gun. I'm not going to let go.

Something hits my leg, right behind the knee. I collapse as if I've lost both my legs.

"Never met a more ungrateful person." Nick's words sound like they're coming through a fog. He looms over me, his expression twisted with anger. The armband glows yellow-white, and … it's in pieces. Seven fragments spin around Nick's wrist, clockwise, emitting a low hum. "After all I've done for you, when it comes time to offer yourself in service, you betray me. Betray us. Well, it doesn't make any difference. I'm sending you home."

He seizes me by the back of the collar, drags me across the floor. The revolver's gone. The loft tilts crazily. There's Chris, leaning against the couch, free hand pressing against his side. Blood oozes between his fingers. He's still got the pistol trained on me.

I scrabble against the floor, desperate for a handhold. Meanwhile, the wind swirling about us has reversed course. It pulls, howling as the intensity increases. I roll onto my side and gaze up into the center of the sphere.

A sunburst shines from the center of the darkness.

"There's a decent chance you can stay ahead of them!" Nick cries. "But I wouldn't say more than a day or two! Say hello to Loredana for me!"

He slides me through the wall of the sphere.

Something pulls me up into the air. My chest, arms, torso, all begin to float. I once saw a YouTube video of astronauts pinwheeling across a common compartment of the International Space Station. This must be what it feels like.

Within seconds, I'm suspended inside the shell, yet buffeted between it and the dark core. Sounds and smells and sights melt together in a nausea-inducing torrent. Behind me—or above me?—Nick is laughing. That sound. I twist, trying to orient myself. I might as well be swimming in a room full of bedsheets.

But I manage to wind up facing his direction. He's grinning. The components of the armband spin faster.

He snaps his wrist back. The components clamp shut, reforming the original band.

White light explodes around me. Nick, Chris, the loft—everything vanishes, wiped away by an unyielding brightness that stabs into my eyes. Heat builds until it tears at my skin, ripping deep into flesh and bone.

I scream, but there's no sound.

My mind dissolves.

Gone.

I hurtle along a tube.

Or a tunnel. Makes me think of driving I-70 through the Rockies east of Denver. Lights whip by, reversing course, smearing colors.

Outside.

Flying through a clear pipe. Fingers slide along the outside wall. They leave ripples in their wake, churning rainbow lines like the surface of a soap bubble. My breathing reverberates, all around.

Above and beyond, stars and fog. Craggy landscape stretches endlessly, black peaks streaked with violet and slate. White lightning edged in blue crackles in the distance, casting shadows and illuminating hideous shapes. Tentacles and teeth. They lash at the tube as I soar past, to no avail.

More beings—but are they? Strange forms, apparitions at first appearance, and yet, there's a sense of ravening hunger that's all too palpable.

One moment I feel I'm moving at breakneck speed, impossible to stop. The next, everything pauses.

I age and shed years at once.

My mind can't comprehend. Madness submerges rational thoughts. I dive inward, away from the gibbering emotions that wrack my consciousness, for long-buried truths.

Prayers. Hymns. *Anything.*

Time and light snap me forward, down a narrowing stretch, until I hit a wall with the force of a sun's fusion.

Darkness. Black. Nothing.

A thunderclap. It resonates throughout. I'm trapped inside a giant horn. Every cell vibrates.

Then a pulse of light impales me.

I land on uneven boards. Splinters cut my hands.

This place stinks of smoke and garbage. Burning garbage. Where am I?

My arms refuse to work. Same with my legs. Rolling over requires every ounce of strength.

It's cold. Bitter and damp. Cold drops hit my face. Snow.

I open my eyes. They almost refuse to work and feel as if they've been taped shut for days. Pretty sure I lose a few lashes in the process.

Another few minutes to adjust vision. Brick walls. Wood floor. Pale, grungy sky through broad windows.

All that, and I'm still in Nick's loft?

I hoist myself on unsteady legs. Blink away the smears of color.

The bricks are crumbled. There's huge gaps smashed in them. The floor around me is rumpled, missing large planks, and others are shattered. None of the windows are intact, save for a few fragments of glass. There's a yawning hole in the roof overhead, revealing bent steel beams and the wooden supports alongside.

No furniture, except for a sodden, collapsed couch. It looks nothing like the couch in Nick's apartment. And yet … I stagger. The soda pop advertisement is painted in the same place. The paint's even more faded than I remember.

Beneath me, there's a circle of pale wood. The illusion disappears.

Not an illusion. There really was a circle. Not just here, but in Nick's apartment.

But this is Nick's apartment. Isn't it?

How long was I unconscious?

I limp to the window, mindful of the holes in the floor and the bounce to the boards. My head throbs. Blood cakes the side of my head. Hearing's returning—hopefully there isn't permanent damage. I pat down my pockets. Nothing. No wallet, phone, keys.

Except …

The Swiss Army knife. I'd grabbed for it when Nick tossed the change of clothes onto the pile of my belongings. In the tussle, no one had found it. Small consolation.

My crucifix is wrapped around it. Hadn't intended to rescue it, as my priorities were elsewhere in the moment. But I'm glad it's here. I loop it around my neck. The return of its weight adds another bit of normalcy to a strange situation.

Now, if I can get some help …

A distant rumble breaks my reverie. Sharp cracks, infrequent, follow up. Another rumble.

Black pillars of smoke appear on the horizon.

And that horizon is wrong. It's Rampart City—the skyline against the distant hills and plains is recognizable. But buildings are in the wrong place. Many that should be there, are gone. Dozens more are hulks, windows gone, walls collapsed.

As I stare, an orange fireball blooms across the Van River, near Holloway Park.

Only there's no park. Tanks thunder across a scorched plain. An attack helicopter, gray and spindly, wheels overhead.

I lean against the wall, mouth agape.

What happened to my city?

CHAPTER SEVENTEEN

The stairs sway as I leave Nick's apartment, or rather, the ruins thereof. I stop halfway down, breath feathering. The door to the street is gone, smashed off its hinges. Snow has drifted into the entryway, piling in the corners.

I place a hand to my forehead and squeeze my eyes shut. Whatever happened left me dizzy, but balance is returning, albeit slowly.

I suck in air greedily. It's accompanied by smoke, which sets me coughing. There's enough oxygen left for the last mental blurriness to focus.

The street is deserted. Six cars line the sidewalks on either side, however, each one is a burned-out wreck. Glass glitters on black stretches of pavement uncovered by snow. Buildings shelter the street from the harshest wind, leaving a chill breeze that brings flurries.

I don't recognize half the business names. All of the storefronts are abandoned. Most display windows are reduced to jagged maws with broken glass as teeth. The electronics store just below Nick's apartment is still there, but it's empty except for a handful of vandalized televisions. The sign is riddled with bullet holes, the paint melted.

Scraps of refuse tumble down the street—food wrappers, bits of paper. Snow slumps, gray and brown, into potholes all along its length.

I zip the jacket against the winter weather, wishing for a pair of gloves and a hat. The sun peeks through the milky white haze overhead, setting the street sparkling.

Federal is a block away. If there's any chance of obtaining help, it has to be there.

I traverse the street and alley with care, glass crunching underfoot. A pair of mangy cats, skin stuck tight to their ribs, yowl at me from behind a toppled Dumpster. More yowls answer from farther down the street, perhaps in the very building I left. Other than that, there's no sign of life.

Gunfire erupts in the distance. I pause in the alley, listening. It's like a brief fireworks display, this one devoid of bright lights and cheering crowds. There could be shouts with it—I cannot tell from which direction it's coming.

Whatever conflict this is gets settled by another rumble, like the ones I heard when first awaking. The gunfire abates.

Is it a terrorist attack? I shake my head. Too much heavy firepower. How would terrorists get tanks into the city? And helicopters? Perhaps it's the National Guard, or the Army proper.

Federal Avenue is in worse shape than the last block.

Whole buildings are leveled. Not a wall is left standing. Here and there, a few structures brace themselves against their fallen comrades. Brick guts spew onto the asphalt. Broken pipes stare out. Deep black shadows reign where shoppers and diners used to congregate.

I stop by a wooden door that's broken, lying discarded across the curb. Caerphilly. I kneel and place my palm on the cold surface. It's warped, as if it's taken far more abuse exposed to the elements than it had in its frame.

The destruction doesn't look new. There's places where the road has buckled. Dead plants poke their way between crumbling pavement. When did this happen? How did it happen? I couldn't have slept through it.

That's all I can figure. Nick put me into a coma, or something similar, inside that bizarre sphere. The madness of being trapped in it, coupled with the armband's role, must have left me with more questions than I have time to answer.

What I need is someone to help.

Unfortunately, the only sign of law enforcement is an overturned Rampart PD cruiser, sans tires and windows. The paint's peeling and bubbled away where fire scorched it.

Despite all the carnage, there's very little trash. Aside from handfuls of stray litter, there's no garbage piled up. Broken glass, crumbled storefronts, and wrecked cars abound, but none of the signs of everyday human habitation.

Something crunches underfoot, and it isn't glass. I sweep snow away with my boot.

Bones. Could belong to a dog.

Think. The nearest police station is twelve blocks east of here. One would think with all the destruction they'd be full out, with sirens wailing across Rampart. Of all the sounds of this new environment, however, that's the one missing and the one I most want to hear.

I would even take an interrogation by Sergeant Ambrose, for a familiar face.

There's no people. Only empty buildings.

Snow shifts. I'm surprised I can hear something so soft, and when I turn, there's only a cat scooting across a broad, empty stretch of Federal. Never experienced the main drag so quiet. The absent thunder of constant traffic is unnerving.

I should start for the police station, but instead I head west. Dualpoint is closer, by far.

Every nerve is raw, aware of the smallest sounds. Each shadow portends danger. A flock of pigeons startles me into reaching for my knife. Ridiculous as it seems, clutching this small, sharpened piece of steel, its weight comforts. It's the only thing I have left that reminds me that I'm me.

Otherwise, I look like Nick.

Thoughts whirl like blown snow as I trudge for the office. Why did Nick toss off that comment about Loredana Lark? Did Procyon have something to do with the devastation? I stop a few blocks from the office and frown at my surroundings. Maybe I took a wrong turn. This neighborhood seems unfamiliar.

No, there's a pair of apartment buildings and the gas station next to the fast food restaurant. Next to that is …

There's no orthodontist office.

I can't comprehend the squat, two-story tech firm I'm staring at. This should be a single-level orthodontist's office. A doctor from Colorado Springs moved here five years ago. He started out taking appointments out of Dr. Huang's office before he obtained the loan needed to open his own place. I spent months designing it. He'd requested peaked roofs and a pair of bay windows, so as to emulate a house. Anna's interior layout reminded patients of a living room.

It isn't there.

I trek onward, picking out another missing structure. A thought strikes me. Rampart's skyline. When I first awoke, it seemed … off. Now, gazing back at the tallest buildings of the financial district, I realize why.

The ones I made are gone.

Yet, it doesn't seem they were bulldozed, then replaced. This is a matter of them never having existed.

I press my hands to the side of my head. What is this place? Wherever I am, it isn't Rampart.

Perhaps this is part of Nick's manipulation. He has me drug-addled, trapped somewhere, stuck in a bizarre dream. Or he's plugged me into some kind of virtual reality program, latched a headset to my face …

None of those sound plausible. Of course, neither does traipsing around a desolate version of Rampart that shouldn't exist, absent all the structures I've spent my entire career designing.

And it's worse.

Dualpoint is missing.

A seedy liquor store stands in its place. Not even a functional one—like most buildings still standing, this one is battered, broken, and missing a wall. I don't want to think about what weapon caused enough devastation to do that and leave a gaping crater where the parking lot should be.

I slump against a lamppost. It bobs under my weight. Dualpoint can't be gone. Not the place that is my home away from home, where I spend more waking hours than anywhere else. Every corner, every snag in the carpet, every flickering light, every smell from every room—they don't exist. All I have instead are broken bottles and a sickly tan floor splotched with coagulated puddles of beer and wine.

And still no people. No sign of human habitation.

I've got to find Jess. She should be at home …but it isn't dark. When I left it was late in the evening. Now … what time is it? No watch, no phone, mean I'm disoriented. It could be another day of the week.

A composed part of my disoriented mind, tucked deep in the back, wonders idly what project I had scheduled for tomorrow.

First things first. Find Jess. Get in contact with the police. And Curt. And see what's become of my co-workers.

Father Hamra. He might be of help. I frown. Though Nick wasn't at all surprised by the revolver. Likely he'd spied on my visit to the church, too, but he must have snooped at the parsonage.

A whimper interrupts my feverish calculations of how long it will take me to walk home. A dog runs out from a side street, limping badly on its right rear leg. Barks and growls chase it. Bedraggled, with brown and white fur, it stumbles into the remains of the liquor store without a glance at me.

His pursuers aren't as unobservant. Four dogs—big ones—pause at the street's outlet. They're of various breeds. The one in charge isn't as mangy as the others, standing taller, not nearly emaciated. All bear scars. Matted fur indicates dried blood.

He snarls at me.

I should stay put. Do not smile at him. Do not make eye contact. Do not show fear. There's enough of the liquor store remaining I could use it for shelter. Of course, the injured dog is in there, some-where, and there's no sense removing myself from one potentially hostile dog into the reach of another.

I start walking away, anywhere but the site where my workplace should be. If Sammy were by my side, this would be a different matter. The two of us could make a stand, give these mutts a clear sign we weren't going to back down.

But I'm on my own.

There's plenty of abandoned houses on the next block. Some are missing doors. A few still have them shut. Not worth the risk to fiddle with a lock.

I glance back, with as much nonchalance as I can muster.

The lead dog is following. His pack hangs back. They sniff at the liquor store dog, perhaps trying to see if their original quarry is still available.

There's a two-story Dutch Colonial Revival hunkered amidst the modern dwellings. All three dormer windows upstairs are shattered, as if someone has shot them or punched holes with rocks, but the downstairs windows are intact. More importantly, the front door appears unharmed, and it's ajar.

I increase my pace, altering my trajectory so the dogs are visible in my peripheral vision.

The lead dog barks. Nasty, ragged. It isn't the bark of an animal getting my attention. It's a sharp warning.

He lunges.

The pack follows. They kick up snow where it's covered the road. Claws clatter.

No use playing it cool now. I sprint for the sidewalk.

They're right behind, and a quick glance pinpoints the lead dog only a dozen feet behind me. His pack is considerably farther back but gaining.

The house's front steps are near enough I'm sure I could leap the last thirty feet and land on the porch. But I won't make it before he gets me. Outrunning a dog is a stupid idea. There's no way to do it.

Unless one has a head start.

I dig into my pocket for the knife, hop the curb, and turn.

The dog is right there. He slams on the brakes, snapping, dripping saliva from yellow teeth.

"Back off!" I snap. "Get back!"

My shout echoes across the neighborhood. He doesn't do what I ask. Instead he aims for a bite.

I should be curled up in a ball, for maximum protection, until he doesn't feel I'm a threat. But I'm not in any mood to take this lying down.

I kick out. My boot connects with his face. He yelps and scampers back.

Go!

I hurtle for the concrete walk to the front door. Take the steps two at a time. The door's wide enough open I ram my shoulder through.

Teeth tear at my pant leg.

I whirl and slam the door shut. There's a tremendous collision, strong enough to rattle the tiny window inset at the top. But the door holds. The hinges are all sturdy.

I press against the door, panting. The dogs outside bark, scratching at the other side, but after a while they lose interest.

I head for one of the living room windows. They're gone, off to the west, crossing unimpeded over lanes that should be full of traffic.

The living room's in decent shape. The couch is in shreds and the chairs toppled, but walls and windows aren't broken. Given everything else I've seen it's downright inviting.

The kitchen is another story. Opening the fridge nets me a gag-inducing stench. What little is on the shelves isn't fit for consumption. Empty cans are strewn about, as is garbage. Upside, the back door is locked.

A quick check of the phone dangling off a counter confirms my suspicions—Dead. Haven't seen a single wire in its proper place during my walk across town. Whatever chance I have at contacting help has to be in person.

I hope the former owners of the house wouldn't mind me pillaging what's left of their pantry—canned mandarin oranges and olives, of all things. The Swiss Army knife's can opener tool makes short work.

I sit on the living room floor, leaning against the smashed remnants of the couch. The sky's a vivid pink shot through with orange. The windows rattle when a distant explosion sends up a new cloud of black smoke.

Sleep could be a problem.

I spend half the night shivering, bouncing between fitful sleep plagued with nightmares and wide-awake panic. Light flashes across the sky. Not a storm. Some of the bursts remind me of the green tracers shown on CNN during the Iraq war.

Twice, vehicles rumble by. Both times, they're slow, searchlights panning the houses. I stay low, tucked in a corner. Blankets salvaged from the upstairs bedrooms fend off hypothermia.

When dawn finally breaks, I stagger out the back door. My mouth's filled with a disgusting aftertaste. Dinner wasn't the best combination of flavors. I turn on the sink, pining for a drink, but the faucet emits only a burst of air. I drink instead the sticky remains of the oranges' can.

I tread carefully out into the city, hands tucked deep into my pockets. The smallest, shortest blanket acts as a passable poncho, thanks to slits I cut with my knife. I'd rather it be less obtrusive, but red fleece will have to do.

Still no sign of people.

A verse comes back to me, one that proclaimed a new heaven and a new earth. Is this the windup before the pitch? Has the slate been wiped clean in preparation for the end of the old?

"I could use some answers." My voice is hoarse. It surprises me with its volume. When there's no one else to talk to and one isn't given to talking to oneself, the sudden sound of speech is as loud as gunfire. "Can you hear me? Tell me what's going on! Tell me what I should do! I don't have time to wander the entire city!"

Here I am, snapping at the blue-gray sky like one of the feral dogs I confronted. My face heats with embarrassment, whether at talking to myself, or at the tone I've taken with the one Sovereign Lord, I can't decide. Either way, none of the dogs show up. A small blessing.

Lacking any thunderbolts from the heavens, I strike out down Federal. It's a long walk to Pinnacle; the cliffs loom in the distance. Even their solemn, craggy faces haven't escaped damage—black streaks mar the pale tan. There's a greater problem, though.

I don't see any houses.

That's wrong. Some of our neighbors should be visible from this distance. The splintered remnants of Fort Rampart are there, to the southeast, in roughly the same configuration as I remember. But there's no houses.

Panic seizes me. No houses means no Jess. What if she lives somewhere else? This nightmare's full of oddities, but I can't shake the feeling she must be somewhere nearby.

Okay. Try a new angle. Curt's condos should be toward the river. St. Lucius Church and Father Hamra, farther west.

Or should I head back into the city? Try for the police?

The homes appear more intact farther from the center, so that's where I pin my hopes.

Hours of trudging down abandoned side streets gets me nothing but tired. It also doesn't get me any human contact. Not too surprising, given the sporadic weapons fire coming from all edges of the city. Whatever's going on, Rampart's center must be a no man's land. Perhaps if I keep going, I'll find one side or the other to this conflict.

I shake my head. Give me back my office, my car, my house. I should be coming home to Jess and Sammy or grabbing a drink with Curt. What are Kaminsky and Anna doing at Dualpoint with the Procyon project? Where is Dualpoint?

Those questions drop away when the first truck rolls into the end of Anspaugh Drive.

I don't recognize the model. It reminds me of a Jeep on steroids, yet it looks nothing like a Humvee, boxy rather than sloped and armored. It's painted a mottled green and gray. So is the second one and third behind it. American flags are etched on the hoods, in black silhouette.

They accelerate once they're within sight, engine noise reverberating off the empty homes. Relief buries me. I wave, both arms. "Hello! Hey, I need some help!"

None of the trucks show signs of stopping. If anything, they speed up, and break formation, so they're taking up both lanes.

I pause, hands spread. Waiting on the dogs was harder. Perhaps I should sit by the side of the road. It might reassure them I'm no trouble.

The first truck slams on its brakes sixty feet away, twisting its back end. Four soldiers pile out, all in mottled gray and tan fatigues thick with armor and faces half-hidden behind visors. Guns point in my face. "Get down! Down on your knees!" one of them shouts. "Keep your hands up!"

"What? I haven't done anything. I said I need some help." I do, however, follow instructions.

One of the soldiers wrenches my arms behind my back, at such an extreme angle I'm sure both will be torn from their sockets. He zip ties my wrists together.

"Hey! That's enough. If you're going to arrest me, someone had better read me my rights," I snap. "Where are the police? I was abducted and dumped in a—"

The stock of a rifle slams into my gut. Whatever tirade I had stored up gets blown out with all the air left in my lungs. I'm left bent in half, gasping.

"Shut up, or there's a bullet to go with those cuffs," the soldier snarls.

"Check him for weapons." This comes from the one in charge.

He has a lieutenant's bars on his shoulders, black rectangles hidden among the camouflage.

The soldier, a young black man, pats me down and inspects every pocket. All he comes up with is the Swiss Army knife. "That's it, Lieutenant."

"Hang onto it. Get the captain on the box."

"Yessir." Another soldier gets back in the truck. Hushed tones murmur out the open door.

Meantime the other two vehicles cordon the area. Eight more soldiers spread up and down the sidewalks. They move with sharp, quick motions, like birds caught out in the open. Guns aim to broken doors and open windows.

I stay perfectly still. Whatever's amiss, these men aren't interested in my protests or my tribulations. It's possible the chaos affecting Rampart has them on edge, to the point of treating everyone as a suspect in—this mess.

"Captain says he'll be here in five," the soldier in the truck calls out. "Caught a mortar ambush by the old highway."

"Roger that." The lieutenant looms over me, his weapon held at the ready. The gun's as unfamiliar as his truck. It looks like a mashup between an M-16 and AK-47. All the soldiers have the same model, though each gun seems to be slightly different. Some have more scratches, while others have been repaired with newer parts.

The same goes for their uniforms. Extra padding buffers a handful of the men. There's few identifying markings on their clothes, other than the American flag and rank insignia. I can't see a single name patch.

They've all got the same symbol on their shoulders, though—a four-pointed star outlined in black, with twin parallelograms bordering the right side.

I stare at the lieutenant's arm. That's the same emblem I saw on dozens of pages coming across my desk and through my email for the past couple weeks.

Procyon Foundation.

The lieutenant tracks my line of sight. There's a curious expression in his eyes, evident even partially obscured by the visor. "That's right. You're not lucky enough to get picked up by regular Army, Zein."

Zein? "You know who I am? Thank goodness. How long have I been missing?"

"Maybe he's gone nuts," the younger soldier mutters.

"Can it." The lieutenant prods my shoulder with his gun. "You too."

Another truck rumbles in from the opposite direction. It's an armored scout vehicle, with much taller wheels—six of them—and sloped sides. Dents and scorch marks indicate a rough time. When it blocks off the other end of the street, a rear hatch lets another three soldiers out.

They're joined by a man wearing a black beret. His chin is smooth as if he just stepped out of the bathroom after a good morning shave. Can't tell if he's bald or not, but his eyebrows are fiery orange. Bright blue eyes pinpoint me with as much emotion as a gunsight. He's a huge man, muscles bulging against a uniform in better condition than those of the other soldiers.

"Sir." The lieutenant salutes. "He was coming up the middle of the road, waving."

"Nice work." The captain faces me.

It's my best friend, Curtis Marin.

"Curt?" My voice squeaks worse than a teenage boy hitting puberty.

He glares at me with the same intensity he reserves for people who park in handicapped spots, or teens who giggle over the blue rectangles of their cell phone screens in dark movie theaters. He clasps both hands behind his back, standing ramrod straight. The soldiers around him take a step back, as deferential as peasants in the presence of royalty.

"I don't believe it," he snarls. "We finally got you."

CHAPTER EIGHTEEN

Curt is … in the Army?

I'd be less surprised if I were surrounded by a pack of speaking dinosaurs. This is the same man who named his Jeep in loving honor of a famous singer. The Curt I know is a bit on the hefty side, not out of shape but not in the best of it, either. He's grins and laughs, boisterous, like the waves at the beach.

This man could be carved from the same stone as Pinnacle.

"You've got a bigger pair than I ever thought, Zein, to put yourself in broad daylight," he mutters.

"Curt, listen, I don't know what's going on but—"

He pistol-whips me.

The pain lances through my jaw. There's going to be terrible welt there and soon. "No one gave you permission to talk," he says. "Fact is, your talking never does anyone any good. Lieutenant, did you search this man for weapons?"

"Yessir. Didn't catch anything on the pat-down except this pocketknife." The lieutenant hands it over.

"He could have men hiding. Check the perimeter."

"We did, Captain. No sign of IEDs, though I was about to call in a bomb dog to sniff around."

"Don't bother. If they were going to blow us up the Thudder

would be in splinters." He checks his watch. "Get him loaded up. Sooner we've packaged him off to HQ the better."

"Sir, yes sir."

Two of the soldiers jerk me upright. They don't bother helping me gain my footing—rather, they drag me to the nearest truck with my boots scraping behind.

"Hold up." This rock-solid, stern version of Curt probes about inside my mouth with a finger. "Bite down and you get a repeat."

I nearly gag, but he finishes the disgusting approximation of a dental exam.

"No pill." The other-Curt sneers. "Wouldn't want you foaming at the mouth and flatlining before we turn you over."

"Curt, please. Let me explain."

"You'll address me as Captain Marin, if and when you're required to speak." He shoves me along.

As the soldiers strap me into the armored six-wheeled truck, I glimpse the rest of the contingent returning to their vehicles. Curt—Captain Marin's voice filters through the gap in the hatch. "Base, this is Marin. Confirmed: we have the King of Spades. Coming home."

Our passage through the western half of Rampart is done in silence. It would have been difficult for me to say a word over the growl of the engines, anyway. The compartment stinks of sweat and grease. Two soldiers flank me. Captain Marin sits across the narrow aisle, glaring, with a soldier on either side. His knees bump mine as the truck jostles across rough terrain, through a wide turn.

The radio mounted to his shoulder keens. Marin wears a headset, a bulky, gray version of the same kind Cassie our receptionist uses at Dualpoint. The foam on the microphone is ripped. He has to yell to make himself heard. "Go ahead."

Whatever the incoming message says, it isn't good, because Marin spits on my boot. "Fantastic." He reaches over the soldier beside him and bangs on the metal railing behind the driver. "Corporal! Take

West Randolph. Got insurgents in Sector Five."

"Yes, sir!"

"All units make for the bridge with best speed," Marin snaps into his mike. "Foxtrot, watch our six."

"Must be looking for him." The soldier to my right, a lanky black man, studiously avoids eye contact. Something about his profile clamors for my attention. Perhaps I've passed him in traffic or seen him walking Rampart's streets. "Maybe we ought to let him ride the curb. Sir."

"Enough of that, Sergeant. This is a high-value target." Marin folds his hands. "I want him intact, as does HQ."

"Understood, sir."

The engine's rumble becomes a flat-out roar. The driver and his passenger exchange heated words. Whatever they're talking about isn't the weather, or traffic conditions, because the passenger soldier gets out a gun.

"Curt …" His deadly expression cuts me short. "Captain, I have a few questions. What's happened to Rampart, for starters?"

The troops around us are quiet. It isn't all fear-based reaction to Marin's orders, I think. The black soldier next to me fiddles with a ring on his right hand. The lieutenant stares blankly at the compartment ceiling. Another man—boy, really, no older than eighteen—pinches his eyes shut and murmurs what I assume is a prayer as he caresses a crucifix.

My fingers ache for the one around my neck.

"You heard the expression, 'silver tongue'? Knew you always had one, Zein, but you sure can lay it on thick," Marin says. "Okay, I'll play. Rampart looks the way it does because the Home Guard and HQ have stopped your crew in their tracks. We're holding the line up and down the Colorado East, pushing back the bulges you Sierrans have gouged out of our country. Give us time and we'll have every last one of you refugees clawing at the Cali Sink."

My mouth works but I can't find the words to fill it. One question has given birth to a dozen more. "That doesn't make sense. You know

I'm not a refugee. I've lived here for years. My grandparents are—"

"Don't. Final warning."

The urge to argue with Curt is overpowering, but not so much I'm willing to ignore the weapons held by every person in this vehicle except for me.

An explosion rattles the truck. It lurches, left, then swerve right. Curt reaches for a handhold. "Keep it on the road, Corporal!"

"Sorry, sir, we're taking fire from both sides! Multiple contacts from—"

A second explosion, this one seemingly closer. The interior lights up with an orange flash. Everyone's shouting at once. We drive past and over some obstacle that the truck's wheels batter.

Flames lick the tiny portholes.

"Squad Two's Thudder got hit!" the driver says.

"Survivors?" Marin has a hand to his headset.

"Nothing left but scraps and rubber, sir."

Marin closes his eyes. "All units, this is the captain. Scatter and run for it. Do not, repeat, do not stop under any circumstances." He twists a dial on his headset's earpiece. "Base, Marin. We're under fire. Location—mile and a half from the bridge. One Thudder lost, four men KIA. Request immediate gunship support."

The reply doesn't encourage him, because he snarls, "I don't care if it's a potential risk of resources! You let any more of my men die and I'll personally remove your resources! Marin out!"

The truck skids. The lieutenant braces me, arm across my chest, as we teeter on three wheels instead of all six. The vehicle slams back down, rattling my teeth, and we speed on.

"Roadblock ahead!" the driver says. "Sir, our trucks are penned in!"

Another explosion. Then everything goes sideways.

Time crawls as we tip over. I could be reclining in a comfortable chair, suspended in midair of the drop. Marin locks his gaze with mine and in the second before we slam down onto pavement, I find the stunned gape of my best friend.

The impact is thunderous. Metal lets off a terrible squeal as we scrape along the street. The *thwap* of bullets against the armored body intensifies, until we're enveloped in a hailstorm. Shouts and crackling gunfire, much closer than the initial attack, answer.

Soldiers groan. The only light filters through smudged portholes, streaming through the dark. "Watch it when you unstrap," Marin orders. "Anyone who crushes the prisoner gets to walk back without his vest."

An urgent knock hammers the back hatch. "Captain! Sir, we got to get you all out!"

"Hold that position, Franklin!" A belt clicks. Marin crouches by my knees. "Jacobs, get him unhooked. You're with me."

"Sir, yes sir." The black soldier hoists me free of my seatbelts and keeps a firm grip on the jacket's fabric. "You stay close, because if they don't kill you, I will." This statement's a whispered threat, out of earshot of his commander.

The rear hatch screeches open. A soldier, face smudged with soot, beckons us out.

"Move, move, move!" Marin shouts.

I'm thrust forward, stumbling along the walls—now the floor— of the truck. Out through the rectangle of light I go—

Into a war zone.

No more distant clatter of shooting. Here it's visceral, the echo of gunshots reverberating deep in my guts. I swear I can feel bullets winging past. The soldier who let us out of the truck shields us, along with the propped open door, his rifle banging out continuous fire. Marin's yelling at everyone but I can't hear a thing except sounds worse than the strongest, most intense thunderstorm I've ever encountered.

Jacobs hustles me to a broken building. The lieutenant's right behind us. He drops in a crouch to fire bursts at the opposite side of the street. I glimpse shadowy figures ducking behind crumbled walls and popping out of empty windows. One of the convoy's trucks is a twisted, blackened heap enveloped in flame. The acrid stench of burning materials fills the air. Black smoke writhes as a breeze off the river catches the column.

The other three trucks have stopped to the right, arrayed in a loose barrier. Ahead, two school buses stripped of all but a few scraps of yellow paint are parked end to end, completely blocking the road. The banks of the Van River lay just beyond.

Our truck is on its side, left side scorched. Armor panels are missing. The driver's side windows are smeared red.

Marin bashes the remnants of the crumpled windshield aside and drags the passenger soldier out. Another soldier runs up from the cordon of three trucks and helps drag the man. His leg must be badly injured, for it's bent at an angle that doesn't look natural.

"Keep your head down!" Jacobs shoves me ahead, and together we tumble over a low wall. This looks like a bookstore, though which one, I couldn't say. I don't recall any such shops on West Randolph. I land atop moldy, tattered pages. Dust obscures my vision.

Marin and the other soldiers join us. Soon the entire contingent that picked me up—minus six men—is returning fire. Muzzle flashes ripple up and down two storefronts.

"Don't mind saying, sir, we're way too exposed!" the lieutenant says.

"Copy that." Marin lines up a target in his sights and fires. A silhouette jerks back, disappears from view in one of the buildings across the street. "Just need to hold out until the gunship gets here, then we make for the bridge."

"Long swim if they took it out already," Jacobs mutters.

"Ty, you better shut your trap or pray for forgiveness," the crucifix soldier says with a nervous grin.

Ty. No wonder the soldier caught my attention. He's got the same sour, pinched look on his face in this deadly moment as Tyson Jacobs does when things go particularly bad at Dualpoint—like after a meeting with a nasty-tempered client. But he can't be Tyson. He's far too young.

Unless …

A steady *whup-whup-whup* grows. My only experience with helicopters is hearing life flight choppers landing at or taking off from Plains View Regional Hospital. Once in a while they buzz downtown, rotor noise thumping off the storefront windows. This machine, though, has a raspy growl to it, and the aircraft that wheels into view is nothing like the graceful white and red emergency choppers. This is a slate gray weapon, spindly, with a bulging engine under whirling blades. Two huge machine guns and pods of what I assume are rockets dangle from either side. It hovers over us, pointing at the opposite side of the street.

Marin—*Curt*—grins. He could be celebrating the five ball in the corner pocket.

"Light 'em up!" Jacobs whoops.

The machine guns tear into the abandoned buildings, streaming bullets faster than any gun the soldiers have. A pair of rockets shoot off in puffs of white smoke, streaking between broken walls. The explosions send us all ducking for cover. Dust rolls across the street, making visibility next to zero.

"Move out! Make for the bridge!" Marin's order rings in my ears. He's right there, grabbing my arm, and Jacobs huffs with exertion on the other side.

Our trio weaves between collapsed walls, over broken glass, through the drifting smoke. Bullets zing here and there. I can't see much, though I can hear plainly the shouts and the gunfire. The busses appear suddenly out of the gloom.

Four men are right there.

They aren't with Captain Marin and his soldiers. For one thing, their uniforms are far less, well, uniform—a motley collection of urban camouflage and black, with different style hats. Only one has a helmet. The rest wear black ball caps. They're masked, either with full face coverings like Curt and I use to wear to paintball matches, or with simple scarves.

The same patch is sewn on all of them, however: three white triangles, with an orange sun setting on the leftmost, on a dark blue background.

Nothing happens in one frozen second. They must be as surprised by our materialization as I am by theirs.

Captain Marin is less startled than all of us. He fires on the closest man. His target crumples in a pool of deep crimson blood.

Sergeant Jacobs flings me aside, slamming my shoulder into a wall. He guns down a second man, but the other two are so close they charge in. Guns become cudgels. Knives flash. The four of them are a flurry of punching and kicking limps, slashing blades, and grappling fatigues.

I can't tell friend from foe. What I can do is run—but to where? Marin said his people are waiting on the other side of the buses, across the Randolph bridge. They could be gone, however. With the helicopter still firing overhead, and the fighting raging around us, I'm fully disoriented.

Marin leaves the man he's fighting with a huge knife buried in his torso. He draws a pistol and aims for Jacobs, who's still wrestling with the last remaining man. I'm certain he's going to shoot his own soldier, until Jacobs pivots on his right heel, and lets the man he's fighting twist around.

Two shots put the last of our opponents on the ground.

"You hurt?" Marin's words sound as if they're coming from a mile away.

"What?"

"Are you hurt?"

I shake my head and tap my ear. "Can't hear."

"Lucky to not go completely deaf," he mutters. "Come on, let's get to the buses."

Jacobs drags me through the gap between the first bus and the buildings. The bridge still stands, its railings poking out of the haze all the way across the Van River.

"Where's that backup?" Marin shouts into his headset microphone. "We are engaging hostiles, unknown number! Requesting immediate extraction!"

Engine noises sound nearby, but I can't tell if they're coming from the other side of the river, down the block we'd just traversed, or some other unidentifiable direction. My head's spinning, I'm limping, and my shoulder's on fire. Jacob's grip is as dogged as any Labrador's.

In the midst of the chaos, three more men materialize from the smoke. Marin and Jacobs swing their weapons to cut them down.

"Captain!" It's the lieutenant. His face is streaked with blood. So is his uniform. "Sir, you're okay."

"If I wasn't, you'd be giving the orders." Marin counts off. "Where's everyone else?"

"Farago and Cruz bought it. The rest are coming up the other side of the street. Building's cleared out. Gunship's been chewing up those old apartments. I don't think there's two cinderblocks left atop each other."

"Good news, finally." Marin peers around the side of the bus.

"Any word about backup from HQ?"

"You know them. Wouldn't tell us the forecast called for rain if we were standing knee-deep in a downpour." Marin scowls. "Jacobs, soon as we get the high sign from the other squads, we're over the bridge, understood?"

"Yessir." Jacobs gives me a sideways glare. "You'd better keep up."

"That's your priority, Sergeant." Marin glances at the lieutenant. "Got waylaid by four Sierrans."

"Took care of them, I suspect, Captain."

"They were sloppy. Jacobs himself could have snagged the whole quartet." Marin stands in front of me. "Didn't seem like they cared if you got hit or not. Jacobs had to remove you from the line of fire. Have a falling out with your superiors?"

I make a face. "I don't know who you think I am, but I have nothing to do with those men. Why are they attacking Rampart? You called them Sierrans. Is it a terrorist organization? Like ISIS?"

"Like who?" Marin shakes his head. "Forget it. My orders are—"

"Sir!" Jacobs whistles, and makes a quick gesture with his right hand.

"Go, go!" Marin pushes me ahead. All of a sudden, we're out in the open, sprinting across the rubble-strewn intersection. The smoke's clearing away. Blue sky even elbows aside the thick cloud cover. Everything goes eerily silent—no gunfire, no explosions, only the approaching vehicle engines and the rough scraping of boots against the road.

They're too numerous to be just our boots, I realize.

A gunshot cracks from somewhere behind us, echoing down the street. At the same moment Marin's lieutenant stumbles, a spray of blood spurting out of his neck.

"Sniper!" Jacobs shouts.

"Keep moving!"

Another shot, then another. Two more, overlapping. Multiple gunmen? I don't stop to think, or question. All I do is run, aiming for the bridge.

There's a ruined Subaru tipped on its side just over the expansion joint. A bullet ricochets off the hood. Jacobs plows me into the crumbled concrete behind it. He props his rifle on a deep dent and returns fire. How he expects to hit anyone is beyond me.

Marin and another soldier drag the wounded lieutenant into cover. "Where's that gunship?"

The helicopter spins over the block, ripping apart walls with its machine guns. The snipers must have decided it was no longer worth the risk to attempt our assassination, because once the chopper completes its pass, there's again silence from the ruined block.

The engine noises I've been hearing at last become clearer. A pair of the armored six-wheeled trucks, same as the ride we were in that was blown out from under us, speed onto the center of the bridge. Together they execute a tight turn, wheels skidding across the road, and wind up with their back ends facing perpendicular. Hatches slam down, and two soldiers each come pounding down the metal extrusions.

Marin shepherds me and the rest of his troops aboard. As we're loading, four more of the large Jeep-like vehicles go speeding past us. One of them has an extended rear cab and is emblazoned with a red cross. All the while, the helicopter hovers low over the streets, rotors kicking up bits of concrete and whipping clouds of dust. A second chopper joins it, coming in from the southeast.

"Direct to HQ," Marin says to the driver.

"Sir, what about the rest of our people?" Jacobs lingers at the open hatch, foot braced on the ramp, as if he's ready to run back out.

"Medics will get them." Marin's expression is taut. "I hate leaving them this way, too, Private, but we have our orders—and our priorities. Intel comes first."

"Thank you for rescuing me," I say.

Marin slams me up against the inside of the truck, fists bunched in handfuls of my jacket. His nose is inches from mine. I've rarely seen Curt this angry—but the wild exasperation in his eyes, the way he breathes between his teeth—I know it. Doesn't matter if this Curt Marin is a captain in some strange version of the Army, with Procyon's label on his arm. He's still Curt, in a way.

"I'll make this clear," he hisses. "Too many of my friends have died from Sierran bullets. If I had my way right now, I'd kneel you at the edge of the bridge, put one in the back of your head, and drop you into the Van, so they could find your body floating among the rocks, bloated and fish-chewed. But we need what you know. Your brain's worth more to us intact than with a hole in it. So, King of Spades, I'll keep you safe, hand you over to HQ, and let her drain every scrap of actionable intelligence."

Her? "I … I'm sorry. I don't know who this King of Spades is, or how I can help you, but you have to believe me. I just want to get home."

Marin stares at me, jaw clenched. He lets go. "You're not going home, Zein. Ever."

He digs into his pocket. Why's he carrying around a deck of playing cards? Marin fans them out and turns one over.

King of Spades. I'm smiling out at me from the face. Only, it isn't me. The physical resemblance is uncanny, but this man dressed in immaculate military garb, with slicked hair, and sunglasses dangling from a pocket, isn't me.

It's Nick.

CHAPTER NINETEEN

Without a watch or my phone, I have no idea how long we drive. It feels like a half hour, but it could be less time, stretched out by fear and weariness.

The truck's tiny portholes admit only murky light, tinged yellow. Buildings have stopped flicking by. The occasional utility pole whips past. We make several turns, and at one point I'm convinced we've gone in a circle, because it feels like the driver makes a continuous right for a long time.

No one says anything. The men are glum, staring at their boots, or at the walls, at anything but each other and especially not at me.

Light outside the truck dims. Sounds echo. We're inside a garage, or a tunnel.

A few minutes later, our vehicle halts. Everyone disembarks, except Marin and Jacobs, the latter of whom pulls a black bag from between the seat cushions.

"No need," Marin says.

Jacobs seems perplexed, having paused with the bag spread open. "Sir, it is protocol—"

"We're not worried about him giving away any secrets about our location, Sergeant."

"Yessir." He tucks the bag away. Instead of covering my face he pulls me out of the truck. He's gone somber, without any side commentary.

My suspicions were correct. We're inside a huge space, cavernous, but manmade. Concrete walls form a long rectangle. The floor is asphalt, and the ceiling metal. Girders and catwalks crisscross in an elaborate web. Fluorescent lights high above illuminate the garage.

All kinds of vehicles are lined up along the sides, or in neat rows down the middle. There's dozens of the four-wheeled Jeeps, plus perhaps twenty of the Thudders, as Marin called the six-wheeled trucks. Eight more vehicles, even larger than the Thudders, are parked in pairs along each side. These monsters have eight tires, and sport giant gun turrets that give the impression someone wanted a fast-moving version of a tank.

There's also easily a hundred people, mostly men, some women, of all ages and ethnicities, though the majority are white and Hispanic. They're either dressed in fatigues like my escorts, or rumpled gray coveralls stained with grease. Some are checking what appear to be supply lists, while others are inspecting weapons, and still more are repairing damaged vehicles.

Every single one stops and looks up as we walk by.

Tools cease clattering. Chatter dries up. The sudden silence is more terrifying than the pack of feral dogs preparing to pounce.

Marin doesn't seem fazed. If anything, he's proud as a man returning from a successful deer hunt. "That's right, folks. We've got him."

Cheers explode. People are whooping, cheering. Applause thunders to the ceiling. The tumult surrounds us as Marin and Jacobs, cordoned from the working crews by their squad mates, take me out a set of double doors.

Those doors are as thick as my arm, solid metal. Beyond them lies a dark corridor, and rocky walls. The floor is metal grating that clangs with every step. More rock is visible beneath it. Water seeps underfoot. The air's damp.

There's no way we drove long enough to get somewhere this

humid. It must be underground, deep enough for moisture to collect. It certainly looks as if it were cut into existing caverns.

Shorter corridors branch off this jagged, twisting hall at odd angles, some going up slopes and others banking down. Most lead to closed doors. Jacobs prods me along until we reach a 90-degree turn. Here, on either side, the walls are lined with identical doors—flat gray rectangles, with smaller rectangular slits cut at eye level.

Marin opens the one labeled "13." There's a cot bolted to the left-hand wall. It has a thin, rumpled white sheet, and a lumpy pillow that looks as if someone thrust their dirty, unfolded laundry into a sack. On the other side is a toilet—a portable composting unit. Water has collected in the corners of the cell, where chipped, pale-green paint floats atop tiny, scummy ponds.

Jacobs shoves me in.

"Take his belt and his shoelaces," Marin orders. "The cross, too."

I stand stock still as Jacobs obeys, but it seems I'm having trouble keeping quiet as my civil rights are trampled. "Please, let me keep the cross. It isn't a weapon."

"Neither are your laces or belt. Suicide watch."

I gape. "This is insane. I'm not suicidal! I was looking for help! Rampart is in ruins, and you people are fighting a war in it! I woke up not knowing what's going on."

"Fine, keep the cross. It'll break before your neck does." Marin snorts. "You're determined to keep up this amnesia thing, aren't you?"

"I don't have amnesia. I'm Dominic Zein."

"I know. That's why you're in custody, and not shot dead like a rabid animal like your comrade Sierrans."

"You keep saying that. I don't even know what a Sierran is! You have to tell me what's going on! If I'm under some kind of arrest, isn't there a lawyer I can contact? What about the police?"

"Police left a long time ago. We're in charge of this region, so if you have any legal concerns …" He shakes his head. "Never mind. Those don't apply to your status."

"My status."

"Prisoner-of-war. Recall the card?"

This is the difficult part. "Yes, I understand your confusion, but that isn't me. That man … he looks like me, and he can be me if necessary …"

Marin produces the card. "This is you, Zein."

"No, it isn't! I mean, it is …" A headache splinters my thoughts. "I'm really confused."

"Don't worry. You'll get some answers, right after we get ours."

He slams the door shut, leaving me one sagging bed and one reeking toilet as company.

There's no way to tell how long I've been in here. The flickering fluorescent lights threaten to induce nausea. I wonder if they're the reason I've sustained a throbbing headache.

Some of that I chalk up to the head wound I suffered before getting—wherever this is. A medic has cleaned and bandaged the cut. That's the only comfort I'm afforded.

I'm rousted from sleep by rough hands. Didn't notice the door opening. Soldiers strip the clothing Nick gave me and toss a plain yellow jumpsuit at my feet. I'm getting dressed when Jacobs enters.

"Hey." He pokes the crucifix on my chest. "Still putting on a good show for us?"

"It's not a show."

"Better be for penance. Keep it outside your shirt, then, so we can see it at all times."

I nod.

They gather up my clothes and leave me in baggy prison garb, with ratty slippers.

Time passes without recognition. Eventually, in the middle of my daze, the slit at the top of the door grinds open. Brown eyes peer through. "Meal."

Sounds like Jacobs. I press my back to the far wall, hands spread on damp rock. This is the third or fourth such visit. I think. Or is this the first?

The door creaks open. It is Jacobs, flanked by two more armed soldiers. He carries a tray. My sole source of nutrition—store-bought bread, of the stale variety, plus a foil bag of chips, a can of flavored sugar-water that reminds me of sour Gatorade, and a mealy apple. Same food every time.

"I need to speak to whoever's in charge." My voice is raspy from disuse. That's become the question of the day—for however many days it's been.

Jacobs sets the tray on the bunk. He motions to the soldiers. "Kneel. Arms on top of your head."

I sigh. At least it's a change from what's become routine. As soon as I comply, the soldiers handcuff me, then link those to shackles around my feet. One of them grabs me by the arm while the second remains at my back, presumably so he can shoot me if I try to escape.

They must be joking. Where would I go? This place could be a mile underground, or dozens of miles from Rampart.

I'm on my own.

They drag me down the main hall, past the cells, then around a dizzying set of corners. Still don't bother with a blindfold, or a black hood. They're not worried about what I see.

Marin's terse answer to Jacobs' question when I arrived haunts me.

"In here." The soldiers plant me on a metal chair in the center of a brightly lit room. My eyes water at the sudden change from my murky cell. It's a bare box, except for the two chairs facing each other across a steel table. The room reeks of body odor and is musty like wet carpet. I find myself staring at my reflection—the opposite wall isn't rock, like the others, but also metal, with a long mirror inset. A crack bisects it, from corner to corner in a diagonal slash, giving my haggard face a twitching, manic appearance. Having several days' worth of accumulated scruff on my chin doesn't help.

Jacobs shackles my wrists to a rusty bar running the length of the tabletop. "Stay put."

As soon as he's gone, I test their weakness. The bar doesn't budge. Neither does the table. Frowning, I try scooting my chair. No such luck. I duck under for a look. Ah. All eight legs are bolted to the floor.

Eight, not twelve. The other chair sits cockeyed to the opposite side of the table. Scratches mar the floor where it's been dragged.

The door bangs open. I can see the shoulders of two troops outside. Marin strides in. He's shaved completely bald, like the real Curt. The only red hair are those same eyebrows. Marin pauses by the threshold. He twists a knob on the wall.

The light intensifies.

It beats down from a single spotlight above the mirror. The angle is such that it hits me square in the face. After however long I've been locked up, I could be squinting into the face of the sun.

Marin disappears into a dark blur under the light. His chair's legs screech across the floor. A drip echoes somewhere in the room.

"Captain, I …"

"Zip it. Why were you on that street?"

"I needed help." The words tumble out, immediate and hurried. I haven't seen Curt—Marin—since we arrived at this base. If anyone's going to believe me, it's him. "I was visiting … an acquaintance and was attacked. He threw me into a circle, an illusion, I guess, and next thing I know, I've woken up in a ruined version of his loft. Rampart's destroyed. You're running around with the Army."

Marin makes notes with a pen. The tip scratches, like a mouse behind the walls. There's a manila folder underneath, bulging with papers.

"Captain?"

"Why were you on that street?"

His manner is so calm, so infuriatingly conversational, it rips apart the last shreds of self-control I possess. "I told you already! I was attacked!" I yank on the shackles, rattling them over the table. "Would you get it through your thick skull? I'm not anybody's enemy!"

"You're lying." Marin's unfazed by my display. "Dominic Zein doesn't need help from us. He's always a step ahead. Always gets intelligence on our operations before we can conduct them. You've left a trail of bodies from the Cascades to Colorado's Front Range."

"I have no clue what you're talking about, Curt—" I cut myself off.

"Don't call me that!" he snaps. "You don't get that privilege. There's dead men and women a hundred times worthier. You're not fit to guard their corpses."

"That is your name. That's the name I've known you by for years!"

"Shut. Up." Marin takes more notes. "Answer my question."

"You won't get the answer you want." My body aches. I can't think straight. Images of Rampart flash through my memories. Pictures of the city, of busy streets, its people, Kaminsky and Anna and yes, Tyson, even obnoxious clients—the Vitalis, so help me. Fragments of my life, one I have no idea if I'll see again, assail me. Then there's Curt—the Curt I've laughed and driven and drank with—melting over the grim, shadowed visage of this military double.

Double. Nick.

He could be with Jess right now. She'd have no clue as to his real nature. Why should she? Everyone else fell for it.

But Jess …

I strain at the shackles.

"They won't break."

"I have to get out of here, Curt."

"You do have a death wish, don't you? I'd oblige you but for the intel."

"Enough." Maybe I can get through to him. "Don't you remember? We went to CU Denver all four years. Graduate cum laude."

"Whatever you're trying won't work. They picked me for this interrogation because they know I don't fall for that kind of smooth talk."

"We threw our caps and cheered together! Went out and got so wasted we woke up in Centennial Gardens …"

"Shut up!" Marin snaps. "Give me the location of your base. I want troop strengths, deployment plans, supply routes. I want operative cells—every man and woman you've infiltrated into our ranks, the informants you've planted among the locals. Names!"

"I don't have anything! I don't know what you're talking about, I already said so! You've locked me up, starved me, and now you're barking nonsense! I told you the truth—the man on the card isn't me. Yes, he looks like me, and can portray me, but he's someone ..." Realization dawns as I stare at Marin. "He's someone different. A doppelgänger. A twisted version of me. Just like you. Just like everyone and everything here."

"Cunning doesn't begin to cover it." Marin shakes his head. "Knew you would try to mess with my head. HQ warned me. Look, Zein, this is your chance to tell me what you know. Once I turn you over, they'll strip it out of your brain, and it'll way worse than this. Doing things my way guarantees you won't spend the rest of your life as a drooling zombie."

I sag against the chair. What's the point? "You don't have any intention of letting me leave or live, do you?"

The random dripping from somewhere in the room is as loud as hammer blows. Marin writes more notes, apparently ignoring my question.

"No mask?" I rattle my shackles. "Wherever this secret base is, you'd never let someone as supposedly dangerous as me inside without making sure I don't see something vital. So, I'm either never going to leave, or you'll kill me."

Marin slides a paper out of the shadows. Sheet after sheet follows. They gleam in the light.

They're satellite images, and photos. Los Angeles, submerged. Reno, pockmarked with craters. Denver, burning. Mass graves. Dead soldiers.

And me.

No. Nick. He stands before a kneeling prisoner, an older man with pale gray hair. The soldier wears fatigues like Marin's, though with a silver bird on the visible shoulder. His glasses are broken, askew on his nose …

My hands tremble as I pick up the photo.

It's Kaminsky.

"One of our finest officers." Marin's tone is subdued. "Colonel Kaminsky was a lifelong National Guardsman. Transferred to Home Guard when things really went south. That image is from his last command, a raid deep into Sierran territory. Took a company of his best soldiers, top techs, and laid waste to that massive supply depot your people had secreted behind Vegas. Set back your offensive by a couple years. That's why we've been able to hold the line at Rampart for so long."

Kaminsky, a colonel and a leader. I can see it.

But I wish I couldn't see the pistol Nick aims at his head.

Another paper slides across.

The trigger's been pulled. Kaminsky's neck is bent, eyes vacant and pointed skyward. A black spray haloes him.

"Surveillance drone caught these. If you're wondering why we took such a keen interest in your whereabouts, Zein, this is the icing on the cake."

I have no cutting remarks. If there was lingering doubt as to Nick's intentions for my life, these photos banish them. He's a murderer. I don't know much of history or modern military practice, but I do know it's immoral to execute a prisoner-of-war. You don't shoot a man who's surrendered.

Especially not one as kind as Kaminsky.

I rub the sides of my head. Who am I kidding? Kaminsky could be a serial killer here. "What is this place?" I murmur.

"Your permanent residence." Marin crosses to the door. He turns the knob.

The light fade. I blink to adjust my vision.

"Last chance to do this simply, Zein." He returns to the table and pushes the notepad into my space. It's blank. He tips a pen in his hand. "Give us what we need to turn the tide."

I meet Marin's gaze. "If I could help you, Captain, I would. But there's nothing I can do."

He scowls. "Fine then. Looks like I'll have to come up with some other way to induce your cooperation. Won't be fun."

Marin gathers up his materials, leaving the photos of death and devastation strewn about. He's got the door cracked open when I make a last, desperate attempt. "Captain?"

"What?"

"Don't strain your brain."

His hand's braced on the frame. Marin narrows his eyes, his expression softening from anger to puzzlement. He opens his mouth, and I can imagine him saying, "Z? It's you!"

Instead he shakes his head and closes the door.

It's over, then. There's no hope of Curt recognizing me, or this version of Curt, I suppose. He doesn't have an ounce of compassion.

The sight of Nick's execution photos turns my stomach. Perhaps, that lack is understandable.

This isn't a problem I can fix with a soothing phone call to a vexed client, or a late-night redesign of a flawed proposal. I can't do anything, and there's no one to help me.

Death seems imminent.

The crucifix weighs a hundred pounds. "Please," I whisper. "Save me."

It's the pathetic cry of a man with no options. As soon as I say it, I feel wretched. Of course now, that I'm in danger, I whimper for assistance. Where was that conversation, that prayer and thanksgiving, when everything was right with the world? I showed up in church Sunday morning with Jess, nodded and smiled, shook hands and joked, while Father Hamra's homilies rolled by like distant semis on the interstate. I was a servant who grumbled at every attendance to Stewardship committee, as lackluster a follower as those in the Christmas and Easter crowds.

Nick may have usurped my place, but I'm as much a fraud as he was to everyone around me.

Helpless as I am, I can only rest my head on my shackles and pray.

Boots thump in the hall. Voices murmur outside the door. One raises in response, infuriated, but the steady, softer one brings it back down. Someone has lost an argument, with perhaps a person in greater authority.

The door opens again. Marin's neck is red, his cheeks flushed. "I'm ordered to turn you over to HQ." Every word clearly galls him, the way he chews on each one.

Hope. Finally.

Except I remember what he said about what awaits at HQ. Drooling like a zombie, wasn't it? Doesn't matter. I need someone else to talk to. Marin—not Curt—isn't listening.

"I will take matters from this point, Captain."

Her order is as startling as her appearance. Loredana Lark steps past Marin, wearing a suit identical to the one in which she was attired before this whole mess, except it's a deep, charcoal gray. Red hair gleams like a campfire, cut shorter than I remember but with the same curls at the end.

"It's true." Never thought I'd be so glad to hear a stranger's lilt. "You've captured him."

"Was more like picking up the worst hitchhiker ever," Marin grumbles. "I've questioned him."

"I'm sure you have."

"He didn't give me anything. Only an identity crisis. So he says."

"An identity crisis? How curious." Lark tilts her head. "Well then, I suppose I'll have a go."

"I'm not okay with this. I lost men bringing this filth in. He shouldn't be at HQ at all, yet you had me parade him around—"

"That's quite enough, Captain. You'd do well to remember to whom the Home Guard answers. Procyon Corps will not tolerate insubordination."

Marin grinds his teeth. "Yes, ma'am."

Lark waits until he's long gone down the corridor before she taps one of the soldiers. "Corporal, unshackle this man."

"Umm … Captain's the only one to give that order."

A glacier wouldn't be nearly as cold, and less intimidating. She doesn't move, nor does she blink.

"Right. Yes, ma'am."

Keys jingle. A few seconds later, I'm rubbing my wrists. Without the shackles I could go running. "Thank you."

"There's no need to thank me. Not yet. Why, we haven't begun interrogation." She smiles, thin-lipped. "First, I offer you the chance to answer any questions you may have of me."

I blink.

"Usually when I offer prisoners such a favor, they are quick to plaster me with inquiries."

"Sorry. I haven't been …" I shake my head. "This has all been insane."

"Yes, I imagine it has. But as I said …" She motions with her hands, as if I'm to continue.

Questions? Plenty. "Fine, then. What's happened to Rampart? Why is everyone so different?"

"Because you don't belong here, Dominic Zein, architect with Dualpoint." Lark sits across from me. "The other you should be the one in chains."

"You mean … he calls himself Nick."

"Yes. Commander Dominic Zein, Sierran Intelligence. Greatest threat to the United States' continued existence."

"You believe me. No one else has."

"That's because I know why the Home Guard has been unable to apprehend the commander for some time now, and why he seemingly vanished from our reconnaissance without a trace. He's no longer here, and no manner of patrolling by Captain Marin and his men will uncover our enemy."

I nod eagerly. "Nick's in Rampart. The Rampart I know, not this wreck. Where am I?"

"On the wrong Earth," Lark says. "And if you want to return to yours, you'll have to do exactly what I say."

CHAPTER TWENTY

Lark relocates me to a classroom. Rows of chairs, the chrome chipped off the legs, stand in perfect formation. Desktops hang forlornly from hinges. A marker whiteboard covers the front and side wall. Bookshelves line the back. The titles run the gamut from world history to military tactics and geography.

"Wrong Earth." I lean against the wall.

"Wrong to you, but all we've ever known. Yours would be the precise opposite if I were to venture there, as Commander Zein did." She purses her lips. "Let us refer to him as 'Nick,' as you do, for ease of communications."

My head throbs. I could use a drink of water. "Yes. Let's."

"As I was saying …" Lark uncaps a black dry erase marker. It squeaks as she draws two large circles, one on either end of the board. "Two Earths—yours, and ours." She marks the leftmost circle "Ours" and the rightmost, the one nearest me, "Yours."

"And you're saying I've transited between these two worlds."

"Yes."

"Well, I can't say it's any crazier than thinking I've been trapped in a coma or terrible nightmare this entire time."

"I'm pleased you're able to cope." Lark draws four lines, joining the two circles with a diamond. "This dimension links Ours with

Yours. Procyon terms it the Interstice."

"What is it?"

"A dimension in which the rules of time and space are mere suggestions. We know little about it, other than it is …unfriendly to human life. To most normal life, I suppose. What does dwell there isn't cordial."

The strange dream I had after Nick tossed me into the light sphere returns—the trip through a corridor and hungry tentacles extended toward me. "I may have seen some of it."

"Indeed you did, if you went through the portal opened by the Echo Watch."

"Echo Watch."

"Nick used it to send you here. Its absence is how I knew you were not him." Lark encircles her wrist with a free hand. "Presents as an armband, most of the time, until it's deployed for that purpose. It can also be weaponized."

My sides twinge, with involuntary memory. "Yes, I've experienced that mode firsthand."

"We don't know where it comes from, but we do know it opens and closes the Transect between Yours and Ours. It transits through and across the Interstice. Nothing can breach it either way—again, as far as we know."

"Procyon Corps. It's a foundation on Yours—I mean, my Earth. I'm in the midst of designing their building. Rather, I was." Seems quite a bit mundane, compared to everything I'm facing here.

"I'm well aware of Procyon's role on Yours," Lark says.

"Oh." I consider this. "How is that possible? Nick has the Echo Watch."

"Yes. Times change."

"I see."

"The situation is not ideal. I've lost all contact with my counterpart, and that has proven most disagreeable." Lark shakes her head. "It leaves Procyon Corps without the slightest clue what's transpiring on Yours."

"Why do you even care? It seems your Earth has enough problems with which to contend without bothering about ours." I frown. "And you expect me to believe you maintain sources on the other end of this corridor—in my Earth?"

"The Transect's focal points are honed, Dominic. In times past its accidental discovery wasn't a problem, because it was 12 feet in the air."

"Until someone happened to build an apartment building in the best place to allow concealed access."

"As you say." She smiles. "Happened."

"Who have you been talking to on our side?"

"Irrelevant to your current situation. All you need to know is my source cannot be any more reliable. Why do you find this hard to fathom? You met our world's version of you. He convinced you of your relation—enough that, I assume, he was able to pass as you."

"He was." Heat flushes my face. "I thought it seemed a good deal. He took the pressure off the busiest points of my life, allowing me to spend more time with my friends and my wife."

"Quite noble. All in exchange for nothing?"

"I thought so." I pluck at the prison garb. "Until he forced me to dress like him and tossed me through the Transect."

Her lips twist. "A devious plan. Travel to Yours and find his doppelgänger. He could have simply killed you, but it seems he took his time to research and replace. That would make him more difficult to detect once it came time to make the transition permanent. Did he give you any sense of why he gave up your mutual arrangement for a more direct kidnapping?"

"No. He gave me the impression he was on the run."

"You understand why that's true."

"Captain Marin showed me the photos. Am I—is Nick really responsible for all he claims?"

"I'll elaborate soon enough. First, you must understand one fact clearly—you cannot return to your world without the Echo Watch."

My heart sinks. I bend over, bracing my hands on my knees. No way back. "It's stuck there with Nick. He's not going to give it up."

"Of course not, but you needn't give into despair. If we can get our hands on the second Echo Watch, there's hope."

"Second." I stare at her. "There's two?"

Lark smiles again. "Come with me. There's more about Ours you need to comprehend."

It's an odd sensation, following her about the base with no shackles, no armed guards. We could be colleagues on our way to a board meeting, except one of us isn't dressed business casual.

The deadly looks troops and technicians give us as we pass make me wish I still had the guards.

Lark pauses outside a set of glass doors set in a thick metal frame. The Procyon logo is etched ghostly white across them. They're tinted, but I can make out a bustling command center beyond—people in uniform carrying papers back and forth, clusters of broad television monitors slapped on the far wall, rows of desktop computers. For all the hardware, though, the room has a decades-old feel. The computers, though numerous, appear cousins to the first one my mother bought when I was a high school junior nearly fifteen years ago. Though filled with data, the screens are boxy, the graphics cluttered and clunky.

"Ma'am, I strongly advise you lock him back up." Captain Marin hurries from the far end of the hall, with Sergeant Jacobs at his side. No other soldiers, however, which I take to be a good sign, "This man has no business in Ops."

"If you're so concerned about him acquiring vital information from us, Captain, you should have blindfolded him the moment you picked him up like a stray dog." Lark's tone is icy. "We've already established the consequences. If he were indeed Commander Zein, we'd mine his brain for intelligence and dispose of whatever remains. No need to fuss about leaks."

Jacobs shifts his weight, abashed. Marin glares at us both, but finally nods. "All right. Fine. You want to give him the grand tour? Then we clean everyone out of Ops."

Lark smiles. "Exactly what I would suggest. The sooner the better, please, Captain."

Marin and Jacobs hustle their people out of the center. It doesn't smell as musty as the rest of the base and appears a great deal cleaner. With all the computer hardware around, however outdated, they must be safeguarding against technical failure. Once everyone is gone, Marin closes the door behind us. "What's the angle, ma'am?"

"The angle, Captain, is that this isn't Commander Zein, as he's repeatedly insisted. This is his doppelgänger, from across the Interstice."

Marin watches me, arms folded, as if I were a bird hopping about the yard and he were a hungry cat. "You're kidding."

"Surely not. You know as well as I the Interstice can be transited."

"Yeah, I've seen the math, but …" Marin steps closer, near enough I imagine he'll grin and shake me with a back-slapping bear hug. But he isn't Curt. "You're serious. This is a different Dominic Zein."

Lark nods.

"Sure explains why he didn't give me the creeps. I've met Commander Zein once, on an undercover op. He made us later, and it went bad. Got away. But you …" He holds out a hand.

A greeting? I grasp his. We shake firmly.

His eyes narrow. "Weird. You shake different than he does. Good shake, yeah, but … the pressure's different."

"Thank you, I think." I let go of his hand. "As far as I know no one else has been able to determine the difference between Nick— Commander Zein—and I in the same way."

"Been trained to profile individuals. It's helpful with interrogation and infiltration." Marin smirks. "I can see, though, Commander Zein had a better idea. So that's it? He hopped across the Interstice and sent you over here in his place?"

"More like threw me over. His buddy Chris …" I ponder that. Chris looked like the dead homeless veteran in the Estes Park newspaper. "Did Nick have a right-hand man? A trusted bodyguard?"

"Krzysztof Niemec. Polish national, ex-Spetsnaz GRU. Skipped out on the Soviets during the Chinese frontier campaigns. Didn't like seeing his comrades get chewed up by the warlords squabbling over what's left of the Middle Kingdom." Marin rubs his chin. "Chris, huh? We thought he was on reassignment after Zein disappeared. He went over the Interstice, too."

"I think so."

Jacobs makes a noise, like he's disgusted with the menu at a restaurant. "This is nuts. I'm sorry, sir, ma'am, but this Zein guy is pulling a fast one."

"The Interstice is fact, Sergeant, and there is no disputing travel across it is possible."

"Okay, but doubles? Of people?" He snorts. "You mean there's another me running around over on some other planet?"

I clear my throat. "Actually—"

"Not a topic for discussion, Sergeant." Lark shoots me a warning look that, if capable of throwing projectiles, would have killed me. "Security clearance is one thing. Gauging what's need to know is another."

"But you never said that world was identical to ours. Ma'am."

Marin glares at Jacobs, who takes the hint and clams up. But Lark seems more interested by the question raised. "Very similar, not identical." She turns to me. "You have no doubt noticed such differences."

"Yes, I have. It's a war zone, not the plains of eastern Colorado I know."

"Up until sixty years ago, you would not have noticed much difference between the two. The date to keep in mind is August 10, 1948. No one was watching the skies as closely as they should have been back then—not like they do now. The first sign of the impending impact was a flare on the horizon above Chile."

Lark leads us to the left side of the room. The televisions are filled with images of ruined cities, and some that are much more intact, as well as scattered video I assume to be from operations in progress— soldiers on the move and such. But I tune those out as the map before me takes my full attention. It's of North America, though I only recognize half the boundaries. A jagged red line slashes down from the Canadian border, halving Montana, Wyoming, and Colorado, then jogging sharply southeast to the Texas north border. No states exist on the west side of that line, except a version of Utah's outline that's missing chunks. It's surrounded by the region colored in pale orange. Texas is outlined in blue. There's a long brown swath along the West Coast, labeled "Recovering."

Everything in orange is called "Sierran League."

"The asteroid splashed down in the Pacific," Lark says. "No one knows the size, but estimates place it at a mile or two. It would have been less catastrophic had it not shattered in multiple airbursts just above the surface. Shock waves and tidal waves devastated the entire Pacific rim. In a matter of days, the U.S. West coast was wrecked. Japan and Australia were all but wiped out. China and Southeast Asia grappled with the aftereffects for years before national governments collapsed into feuding regional dictatorships."

I can't imagine the scale of such a disaster. Nothing like it ever happened in modern history. "Were the aftereffects in America as severe?"

"Not enough to collapse the country." Lark draws a rough map of the continental U.S. She shades in a long stretch from Seattle to Los Angeles. "The federal government, coupled with nearby states, got as much aid as they could to disaster areas, but looting and fractured communities proved too dangerous to handle. The final solution was to partition the West Coast off from the rest of the country. Aid efforts continued."

Lark reaches for a computer atop one of the desks. It's a clunky laptop, the size of a briefcase, and when she opens the lid, the graphics look worse than those of the used model I had in college a decade ago. It hums like an electric scooter. She types a string of commands.

The television monitors wink out, their live and recorded images replaced by grainy newsreel footage. Wave after wave of airplanes drop boxes with parachutes attached; convoys bearing Red Cross insignia roll along rutted roads lined with toppled trees; soldiers and civilians pick their way through flattened houses.

"Nothing but a shame the way it was abandoned," Marin mutters.

"It seems the government did the best it could at the time." Though even as I say it, the images make me wonder. There's plenty of scene depicting material aid coming in, but signs of rebuilding are oddly absent.

"Many disagreed. Representatives and senators from California, Oregon, and Washington stopped showing up for Congress. You must understand, millions were dead, but millions more were dispossessed, homeless, jobless, among a catastrophically damaged environment. They were desperate." Lark tapped a key. "One man capitalized on that desperation."

I'm drawn to the face of a tall, broad-chested man in an immaculate suit. The Technicolor feel to his photo emphasizes the youthfulness of his face and the fullness of wavy brown hair. "Senator Thomas Michael Benton, of Arizona."

The way Lark spits his name, coupled with the tension roiling off Marin and Jacobs, fills in more than any of them can explain. "I take it he's responsible for your Sierran problem."

"Man singlehandedly organized the League," Jacobs says. "He was a young go-getter, first term senator. Born after the Blasts. Went into the damaged zones, rounded up survivors, used a personal fortune to rebuild. Kicker was, he got the remnants of National Guard units west of the Sierras to sign on. Kept his new groups loosely affiliated, but loyal to him."

"By the mid-1970s, he launched his first offensives. There's some who suggest the government was considering nuking the ragtag armies, but the political will wasn't there." Marin shrugged. "Couldn't blame them. What with the World War II still fresh, and units operating in Europe against the Slavic revolts, nobody wanted more war. By the time leadership struck back, the Sierrans had footholds among the Rockies."

The implication is staggering. "Decades of war."

"Off and on. There've been truces, cease-fires, attempts at negotiations. Most fail every time Washington pushes for them rejoining the U.S." Marin shakes his head. "Hit a decent spell a decade ago. Then the terrorist attacks in Baltimore and Chicago got our attention again. Guerrilla strikes started. The Sierrans pounce. Their new offensive these past five years has been near unstoppable."

"We have your friend Nick to thank," Lark says quietly. "Benton gave him regional command along the Southern Rockies. One need only walk downtown Rampart to see the effect."

"He's a killer and a thug," Jacobs says.

"As you were, Sergeant." Marin pins him with a sidelong glance.

Too late. I'm reliving the image of Nick shooting this world's Kaminsky in the head. It could be me. Nick claimed we are one and the same person. But I could never do something so callous. Father Hamra's comments about the soul chime in.

What am I capable of?

"You see the predicament we face, Mr. Zein," Lark says. "With the commander in possession of the Echo Watch, he can travel between our two worlds at will. He can help his compatriots escape to Yours with impunity."

"But you said he's key to the Sierrans' success. If he's gone, won't their movement collapse?"

"It is possible, yes, but at its core the Sierran League is Benton and his family. Commander Zein is a skilled tool, but only one of many. We must staunch the flow out of our world. The only way to do that is to regain control of the Echo Watch."

"Watches. You said there were two."

"Yes. I did." Lark glances at Marin. "The other, its twin, is in the hands of Zein's compatriots on this world. Hence Captain Marin's previously mentioned undercover operation. We know who has it. Retrieving the Echo Watch has proven difficult. We want you to get it."

I burst out laughing. It's a long, gut-shaking laugh, something I haven't had in … I wipe tears from my eyes. "How many days have

I been here?"

"Sorry?"

"You heard me."

"Three."

I'm still laughing, but it's the only thing holding back the onrushing flood of hopelessness. "Three days. Nick has taken my place, doing God knows what on my world for three days. He could be at my work, living in my house … with my wife …"

The dam breaks. I lash out and knock the laptop onto the floor. Its screen cracks. Benton's picture fizzles, then vanishes from the television monitors.

Marin goes for his sidearm.

"Don't be an idiot," I snap. "I'm not going to try to kill anyone. That's Nick's plan, it seems—to kill and hurt."

"Mr. Zein, I understand you're upset," Lark says. "Consider our perspective—you appear, dressed as the Commander, in the midst of our war's front lines. We had to keep you under close observation until I could be sure—"

"Sure of what? That I wasn't that lunatic? Well, I'm not. Feel better?"

"Calm down, man." Jacobs reaches for my arm.

"Don't lecture me," I snap. "You don't even exist where I'm from."

The room goes silent and cold. Jacobs stares, wide-eyed. Lark's expression is more a promise of death.

Marin throws up his hands. "Seriously? You let this amateur into my Ops, he loses his cool, and he's supposedly our best candidate? Give my people another shot."

"You had yours, and you failed," Lark says coolly. "Mr. Zein represents our final chance to reclaim both the Echo Watches—if he agrees to the mission, of course."

I jab a finger at Lark. "I want out of here. You said the Echo Watch can take me home? Fine. Tell me how we retrieve it."

"This isn't a simple matter of knocking on the Sierran base gates and politely requesting its return." Lark hasn't even flinched. "Nick entrusted it to the one person he knows wouldn't betray him, which is why we have to send you. Only Nick can get the Echo Watch back to us."

I nod. It's fitting. Nick has used subterfuge to take everything from me. If I can return the favor and put a stop to his rampages, all the better. "You want me to be him? Fine. I will do it. I'll put on his smile and his walk and lie to whomever you need. Just tell me where to go."

Lark smiles. "Good. Very good. Captain Marin, do you have a spare deck?"

"Yes, ma'am." He digs the pack of playing cards from his tunic. I accept it from him, but he doesn't let go. "Have to go on record as protesting this action. Real Commander Zein or not, this guy has no experience with our operations."

"Which will make him all the better an infiltrator. He's dealt with Zein on a level none of us have experienced—a personal friendship."

Marin frowns. He lets go of the pack.

I open it. Every card carries faces—men and women, old and young, most dressed in military garb like Nick's, though some wear civilian clothes. I pause to glare at Benton's aged face on the Ace of Spades. My hands shake as I turn over the next card, the King.

Nick.

"Your target is the Queen of Spades," Lark says quietly. "She keeps the Echo Watch on her at all times."

"That's going to make it harder to steal it." I flip the card.

"You're not going to steal it. She'll willingly give it to you."

The image stops my heart. Her face is more severe than I've ever seen it. She wears a black turtleneck, with a pin of the Sierran flag on her collar. Black eyeliner, deep maroon lipstick, hair grown longer and worn loose—none of those are familiar.

But the smile. The tilt of the lips. The lift of the chin.

The card reads, "Agent Tabitha Boutros, Sierran Security Bureau (SSB)."

It's lying.

The woman is not some mysterious enemy.
She's Jess.

CHAPTER TWENTY-ONE

Captain Marin sets a file folder bulging with papers on the desk in front of me. "Study up. This is everything we have about Commander Zein."

We're back in the classroom. Jacobs stands guard outside the closed door. The room still stinks from Lark's liberal use of the dry erase marker during our earlier briefing. The ventilation shafts overhead rattle and click as warm air wafts down.

I open the cover. Nick smirks at me, from a larger photo the playing card must be based on. The first few sheets are crammed full of details—vital statistics including place of birth, family, blood type, and the like—followed by more in-depth reports on eating habits, travel methods, and personal quirks.

One of them makes me shiver: *Subject prone to tugging at left pant leg with left thumb and index finger when anxious.*

"Internalize every word," Marin says. "You've got to know this stuff. How good is your memorization?"

"Hmm?" I've reached the page discussing Nick's marital status. *Single.*

"Hey." Marin kicks the chair. I lose pages on the floor. "Wake up. You're going to infiltrate the enemy compound and I can't be there to babysit you. I had my chance, remember? The Sierrans know me.

Lucky enough to have made it out of their midst last time, but it means I can't go back in."

"Yes, I understand, thank you." I retrieve the fallen papers. They're Nick's service record. Very little in the way of military training, though what there is suggests hand-to-hand combat.

"You're not focused."

"Can you blame me? You people just told me I have to steal a portal-opening device that doubles as high-tech Taser from my wife! You could have mentioned her face was among the cards."

"Ah, that's what's got you bent. Don't worry about it."

"Oh, of course, there's nothing to worry about. Why should I worry about having to fool the woman? She's my wife!"

"No, she's Nick's girl, and if you keep referring to her as your wife you're going to get shot." Marin slaps both Nick's card and Jess's—Tabitha, I must remember—onto the open files. "Get that drilled into your head. This is Tabitha Boutros. Her specialty is logistics and analysis. She's Nick's catalog—anything the Sierrans plan, in terms of covert operations, goes through the pair."

"Every time I look at her, I think of Jess."

"You're not listening. Lark said it—this isn't your world. It's ours. People are different here. Me? I'm not the same Curtis Marin as the Curtis Marin who exists on your world, if he does exist, or if he's still alive."

Lark hasn't told him, then. "I know Curt where I come from."

Marin shakes his head. "Don't. I figured as much when you started rambling about the good old college days. Me? Never went to college. Most of my high school friends are dead or moved East to get away from the front. A few hopped the border to Canada to escape the draft. Whatever you think you know about me—about Agent Boutros—is wrong. We're not them. I'm not Curt. She's not Jess. Got me?"

I nod, staring at the strewn files. Was this how Nick got his claws into me? Did he spend his nights in his Rampart loft, beer in hand, poring over the minutiae of my life? Obviously so. Directly spying on me helped, too.

He could still be spying on Jess. Why would he need to, though? Three days in, he was living with her.

Hot, sullen anger sinks to the pit of my stomach. I'll get this memorized. "I take it the plan isn't as easy as just driving into their base. After all, we have to find it first, otherwise you wouldn't have interrogated me for its location."

"Actually, we know the coordinates." Marin leans against the white board. "Have for several months now. That's part of how we knew Commander Zein, your Nick, had vanished. I threw that out there for you to see if you'd let anything slip, maybe get into negotiating mood if you thought you knew something vital that we hadn't uncovered."

"Where is it?"

"Don't worry about that until you hit the road. Your escort will know the way. Stick to the story: you were detained by our forces, and we managed to drag you away into captivity after the firefight downtown. But you escaped from our custody when we stopped to fix a mechanical failure en route to HQ. You spent the last several days evading capture."

"All right. How did I do that?"

"Dunno. Make something up." Marin rolls his eyes. "Come on, Zein. You had plenty of exposure to Nick. Should give you some hints on how to manipulate people."

"Yes, it did, but spinning bald-faced lies in the face of enemy soldiers doesn't seem the best idea without a solid plan behind it."

"So write it all down."

"You're not instilling great confidence."

"Quit worrying. Consider this cramming for an exam, only it's the worst exam you've ever taken, and if you fail, you die. But you won't die."

"That's better."

"Like I said, you were around the guy. Better than that, you were partners. He confided in you, I assume, to get you to believe he was a teammate. Did he fool everyone around with ease?"

"He did. I didn't think it was possible my best friend—and my wife—would be taken in by a false me, but it was." The image Nick sent to me, of he and Jess at lunch, still burns. Let him gloat. It wouldn't be for much longer.

"Keep that in mind when you're portraying him. Whatever you say about the scum, he had tremendous nerve to pull it off, to gallivant around a world he didn't know, interacting with people who were altered versions of the ones with whom he was familiar."

I nod. "I'm assuming you have a new uniform for me, credentials."

"Sort of. You'll go out in one of our uniforms, complete with blood stains and a bullet hole. You shot a Home Guard soldier and stole it." Marin grimaces. "Figure on whoever picks you up being suspicious of Nick returning in the same clothes, after spinning a tale of capture."

"But they know he's been gone, yes? They know something's amiss."

"There's chatter across Sierran communications about Nick, yeah, but it's indeterminate. I can't tell you whether or not they're aware he's gone to your world, or even if they know of what he can do with the Echo Watch." Marin points. "You got to keep an ear to the ground while you're there. Pick up whatever intel is available."

"I think I'll have my hands full deceiving my wife—that is, Tabitha Boutros. Agent Boutros."

"Tabitha. He calls her 'Gracie' when he's in a good mood."

"Gracie." I stifle a smile. "That fits."

"Oh yeah?"

"Tabitha's a name derived from Hebrew. It means beauty, also grace, sometimes gazelle."

Marin snorts. "Well, she's gorgeous, I'll give you that. Still didn't take her but five seconds to fling a knife at my head when she found out I was a spy."

"She was the one?" My stomach churns. If she spotted Marin despite his disguise, I didn't hold out hope for me. Of course, my face would have more appeal than his.

"You bet."

"How'd you get away?"

"Explosions. Lots of them." Marin shrugs. "That and gunship support. Never underestimate a decent rocket strike from a Comanche chopper."

"If you could have one of those ready to follow me, I'd be grateful."

"You'll do fine. Count on it."

"How can you be sure?"

"Because you got the looks for the job." He grins, a wolfish expression I've not yet seen on him. "Also, it takes guts to shout down Miss Loredana Lark. Consider me mildly impressed."

I return the smile. "Here's hoping I don't disappoint, Captain."

He heads for the door. "You avoid getting dead, Dominic, I'll buy you a burger. Not one of those cardboard patties we get in the MREs, either. Real cow."

The sound of the door banging shut wipes the smile off my face. I'm left with the overwhelming piles of paragraphs telling me everything I could every desire to know about Nick. His father didn't leave him, it seems. Stuck around and is still in close contact with his son, or as close contact as Nick can manage being a spy and military commander. Mother and Father are married, with three children.

Three children.

There's photos.

A woman, impish face, short hair, three years younger than me, and a man, five years younger. She has Mother's smile, and he has Father's proud nose and cheekbones. There's hints of me, of Nick, in both.

An invisible hand clenches my heart. Nick has siblings. A large family. Are they happy? They're all living within the Sierran League.

I slid another sheet next to it, a list of Nick's operations that have led to Sierran victories on countless occasions. Few were counteracted by the Home Guard. The tally of casualties runs into the thousands over the past decade.

All this time, I fretted about burying myself in building designs. I moped about hours spent away from Jess, without friends, giving everything to the job. My life needed more relaxation, more fun, more … self.

A world away, across an incomprehensible gulf, Nick was singlehandedly waging a war.

I shudder. No wonder those troops fought so desperately against Captain Marin's men in Rampart. Nick must be invaluable to their efforts.

And yet, he chose to leave them.

Was it as he claimed? To rid himself of pursuit? Marin didn't make it seem like the Home Guard or Procyon were planning to capture him soon, no matter how high a priority his defeat was. I saw no evidence of plans. Not yet.

Perhaps Nick wanted, like me, to get away from his life.

There's a knock at the door.

"Come in."

Jacobs elbows it aside. He's got an electric razor and a mirror clasped in his left hand. There's a garment bag clutched in his right. "Cleanup time, sir."

"I warrant a 'sir,' now, Jacobs?"

"Since you're playing for our team, you get a temporary one." Jacobs hands over the razor. "Got to make you look like … you, or Commander Zein. Both, I guess."

"Thanks." I prop the mirror against the board and set to trimming off the several days' worth of whiskers forming a scruffy beard and mustache. The razor buzzes angrily.

"You got a recent photo in this file?" Jacobs pokes a finger under the pages.

"There is one, yes, but I saw Nick less than a week ago."

"What'd he look like?" Jacobs sets the garment bag on a chair next to my desk. "I mean, besides like you, sir."

"I don't catch your meaning."

"I've seen the photos, the cards." He pats his chest pocket. "Got my own deck, just like everyone else in the Home Guard. I mean, what's he look like when you're face-to-face? He's killed a heap of our people. Lost three friends over the past eighteen months to his squads. The captain's been there, right with him, but he won't say anything about it. Classified."

"Ah, well, I don't think I can be much help."

"Just … looking for something about the real man. Not the monster I … we keep imagining, sir."

"There isn't anything I can say about the monster, Jacobs." Nick did kill a man or have him killed. And Mrs. Cortez's dog was Chris's handiwork. "I saw him fight. Hand to hand, against men trying to steal my car. He had skill. Of course, the Echo Watch proved an unfair advantage. Other than that, I found him charismatic, manipulative, but very much a man like you and me. He has an artistic side. The file doesn't say anything about formal architect training, yet he produced work as inspiring as any I'd seen."

"Ms. Lark said you were an architect."

"Yes." I rub my chin. Looks like I'm ready to kiss Jess good-bye, grab my laptop bag, and start up the BMW. None of those things are anywhere nearby. Something brushes my leg, but it's a phantom sensation—Sammy's not there begging for a scratch good-bye.

"So … you got no combat experience."

"Not unless you count my brief fight with Nick and his bodyguard. I had a gun. It didn't matter."

"Hey, you went up against an ex-Spetsnaz Commie soldier and the warlord's favorite hatchet man." Jacobs unzips the garment bag. I catch a glimpse of gray and green fabric. "The fact you get to jaw about it instead of being dead's pretty dry."

I've retrieved Nick's file and have paged through it when his comment makes me pause. "Dry."

"Yeah. You know." Jacobs raises his eyebrow. "Outstanding. Cool."

"Oh. Yes. Why 'dry,' though?"

"Means you didn't get run over by a tsunami after the Blasts."

I wince. "Right. Sorry."

"No sweat, sir. My family's all Chicago and East. Here. Should be the right size for you." He hands me a set of fatigues identical to the Home Guard soldiers, including a private's insignia and the faded Procyon emblem. Marin wasn't kidding; I poke my finger through one of several bullet holes. The cloth around the holes is crusty with what I hope is not really dried blood. Given Marin's insistence in preparing me for this mission, though, I wouldn't be surprised if it were.

"Looks about right."

"We'll get a pair of boots up here. Wrong size, but we don't want it to seem too convenient you found a set that matches." He holds up a pair of black boxer briefs. "And these."

I frown. "What's wrong with the regular boxers I wear?"

"Nothing. Commander Zein doesn't wear them. These are the Sierrans' standard issue for officers and SSB agents."

"Oh." I hold the underwear at arm's length. All this anxiety over portraying the man I thought was an ally and is now my enemy, seems absurd when dealing with a pair of shorts.

"Get changed. I'll make sure you match up." Jacobs opens the door. "Uh, sir?"

"Yes?"

"Back in Ops, you said something about me. About your world."

"I shouldn't have opened my mouth, Sergeant. I was angry, and tired. Still am. Ms. Lark …"

"Yeah, she's warned us about stuff like that ever since Procyon brought in Home Guard on their Interstice project. But …" Jacobs drums his fingers on the door. "Sir, I got to know. I don't exist there?"

Many times, I've regretted the things I've said, especially in the heat of the moment to people like Jess, and Curt. This is as bad. "As far as I'm aware, you don't. I worked with your father, Tyson Jacobs."

"Tyson Jacobs, Senior."

"No. Just Tyson Jacobs. Never married, childless."

"Oh." Jacobs blinks. "Really? So me and my sisters—we aren't in your world at all?"

I shake my head.

"Huh. And Dad—I mean, your Tyson Jacobs, he's an architect, too?"

"Yes. Is he alive here?"

Jacobs sucks in a breath. "Dad's *dead*?"

"No, that is … he isn't your father there. He's a different man." Yet if Tyson walked into this room, Jacobs would no doubt greet him as the person who raised him. "I suspect that's true of everyone."

"Yeah, I guess. It's funny to think of Dad as something other than a preacher."

For a moment I consider the possibility I really am dreaming, because this mirrored world just got odder. "Did you say preacher?"

"Yep. Baptist. We see him from the front pews every Sunday. Well, my sisters do. I haven't been back home for a while now." Jacobs smiles. "Funny how these universes work, isn't it?"

"How is that?"

"If you hadn't come across, who knows what Commander Zein would have gotten away with?"

He leaves me alone with the costume. I change in silence, listening to the depth of my breathing, the rustle of the clothing, the throaty rasp of the ventilation.

When the last zipper is zipped and button is buttoned, I study the files until my eyes feel rubbed raw with sandpaper. I'm parched. My stomach rumbles. There's no clock; I don't have my phone or watch. However long I've been at this, it doesn't matter—I've got to remember everything I can.

Finally, I glance up at the mirror still tilted against the board. The reflection is me, clean-shaven, hair swept in the correct fashion. Dominic Zein.

Feels like eons ago I sat at the table in Caerphilly, waiting for Curt, watching the evening passers-by. Nick had walked by. He gave that sly smile of his, the one that ceded notice of you, yet gave nothing away about himself. Confidence. What was the word? Bravura.

I try it on.

Doesn't look right. It's smug, yes, but too much so. Too much like Tyson when he's won out. No, it has to be tempered with assurance that I'm right, that my way is not only the triumphant way, but the only way.

There he is.

Commander Dominic Zein.

Me.

Jacobs is my escort. He gets a new change of clothes, too, albeit a stolen Sierran uniform. It's been ripped and sullied. I don't ask if the cosmetic changes were applied before or after it was stripped from a dead enemy soldier or if it came from a captured supply truck.

He and I stand side by side next to a Thudder. I saw this vehicle tipped on its side, undergoing heavy maintenance when I first arrived at the base. Whatever repairs were needed did not include the exterior, which displays the scars from numerous bullets, plus scorches from a handful of explosions. It stinks of sweat and oil.

"You must get Boutros to give you the Echo Watch." Lark paces a short line in front of us. Marin waits behind, at parade rest, jaw clenched. "Elsewise the only way to get the device is to remove her arm."

"It won't come to that, ma'am," Jacob says.

"Thank you, Sergeant, for the assurance of things yet unseen. Your charge has made quite the convincing transformation."

I flash that smile. "Hey, relax. We'll be in and out before anyone suspects the plan. Just be ready to pick us up."

Lark raises an eyebrow. She says nothing to me, but directs her comment over her shoulder, at Marin. "Convincing indeed. I've half a mind to slap him in irons again."

"Yeah. He's great." Marin scowls. "What's your wife's name?"

"Gracie's my love," I say, "But she's no wife. Not her style, or mine."

"And where have you been?"

"Holed up between Ovid and Julesberg, on the Nebraska line. I thought I was going to hike all the way back to base before one of our loyal Sierran fellows retrieved me."

"That's great, but I meant in the weeks before."

"The mission is none of your concern." I pour every ounce of conceit into my voice, reserved for the occasions I'd had to shut Tyson down. There's a twinge of guilt. Can't believe I'll miss the interaction. "It was sanctioned by Benton himself and, therefore, so high above your pay grade you'll wrench your neck trying to crane it. Suffice it to say I was captured, escaped, and need the Echo Watch to retrieve ours before Procyon can dissect it."

Lark smiles. "I daresay he'll do fine."

"Got a creepy edge, that's for sure," Marin mutters.

"I appreciate the compliment," I say. "I think."

Marin faces Jacobs. They salute each other. "Good luck, Sergeant."

"Godspeed, Captain."

Jacobs climbs into the driver's seat. The engine coughs to life, a throaty rumble echoing throughout the chamber.

"Dominic." Lark takes my arm. She leans in so I can hear her over the noise, yet no one else can discern. "I must reiterate—Agent Boutros must give you her Echo Watch. Even considering the alternative …"

"I can't say I have the stomach to dismember her." Sierran Security or not, Tabitha looks like Jess. Whether or not she *is* Jess remains to be seen. My wife and I have never raised hands against each other. But if the woman possesses the only way for me to get home, to my real world …

"There is no guarantee we can make the device work if it is attached to her person and not rescinded. It needs an adjustment period before you can use it." Lark holds out her hand. "Sergeant Jacobs knows the return route. We will not risk a rendezvous at headquarters."

We shake. "Thank you."

"Don't thank me yet." Her smile is enigmatic. "You may not enjoy the consequences of your and Nick's actions."

Jacobs drives us up a series of switch backs, concrete ramps making a 180-degree turn. Bright light floods the dim tunnel from a slit that grows wider. A metal door rolls up, the abrupt daylight making my eyes water. The Thudder rumbles out into the open. I glance behind us. The door closes, disappearing behind a bend in a broad dirt road rutted from repeated use. Aspens hem us in, as we drive over a rusty bridge spanning a broad, rushing creek. Even sans leaves, the trees form a barrier on the opposite bank, concealing not only the long, low mesa into which the cavern is apparently dug, but the road itself.

I notice a lack of timepieces in the car. If Jacobs has a watch, he isn't sharing. "How long?"

"When we get near enough, you'll know." He fiddles with a dial on the dash-mounted radio, completed with CB handset. "The Sierrans might be sloppy, but they're not sleepy."

The road is long enough, and light fading. Late afternoon. The sun's turning the snow-coated plains golden. I rest my head against the cab door. The Thudder's swaying does the rest.

A loud honk jolts me awake.

Night. The sky's inky black. I suppose there's piles of stars, but the searchlights glaring through the windshield wash away any indication. Off to the left, past Jacobs, are the ruins of Rampart, illuminated here and there by more searchlights.

Jacobs has his hands raised.

Sierran soldiers, all in the urban camouflage and rag-tag accessories that seem standard, swarm the truck, three to each side. They whip our doors open. "Keep your hands up! Get out, slow!"

"Sir!" The voice to my right squeaks. "It's Commander Zein!"

Exclamations and hoots ripple through the men approaching the truck, but they don't impress the hulking Latino soldier who drags Jacobs onto the dirt. "Secure the intruders and *then* establish identity, Private!"

"Sir, yes, sir!" Gloved hands yank me roughly from the cab. Gravel scrapes my knees. Gun muzzles glare at me.

There's a tall, chain-linked fence topped with razor wire just ahead. A motley collection of military and civilian trucks are arrayed behind it. It seems all have machine guns mounted above their roofs.

A flashlight dazzles me from inches away. "You weren't kidding," the Latino soldier says. "It is you, sir."

I blink away spots. The nametag says "Vega." The name hurtles at me from Nick's files. Lieutenant Arturo Vega, Sierran Army, aide to Commander Zein. Nick calls him Vega, nothing else. "It is indeed, Vega, so how about you stop blinding me so I can see the home team?"

Vega lowers his flashlight. He's got a broad grin and a thick, black mustache. "Good to have you back, Commander." He helps me up. "Who's the newbie?"

"Ty Jackson," I give as Jacobs' alias. "Local adherent. He picked me up. Kind of him to not let me walk all the way back to camp."

"What happened? We heard you were on mission, then maybe captured."

"That's what I would like to know."

The voice is a lash. Even in this alien setting, I know it. My heart won't cease pounding.

Jess.

She's dressed in the same black turtleneck with Sierran flag pin and camouflaged trousers. Her posture's ramrod straight, hinting at the military training she's received, yet the sway to her steps is unmistakable. This is my Jess.

No. Agent Tabitha Boutros.

"Isn't this a remarkable sight." The vocal resemblance is uncanny— same tones, yet with a hard edge I've never heard. Her students would no doubt cringe. Certainly the soldiers around me miraculously improve their posture. Even Vega stands lock-still. "Off on secret assignment for weeks, and here he is, in a stolen American vehicle with an unknown face as chauffeur."

I give my best Nick smile. "Missed you, too, Gracie."

There's no reciprocation. All she offers is a stern glare. "Take the driver to a holding cell. We'll determine if his identity is true. If not, I know where to dump unwanted bodies."

Soldiers escort Jacobs away. He and I share a look. Not a sign of panic on the man's face. I won't let him down.

Tabitha approaches. It takes every ounce of calm to maintain an indifferent, casual stance. "You didn't communicate."

"Couldn't. Betrays the notion of a secret mission."

A smirk creases her lips. "Then let's debrief."

CHAPTER TWENTY-TWO

Base is a misnomer. The compound into which Tabitha leads me is a collection of metal containers welded together, elevated on trusses. The boxes are joined in a maze, the whole thing a series of sharp turns. It's reminiscent of the Home Guard-Procyon caverns, minus the proliferation of rocks.

She leads me past various rooms, some of which are packed with foodstuffs, others with medical supplies, still others with racks of guns. Soldiers stare at us from them. They're a curious mix of ages—late teens, 40s and 50s, men and more women than the Home Guard evidenced. None seem in the best of shape. A few are downright overweight. Their appearance contrasts sharply with the fit troops of the Home Guard.

Tabitha makes a final turn at a T-intersection. Two big men stand guard. "Have Lieutenant Vega wait outside when he arrives."

"Yes, ma'am."

One opens the door for us. There's an antechamber beyond, with coat hooks and a bench with boots tucked underneath. Tabitha waits until the door shuts, then opens the next one.

It's a penthouse.

Thick, soft carpet. Tile floor in the kitchen—and it is a full kitchen, complete with stainless steel appliances, granite countertops, and a stove tucked into an island. Twin couches face each other, framing a faux fireplace. A broad screen hangs over that, displaying a gorgeous night sky over a distant beach. There's even a chandelier, illuminating the entire room with a soft, golden glow. There's two doors to either side.

More surprising? The eight framed drawings festooning the walls. Each one is a gorgeous rendering of a building, from majestic skyscraper to humble cottage. Sketched in pencil, brought to life with watercolor paints. After everything Procyon and the Home Guard drummed into me about Nick's life on this Earth, I nearly forgot his early training in architecture. Apparently, he's kept it going, albeit in amateur fashion.

Speaking of Nick …

What would he say? How would he react to being home?

Tabitha's hand touches mine. It's like a hot iron.

I pull her close and kiss her.

It happens before my mind can catch up with what my body's doing. I've missed Jess so much. To have her in my arms again is intoxicating. The only thing that would make the feeling complete is Sammy barking for my attention—

She isn't Jess. Captain Marin's warning whispers through my head.

We part from each other. She touches her lips, eyes wide. "Hello to you, too."

Have I overstepped? If she and Nick were having problems, Marin's intelligence may have missed the signs. *Don't worry. Be Nick.* I grin. "Who do you think was on my mind the entire time? It wasn't Benton."

She grins back and kisses me again. This time I break away, winking at her. Inside my guts and emotions are a whirlwind. Jess, but not. Here she's Nick's woman, not my wife—but I'm Nick.

I flop onto the couch, kick my feet on the other end and sigh. "How I missed this place. You would not believe the privation I've faced, Gracie."

She stands over me, arms folded. "Where have you been?"

"You wouldn't believe me if I told you the truth."

She raises an eyebrow. "As if you've ever told me the whole truth, Dom."

My head spins. Dominic, Nick, Commander Zein, Dom. Too bad there isn't time to write them all down on my arm for reference. "You know how it is."

"What about Niemec?"

For a moment I stare at her, mind blank. I buy precious seconds by rubbing my hands across my face. Niemec? Think back to what Captain Marin said. Krzysztof Niemec. Soviet military. Special forces. He's the one Nick calls "Chris," who killed off his double on my world. "Still there. I don't know what's happened to him. Probably nothing good."

In a sense, it's the truth.

"He was a fool," she murmurs. "I told you it was easier to take Vega along. Niemec was just muscle, but you insisted on him instead of your right-hand man."

Why would Nick have done that? It clicks. The homeless veteran. Nick likely knew Chris had a double. Perhaps Vega's wasn't around—or Vega didn't exist on our world. "The situation called for someone of his talents. Vega would have been a problem. Besides, I needed someone I trusted back here making sure you were okay."

"Thoughtful of you." She traces a line down my chest.

Can't help but feel strengthened by the praise. "It is, isn't it?"

"If you're here, without your Spetsnaz puppy, I imagine you don't still have it."

Ah. "There were some—complications. I had to give it up, under duress."

"They followed you even there?" She crouches beside me, a wild hunger in her expression. "The other Earth?"

In a manner of speaking. "Took the Echo Watch and tossed me back. Who knows what they have in mind with it?"

"Procyon." She spits it.

"Yes. I'm sure you recall they have agents on both worlds." And this sets me thinking—how much does Loredana Lark from my world know? This place's Lark certainly hinted at two-way communication between both places. "They tracked me down, despite my efforts at concealment."

Tabitha reaches for my right arm. "You gave it to them."

"It was either that or be cut apart as a guinea pig for their experiments."

She frowns. The disdain is a mirror to Jess's. "You shouldn't have given it up."

"True, but I'm fond of my limbs."

"All right."

"So, we have to retrieve it."

"No."

"No? You're kidding. If we leave them with one and us with the other, we lose our advantage."

She rubs a hand along the sleeve of her left arm. There's a bulge there, obvious to the most casual observer. A glint of silver emerges by her wrist. "And if we travel there to do so, we could lose both."

"It's an acceptable risk. Do you really want Procyon and Home Guard hopping back and forth? Who knows what kind of help they could recruit?"

"Yes. We have no idea. But that doesn't mean we should throw away what we have here for some nebulous gain."

I grit my teeth. Nick's file states that he and Tabitha consider each other on equal footing when it comes to tactical considerations, and their debates are the stuff of legend. I feel like I'm having the same argument with Jess about whether or not we should have a family. Only, in this case, the stakes are much greater. "Gracie, come on. Let's use yours, go over there, and get it back. We can't be without this power."

She eyes me with cool consideration. "Power? The Echo Watches aren't the power with which we should be concerned. Our project's near completion. Doesn't that worry you at all? Of course not. You never worry."

Project? What project? Panic seeps through my barricades. Easy. Focus on being Nick. Find out what she means. Carefully. I smirk. "There's a shocker. Why should I? We have the Home Guard where we want them."

Tabitha chuckles. "Ah, yes, there's the bravado."

"I assume you've made progress in my absence."

"Such little confidence."

"Show me what's been done."

She kisses me again. Her lips linger against mine. "I promise, you'll like it."

I lean against the couch as she slides aside the projection screen. There's a wall safe behind it. She turns the tumblers to the correct combination. A click. She opens the door and extracts a thick folder.

All this time, I've seen little evidence of information technology. The computers at HQ were antiquated. There doesn't appear to be a single electronic device in this suite. Paper files are the norm. Perhaps, after the cataclysm, the technology didn't advance as quickly as it did on my world. Or, maybe the risk of espionage is so great that hard copies are more secure. No chance an enemy can steal secrets from a distance if they're kept off a computer network.

"We made it past the last phase," Tabitha says. "The one that had given us such a headache before you took off. It shows great promise."

She opens the folder.

There's a man there, a body, lying on an examination table. The room is all linoleum floors and metal walls—except the walls are covered with small, square doors.

I tighten my lips, so I don't let my disgust show.

The body is covered with oozing, raw red sores. Clumps of hair have fallen out. His eyes stare sightless at the ceiling, black and red, with blood oozing from the corners.

There are other people in the room, all clad in full-body suits with plastic face shields. It makes me think whatever killed the man is a disease, or radioactive. "Well, that's progress, as you say."

"I know." Tabitha smiles. She pages through more photographs. Each one is a person, dead, horribly mutilated by whatever ended their lives. "The fatality rate is pushing 90 percent. Dispersal is a problem. The tech boys think we can do something with UAVs, if we can steal a few from Reconnaissance. Benton wants a field test in the next few days."

"Do you have a target in mind?"

"That hasn't changed." She glances at me. "Home Guard positions to the northeast of Rampart."

"Surely they'll be prepared to repulse such an attack."

"Yes, I agree. I don't want to underestimate them, either. That's why Benton's approval for the double strike is so important. He agreed to your plan."

"My plan. He did?"

She nods, her eyes wide with an eagerness that turns my stomach. "We'll hit the Home Guard emplacements and the refugee camp behind it, simultaneously. The resultant chaos will give us the opening to finally overwhelm their lines."

"I see. Well, that is good news." How can Nick contemplate these horrors? Refugees. I don't know whether she means the former inhabitants of Rampart, or people who've fled east in the face of the Sierran advance, but either way, it's unconscionable. The idea that the two of us are the same man makes me ill.

"Are you all right?" Tabitha puts her hand atop mine. "I knew we should have taken you to the medic first thing, but I figured you would argue."

"You do know me." I stand up. Air. I need fresh air. There's a vent nearby, but no windows anywhere. Reasonable, given Nick's and Tabitha's rank with SSB. "Let's take a walk. I want to see the project firsthand."

"You're sure." Tabitha packs up the folder. "You've barely reviewed the details."

"I've been over them a hundred times and reading them a hundred and one until I get a headache won't change anything, now will it? I want the first-hand update." And make one more push with an extra helping of Nick's personality. "Besides, if this is going to kill as many people as I hope it will, I've got to shake the hands of the people doing the grunt work."

She smiles. "Let's go."

Vega is there, standing at parade rest. "Sir, is there a problem?"

I smile. "Not at all. Agent Boutros is getting me up to speed on our pet project."

His expression stiffens. "Yes, sir."

"You can wait here. We'll return shortly," Tabitha says.

He salutes. "Ma'am."

I let Tabitha stay a half-step ahead, seeing as how she's intimately familiar with the base and I'm a complete stranger—on the inside. Part of me wonders if Marin was this terrified when he strode through the enemy's complex like he owned it. Likely he was more so, lacking my similarity to Commander Dominic Zein.

After a few twists and turns down unmarked, dingy corridors, we exit a door to the outside. Snow spirals in the glare from blue-white searchlights set at corners around a fenced yard. More vehicles are parked back here. They're crawling with soldiers, a hive of repairs just as frenetic as the Procyon/Home Guard garage. The difference is the lack of standardized supplies. Everything appears to have a different source, as if the quartermaster raided a dozen gas stations.

There's a concrete bunker partially buried in a hillock. The falling snow can't conceal the freshly turned dirt, something I've seen at countless building sites. The concrete's a bright, uniform color. I drag a finger along the edges as more guards admit us through a hefty steel door. It's new, all right. There's no weathering. Is it a month old? Marin's reports didn't mention it.

The hallway slanting down is metal, with caution stripes of black and yellow lining the walls. Tabitha taps a biohazard symbol. "About time they got these up. Coming in here, knowing what's stored below, always makes my skin crawl without the proper warnings." She glances at me. Is she expecting a response?

Think. I shrug. "Stickers won't help anyone if it gets out. Dead's dead, with or without warnings."

She shakes her head, but there's a smirk on her lips. "How I've missed your attitude."

"Sure that's all you missed?" I wink. "I know on my part, *your* attitude wasn't the primary thing I pined for."

She opts against a response, but the smirk remains.

Then we round a corner straight into hell itself.

The right wall is glass, blocking us from accessing an empty corridor. Beyond that, a second glass wall seals off a laboratory. I say it's such because it's the most clinical descriptor I can find for a torture room. Four people clad in the same environment suits as I saw in Tabitha's project photos move about, one taking notes on a clipboard, another mixing liquids in pipettes, two more using the biggest needles I've ever seen to inject test subjects.

Two of them are strapped to tables—a man and a woman, both white. They're insensate, eyes half-shut, unfocused as they face the ceiling. The man must be dead. The same hideous markings cover his body where the skin is visible. The woman, though, doesn't show signs of the ailment. Not yet.

"They tell me transmission is still a factor." Tabitha could be discussing our dinner options. She inspects the edges of her fingernails. "We have initial success with infection, but the virus won't leap from one victim to the other with rapidity. I suppose that's to be overcome by dispersing it in aerosol suspension."

"I suppose." I fold my arms, to put on a show of being frustrated, when I'm really trying to hold back outrage. "How's our volunteer supply?"

Tabitha glances at me. "Your sense of humor needs retooling, Dom. Keeping the prisoner population available for testing has reduced turnaround time. I'm certain Benton's pleased with your suggestion. We don't have to wait nearly as long to complete the cycle when we can use Home Guard soldiers for our purposes. Not ideal as far as screening candidates goes, but when operating in field conditions, one makes do."

"Obviously." *Murderer.* The word churns in my head like a summer storm cloud. There's no end to his crimes. Nick has killed untold numbers, not only through indirect tactics, but by injecting them with—whatever this is. My next goal, it seems. And where have they taken Jacobs? If we're going to make it out of here with the Echo Watch, we have to do so together. "How fast acting is it?"

"Minutes. This is a more aggressive strain of smallpox, like we requested. I'm amazed they've done so much in such a short time."

Smallpox. Thousands could die—or millions. I don't know whether or not smallpox is as virulent as it was a hundred years ago. What I do know is it had been locked away in American and Russian military labs, sealed off from the rest of the world. The fact that the Sierrans are not only experimenting with it but intend to deploy the virus against soldiers and civilians alike, means they're more desperate than Home Guard-Procyon realizes.

"This is all very impressive, but at the same time, bland," I say.

"Bland?" Tabitha scowls. "How can this be bland? Our weaponized smallpox will provide Sierra the leverage needed to finally win."

"Of course it will, but you know as well as I it's only a temporary boost. Vaccines exist. And someone will find an effective way to counter the aerosolized version. It's a matter of time." I rub my arm. "*This* is of greater concern."

"We've been over this."

"Yes, and I'm dissatisfied with your answer. What's made you so weak?"

She straightens up, a soldier under review. "I am not weak."

"You sound like you are. Did missing me override your sense of duty with sentiment? Our objective is the Sierran League's supremacy." I wave a hand dismissively at the horror show behind the glass. Welts arise across the infected woman's arms and face. She gasps for breath. I want to break through, drag her to safety, or force those working in the lab to do something. But I can't. I'm not Dominic. I'm Nick. And Nick's the one who came up with this gruesome plan. "What better way to achieve that supremacy with the Echo Watches? With them both the two of us can travel back and forth between the Earths."

"Fat lot of good that will do us, besides costing us one of the two."

"That's why we need to retrieve my Echo Watch. Keep them both from Procyon, only this time, we don't waste our advantage."

"How would you have us do that? Ignore our responsibilities here and hide on a different world?" Tabitha pokes a finger at my face. "Fess up, Dom. I know why you went there. You were on the run. There was no secret mission. You were setting up another life, some kind of grand plan to hide yourself from all this—from me."

I stare at her. Not the kind of argument I thought I'd have with an enemy spy, about a device that can open cross-world portals, outside a laboratory devoted to creating weaponized smallpox. As thoughts careen inside my head, searching for a sensible response, motion in the lab distracts me. The woman lays limp against her restraints on the table. Her head lolls to one side, gaze unseeing.

She's dead.

The technicians sealed behind their suits confer over clipboards. Are they pleased with their success? Are they happy the virus kills faster? Do they celebrate results with loved ones?

I focus on what Marin said. These aren't the people from my world. This woman, standing before me with hurt etched on her face, is not my wife.

Yet, she is a person. She's Nick's love. For whatever reason, he left her here to oversee the machinery of war, while he plays at being me. What's his endgame? Is it part of a devious plan?

Or did he just run away?

I take Tabitha's hands, clasp them in mine. Her fingers are like icicles, at least until mine warm hers. It makes me smile. Jess's are the same way. "Gracie, listen—I would never abandon you. We've been through so much together. You're my partner, and more than that—my love. That's why I need your help, to use your Echo Watch to get mine back, because whatever's going to happen, it needs to involve us both. Let the lab rats play around with the virus. When the time comes to attack our enemies, we'll lead the way, side by side. The Echo Watches are the only true power we need concern ourselves with. Let's use them to bolster our power so that no one can ever separate us."

She breaks into a smile. No tears, though her eyes glisten under the sickly bunker lights. "I should know better than to doubt you. All the missions you've undertaken, all the times you've disappeared, I've always gotten you back. But this time—Dom, we can't fail. Benton has a lot riding on our project. The front lines are static. We need this breakthrough."

"And we'll get it, in more ways than one."

Tabitha nods. "Tell me what's next."

My heart's pounding, because I have no idea what's next—other than to grab the Echo Watch and escape. I simply extend my arm.

"All right. Hold on." She clasps my arm. Her fingers tremble.

"Hey." I brush her cheek. "I love you."

She leans into the gesture. "And I you."

Then she sets her other hand atop the Echo Watch.

The metal band melts. It seems impossible, but one moment it's a solid object braced around her wrist, and the next, it's flowing across her knuckles as if it were poured down a counter. It streams onto mine. I gasp. Dunking my hand into Arctic waters would no doubt feel like the Caribbean by comparison. The sensation intensifies until I'm squeezing Tabitha's hand with everything I have. She grimaces, her face paling, but she doesn't withdraw.

Needle-like cold stabs through my wrist. The Echo Watch springs to life, pieces spanning and spinning until it resembles the deployed mode I saw when Nick opened the portal to the Interstice. Suddenly the cold swaps to a searing heat. Hundreds of tendrils flail from the pieces.

Then they constrict my arm like a snake striking.

There's a moment of blinding pain that makes me stagger, but it's gone in a second. A throbbing ache sets in.

Jess—Tabitha—rubs her wrist. "That was unpleasant."

"Certainly was."

"Give it a moment to adjust to you. Then test it."

"Test it?"

She smirks, and pantomimes shooting.

Yes. The Taser function. I aim my wrist, imitating Nick's stance. Of course, I have no clue if there's a trigger. Or batteries. Or—whatever.

But even as I think it, I see myself firing successfully. It's a hazy image, cleaner than a memory, yet not enough I can tell whether it's imagination. It feels—real.

I flex my hand, just like in the image.

A flattened disc of yellow-white sparks hurtles from the Echo Watch. It leaves a charred, shallow crater on the concrete wall at the end of the wall.

The rush that accompanies it overwhelms nagging anxieties about my assignment. Who made this device? I've seen what it can do, but to experience it firsthand …

I'm thankful it's no longer in Tabitha's possession, but she's only half the picture. I have to get back to my world, find Nick, and stop him.

"That worked well." Tabitha stands before the glass. "Let me finish with the prep work for the demonstration, then we can make a foray into the city to the transit point. I have to admit, I'm excited to see the Echo Watch in action for the first time."

"It's like nothing else, Gracie," I say. "Keep an eye on these lab coats. I'm going to check on my Good Samaritan."

Her gaze flicks to me, then back to the laboratory. Suited figures roll away the tables, still laden with their dead bodies. "Come see me when you're done."

I keep my stride even as I leave the bunker, eyes forward, shoulders back, with all the Nick-like swagger I can summon. See her when I was done? Not likely.

I have to find Jacobs and get us both out of here, so the Home Guard can bomb this nest of pestilence into oblivion.

CHAPTER TWENTY-THREE

It occurs to me I have no clue where to look.

Last I saw of Jacobs, Sierran soldiers were escorting him into the base. Under armed guard. It's unlikely he's sitting in their version of a break room, sipping coffee or munching a doughnut while he regales his supposed comrades with tales of derring-do.

More probable? He was being questioned. Harshly.

I lose too many minutes storming through the maze that is the main base, tossing sloppy salutes at nervous soldiers who snap to attention as I pass. Eventually I ignore them, scowling instead. Nick would scowl. He doesn't strike me as a person who's big on military protocol.

Enough markings become familiar that I wind up in front of Tabitha's and Nick's room. Vega's still there, conferring with a pair of young soldiers. "Vega."

He turns around, doesn't bother with a salute. He knows Nick well enough. "Commander. I thought you and Agent Boutros were occupied."

"We were. Now I'm not. Tell me something: where's the soldier who drove me in tonight? I need to speak with him."

"Interrogation Three."

"Interrogation?" The spike in blood pressure isn't faked, but I vent my anger with more intensity than I'd allow over something more trivial—say, a colleague stealing my designs. "That's unacceptable. If he hadn't grabbed me from the side of the road, I'd have been picked up by Home Guard again and back in Procyon's hands. You think Benton would like that? Perhaps he'd like to hear how you treated the young man who risked his life to save mine."

Vega's expressionless, but his posture solidifies with every snide word until he's welded in place. "Sorry, sir."

"Take me to him. *Now.*"

Vega hurries off into the maze, with me trailing behind. Here's hoping he doesn't realize the only reason I'd given the order was because I was lost. Yet, as we continued making turns, I pieced together a rough map. Down that hall was a room full of weapons. Around the other bend, the doorway that led outside to the bunker and the horrors it contained.

All the way, the Echo Watch pulses.

It's a second heart, a slow, steady beat. Faint, but unmistakable. The warmth is distracting. I should be making mental note of my surroundings. Having the thing clinging to my forearm like some kind of sessile pet doesn't make it easy to keep up false pretenses.

Vega stops outside a thick metal door, with "I-03" spray painted in white from what was apparently a stencil. He raps under a narrow hatch. "Lieutenant Vega, with Commander Zein for the prisoner."

"Prisoner?" I snap.

"Sir, it's protocol," Vega says. "In the event of an unidentified individual gaining access to the base, we perform interrogation to determine his true identity. Security demands I keep you from the room—shouldn't even let you near it, for your safety."

I put myself toe to toe with Vega. After everything I've seen, everything I've undergone, to have progress stymied by a rules-spouting enemy of my country doesn't improve my mood. Imagine that. "Listen. The only person's safety with which you should be concerned is your own. Open the door, let me in, and leave us be, or I'll have you report to Agent Boutros for a firsthand inspection of our project. On the table. Understand?"

Vega's eyes widen. Whatever loyalty he feels toward Nick, I don't doubt I'm pushing it to its limits. I don't care. The Echo Watch is on my arm. I have to get across the Interstice, back to my world—to Jess, and Curt. "Sir. Yes, sir."

"Stop with the 'sir' and let me in, Vega."

Vega opens the door. There's a young soldier, blond with neatly trimmed beard and mustache, hand raised to the latch. He must have been answering Vega's knock. "Is there a problem, Lieutenant?" His tone is nasal, with a sharp stridency I recognize as being native to the Philadelphia region. "I don't like having interviews interrupted."

Blood's on his pale knuckles. The skin's reddening around them. I sidle up for a look. Jacobs has a swollen eye, and nose. He glares at the blond soldier, but sees me, because he throws a wink when neither of them are looking.

"Major, Commander Zein requested it." Vega's smug, even though he's talking to a guy with a gold leaf on his shoulder. "I didn't think it smart to refuse."

The blond guy finally sees me. "Commander." A salute follows, belatedly.

His nametag says "Shipley." Here's hoping Nick's pattern is to be condescending with emphasis on surnames. "Major. How's about you step aside and give me a moment with our guest, in private."

"It's against protocol—"

"Couldn't care less, Shipley." I brush by him, into a room that stinks of sweat, certain he's going to detain me. But Nick must carry a great deal of clout, because no one stops me. I'd be lying if I say the unfettered access to things most people would be arrested for trying doesn't fill me with a surge of pride. No wonder Nick oozed confidence. "And when I say privacy, I mean complete. Shut off whatever cameras you have in here."

Shipley frowns. "For Interrogation Three? Not unless you've loaned us some of the cash you and Agent Boutros get to play with. Sir."

"Fine. Get out. Both of you."

Shipley looks at Vega. "A word, Lieutenant." Then he's gone.

"Commander." Vega leans in the doorway. "Are you all right?"

"Sure, Vega. I've been held captive by our enemies. Got me tense. That's all. I need to ask this young man what he knows about the situation, without smacking him first. It's the least I can do for someone who saved my life."

"Yes, sir. I'll be outside if you need me." Vega closes the door.

I blow out a breath and sag against the wall.

"Nice." Jacobs grins. He isn't shackled, surprisingly. "You're doing good."

"We'll discuss my potential Oscar later. Can you walk?"

He raises an eyebrow. "Serious? The major's an amateur. I've been beaten by pros. This was a love tap." Jacobs hops up from the chair. "Room's got no surveillance, and Shipley wasn't recording."

"How do you know? He could have them hidden."

"Not likely. You seen how huge those things are?"

I'm puzzled, until I remember the differences in technology. Whatever passes for a digital recorder—or perhaps they still use tapes—it isn't a cell phone one can drop in one's pocket. "I'll take your word for it."

"How'd your end go?"

I lift my sleeve.

"Wow. Oh wow." Jacobs gets so close I can feel him breathing. "It's … to be honest, I thought maybe the captain was joshing us. Like the Echo Watch was some kind of objective, or theoretical device. But it's really … real."

"Yes. And before you ask, it works. Well." I gesture to the door. "Shall we go?"

"Sure. First I got to retrieve something from our truck."

"What? Why? We're taking the same one back out, aren't we?"

"Uh, no. It's staying as a present for the Sierrans, and a signal for the captain. All we got to do is grab the remote and throw the switch."

"Switch."

"As in … detonator?"

Jacobs pantomimes an explosion. "Boom."

I slap my hands to the sides of my head. "I would have felt better knowing this ahead of time, Sergeant!"

"Yeah, well, captain said it was need to know. Said you'd have enough stress without—"

"Knowing I hitched a ride on a bomb? Yes, I'd agree." I pace the room. "So the plan is to blow it up, and he'll see the flare. Do we have a say in where it's placed?"

Jacobs frowns. "I suppose. Does it matter whether we light it off in the front yard or the back?"

"Only when one considers the backyard has a biological weapons lab buried under it."

"You're kidding."

I shake my head. "Smallpox."

Jacobs puts his hands on his hips. "Okay. That complicates things. A lot. But let's make do. I'll need some more fuel tanks. Like, an entire fuel *tanker* would help."

"Well, they have a bunch of vehicles parked out there. I'm sure you'll find something you like." I place my ear against the door. Murmurs, indistinct. Vega and Shipley are still waiting. "Meanwhile, I suggest we come up with a plan for getting past these two."

"Serious? You're supposed to command them to get out of our way. You're the Commander, sir." He salutes.

Of course. I exhale. It was such a welcome feeling to put back on Dominic Zein after wearing Nick for several hours. Apparently, that long is enough to make one's skin crawl. "Follow my lead, please."

"Sure. But Commander Zein wouldn't say please."

I open the door. Shipley's gone, around which corner in which hall I haven't a clue. But Vega's there, waiting at parade rest. He steps forward as soon as I exit with Jacobs in tow. "Sir, everything all right?"

"Absolutely, Vega. Escort Jackson here to the truck he liberated from the Home Guard. He's got to retrieve important intelligence from it. I don't want him accosted. See to it."

"Yes, sir." Vega stays still. "Did Major Shipley clear him?"

I can't think of another argument without becoming a broken record, so I just imagine Tyson Jacobs from my world remarking on my family origins and give him the sharpest glare I can summon with the resulting anger.

Vega nods. "Understood. Jackson, follow me."

Jacobs tosses off a wink as he trails Vega away from Interrogation Three.

But it's occurred to me, if Jacobs and I are to destroy the lab, Tabitha's files could offer a refined approach. The technicians there are handling a weaponized version of a dangerous virus. Surely, they've got a failsafe in place to eradicate it if containment is breached.

Holding the hope close in prayer, I make my way back to the quarters Nick shares with Tabitha. It only takes two wrong turns, which I count as improvements. The young soldiers standing there salute and let me pass without question.

Fortunately, Tabitha didn't lock either door. Whether the guards can be trusted so well with secrets because of their innate loyalty, or abject fear of Nick's reprisals, doesn't matter to me in the slightest.

Also, the safe is still cracked open.

I smile. Nick's reappearance made her a bit too trusting.

I grab the folder, and page through. There's plenty of information, most of which escapes me. I'm an architect, not a doctor. What's obvious, though, is the stapled document entitled "Security Precautions." There's a table of contents. One of the last bulleted items is, "Containment."

"Perfect," I murmur.

"It is perfect."

I spin around. Tabitha's standing in the open doorway, hands clasped behind her back. She could be Jess clad in black and camouflage, ready for an evening by the fireplace in our Estes Park cabin. But the tension in her stance, and the gun riding in the holster at her hip—neither of which were there before—shatters that illusion.

"You were gone for so long without word of your mission, not even a hint scribbled in a note on the pillow," she says. "Naturally I assumed it was something dire. Perhaps Benton himself had tasked you with a deep cover assassination. The more I considered it, the more I dismissed the supposition. Even when you'd had assignments from him in the past, you'd always found a way to let me know. This time? Nothing."

She comes closer, every click of her boots on the flooring a metronome pronouncing my imminent death. "I'd stood on the edge of hopelessness for the past few days. I've never lost it before. Yet, there I was facing two prospects—you'd abandoned me and the Sierran cause forever, or you'd been killed. Either one was enough to cut my heart out."

As she says it, there's no tears. There's nothing on her face that reminds me of when Jess was upset. *Jess.* The Echo Watch rubs against my wrist. I clutch the folder to my side. "Listen, Gracie—"

"Don't call me that." She whips the pistol from its holster with such speed I think I feel the breeze from her arm in motion.

I snap my wrist up, too, and heat builds in the Echo Watch. Yet, I didn't think about blasting her with it. No conscious effort that I recall. Reflex?

"Don't *ever* call me that again." Tabitha's words spit between clenched teeth. "Because you're not Dom. Whoever you are, you're not Commander Dominic Zein. Which leads me to believe one of two possibilities—you're either someone who Procyon invested a great deal of time, money, and the best plastic surgery possible in creating, or you came back from Yours."

Her use of the pronoun shoots a spike of fear up my guts. Only the Procyon-Home Guard crew working with Interstice travel referred to it that way—and more than that, they're the only trio on this world who've admitted the Echo Watch can achieve the trip.

"Tell me now, and I'll let you live long enough to see Dom returned." Her finger flicks the safety off. "Do it."

I have no doubt I can hit her with the Echo Watch's burst. We're only six feet apart. But I'm equally certain she's more familiar with the weapon capabilities than I am and is also a better shot. My attack would likely end with my skull punctured. I slowly lower my arm. "All right. Yes, you're correct. I'm not your husband—boyfriend. The commander. My name, though, is Dominic Barnabas Zein."

She raises an eyebrow. "Impossible. They brainwashed you?"

"No. I'm entirely separate from the commander—I call him Nick."

"You've—met him?"

"Met and dealt with for a good week and more. Nick took my place at various meetings and work functions, freeing up my time to spend with … my wife, and my friends. He gave me room to breathe." It seems so childish now that I finally admit it to her, and yet, it's also liberating. A weight seems to fall off my back. I stand straighter. It's bothered me that I couldn't—or wouldn't—tell Jess what's really been happening, especially after Nick had the gall to take her on a date. I couldn't say anything face to face.

Until now.

Tabitha frowns. "Dom went on a mission across the Interstice. You told me that."

"I stretched the truth. He did come across the Interstice, but not on any mission I know of. He said he was there to help, but all he wound up doing was throwing me over here. With no hope of return." I shake my sleeve back, so she can see the Echo Watch. "Until now."

"No." She still won't lower the gun. "He was coming back. He had to be on assignment for Benton."

"He and Chris had something in mind, but I don't know what it is."

"You're lying!" Despite the anger quaking her voice, she aims at the floor. Tabitha steps even closer. "Dom wouldn't leave this—or leave me. Us. We're partners. We dreamed up every action together, every sacrifice for the Sierran League, every step of the smallpox project. I won't believe he ran off like a bored child."

She isn't disarmed, but the lack of an impending gunshot emboldens me. "It doesn't change the truth. He said he was in hiding. Never mentioned you, or any details about this world. He and Chris, this Niemec guy from your team, were staying below the radar, for the most part. And frankly, I could have cared less. All I wanted, and still want, is to get back to my world. To my friends, and Jess."

Tabitha looks me straight in the eye. "You mentioned the Good Samaritan."

"What?"

"The Good Samaritan. That's how I knew you weren't Dom. It's a church story."

That throws me. "It's hardly *only* a church story. Everyone knows it, by and large."

"Yes, but Dom hates all things church with a passion exceeded only by his disgust for Procyon. He's taken great pains to banish all references from his talk, and even when I've slipped, he's lost his temper." She bites her lip, and in that second, she's the woman I know and love. "You also said 'Jess.'"

"My wife. Jessica Zein."

"Jessica—Boutros?"

"Before we were married, yes."

Tabitha deflates. "My parents fought over my name. Mother wanted something more Americanized. Father preferred Biblical. When Mother died in a U.S. air raid that came in retaliation for Sierran bombings, Father obviously didn't worry about her preferences."

I can't help it. I place my hand aside her chin. "I know you're not her. That you and Jess are two people, two souls. But there are pieces of her you share. I've looked at you and seen those. Nick was wrong to leave you behind, no matter the dark things you two have committed. He promised more than that."

Heat floods her cheeks. "We never married."

"That doesn't matter. Running away makes him a coward."

This time, there are tears, if only the hint of them. "What does that make you? You're going back to your world, with the Echo Watch, and leaving a war over here."

"Not anymore." I hold up the folder. "I won't show my face back there until I know I've set right at least one of Nick's wrongs. He's hurt too many people. He can't be allowed to continue."

Tabitha kisses me.

We linger together, holding each other with our free hands, even as she presses the gun to my abdomen, and I refuse to relinquish the files about her weaponized smallpox.

Her? Hers and Nick's. That makes it mine.

But she's not Jess, even if I can glimpse my wife in this woman.

I part from her, our lips brushing with a spark. "I'm sorry. For everything."

Tabitha steps away, her eyes glistening. Her finger tightens on the trigger.

A moment before the gunshot, all I can think is, *I've failed*, followed by, *Forgive me, Father.*

But she doesn't shoot me.

She drops to her knees, spinning around, and raises the gun to shoulder level. Three shots explode in rapid succession.

At whom? The guards?

No. They're prone on the floor, beyond the outer hatch. I glimpse Jacobs ducking around the corner.

Now. Do it!

I level the Echo Watch, Tabitha's head positioned above my knuckles. The thoughts barraging me don't make it easy to aim or activate.

I can't kill my wife.

She's not Jess.

How can I shoot an innocent person?

Not innocent. A killer, or at the very least, the aide to one.

I cannot kill Jess.

She isn't her!

No.

Shoot!

I won't kill her.

Now!

Tabitha turns, and it's as if I've slowed time.

I shoot.

The swirl of yellow-white strikes her in the side, below her left arm. The only thing more heartbreaking than the astonishment in her expression is the sound her body makes when it hits the floor.

I drop by her side. Please, don't let her be dead. I place my hand by her mouth.

Warm air tickles the hairs. When I finally locate her pulse, it's slow but steady.

"Hey!" Jacobs's in the door, gesturing with a rifle. "You done in there? Let's move!"

"What happened with the truck?"

He raises a black device with an antenna as long as my forearm, grins, and flips a red switch.

A resonating *BOOM* makes the entire complex shudder. Lights flicker. The ground shakes, making even Jacobs stagger against the wall. More explosions follow, interspersed by shouts. A loud, grating klaxon starts up. The lights in the room and throughout the halls go red.

"We should go," I say.

"You're the commander!"

Together we run down the halls, side by side, as I desperately try to remember the right way to the bunker.

A soldier appears around a corner. Major Shipley. He comes up short, pistol raised. "Sir! Commander, we're under attack!"

Jacobs cuts him down with a burst from his rifle. The sound's shockingly loud in the confined space. More shocking is Shipley, dead on the floor. His chest is a dark smear of blood, spreading from four holes. He stares at the ceiling, mouth agape.

"You killed him!" My stomach heaves. This is insane.

"Get in gear!" Jacobs shoves me across Shipley—across his body— and forces me out the back door.

The yard is chaotic. Soldiers must be nearby, running amongst the vehicles, because I see fleeting shadows cast by the glow of orange flames.

Flames?

Behind us, a huge fire reaches for the night sky. Several smaller fires—and by smaller, I mean those barely cresting the roof, not towering dozens of feet into the air—light up the base. The heat rolls over me like a Colorado summer.

"Come on!" Jacobs runs for the bunker doors, which are wide open. A trio of technicians, no longer in protective gear, come stumbling out. Jacobs fires over their heads. They accelerate their escape. "I've got to plant a transponder."

"What for?"

"So Captain Marin can bomb this heap to glass!" Jacobs shouts.

"No!" I grab his arm. "You can't."

"What?" Jacobs jerks free, his face golden in the flames' light. "Don't tell me you've gone Sierran. 'Cause I *will* put you down with those dogs."

"No, that isn't what I'm saying." I slap the folder against his chest. "We have to clean this place from the inside, or we'll kill everyone in a ten-mile radius."

CHAPTER TWENTY-FOUR

The bunker is abandoned.

Whatever protocols the Sierrans have in place for an attack on this base, securing the smallpox project is not high among them. Or perhaps the sheer surprise of the explosions convinced the technicians their lives were worth more than their patriotism.

Either way, we're unopposed.

"Hurry!" Jacobs's pacing the concrete and glass corridor.

"Will you please shut up?" I'm scanning the security protocols for containment. Down at the bottom, toward the back. "Here it is. We have to purge the oxygen tanks and ignite the lab's air afterward."

Jacobs's eyes go wide. "Serious? You know what that'll do, right?"

"Of course. Oxygen's flammable. It will burn every last trace of the smallpox."

"Yeah, and our butts if we're still down here. Plus, I bet it's gonna leave a really big crater."

There are dozens of oxygen tanks lining the back of the lab, and there's a storage room across the hall filled with even more cylinders. I can't make out the markings on all of them.

Then I remember the dead man and dying woman.

"Nick intends this stuff to kill your soldiers, not to mention every civilian refugee nearby," I snap. "A little fire's the least of our worries."

"Relax, sir. I'm just making sure you know the stakes."

"Trust me, I do." Tabitha's prone form fills my mind's eye. "Help me find the valve."

The blaring alarm outside and accompanying shouts make the task harder. I'm muttering under my breath when I come across a row of wheels, one of which is helpfully labeled "O2." I start cranking. The oxygen escaping hisses softly on the other side of the glass.

"Sounds like you got it," Jacobs hurries to the end of the hall. "I'm going to watch our exit. You got a plan for lighting it off? I'm not packing grenades, otherwise I'd offer."

I join him, then aim the Echo Watch at the stacks of cylinders.

"Oh." Jacobs tightens his grip on his gun. "Yeah, I was afraid of that."

The intensity builds in the Echo Watch until a hum fills the air. The heat's searing, yet my skin doesn't even redden. "Run."

Jacobs complies.

I fire the burst, and sprint after him, up the concrete ramp, straining for the black rectangle of the yawning door.

The explosion makes me stumble. Heat builds behind. There's a monstrous roar.

We hit open ground and run flat out toward the side of the base.

The shockwave lifts me off my feet, and for a single, scalding second, I imagine flying to be a glorious thing—until I tumble onto rocky ground slick with a thin layer of snow.

"Ow," Jacobs groans.

We were far enough away the impact didn't break any bones, but regaining our footing takes longer than I'd like. Flames churn through the bunker's entrance, sending a huge column of black smoke aloft. Terrible as it looks, I know it's doing its job to eliminate the virus.

Doesn't mean I want to stay anywhere near it.

Helicopter blades thump the air. It sounds like far more than the one I saw when Captain Marin's troops rescued me from downtown Rampart.

Jacobs waves me along. "Sounds like our boys are bringing the big guns!"

It's more than I could have imagined. Twenty attack helicopters fire on the base, demolishing vehicles, sending Sierran soldiers scattering into the dark countryside. The opposition is not without teeth, though; anti-aircraft guns and rockets slash through the night. Four helicopters go down.

The base. Tabitha. "This way!"

"What? We're not supposed to be heading *inside!*"

He's right, of course, but she can't die.

Choking on smoke, we forge through the halls, some of which are lopsided. At one point I jump over an open door. But the Zein quarters aren't damaged, not yet. Red emergency lights cast everything in a bloody gloom. Tabitha's still there, unhurt. She groans when I pick her up.

"Easy," I order Jacobs. "Grab her legs."

Muttering something I can't hear and suspect I'd rather not understand, we work our way back out.

Sierran soldiers defending the base pay us no attention, thankfully, and a few even direct us away from the fighting. Constant fire from both sides flashes back and forth at the front gates. A section of fence has collapsed; Jacobs and I trod it to freedom.

"All right. So, what's the extraction plan?" I huff.

"Not to save Commander Zein's twisted assassin girlfriend!" Jacobs grunts. "I get it, she's pretty and all—"

"I'm not leaving her to die!" I snap. "Besides, she'll have more intelligence for your war. Isn't that enough?"

"Just making sure you know what you're doing."

"Me too." Right now I'm wishing I was back at my desk, nitpicking a final design, or even soothing a set of argumentative clients like the Vitalis.

Because dragging the doppelgänger-spy version of my wife across a battlefield outside my city limits with my rival's should-be-non-existent son pushes the bounds of what my mind says is rational.

Engine noises build in the distance. Something large is coming our way. Before I can discern what's hiding in the black, flashes of light illuminate tanks. Big ones. A few seconds later their shells blow holes in the Sierran base. They rumble up the road, with the helicopter gunships wheeling overhead. The big Jeeps and armored, six-wheeled Thudders follow.

However many troops the Home Guard had brought to this raid prove too many for the Sierrans. They're melting into the distance, keeping up covering fire to shield the withdrawal. I'm keeping my head down as Jacobs and I carry Jess toward Rampart. I can't tell where we are compared to the city, other than on the west side. We could be on either bank of the Van River.

"Hold up." Jacobs drops Tabitha's legs. He unlimbers the rifle from around his shoulders, and crouches against the hillside. "We've got incoming."

I ease Tabitha to the ground. Her eyelids flutter. I'd rather she stay incapacitated for this move, because I'm not certain Jacobs and I could fend her off fully conscious. But with headlights sweeping across our hiding place, now's not the time for should-have.

"You gonna lend me a hand?" Jacobs shakes his wrist.

"Oh. Of course." I aim the Echo Watch.

But fortunately there's no need to turn the engine of the approaching truck into slag. It's a Thudder with Procyon markings, and the American flag emblazoned on the flanks, same model as I rode out of Rampart when I first arrived. It halts too close, spraying dirt over us. The doors bang open. Five Home Guard soldiers surround us.

Captain Marin and Loredana Lark are next out of the hatch.

"Sir!" Jacobs is on his feet and saluting. "Captain, it's good to see you."

"Good to see you unsinged, Sergeant." Marin's shaking his head, but he's got a broad grin that reminds me of Curt when we played our last round of pool at Bentley's—well, only a week or so ago. It feels like years past. "I know we discussed a signal flare. Obviously, you made the in-the-field decision one exploding truck wasn't sufficient."

Jacobs shrugs. "You know me, Captain. I aim to please."

"Well done." Marin joins me crouching by Tabitha's side. "And you've brought Christmas early. This is her, right?"

"Tabitha Boutros."

Marin reaches for her wrist. She moans. "Not dead."

"No. I wasn't going to kill her. You can question all you like and … well, I know she has to pay for what she's done. All I ask is she is kept unharmed."

"We have no desire to see anyone treated as the Sierrans treat their captives." Lark wears camouflage like the soldiers, but even those are more neatly pressed. "I am far more interested in the intelligence she offers. Aren't we all, Captain?"

Marin scowls. "Yes, ma'am. Would've been easier if she were killed in the breakout."

"Easier for you, but not for me."

"What'd you do, hit her over the head?"

I lift my wrist, letting the cuff fall back. Seems easier than constant explanation.

"My word," Lark murmurs. "You did it. The Echo Watch."

Marin whistles.

Lark touches the exterior. She shivers. "So cold."

Odd. The heat pulsing through my forearm should be evident to everyone.

"We're doing this, then?" Marin asks.

Lark eyes me in a way that reminds me of Sammy watching his dinner being served—hungrily. "Mr. Zein has kept his end of the bargain. We shall keep ours."

I drag my arm back. "Only if I have assurances Tabitha won't be hurt when I'm gone."

Explosions rattle the night. The pervasive gunfire ceases, but only long enough for a more explosions to fill the gap.

"This is hardly the time to request a notarized contract," Lark says wryly.

"That isn't what I meant. Your word will suffice … and if she's harmed, you won't be getting the Echo Watch back."

Marin and Lark share a look. Neither seems pleased, but with the escalating battle raging, no one seems intent on staying put. "As you wish," Lark says. "I give you my word, Agent Boutros will remain in our custody until such time as she can be arraigned for trial. In the meantime, perhaps we should adjourn to your point of entry."

"Good." I let the soldiers carry Tabitha away. "I'm ready to go home."

A second Thudder shows up, this one marked with a red cross atop a white square. Lark orders Boutros strapped down and manacled. By then, she's regained consciousness.

She stares blankly past me as Lark pats her down. "Clean."

"Okay, load up!" Marin waves us toward the first Thudder. "Last taxi's leaving."

He, Jacobs, and Lark get aboard with the contingent of soldiers. Jacobs waits for me at the back hatch. "You coming?"

"One moment." I stand over Tabitha. "Either way this ends, I will see Nick again."

"I understand." Her tone is hollow. "Don't do me any favors, Dominic. If you have to kill him, you have to kill him."

"It won't come to that."

"Yet, you've already got blood on your hands. Doesn't it make you feel powerful?"

It makes me feel—something. I won't deny, the fear leeching strength from me upon my arrival has abated. Not even the battle up the hill, now moving to the north, frightens me. "I will fight to regain my life."

"Make sure it's worth the price." Tabitha turns away. "Efforts can be misspent."

I touch her arm. She stays quiet, but reaches over, resting her palm on my knuckles.

The ambulance hustles off to the rear of the attacking Home

Guard column.

Our Thudder bounces along the countryside, until rough ground gives way to pavement. Soon we're speeding down the ruined streets of Rampart, the truck swerving occasionally. Dim orange lights are the only illumination in the rear compartment. Everyone's silent. Marin glances at me, nods. Jacobs stares at his feet, lips moving.

Lark rests her elbows on her knees. She steeples her fingers before her lips. "The portal will open at your command," she says. "I trust you've deconstructed the weapons features of the Echo Watch."

"Both incapacitating and destructive, yes."

"Very good. They're quite self-explanatory. But the portal—you must be cognizant of your destination. Lack of focus will find you lost in the Interstice."

"That wasn't necessary when I traversed before. Nick just threw me in."

"Yet he is the one who activated the portal. It was his intent that guided you here. The same applies in your case. One must be careful about navigating the Transect. When we first discovered its existence, there was no way to know whether it opened into something other than, say, a rock pile or thin air a hundred feet up. We tossed a few remote cameras through. Eventually we guided one back with clear video of a ramshackle loft."

I nod. "Not Noah's dove, but a reasonable facsimile."

"Indeed. Unfortunately, when we transported the Echo Watches to our headquarters, Commander Zein's forces intercepted the convoy. Killed everyone, took both. I can only assume he made good use of the data we'd assembled."

"The loft is in far better shape, yes."

"You won't have much time when you return. You must retrieve the second Echo Watch from him, by whatever means necessary."

"And if he won't give it to me?"

"Remove it." Lark leans back and folds her arms.

Jacobs nudges me. "I'd offer you my sidearm, but you've got that covered."

"Right. Appreciate that."

Eventually our truck halts. I step out. It's the same street. The wrecked apartment building looms against the night sky. The northwest horizon glows with the fires from the Sierran base. Gunfire rattles, far too close.

"Area's hot." Marin jumps out, with Jacobs right behind. "Ma'am, you'd better get clear. We'll provide cover."

Lark nods. She extends her hand to me. "Godspeed, Mr. Zein. We will be waiting."

"Thank you for your help."

The Thudder speeds off, leaving Marin, Jacobs, and I on the sidewalk.

"Okay." Marin hefts his rifle. "This is Zein's place."

"It's in much better shape where I come from," I say. "Except for the occupant."

Marin snorts. "Jacobs, take point. I'll flank."

"Roger that, Captain."

Jacobs leads the way up the rickety stairs. A yellow flashlight beam illuminates the steps in sharp relief with the surrounding gloom.

I brush my hands along the wall. Even with it being the middle of the night, I feel more aware of every creak, every gust of wind, every flicker of motion. My senses must have been badly warped when I exited the portal and stumbled out of the building.

Jacobs and Marin flank the door to the loft. Marin gestures his orders. Jacobs nods, then steps low into the room, flashlight beam sweeping across the space as he shifts his rifle from corner to corner. Marin follows, his gun aimed high. Their boots scratch on debris. Our breaths feather white in the cold air.

I pause in the ruined kitchenette. As devastated as the loft first appeared, it's oddly reassuring to be back atop the rumpled floor, boots crunching on broken glass. Stars peek through the clouds visible in the hole overhead. Loose fabric on the derelict couch flutters in the frigid breeze.

But I must watch where I step. Somewhere among the wreckage is the portal.

"Any time you're ready," Marin murmurs.

"One second." It appeared as a discoloration of the wood planks whenever I visited Nick. With it being so dark, tough … "Shine your lights over here."

Jacobs shifts his aim. A broad swath of the floor turns yellow. The beam drifts along, until I glimpse an arc between darker wood and lighter wood.

"Stop there."

The beam pauses. It takes a moment, but the arc disappears, until there's no variation in the wood.

"Right here." I step to the edge. I can't feel anything, even when I sweep my fingers through the air. The Echo Watch must detect the portal, somehow. I slowly raise that wrist.

The arc snaps back, more distinct than ever. The same pulsating bubble forms, and in its swirling surface are three faces—mine, Jacobs', and Marin's—staring in awe. Their clarity and that of our surroundings smears away, blurring across the outside the sphere, until the black shadow deep inside beings absorbing light.

"This is it?" Jacobs has to shout over the howling wind. "How do you get through?"

"Working on it!" Lark gave me precious few instructions, but I can recall Nick's stance well enough. I ignore Marin clamoring for my attention and focus on home. On Jess. On Curt. On Sammy. Dualpoint. Anna. Kaminsky. Father Hamra. Even Dr. Huang and the Vitalis.

But especially, the loft. Not this decrepit, sepulchral version, but the bright, relaxing, warm space in which Nick and I shared beers.

Before he conquered my life and dumped me into the one he'd fled.

I have to go back.

The Echo Watch, its heat suffusing my arm, gleams. Lines brighten yellow-white, as they do when preparing to fire, except the intensity builds without any discharge. Pressure ratchets down on my wrist until I'm certain the bones will break. But instead, the Echo Watch bursts apart into seven pieces, each one like a shard of pottery, a sliver of molten metal. They spin clockwise, humming.

It's working.

More flashes—only these are from outside. They twinkle through the open wall and windows, far brighter than the stars. I'd stand there staring like an idiot, except Jacobs pulls me to the floor.

Only then do I hear the gunfire through the roaring storm winds generated by the patrol.

"This is Captain Marin! We need support! Sierran patrol at our location!" He blurts the message into his radio, then props his rifle on the slumped couch. "Zein! Get through that thing! We'll cover you!"

I crawl forward, sparing only a brief glance back at him. His face contorts as he returns fire, the muzzle flashes freezing his visage in the midst of shouting. My brain fills in the gaps by contrasting Curt laughing over a beer, seated across from me at Caerphilly, the night I saw myself outside the bar and thought I was hallucinating.

Jacobs, the son of my rival, who doesn't exist where I come from, crawls toward the window. He hollers at Marin, who rolls something across the floor. I see a metal sphere before Jacobs hurls it into the street. The explosion makes dust fall from the remaining rafters.

The wind catches said dust in midair and drags it into the portal.

More gunfire slaps the side of the building. Jacobs cries out, flattens himself. Drywall and brick dust cloud his position. Bullets chew chunks out of the couch.

There's a meaty *thwap-thwap* repeated as they hit Marin.

He jerks about, a marionette on invisible strings, then flops to the floor when those same strings are cut.

"Curt!" I struggle against the wind's pull, but it's already lifting me off the floor. I dig my fingers into gaps between the boards, straining toward him. There must be something I can do.

He's slumped against the wall, eyes closed. A dark pool expands beneath him.

I anchor myself alongside him, scrambling to find a pulse, a sign of life. Nothing.

"Captain!" Jacobs hurries for us, oblivious to the continued gunfire. He drops to his knees at Marin's boots, teeth clenched. "Sir!"

"You have to go!" I shout. "You have to get out of here!"

Jacobs stares, uncomprehending. Then he digs beneath Marin's jacket, his shirt, until he finds dog tags. Jacobs pulls them free. "No! You need cover! Go!"

Outside, vehicle noises interrupt the weapons fire. More shooting. Shouting. I can't tell which side is winning. All I know is soldiers are coming up the stairs.

The Echo Watch spins faster. It's dragging me back to the portal, the air between us reverberating with the most unsettling vibration.

Jacobs follows, digging his heels so he won't be sucked in, his weapon aimed for the door.

Three men appear in it.

Sierran uniforms.

They exchange shots with Jacobs—and miss, but he loses his footing. He stumbles goes end over end. He hits the sphere and is pulled inside.

I throw myself after him.

No sooner do I grab his ankle, the two of us floating in freefall, then the blinding light builds from the center of the black hole. I squeeze my eyes shut.

Jacobs' cry twists into a long, drawn-out groan, and everything around me ceases as the intense heat sweeps me away.

This time I know better than to leap to my feet. I can't afford to be disoriented.

I open my eyes.

The beams above are in great shape, and even better, there's no hole in the ceiling. Brick walls retain their shape. The wood floor beneath my back is nice and flat, without gap or splinter. No broken glass, either. The windows are intact.

Blue skies. I haven't felt this warm in days.

I ease off the floor, mindful of my head spinning. Yes, all the furnishings are in the right place. Even the faded pop logo adorns the wall. Whatever mess the portal left when Nick threw me into it has been cleaned up. There's no lights on, either, which means Nick and Chris are gone.

Jacobs groans.

Jacobs? I help him upright. "You shouldn't be here."

"Didn't have much choice," he mutters. "Your windy space whirlpool sucked me down the drain."

"Yes, well … let me see what we can do."

"You do that." Jacobs rubs his forehead. "I'm gonna sit here and hold my brains together. And try not to ralph all over this floor … wait a second."

Jacobs squints at his surroundings. "This is … nice."

"It is. It's the way it should be." I cross to the window and place my hand on the tinted glass.

There's my skyline.

Jacobs joins me. "That's—wow."

"Rampart."

"Yeah, but, nothing's damaged. It hasn't looked this good for years, and even then, it didn't look like—the future." He taps the glass. "Those are the cars?"

"Look, we need to get out of here. There's no telling when Chris will be back, though if Nick's inserted himself into my life, he's either at Dualpoint or with one of my clients."

Jacobs nodded. "I'm gonna pretend like that all makes sense. I don't suppose, then, I can wander around town in my stolen Sierran uniform."

"No. I suggest we liberate some clothes from our host."

Together we cobble together outfits from Nick's wardrobe in the other room. He returns the Swiss Army knife to my possession. I find my personal items on the dresser. Odd. Why did Nick leave them lying about for all this time? Well, at least I can dress in my own clothing. No more playing soldier.

"Hey." Jacobs is looking at the wall, in the middle of pulling on a blue long-sleeved shirt. The contents of his Sierran uniform are lined up on the bed, including zip ties and ammunition for the rifle. "What's up with this calendar?"

"What do you mean?"

"Says it's October."

"So?"

"So, the one we've got back at Home Guard says December. A year ago."

CHAPTER TWENTY-FIVE

The first thing I do after returning to my world is dial Jess.

It's a futile effort. A droning female voice informs me the person I'm trying to reach doesn't have voicemail set up.

I try again, and once more, but each time, the calls go unanswered. They only ring twice, too.

Jess never leaves her phone off the hook, so to speak. We're able to text or call each other whenever. It's how I can run errands while out between appointments.

Perhaps more surprising, Nick hasn't canceled my phone.

"I don't suppose you got one of those nice rides waiting for us down there, do you?" Jacobs is positioned by the window, as watchful as a hawk perched on a skyscraper. "Because I'd really like to drive over roads that don't have craters or aren't lined with IEDs."

"I doubt it's still there." The BMW isn't parked anywhere near, up or down the block. Nick's commandeered it for his own uses. That would explain why my keys are gone.

My watch and, thankfully, my wedding ring are on the dresser. Nick has his own, of course, so he has no need of duplicates. His reason for not throwing any of my effects away is likely the same that gave him confidence I'd never go to the police. No one would believe there were two of us.

Fine. I'm resigned to the fact. This doesn't have to involve the police. I can handle Nick himself.

But I cannot do it alone.

I find Curt's contact. <Hey. You have a second to grab coffee or tea this morning? Feel like catching up?>

His contact, like Jess's, is a photo. In Curt's case it's him, bearded and grinning, flashing a thumbs' up. He wears mirrored sunglasses. Where's that picture from? We went skiing, couple years back.

I can't help replacing that face with Captain Marin's as blood seeps from his body and life fades from his eyes.

"Hey." Jacobs taps me on the shoulder. "If this is the place, we've got to move."

"I don't understand it. I went through the portal five days ago, between two identical points. How did I travel a year back in time?"

"Dunno. But like I said, it isn't supposed to be October. It's almost Christmas. By our accounting."

"That's not right."

Jacobs shrugged. "Not even as weird as the calendar saying we're off by twenty-six months."

My mind reels. What I know of theoretical physics could fill my pants pocket, but the portal must have more qualities than what Lark told me. It traverses space *and* time. Obviously those two are more fluid than I'd imagined, if their Earth lags behind ours by hundreds of days.

Wait. Lark. She exists here. And based on what she'd hinted about herself back there, she may be of more help than the average person who's unaware of the Interstice. "We should get to Procyon."

Jacobs frowns. "You think the base is here, too?"

"No. There is no base. But Loredana Lark is in town, as a point person for Procyon to build a new facility downtown. I'm—or was—the lead architect for the project."

"Okay. Yeah, that's a good idea, I guess."

I throw out my arms. "I'm sorry, do you have any input? Because I'm running out of options."

"Hey, this isn't what I trained for." He pats the Sierran rifle leaning against the couch. "This is what I trained for. This is what I know. Every morning, I got up from my bunk knowing Rampart was a war-torn wreck that only rats, feral dogs, and Sierran scum skulked around in. Now I'm drooling on the window because the place where I grew up got a second chance. So excuse me if I'm having trouble coming up with a plan!"

I hadn't considered the effect this transit had on him. It could be worse than mine, especially given that he knows he doesn't exist here and, more sobering, his father is dead. The father whom he idolizes, and who I told him is a first-class jerk. "Sorry, Sergeant."

"Don't worry about it. When you're ready to move out, let me know. Meanwhile, I'm all about raiding this guy's refrigerator. Good-bye, rations."

I brush aside any concerns I have for Jacobs rummaging through Nick's food and instead focus on the fact that Curt hasn't texted me back. My guts twist. He's never this late.

Finally the phone buzzes. <I have free time at 11:30. Shattered Mug. You're paying.>

Right. <Okay, see you then.>

That's it. No Z, no wondering what's been going on. No questions or greetings.

I shove the phone into my pocket and glower. Nick, what have you been doing in my absence?

Time to find out.

I have thirty-five dollars in my pocket. There's an ATM out on Federal, so I lead Jacobs to it.

There's not a cloud in the sky. Aircraft trace neat, white tracks across the brilliant blue. No wind, and the sun's enough to fight off the cool breeze. Everything about this Rampart is better—even the alley is cleaner.

Jacobs can't stop staring. He's physically incapable of closing his mouth. It's worse when we get onto Federal. He stops walking, staring at the people passing by.

"This is—it's how it should be," he murmurs. "No bombs. No rubble. No ambushes. Everyday life."

"You'll have a chance to get your Rampart back that way," I say. "Have faith."

He chuckles. "You sound like Dad."

"Yes. About that …" I shove my card into the ATM.

"Yeah, I know. Won't be seeing him here. And I'm not here either." He frowns. "That last part's a good thing for us, seeing as how the cops won't be puzzled by two of me."

"Good point." Hang on. The card's rejected.

"Problem?"

"Possibly." I pull out my phone, bring up my Amazon account. Password's changed.

"Great," I mutter. "Nick's moved right in. There's no extra money at the moment."

"This mean we're stuck with whatever you've got in your pocket?"

"It does." My credit card comes up as likewise invalid. He's thorough. But he left my phone, which could be either a lapse, or intentional, if he had some purpose for maintaining the old number.

Nick probably has no idea I'd back.

Fortunately the Shattered Mug is a walkable distance from here—not convenient, but walkable. By the time we get there, I've managed to keep Jacobs from stopping and asking about every single business we pass.

Sheryl is parked across Juniper from the coffee shop. I grin. Never thought I'd be so happy to see a Jeep. "Wait in here. I won't be long."

"No way, sir. The captain and Ms. Lark wanted me to watch your back, so that's what I'm doing."

"Curt's going to be mad enough without my having to explain a stranger's presence."

"Then I'll check out the store across the street, but I'm not getting back in the Jeep without you."

I shake my head and give him $10 from my wallet. "Knock yourself out."

He snatches it up and heads for a convenience store.

It's all I can do to not run between traffic, throw the doors to the Shattered Mug open, and give Curt a massive bear hug. Once I get inside, and breath in that sweet, sweet aroma, I realize that's the right decision.

Curt's watching his mug, stone-faced.

"Hey." I sit opposite him. "Curt, it's good to see you. You have no idea—"

"Cut the chatter." He doesn't look me in the eye. "What do you want?"

"What do I want? I wanted to see you. How've you been?"

"Fine."

"Curt, look, I know things might have been confusing lately—"

"Not confusing at all, Dominic. I'm assuming you're here because you want something, but I got news for you: If all you're doing is pumping me for expertise, and ignoring advice, then you can pay for my coffee and walk back out that door."

There's a cold, hard edge to his words. Dominic? He never calls me Dominic unless he's really worried, or very upset. Judging by the way he glares at the table, it's the latter. "Curt, I'm sorry. I tried to explain this to you before—"

"Hey, you know what?" Curt pushes off from the table. Now he does make eye contact, and I'd rather he didn't. "Don't care. Not. One. Bit. You've put everything at risk, and put me in a rough position, so don't try the whole 'sorry' business, because you're not. You're getting everything you want, Mr. Co-Owner of Dualpoint, and if that means you'll just step on the people you used to rely upon—and relied upon you—then I guess we're done."

"Will you listen?" I stand to match his posture, mindful of the curious looks we're getting from everyone in the café. "That isn't me."

"No kidding. It isn't the Dominic Zein I've known half my life." He snorts. "It's the new and improved version."

He stalks off, without finishing his coffee.

"Hey!" I grab his arm as we're both about to leave. "I need your help! That guy, that person who's been doing—whatever it is he's been doing, he is literally not me. He's a double of me, a doppelgänger, from another Earth, and he threw me out of this one. I've just made my way back. Together we have to stop him!"

It sounds even crazier than it did in my head. Curt sneers, reminding me an awful lot of Captain Marin. He yanks his arm free and is out the door.

There's no other options. I have to make Curt believe me. If not my best friend, then who else?

I follow him into the street. Jacobs sees us, crosses from the other side. He's got a *Rampart Post* rolled up under one arm, and a packet of Twinkies in the other. His expression as he takes a bite is rapturous.

"Curt, this is the last time I'm going to ask you nicely." My mounting frustration is burying any concern I have for his well-being.

"Nicely?" Curt turns around. He's got the driver's side door of Sheryl open, his keys in his hand. "What, you're going to fight me? That's funny. Last time we did that we were drunk off our butts and you—"

I stun him with the Echo Watch.

Curt's face is frozen in shock. I catch him, grimacing under his superior weight. The keys hit the pavement.

"This is your plan?" Jacobs grabs his feet and helps me shove him across the driver's seat to the passenger side. "Your big plan? You're gonna ask your best buddy for help then zap him when he says no?"

"How'd you know he said no?" I start Sheryl and slam the door shut.

Jacobs clambers in the back, pulling his door closed as Sheryl's tires squeal away from the curb. "Maybe the part where you two looked like two old ladies bickering over the Bingo scores was the tip off."

"Shut up." I press Sheryl through traffic, barely able to keep her at the speed limit, but at this moment, I'm not concerned about that. I take out my phone, redial Jess.

Still nothing.

"Eyes on the road!" Jacobs snaps.

A car horn honks. I swerve, missing a pickup by a foot. The driver's irate enough I hear his muffled tirade through closed windows.

And now I've run a red light. Perfect.

"What's your genius idea now?"

"We have a vehicle."

"Yeah, until your pal wakes up."

"When we get back to the apartment, go up and get your gun." It sounds like a terrible. Is Sergeant Ambrose and Rampart PD watching the place? Or has Nick kept his—my—nose clean enough they've given up?

Somehow, I doubt Nick's let them finger him or Chris for Tyson's death, the joyride with his truck, or the vigilante attacks I now realize Nick conducted with the Echo Watch. Those could have been Nick testing the weapon aspect.

Great. He's been training.

I skid up in front of the apartment entrance. Jacobs is out before Sheryl comes to a complete stop. For a moment, I wonder how he's going to get through the front door, since I forgot it locks automatically, but Jacobs pulls it open with no problem. A magazine falls out.

He's gone less than a minute, and when he returns, there's Nick's blue jacket, wrapped into a thick bundle. Jacobs hops back in. "Go."

I flip a U-turn, aggravating more drivers, praying the entire time I'm not going to show up in someone's Twitter feed as the Crazy Downtown Driver guy.

"Where's the police station?" Jacobs uncovers the gun and checks the magazine.

"That way." I point as I turn the Jeep the opposite direction.

"Okay …"

"I have another stop to make before we risk contacting them."

I take the next corner so fast, Curt thumps against the door. He groans. "Man, my head."

"At this rate, I think the cops will find us," Jacobs mutters.

The sight of Dualpoint's distinctive roofs makes me want to cheer from the top of the Jeep. I'd feared I was going to make the last turn and see the dilapidated liquor store from the other Earth, where I almost got myself eaten by feral dogs.

Still strange not seeing Tyson's car here—his truck, or the replacement he got when Nick had Chris dump his in the Van River.

This elation is counterweighted by Curt regaining consciousness.

"Did you knock me out?" He stares, incredulous. "I mean, chloroform me or something? No, wait. It felt like you Tased me. Bee stings. Really bad bee stings. I didn't throw up in Sheryl, did I?"

"No. You should be okay. Let me check your pulse."

Curt nods, but then pulls back, suddenly incensed. "Hey, no! You're a jerk. You've been so busy fouling up everything except for work that you've—"

There's a click behind us. The black barrel of Jacobs' rifle hovers an inch from Curt's temple.

Curt's eyes, wide as headlights, flick sideways. "Uh, Z …"

"You stay put and be quiet, Captain," Jacobs says. "I know this is weird but listen to the guy with the gun."

"Captain?"

Jacobs grimaces. "Sorry, sir. Force of habit."

"What?"

"Curt. Stay put. I need to check something. I'll explain everything." To Jacobs, I add, "Don't shoot him."

"You already did."

I leave them there, glad to see my BMW isn't in the lot. Nick must be out at an appointment with a client. One of my clients. It occurs to me I'm not even wearing the same outfit he might don today, which will cause even more confusion.

Doesn't matter.

Kaminsky intercepts me at my office door. He beams. "Dominic! Back already? I wanted to catch up with you about the Procyon designs. Ms. Lark's quite happy with your latest changes. In fact, she's got them fast tracked with her supervisors. Say, did you change your shirt?"

"Stopped home to, ah, change it. Spilled tea." I clap him on both shoulders. "It's good to see you again."

Kaminsky arches an eyebrow, but chuckles as he removes himself from my grasp. "Easy there. You already got your raise. Hugging the old man won't get you more. You'll be all set to talk with Lark about the changes?"

"Definitely ready." I'm overjoyed he's not dead, considering the last time I saw his face it was in a grainy photograph as Nick put a bullet through his skull.

"Good man." Kaminsky leans in. "By the way, this thing with Anna ... whatever your personal life's like these days isn't my concern, but you two work well as part of Dualpoint's team. Don't jeopardize it, all right? I count on you two to smooth things out."

He leaves me outside the office, mouth agape.

Whatever he means, I'll puzzle out later. I grab Sergeant Ambrose's business card from its hiding place on my desk—the desk where everything's in the same place. Nick hasn't rearranged much.

But I take the chance to scan his email screen, which is wide open. Nothing earth-shattering. There are emails back and forth with Lark, talking details about Procyon. Her responses are terser than I remember.

I snap a shot of the exchange with my phone and head for the back door.

Anna intercepts me, by pressing in at a range reserved only for Jess. "Hey. You changed."

"What?"

"Your shirt."

"Oh. Spilled tea." Her hands rest on my chest. They burn like irons "I've, ah, got to get back there."

"Not yet." She pulls me in close for a deep, passionate kiss, her grasp on my collar firm.

Stunned, I don't respond, then let myself sink into reciprocation. It's everything I'd imagined. Not in my wildest fantasies did I think—

No. I break us apart. "Well, ah, yes. Like I said, have to go."

She smirks, lips quirked in a fashion that promises I'd enjoy the situation much more if I'd shut up and kiss her. "Okay. I'll see you tonight. My place."

Her place?

I hurry out to the parking lot. Curt tracks me with an intensity I'd only seen his counterpart Captain Marin reserve for Sierran soldiers. "You going to tell my why this kid's ready to shoot me?"

"Not ready, Captain, just prepared," Jacobs says.

"Curt." My fingers tighten on the wheel. "Me and Anna?"

Curt sighs. "Yeah, what about it? I mean, other than it being the worst idea you've ever had. Also, I told you so."

"But I didn't—"

"Come on. I saw you at Bentley's three nights ago. Like high school kids copping a feel." Curt shakes his head. "I can't believe you did this to Jess."

"That wasn't me. It's someone who looks like me."

"Right. You mentioned that."

"Well, it's true." I get us out of the parking lot and head for Rampart Valley High School. "Who do you think is sitting behind us?"

Curt glances back. Jacob lifts his chin. "I don't have a clue but, man, he's like Tyson Jacobs minus twenty years."

"Exactly that. He's Tyson's son." I dial Jess's number. Nothing. Again.

"Uh, yeah, no he isn't Tyson doesn't have any kids."

"He doesn't here. On the other Earth, he does. And he's a pastor."

Curt stares at both of us, then bursts out laughing. "That's the best explanation you've got for why you've been a complete tool?"

"Yes."

"What did you knock me out with, a hammer?"

"This." I wave the Echo Watch in front of him. "It doubles as a weapon. But it opens the path between the worlds."

"Your bracelet."

I sigh. "Curt, I need you to dial back the sarcasm and work with me. Nick—me—the one you've known for the past week, he's on the run from the people who sent me back. We have to catch him."

"Is that what armed sort-of-Tyson is for?"

"Sure can tell you aren't the captain," Jacobs mutters. "He wasn't denser than concrete."

"Shut up."

"Both of you zip it!" I snap. "I don't need this nonsense! Nick has taken over my life, and judging by what I've just encountered, he's made a bigger mess than I figured. I have to tell Jess, sort this all out, and stop him. You're going to help me."

"Or what? You'll drop me and Sheryl somewhere we can't get in your way?"

"Just you. I need Sheryl."

"Um, no."

I aim the Echo Watch in his face. Heat pulsates around my hand. Sparks dance at the edge of my vision. "Curt. Enough."

He licks his lips. "Okay, take it easy. What did you have in mind?"

"We'll find out when we get there." The high school's five minutes away. I speed up.

I send Jess a text this time. <Come outside. I'm waiting.>

A police car drives by the front of the school, slowly. Whether or not it's Ambrose doesn't matter. I'd rather no one see me. Waiting by Sheryl, with the whole building sprawled in front of me, makes me feel as exposed as running with Marin and the troops under fire.

Jess comes out the front door.

My heart leaps. She's as beautiful as I remember—which isn't that far back a memory to retrieve, since I just spent several hours with Tabitha Boutros. Where she was severe, though, Jess is smooth. She's got on a slim gray shirt, with long sleeves and tall neck, plus a green skirt. Her hair's in a ponytail.

She's walking fast.

I intercept her at the steps down from the front walk. "Jess! Thank God. Listen, I need to tell you what—"

She slaps me.

Open palm. No idea what the mark looks like, but judging by the buzzing of my cheek, it's a brute.

"I can't believe you." She hauls off again, but I catch her wrist before it can connect. Tears stream down her face. "Let. Go."

"Jess, please." I hold on. "Let me explain."

"Explain? How you slept with Anna and made me look like a fool when I denied it? Is this payback for trying to have an honest discussion about starting a family?" She pulls free. "I'm staying at Marisa's until we work this out."

"Work it out? I didn't sleep with Anna! You're my wife. I'd never—"

"Don't. Don't stand there and lie to me again. Over and over. And I never once …" She shakes her head. "Go away, Dominic. Leave me alone."

She storms back inside.

I stand there, alone on the sidewalk. The Jeep's engine rumbles behind me. Sheryl's waiting. I raise my phone to text Jess, or call, but pause with finger over the keys. What good's that going to do? She's a mess. And it's because of my mess.

Nick's mess.

I want to hurl the phone. He's going to pay for this. I'm starting to think it wouldn't be such a bad thing of Jacobs shot him. We could claim he threatened our lives.

Perhaps I should do the shooting.

My phone buzzes. I stab the answer key, not caring who it is, and ready to bite someone's head off. Even Curt's. "What?"

"Morning, Dominic," Nick says. "I see you're back. That's a problem."

CHAPTER TWENTY-SIX

It's him.

"What, no hello? No, how have you been?" Nick chuckles. "I thought we were better friends than that."

"You're insane."

"Name-calling's the refuge of those incapable of forming convincing arguments, Dominic. And it's certainly no way to greet the caretaker of your life."

"Caretaker?" I whirl around, ready to punch Nick, but he's nowhere to be seen. There's plenty of traffic, and dozens of parked cars. People come and go from businesses lining the streets around the schools. He could be standing in one of the apartment complexes nearby. "You took over my life. You ruined my reputation with the people I love."

"You never used to be this prone to exaggeration."

"You literally kicked me out of this world!"

Nick laughs again. "Well, I can't dispute that one. Despite your sudden reappearance and rather cross attitude, I'm actually happy to hear from you. Not to say you being back doesn't interfere with my goals, but I can handle minor difficulties."

"We're going to find you, Nick. I'm sending you back."

"By we you must mean dear Curt and your newfound buddy

from the Home Guard, hmm? Tell me, how is Captain Marin? Can't do the job himself anymore, I take it, so he sends his minions to babysit you."

I may not be able to see him, but he must be near enough to see us. I head for the Jeep, scanning every window, every car, every person's face. None look like mine.

None look like Chris's, either.

Jacobs gets out of the Jeep, sans gun, thankfully. "What's wrong?"

I wave off the question. "You're following us."

"Oh, not visually, if that's what your worried about. I'm not brainless enough to put my man on your tail when you're tooling about town with a member of the local armed forces. No, it's simpler than that."

"Nick, whatever you think you're doing, it won't work."

Jacobs' scowls when I say the name. He motions for me to get back in the Jeep.

"Been working pretty well thus far. Let me see—rising to the top post at your architectural firm? Check. Spending quality time—and I do mean *quality*—with the lovely Anna? Check. Assuming every aspect of your life? Check. Trimming away the excess so your life, which is now my life, becomes leaner and more manageable? Check."

I can't believe he's so cavalier with the things I value most. Then again, I've witnessed how he treats the people he's not trying to hoodwink. There was plenty of fear directed toward me by his subordinates, and Tabitha was crushed when she realized Nick had abandoned her.

"Now your turn," Nick says. "Since I have no intention of returning there, how's life on the other side of the Interstice?"

"Your base is destroyed." The revelation is delicious. "The smallpox project is finished. I assume Home Guard is busy rounding up the rest of the Sierran troops who escaped."

"That's unfortunate." He works to keep the jovial tone, but stern quality creeps in. "The vaunted Captain Marin, at it again."

"He's dead."

"Oh? Silver lining. Though I will miss matching wits with him. The man had tactical skills. You know, that's been one of the oddest things about living as you, Dominic—hanging out with your pal Curt. I almost couldn't stand to look him in the eye, given his double's insistence on making my plans more difficult to fulfill. That's part of why I dumped him. That and his sanctimonious hypocrisy. Telling me not to fool around with Anna, when he's on the constant watch for the next ex-girlfriend."

I start the engine. Curt makes a face. "Who're you on with? What happened with Jess?"

I cover the receiver. "Nick. The other me."

"Don't leave everyone out, Dominic," Nick says, his voice muffled. "Put us on speaker phone."

"You're not—"

"Yes, yes, I know. I won't get away with it. You and your scrappy band will foil my plan. I've heard it before from many individuals. Guess what? They're all dead."

Curt's face goes blank. He points at the phone, then me, then the phone again.

"Now listen, once you leave the high school, do me a favor and stay away from Jessica. She's a great girl. But she isn't Anna. She doesn't get this whole thing I'm doing. Don't get me wrong, it's been nice playing house with her, but as I said, I'm making life leaner."

"You're disgusting. Tabitha's waiting back there for you, or she was, before I told her what really happened."

For a moment I assume he's hung up. When his voice returns, the cheery, chatty version is replaced by the same Nick who threw me into the Interstice portal. "You should have stayed clear of her."

"Sorry, Nick, that wasn't part of *my* plan. It was necessary when I infiltrated your base and snuck a peek at the plans for your smallpox holocaust. She thought you were dead, or at best, on a secret mission." My grip tightens on the phone. "You should have seen her when I told her the truth. She loves you, and this is how you treat her? How you repay her loyalty?"

"Gracie isn't Jess. The two are not synonymous. And she—Gracie …"

"Don't bother. You're transparent, Nick. This is all about you. I don't care whether you're running from your past or scheming for a future. This ends. All of it."

"Yes, yes, fine." Somehow my threats seem less effective when the recipient isn't worried about them. "Tell me this, though: Is Tabitha loyal? To the cause, I mean?"

"The cause? I don't know. She's in Procyon's hands."

"Procyon," Nick spits. "You mean Loredana Lark."

"I mean the very one."

"I'd wondered about her. I assume she's how you got back … Ah. Yes. You took the other Echo Watch."

"I did."

"How badly hurt is Tabitha?" There's nothing akin to remorse in his voice. Only curiosity, like a kid poking an ant hill.

"Not at all. She gave it to me, because she thought I was you."

"Oh, well done. Well done indeed. If you can pass as me, you must have thoroughly enjoyed it all. Enjoyed playing the powerful commander."

I glance around the car. Jacobs is watching out the windows, hand on the rifle, trying to figure out where our opponents are. Curt, meanwhile, looks appalled by everything he's hearing. At least he's not treating me like a pariah. "No, I didn't."

"Sure. Keep telling yourself that. Whenever you use the Echo Watch, don't think about how it makes you the most powerful person on the planet—powerful in a way that fool Benton could never fathom. Funnily enough, only Lark and those in the know at Procyon realize the true potential the Echo Watch represents, which is why it's awfully foolish of her to help you return."

"What does that mean?"

"It means, you idiot, that once I kill your friends and cut your arm off, I'll have both of them. No sharing necessary."

"I don't—"

"Of course you don't." Nick sighs. "That's one of the problems pretending to be you, having to dumb myself down. It's taxing. One of the first things I'll relish doing once I've cleaned your life up to my liking. Speaking of which, I'll make sure to start with my own traitor."

"What traitor?"

"Seriously? Have you not done your homework? Dominic, do you honestly think Chris is the only one of my compatriots I brought through the Interstice?" He laughs. "This world of yours is *crawling* with them. When I'm through, I'll have my new network that rivals anything Benton's built. It's a shame Tabitha can't be part of it, but hey, I've got a replacement or two for her. I digress. Chris is on his way to my traitor's location, and when he's done with him, he's coming for you. Have to say—the technological advances are one of the nicest surprises your world offers. That, and the lack of a war on American soil. Both make it so much easier to navigate."

He hangs up. I scowl at the blank screen. Technology. Navigate. He was very specific.

I flip over the phone, and strip off the case. There's a thick bump on the back, a black object nestled against the battery cover.

"What's that?" Jacobs asks.

"I think he's tracking our phone through GPS."

"GPS."

"Global satellite positioning."

Jacobs whistles. "On your phone? That tiny thing? Wow."

Curt snickers. "Where are you from, the 1980s?"

"You two can it." I fumble for the deck of cards Marin gave me. Nick said something about a traitor. It has to be someone close in his ranks, then. I flip through the cards, fumbling a few. They flutter to the floor.

A somber face stares up at me.

No. I pick it up, feeling increasingly sick. He's not wearing glasses, or the clerical collar, but otherwise, there's no mistaking of the Jack of Clubs.

Father Olin Hamra.

My cell phone is a liability. I throw it out the window. Curt suggests I back over it with Sheryl. I happily oblige his sentiment.

Jacobs has ideas on how to manage our problems, but I don't hear anything except the roar of the engine. I don't stop when we pull into the church parsonage driveway. I ignore Curt's shout when I slam the door shut.

Everything's a haze of anger, bubbling up after weeks of aggravation, boiling over until Father Hamra answers the door. He smiles, but after one look at my face, he becomes as somber as if he were conducting funeral rites. "You've returned."

"You knew." I press into the kitchen. He gives way before me, until his hips hit the table. "This whole time. I came to you, confiding about doppelgängers, and the whole time, you knew he was here."

"It was always part of his agenda, but I couldn't go forward with my part."

"You're one of them!" I snap. "What did you do with the real Father Hamra? Did you kill him, like Nick and his thug killed that veteran so Chris could take his place? How many more deaths are on your hands!"

"None!" Hamra's vehemence halts my onslaught. "I have never killed a man."

"That's why you came here, isn't it? To kill the real Father Hamra, take his place, and then—spy on me, in preparation for Nick's arrival." I shake my head, disgusted with both of us. "That whole story about your family dying, it was all some awful cover."

"No. Every word is true." Hamra sags into a chair. "Only, I did not reveal all of them to you. Yes, Father Hamra's family died, and yes, it drove him to the darkest despair. It was during this time I watched him, became familiar with his routines, prepared myself to step into his shoes. You must understand, I was never a devout man. My childhood beliefs barely survived the wars and struggled under

Commander Zein's leadership. Trust me when I say keeping Father Hamra under observation forced me to answer difficult questions I'd spent decades avoiding."

"Is that when you killed him? When you'd absorbed everything useful?"

"No. He killed himself."

I stare at him, the words dissipating from my mouth.

Hamra points behind himself, to the window. "I was in a car, watching through that window with binoculars. He put a pistol to his head and pulled the trigger. There was surprisingly little sound. Naturally, if I wanted to subsume his position, I could not let anyone find him dead. So, I cleaned up the mess, and disposed of the body. That was when I became Father Hamra, instead of Agent Olin Hamra."

"And … your mission continued."

"No. I freed myself. I posed as this man of faith, imitating him in every way, and one morning, as I stood before the people giving mass, preaching words in which I placed no confidence, I … believed." He smiles. "I cannot explain it. From that moment forth, it ceased to be an act and became a vocation. It unshackled me from my vile mission. Nick, naturally, did not understand, yet he also declined to draw attention to himself by having me killed."

I join him at the table. There's no denying his tale. If it's another lie, it's a very convincing one. Yet, when I saw him with our people, and heard him proclaim forgiveness, it was all the truth. "Two people, two versions of the same person, living on opposing worlds, separated by an interdimensional gap. Who are they? Both share blood, DNA, physical appearances, skills …but are they the same person?"

"What are you asking, Dominic?"

"Would God create two of the same soul? Condemn one and save the other? Or do they share a soul? Were you and the former Father Hamra one and the same? Are Nick and I the same?" I massage my forehead. "I cannot be tied to him for the rest of my life, let alone the eternal life to come."

Hamra gets up, crosses to the cupboards. He searches through them, sliding canisters aside, relocating boxes. The open and shut of the doors provides a steady rhythm. "My friend had a car, many years ago, an Austin-Healey Sebring convertible. It was a lovely vehicle. Dark blue, cream interior. You could have parked it in the Guggenheim and people would have lined up around the block to pay admission, such was its beauty. Rare craftsmanship. He drove it every day, rain or snow, and even the gas shortages during the worst of the fighting didn't dissuade him from taking short trips."

"As with most things, the vehicle deteriorated, its engine failed, and it soon required far more in repair than my friend could afford. The day he sold it to a restoration company, we all joined him for drinks at his favorite pub. The Irish could not have performed a better wake."

Hamra opens one last door. He smiles at whatever he sees. "A decade later, when my friend was in better financial straits, he found another 1959 Austin-Healey Sebring convertible. Imagine his delight as he read the advertisement of identical specifications, gazed at the same blue paint job. It was a duplicate of his car, right down to the stitching on the upholstery. He later discovered it had been manu-factured at the same facility."

He sets a small canvas backpack on the table. Nimble fingers undo the strings. "He paid the cost, money being irrelevant to him at his juncture, and met with the seller for a drive. My friend put the car through every test, subjected it to the same stresses he'd once foisted on his favorite. When he finally parked back in the man's dealership lot, he got out of the car, ran his palm over the hood, and stared at his reflection in the perfect polish. Then he handed the keys back to the dealer."

"The dealer was, understandably, vexed. He had assumed he had perpetrated the perfect sale. 'Sir,' he said, 'This is built the same as your old car.'"

"My friend replied, 'It may drive the same, it may look the same, but when I get behind the wheel, I know something is different.'"

"The situation isn't the same as a used car deal, Father," I say.

"But you appreciate the meaning." He reaches into the bag. "Your soul is your own, Dominic. Our Lord in Heaven made it specifically, without a concern as to what other souls are like. When He knit you together, he put in you that mysterious spark that he placed into no other. Commander Zein has a spark, too, a soul made only for him. Whether or not he has misused it is not your responsibility."

"Thank you, Father, but I feel he is my responsibility. If I can help right the wrongs he has committed—"

"It will not gain you admission to Heaven, Dominic. You have already gained eternal life."

He hands me a tiny book, its cover of faded blue fabric. The pages are browned, but not yet brittle. I open it.

"My father served in the United States Navy," Hamra says. "He carried it with him everywhere. 'A Prayer Book for Soldiers and Sailors.' Do not concern yourself with denominational differences. Take it as a reminder that things from our world and things from your world are likewise ordained."

I page through to the Our Father. Every word is what I have read from childhood through my adult years. "Thank you. And not just for the advice, but for all you've done for our congregation. Whatever you were when you came here, you've become Father Hamra to us all. Consider yourself forgiven for the deception."

His eyes are bleary. "There have been so many nights I have hoped to have heard those words yet found no one here on Earth to whom I could confess. Thank you."

The sound of glass breaking is no louder than someone dropping a bottle on the floor. Hamra jerks. He sprawls onto the linoleum. Blood spatters on my shirt.

There's a small hole punched in the window, cracks radiating outward. I stare at it, stunned into inaction, until I realize the blurred form of a dark blue SUV.

Chris.

I drop to the floor. "Father!" I pull toward him.

He's gasping, face ashen. A shaky hand clasps mine. "Forgive …

me …"

"You are forgiven. Always." I squeeze his fingers.

The grip goes slack. His head droops.

Gunfire breaks the silence. I recognize the sound—a Sierran rifle. Jacobs is outside Sheryl, crouched behind her spare tire. The muzzle flashes.

Curt scrambles out the opposite side, shouting as he runs toward the parsonage door. "Z! Let's get out of here!"

"I can't leave him!"

Curt grabs my shoulder, his face white. "Doesn't look like we can do anything, and if that guy in the SUV has his way, we'll all be perforated."

Two more shots shatter the rest of the window. One explodes a clock on the wall above my head.

We bolt from the kitchen. Jacobs chooses that moment to shoot back, giving us enough time to close the distance to Sheryl. We skid on the dirt, slick where the snow's melted. A bullet smashes one of the passenger windows.

"Who is this guy? Why's he shooting my Jeep?" Curt shouts.

"Because he's trying to kill us." I scoot closer to Jacobs. "Is it just him?"

Jacobs nods. "No one else in the car. But we can't stay here until he runs out of bullets. I've just got one more magazine. Halfway through this one. Could use some more firepower."

"Right." I steady my breathing. Heat builds in the Echo Watch. Conscious focus seems to intensify its warm-up time. Within seconds it's so bright I have to avert my gaze.

Curt, though, has that look he reserves for the most beautiful woman to walk into Caerphilly. "That's … not a bracelet."

"Not now, Curt."

"Does it shoot?"

Instead of replying, I ask Jacobs, "Can you draw his attention long enough for me to …"

"To what?"

"I don't know. Shoot back?"

"Sure thing." Jacobs ducks under the rear fender. "Go."

"Go?"

He opens fire, a pair of short bursts. As soon as he's done, Chris shoots back from the safety of the SUV.

Secure in the knowledge his attention's elsewhere, I flatten across Sheryl's hood and send a blast from the Echo Watch. It leaves me extremely visually incapacitated, to put it mildly. It's worse than accidentally staring into the face of the sun. The pulse melts paint in a long streak over the hood. The result for the SUV is far worse.

The pulse strikes the rear passenger window. Glass explodes in a glittering shower—not just from that window, but the one opposite it. Flames ripple throughout the interior.

Chris tumbles out of the driver's side door. I can only tell because I hear it bang open, and his shoes crunching on gravel. But the fire hasn't persuaded him to get out from cover. Instead, something comes hurtling over the top of the truck. Is he out of ammunition? Sure seems like he's reduced to throwing rocks.

"Grenade!" Jacobs shouts.

Instinct takes over. I aim for the incoming projectile with the Echo Watch—but instead of maintaining its pulse state, the metal drops temperature so fast I'm certain it will give me frostbite. Jacobs pulls Curt from Sheryl's side, but they're moving far too slow. So is the grenade, now that I think of it.

Even the flames slow their dance.

This time, when I shoot back, the Echo Watch emits a shimmering ripple that speeds through the air. Everything accelerates. The grenade is shoved along a new trajectory, returning to its owner.

It explodes against the same passenger door where I first shot.

The fireball jolts the SUV hard enough to lift the wheels from the pavement. The shockwave blasts hot air, singing my face.

The explosion's crumpled the door, blown out more windows, and spread the fire throughout the entire SUV. Flames lick the undercarriage.

"Hey!" Jacobs grabs my shoulder. "We got to move!"

He gets us thirty yards away before the entire SUV goes up in flames.

The roar disguises a pair of gunshots. Jacobs grunts. He goes down on his knees, clutching his side. Where's his rifle? I see Curt, crouched farther away, eyes wild. The rifle's discarded on the grass beside him.

Footsteps.

A blow to my back makes my vision swim. I hold myself on all fours, like an animal, trying not to vomit. A pair of brown shoes, streaked with mud, stop to my left.

Chris stares down at me, with all the feeling of a homeowner preparing to smash a spider. He has a long rifle in one hand, equipped with a huge scope and a thick suppressor. He's aiming a pistol to my head with the other.

For all his preparation and intensity, though, he stands for what seems the longest time. I wonder if the Echo Watch as made things seem this way, as it did when I deflected the grenade, but the roaring flames sound correct.

Gunshots.

I startle, fully prepared to feel the piercing pain. But it's Chris who spawns wounds—four of them, in his chest. He collapses.

It's Curt. He's got Jacobs' rifle propped up, in the same firing stance I've seen him use at the range on the few occasions he's made me go. Can't fault him the practice anymore.

Jacobs rips off part of his jacket. He winces as he presses hard against his wound. "Nice work, Captain."

CHAPTER TWENTY-SEVEN

Jacobs demands we get out of there, without attempting to douse the flames or cover Father Hamra's body. I don't argue.

The only place I can think to go is home.

"Um, how about calling the police?" Curt waves his arms as the three of us walk through the front door. The part of my brain not still reeling from Father Hamra's death notes it's a good thing I'm not locked out, because it's possible Nick could have changed the locks.

"Yeah, you have that conversation," Jacobs mutters. "I'd love to hear you explain the two dead bodies and one blown-up truck."

"There's a First Aid kit in the upstairs bathroom, behind the mirror." I point up the steps. "Do you need help?"

"It's a through and through. Didn't hit anything vital. If it did, I'd have bled out by now. I'll go patch up."

As soon as he's gone upstairs, I head for the backyard. "Sammy? Sammy!"

"Hey, are you listening to me, Z?" Curt trails me. "We've got to get some help, and I mean besides this nicer, marksman version of a young Tyson Jacobs."

"We are getting help. But I need your phone."

"Right. Yours was bugged." He hands over his smartphone.

"Thanks." The backyard's empty. Thick clouds swaddle the sky.

Snow's drifting down, the flakes thickening. The wind from the southwest builds. "Sammy!"

"You dropped him off at the animal shelter two weeks ago."

"I did?"

Curt nods. "You told me his behavior got worse, as in, he started snapping at you and Jess. Now I'm thinking, he was probably snapping at only you. Or, your other you."

Nick wasn't kidding. He really is cleaning out my life. I rest a hand on the doorjamb, remembering how he and Chris first took care of one annoying dog next door and followed it up by killing my workplace rival. "You believe me, then?"

"I'm working on it. Your magic glow band that shoots lasers helped convince me. Plus, I've seen that guy you two called Chris around. You—other you—claimed he was an old friend of the family." Curt snorted. "Sure. Because you and your Lebanese clan have friends who look like Russian mobsters."

"Special forces, actually." I head back inside. "Curt, I'm sorry. There's no other way to say it. This other me—Nick, or Commander Zein—he showed up a month and a half ago. He promised to help alleviate the stress in my life, so I'd be happier. He took over onerous work tasks. For a while, worked great. He fooled everyone."

Curt rubs his shiny pate. "Huh. That explains where you got your abundant free time all of a sudden."

"It does. Again, I can't apologize enough."

"Hey, look, I don't pretend it was the right thing to do, but if I got the same offer from a clone or whatever of me, I might take it." Curt's smile is faint. "We'll work on the forgive and forget later, okay?"

I shake my head. "I was a fool. He's ruined everything. Here I was thinking it was a gift from above, and it's been nothing but a curse."

"Maybe, but maybe you've got a chance to clean it up. You've told me that, from some of the homilies they feed you. Maybe you're the one who's got to bring this guy to heel."

"Thanks, Curt." I pluck Sergeant Ambrose's card from my pocket.

"I'll make this up to you."

"You better believe it. The tab I'll run for you to pay at Caerphilly and Bentley's both will be beyond your wildest imagination." He taps my wrist. "And considering the mess you dragged me into, that's a lot of wild."

The phone rings, but no answer. Goes straight to voicemail.

I stab the End button and redial.

"Z?"

"Yeah."

Curt jerks a thumb upstairs. "Jacobs keeps calling me captain."

"He … served with you on the other Earth. You were a captain in the Home Guard, which as near as I can tell is a branch of the Army overseen by Procyon Foundation in this region."

"Procyon, the West Coast folks you're helping build a massive office complex?"

"Yes."

"Oh." Curt frowns. "You said, 'served' and 'you were.' I'm assuming …?"

"Past tense." I stop the redial. "Captain Curtis Marin died protecting me, so I could return home."

Curt rubs his beard. "Man. That's intense."

"But it's something I could see you doing. This world or the other, there are ties between individuals." I smile. "Between friends."

"That's very Hallmark of you." Curt rolls his eyes, but he's gotten red in his cheeks. "How's about calling the cavalry?"

Before I can summon a third redial, Ambrose calls me back. "Hello, Sergeant?"

"If this is your idea of a good time for a chat, Zein, you've been downing more illegal substances than the lowlifes I'm pretty sure you've slapped around our streets," he growls. "What do you want?"

He's speaking close to the phone. Shouts and hurried footsteps rumble in the background. "I need you to meet me at home."

"We've got what sounds like a small battle at your church, and you want me to drop in for tea and scones? Arresting you is going to be really fun."

"Come quickly, and alone," I press, "before this gets even more out of hand."

The four of us stand arrayed around the dining room table, except Jacobs, who's seated. His shirt's stained with blood, but he has bandages poking from underneath. Judging by the way he scowls at Sergeant Ambrose he's not feeling weakened.

Ambrose, meanwhile, won't take off his ridiculous sunglasses, even as he rubs the bridge of his nose. "Let me run this once more, to be sure of the facts. The person committing these crimes isn't you, but he is you. He's you from an alternate dimension."

"Well, from a second Earth."

"Uh-huh."

I dig out the packet of cards, and flip through them. "Here. You see? Doubles of more than just me."

Ambrose plants his hands on the table as I spread Nick's, Tabitha's, and Father Hamra's face in front of him. He tilts his head. "Neat trick. This one's your wife."

"Agent Tabitha Boutros. She and my wife are … similar. But this." I tap Nick's card. "You see? Commander Dominic Zein. He works for, well, enemies."

"I watch a lot of crazy movies, Zein. Read some far-out books, too. But I'm not going to be thrown off your scent by fancy Photoshop tricks." Ambrose pulls off his shades and fixes that icy glare on each of us in turn. "Of course, this all begs the question of why you're going to great lengths to make up goofy stories. Here's my rationale: you've got a lot you're wanting to draw attention from. The vigilante appearances. The death of Tyson Jacobs—"

"My father, by the way."

Ambrose scowls. "My report stated he has no next of kin."

Jacobs shrugs. "Not from around here."

"So, what, you're one of these double people? Kind of makes you a single." Ambrose straightens. "Look, I've got two more bodies to add to your mess, and you trying to sell me on counterfeit playing cards isn't making your case appear plausible. You want innocence? Give me alibis."

I'm not that fast on my feet. Jacobs isn't willing to break the silence for something as trivial as Ambrose's bluster. After all, he's seen real interrogation.

Curt blurts, "Chris killed Dominic's priest, and tried to kill us. I shot him in self-defense."

Jacobs moans and shakes his head.

"Now we're getting somewhere." Ambrose thumps a finger on the table. "Details, boys. Chris being the guy with four bullets in his chest?"

"If you check with the police in Estes Park, they're investigating the death of an Eric Talbot," I say. "He's the spitting image of Chris, who killed him in order to take his place."

"Stop, will you? This isn't helping." Ambrose produces zip ties from his belt. "If somebody can't give me some facts beyond you three were at this place and one of you shot someone, I'm calling for another car and hauling you downtown."

I storm from the table, toward the back door.

"Okay, have you seen the damage to Sheryl?" Curt sputters. "It's not like we took her for a joyride down the Van River. This was a shootout! The guy put holes in it trying to kill us! And if Dominic says he's linked up with someone who's major trouble, you should go after that guy, not the ones trying to stop it."

"Like I said. Evidence is evidence."

Fine. He wants evidence? We can't be dragged to jail when Nick is loose in this world, especially now that he's lost Chris. Father Hamra can't have died in vain—and yet, that's exactly what it feels like. Chris murdered him, for refusing to do the wrong thing. At least Father Hamra found peace, the eternal kind, and tried to bring the same to the people he served.

I aim the Echo Watch at Ambrose. "Sergeant, I'll give you proof, but you won't enjoy it."

His hand goes to his gun. "Why's your armband glowing? We've gotten weird reports about something like that. Those guys who tried to steal your car complained about their weapons warming up."

"This is what did it. It's the same device Nick possesses, and it isn't of this world. I used it to return to ours. And yes, he's used it as a weapon."

Ambrose draws his firearm. "Put it down."

"I can't. Don't shoot."

"Last warning. Put it down."

Curt spreads his hands. "Hey, let's all not shoot anyone."

"Quiet. Zein, I'm not going to repeat—"

Having no idea how to trigger the same response I saw Nick use against the car thieves, I rely on memory. The scene of that night plays out like a slow-motion film, minus sound. A piece of the Echo Watch detaches, floating an inch from my wrist. A curious blend of cold and warm waves wash along my forearm.

Ambrose's trigger clicks. There is no accompanying thunder.

Instead he shouts and drops the gun. It's glowing orange in the barrel and along the stock. A faint sizzling emanates from the floor. A black burn mark spreads underneath, halting only as the glow fades.

Ambrose fans his hand. The palm and fingers are red. "Going to add assaulting an officer to the rapidly-growing list of charges."

"You asked for a demonstration. You had it. Are you going to help us?"

"Really? This doesn't prove anything other than you're the same person who's committed all those crimes!"

The doorbell rings. Everyone looks around at the other.

Curt nudges me. "Your house."

I'm out in the hallway when Ambrose starts reading Curt the Miranda. An argument breaks out, with Curt's voice the most strident. Jacobs' tone is stern, but unbothered.

I reach for the doorknob but it's already swinging open.

Nick's on the other side. He smiles. "Oh, good. You are home." He whips his Echo Watch high.

I dive for the living room. Lighting flashes around me. Heat tears at my back. The impact breaks a chair, reducing it to tatters.

Ambrose is the first on the scene, having apparently reacquired his gun. Curt's right behind him. They both gawk, proving as useful as mannequins.

Nick sighs and shakes his head. "See how complicated you've made things, Dominic? I wish you'd been able to stick to our arrangement. It worked best when you were banished. This means I've got an even greater mess to clean up."

He aims for Curt and Ambrose, but I'm rolling onto my side before he can fire. I loose a burst with my Echo Watch, one that goes too high, scorching our ceiling.

Ambrose should shoot. He doesn't. Whether my melting effect ruined his gun, or he's too shaken by what he's seeing is irrelevant. He's defenseless against Nick.

A dark shape tackles Nick from behind. Jacobs must have circled the house via the backyard. He grunts as he takes Nick down and clutches his side.

Nick's paying attention. He aims a vicious kick for Jacobs' wound, which connects and frees him from the others' grasp.

Ambrose empties his magazine.

Nick slashes between him and Ambrose with a streak of yellow sparks, a miniature lightning storm. White flashes riddle the air.

Next thing I know, the slide on Ambrose's gun is locked back, and he's out of ammunition.

Nick turns to me. "Being you isn't very much fun when you're still around. I tried giving you a semblance of comfort—as in, remaining alive. That was a mistake."

His Echo Watch pulsates, in the moment before he fires. Instinct allows me only that brief gap in which to mount a defense. Memories of the failed carjacking and the disabling of Ambrose's gun minutes ago merge.

We fire at each other simultaneously.

The bursts connect midair. I expect them to dissipate, to fizzle. Instead they wrestle, then grow, expanding until they're a pale shell crackling with energy. My lungs beg for air. Heat sears my face.

Nick looks as stunned as I feel.

The shell pops. The energy lashes out in concentric waves, shattering windows, and battering people. All five of us are thrown about the living room and hall.

My ears ring, blocking all other sound. Nick's saying something—or is it Curt? Pain lances my neck as I raise my head, desperate to clear blurred vision. Nick staggers out the door. A blink later, he drives off in the BMW.

I've failed again. But we're alive.

Police cars cordon the street. There's a fire engine, plus a pair of ambulances. Ambrose insists we all get checked out. As an EMT records my blood pressure, eyes riveted to the readout, Ambrose engages in a quiet but heated discussion with the younger officers. A sharp hand gesture punctuates every word.

"Stay seated." The EMT is a petite blond woman. Something about her is familiar. I don't dare check the deck of cards. I've had enough of those surprises. "Your blood pressure's elevated."

"Thanks." She leaves me for Jacobs, who's having his wound cleaned and stitched. Jacobs catches me looking, and nods.

"You okay?" Curt leans against the ambulance. He has a massive bruise on his forehead, the size, shape, and color of a smashed prune. "You look awful."

"And you're unlikely to win a beauty pageant."

"It's the beard." His smile fades. "It was all true—the stuff you said, I mean."

I gaze at my house, with its battered door and broken windows. Caution tape bandages it. Explaining this to Jess will be a nightmare. That's assuming she'll speak to me soon, or at all. "Yes. I can't believe it myself, most of the time, but everything I've seen, the people I've met—they're as real as you and I."

"Sure seems like it."

"You still upset with me?"

Curt shrugs. "Probably. Yeah. In your defense, you did try to tell me, but I assumed you were pulling my leg. Having your double show up and try to blast us all to pieces puts that discussion into perspective."

"I've made a mess." Sickness rolls over me. I want to walk down the street, away from the disaster, from the terrible choices, and start again far from here.

Yet, that's what Nick did, too, and it did not turn out well for most involved.

Ambrose walks over. The man exudes frustration. I get the impression he prefers order, and this situation is anything but orderly. "Okay, here's the deal. This is a gas leak. We've shut down the neighborhood. Nobody's getting in or out—not that there's a ton of people around, with it being the middle of the day. We're shuttling your neighbor lady out of the one-block radius."

Mrs. Cortez? A pair of firefighters bundle her off to a waiting car. A young Latino man glares at me from behind the steering wheel. Her nephew, I guess. Nick had threatened his immigration status. Another example of his trying to make my life less complicated.

It was never about that. It was always for Nick's benefit.

"Zein." Ambrose snaps his fingers. I glare at myself reflected in his sunglasses. "Thanks for paying attention. We'll keep this as quiet as possible. I'm not keen on any of you blabbing about what really went on."

"You don't have to worry about that. Are you sure a gas leak will explain away what happened to my house?"

"Unless you think the truth will be more convincing."

So, now he's willing to take our side? I could have used his cooperation before Nick tried to kill me. "I imagine it'd be hard to explain."

"My concern is public panic. Besides, how am I going to put out an APB on you when you're sitting right here?"

A fair point. "I'm open to suggestions on how to handle Nick."

"Oh, no. I'm not saying a word beyond when it comes to specifics. Use your soldier pal. I'll give you a hand with this Nick maniac, but it's not like handing over a blank check. Things get too messy, you're on your own, and Rampart PD will be there to provide the broom to sweep it all away. Got it?"

"Of course, Sergeant. I appreciate your discretion."

"And I don't appreciate your sarcasm." Ambrose stalks back to his squad car, muttering the whole way.

Curt chuckles. "Way to lay on the charm."

"Fresh out, I'm afraid."

"Yeah, well, better find your backup supply, because it looks like you'll need it for this lady."

Lady? The pock-pock of heels on the asphalt should have been my first clue. Loredana Lark closes the distance between her silver Lexus sedan. She's wearing the same suit ensemble she sported at our first meeting, albeit with a white winter coat in place of the jacket. Her hair's a beacon against the humdrum colors of our neighborhood and the falling snow.

"I'm relieved to see you're well, Mr. Zein." She could be discussing the addition of a staff lunchroom to the Procyon building designs. "But waiting here will not solve either of our problems."

"I wasn't aware you and I shared problems."

"Two, actually." She glances at my arms.

I sweep back the blanket issued by the paramedics and let her get an eyeful of the Echo Watch.

"Indeed." She positively beams. "Most impressive. I take it your furlough to the other Earth was successful."

Curt clears his throat. "Is she, ah, one of the double people?"

"My contact with my doppelgänger is sporadic, but at our last contact it was quite clear the Sierrans had possession of both Echo Watches." Exhaustion aside, amusement warms me as she gives Curt a disdainful look reserved for the orneriest student in class. "I was to ascertain Commander Zein's goals on this Earth, a task which was, for a time, perplexing. It took some investigating to realize he wanted to infiltrate this society even more effectively than his operatives on our world had managed. Hence my concern during our brief interactions."

Someone else who knew about Nick before I did? I hated adding another face to the lineup of distrustful people, but I had little choice. "Knowing who he really was could have been helpful. Your compatriot across the Interstice was more forthcoming. I'd expect the same."

"She has a tendency to be too—open. Discretion is vital on this Earth. I understand her choosing you to achieve our goals, and I must say, I admire your ability to obtain an Echo Watch. Let us trust you can put it to good use before Commander Zein does further harm."

"I'm not going to let him do *any* harm beyond the catastrophe he's already caused."

"Then I suggest we move quickly, because what he's done to this point has been child's play." She starts for her car. "Bring your companions, please."

"I'm not going anywhere with you until you explain yourself." I'm through with secret agendas. All I want are answers, and my life reset to normal.

"The explanation I'll offer is that downtown, our mutual acquaintance Nick is readying his other doubles for some kind of action that will kill hundreds," Lark says coldly. "I lack intelligence on what it is, other than the knowledge he removed something from a laboratory that one of his lieutenants was secretly keeping for him."

I'm on my feet immediately. Dark certainty clouds all other concerns. "Come on, Curt. We have to get Jacobs and go with Miss Lark."

"Why? What's this junk about Nick trying to kill people?"

"He's brought weaponized smallpox to our city." It sickens me to say it. "And he's going to use it."

CHAPTER TWENTY-EIGHT

The wind howls across Rampart. What was forecast to be flurries has parked over the city, churning with blizzard forces. Snow sticks to the windshield of Lark's Lexus as we hurry across town. We make a quick stop at Curt's condo so he can retrieve one of his guns, a vintage M1911 that he keeps as well-maintained as Sheryl at her finest. Only then, with all of us armed, does Jacobs deem it less a hazard to confront Nick at his loft.

The sheer madness remains—our quartet, with a woman I barely know behind the wheel, and my rival's nonexistent son-soldier, plus my best friend, embarking on what is essentially a vigilante attack.

I would trade it for a pile of unread emails after a long weekend, and a never-ending stream of complaints from Mrs. Dockery.

It's noon. Traffic is heavy and moving slowly what with the snow flying. But the side street leading to the loft is empty. Snow coats the parked cars with a thin layer. The road's still too warm for it to stick.

I shiver at the memory of the ruined, icy version of the same street on the other Earth.

"Nick seems to have replenished his forces," Lark says.

There are two men in a gray sedan parked in front of the door leading to the upstairs loft. They're crammed inside the front seats like a package too big for its box.

Jacobs secures the magazine to his rifle. "I'll take care of them."

"I don't want anyone else killed," I say. "There's been enough bloodshed."

"Yeah, and what do you thinks gonna happen when they see us coming? Greeting cards and flowers?"

"Yes, I know. But I have an idea. It'll involve your cooperation, Ms. Lark."

"I'm listening."

A moment later, she nods, albeit reluctantly. "It has merit. Very well. We shall try it your way."

"Good. Jacobs, you know your part?"

"Uh-huh. Also, it's stupid."

"I didn't ask."

Curt taps the back of my seat. "I'm all in favor of punching someone if it comes down to it. Just sad I don't have my hands on a pool cue."

"If there was time to swing by Bentley's, I'd be happy to fulfill the request."

Lark aims for the empty spot behind the sedan. At the last minute, she veers sharply right, then straightens out, but her reactions are purposely slowed. The Lexus' bumper thumps the back of the sedan. It's a light enough touch to avoid deploying the airbags, but enough of a nudge to get the attention of both men.

They open their doors simultaneously. I hadn't counted on how large they were—more of the bodybuilder type than, say, the average Sierran soldier.

Lark is first from the car. "I'm terribly sorry, gentlemen. I'm afraid I wasn't paying attention. Text message, you know."

Neither of them chides her for her lapse in driving attentiveness. Instead, as if sharing bodies, they reach inside their jackets.

Lark moves with the grace of a gymnastic. She seizes the leftmost man's wrist, of his hand tucked inside the coat, and shoves it against his chest. Her other hand impales that wrist with a slender knife she's plucked from somewhere inside her jacket.

The guard's scream is enough to draw his partner's attention. He twists, aiming a semiautomatic pistol at Lark, but doesn't shoot, seeing as how she's ducked behind the other guard.

That's my cue.

I pop the passenger side door and brace the Echo Watch on the frame. Two quick bursts leave the men incapacitated on the pavement.

Curt and Jacobs hurry out, grabbing both guards by the shoulders and feet "Tasered," Curt says. "Nice."

"One of many features, apparently." Lark slips her knife free of the man's wrist and chest. She wipes the blade on a handkerchief, tosses the soiled cloth aside, and secrets the blade wherever it had originated. "I suggest confining them to their vehicle, sans keys, of course."

"Read my mind." Jacobs tosses Curt a set of zip ties.

A few minutes later, both men are slumped inside the truck. Their wrists are manacled to the steering wheel and passenger door handle, respectively. Curt pitches the keys into a storm drain. He hands Jacobs one of the pistols and offers Lark the other.

"No thank you. I have my own."

"Okay." Curt turns to me. "And you're all lasered up, so …"

I shrug. "Come on."

Curt ditches the last gun and we head for the loft.

The door is unlocked. I take this as a bad sign. It means either Nick expected his men to protect entry, or he's expecting us upstairs.

No one accosts us on the climb. Jacobs is first to the apartment door. He gestures. There's a sliver of light between the door and the frame. Ajar.

I nod.

Jacobs kicks it open. He barges in, rifle raised, sweeping his aim around the room. Curt follows, mimicking Jacobs with the parody of someone who's obviously never had military training, but thinks they've played enough video games to approximate. Lark draws a tiny silver revolver from her pocket.

Nick's standing by the window. He turns around, and smiles. "Hey, Dominic."

It would be easy to incinerate him right now, if not for the three armed men surrounding him.

Unlike the bodyguards downstairs, they're of varying shapes and sizes—one tall, black man who's baldheaded, a stout brown-headed man in a fleece jacket, and a pale, redhead with an athletic build. Their faces carry similar stern scowls, and there's something unsettling about their appearances, even more than the MAC-10 machine pistols pointed at us.

I've seen them before, when Marin and I flipped through the deck of cards. These men are all in there.

Nick watches me. "I can see those gears turning. If you're wondering about my associates, and the boys downstairs—nice job dismantling them, by the way—yes, they are from my Earth. They're not the only ones. I meant to keep them all secret but seeing as how you've forced my hand …"

"You had Father Hamra killed."

"Like I said, he's a traitor."

"He's a better man than you'll ever be."

Nick loses his smirk. "If you mean better in that his interference cost me a perfectly good soldier, then yes, he was. Chris's loss necessitated my activating some of my longer-term assets I'd stashed away for a rainy day." He gestures at the snow blowing sideways in great sheets outside the window. "Close enough."

I'm more concerned by what's in his other hand. It's a set of three vials, linked together with a lumped device. Wires twist from one end to the next.

"That would be our reason for coming," Lark murmurs.

"Loredana, how nice to see you again," Nick says. "Though I suppose it's your first time to see me."

"Hardly." Lark shifts her stance so she's aiming for his face. "I'm kept quite aware of your goings-on by my counterpart. It was something of a surprise, however, to meet you in something as mundane as a building plan session."

Nick laughs. "You know what they say. Don't quit your day job. In my case, I had to find one. Dualpoint works nicely as a cover."

I hold out my hand. "Nick, give me the vials. You don't have to do this."

Nick laughs, as happily as if he were opening birthday presents. "Give them? You have a great sense of humor—you, the man who destroyed this same project where I came from. Relax. These aren't meant for your world—our world. I live here now. They're going back to the mess I left, so that I never have to look over my shoulder."

The idea's appalling. Those people on the other Earth have suffered so much already.

"You can't!" Jacobs snaps. "There's a ton of refugees and—"

"Refugees. They have nothing left. Better they're put out of their misery. The strong who survive can be conscripted by the Sierran Army." Nick shrugs. "Assuming my old compatriots survive, too."

"You'd destroy your own home?" I can't fathom his mind, the mind we supposedly share.

"No. I'd level the wreckage of home. There's no fixing the broken there. Everything and everyone is tainted by the Blasts. Here, the world's clean. It's fresh and alive"

Overpowering him doesn't strike me as an option. Jacobs keeps his rifle trained on the three men, but they, too, pivot their guns to bracket all of us. Curt has his pistol in two-handed grip, eyes wide with fear, shifting his gaze from person to person. Lark's arm never wavers as she stands sidelong to us. Her silver revolver catches flashes of white from the blowing snow. Anything we start, or they start, is going to end in death.

Unless I can disarm them.

"Please, reconsider. Put the vial down and we'll let you go." I can feel Jacobs and Lark cooking me with their glares. "We won't follow you back. You have my word."

"Z," Curt mutters.

"Shut up." The Echo Watch vibrates my forearm. I keep it at my side, ignoring it, watching for Nick's reaction. If he has any idea what I'm planning …

"You're not listening. I'm not going back. If I go anywhere it's going to be a sunny beach. Normally I'd be intrigued by an offer of amnesty, but you'd need something with which to bargain. Money. A fast car. Both, and a woman, preferably." He sneers. "But then, I've already got two of the latter."

It takes all my restraint to not burn the smug expression off his face. Heat builds in the Echo Watch. Instead I concentrate on all three guns pointed our way.

"No, Dominic, our time together is at an end. Can't stall."

He sweeps up his arm, and I expect the portal to spring open—yet his Echo Watch isn't pulsating in the way it should. That's not the plan.

I mimic his move.

All the guns in the room, theirs and ours, glow like coals. Curt yelps and drops his pistol. Two of Nick's men react with the same surprise.

One of them fires.

The shots go wide, but not by much. They buzz near my head.

Jacobs still has his weapon. He grits his teeth, smoke rising from his palm, and unloads a burst at the brown-haired shooter. The man is cut down in a spray of blood.

Lark pulls her trigger once, but only once, before she snaps the gun aside. She grimaces. The revolver winds up under the pop logo.

Nick's already sweeping his Echo Watch between us, the same way he disintegrated Ambrose's bullets. Lark's single shot fizzles midair.

The bald man and the redhead pounce.

Jacobs rolls backward under the redhead's attack. He sweeps the assailant over, onto his back, but loses his rifle in the process.

A well-aimed blast from Nick's Echo Watch reduces it to slag.

Curt throws a punch at the bald man but misses. His opponent lands two better-aimed blows, bending Curt over with a great gasp.

Lark's knife reappears. It spins end over end through the air.

The blade stabs into Nick's shoulder. He yells, reaches for it with his Echo Watch-equipped arm.

I lunge at him, slamming us both against the window. Cracks spider web the glass. The vials are right there, under my fingertips.

Nick's blow knocks the wind out of me, and we're reverse. My head rebounds off the window frame. Nick's Echo Watch sizzles inches from my chin, at just the wrong angle to hit.

Lark hits him from behind. Her knife flashes across the room, discarded.

He whips her across the jaw with the weapon, sending her sprawling. The vials fall from our grasp, bouncing across the floor.

Everyone freezes in the middle of their fights, certain the container will crack, and we'll all be exposed.

But the vials hold. They spin away.

"Perfect." Nick slams his elbow into my chest. I lose my grip on his arms.

He dives for the vials.

Desperate, I fire the Echo Watch, scorching the wood planks black. But the sphere appears, right over the discolored flooring. The rest of my blast fizzles out at its edges.

Nick's floating in the space between, Echo Watch a blur of spinning pieces. The blinding light flares behind him.

Gunshots boom like cannons behind me. The window shatters. A winter storm roars in, tossing papers, spattering us with snow.

"Nick!" I shout.

There's a flash of light. Nick's gone.

"Go!" Jacobs has his arms braced around the neck of the bald man. "Get him!"

Curt shouts a warning. He hurls himself at the redhead. That one aims a gun at me.

I dive through the portal, letting the Interstice drag me through the stinging heat. My world blacks out.

A gunshot echoes.

Time and space bend around me. I soar through the Transect, the ripples slipping along the outside wall. Once more, my breathing rumbles around me like an orchestra.

Yet the pain of the transition doesn't fade. Instead, it digs deeper into my abdomen. I reach for my lower back. The palm comes away bloody.

Lucky shot.

Nick is an apparition flying ahead of me. His outline is identical to the soap bubble that surrounded the portal and makes up the Transect's shell. My hand is the same way. So is every inch of my body.

Have to catch him. As soon as I think it, my velocity increases. The Echo Watch pulls my arm ahead, and together we rush after Nick. It's a slow gain, but we close the distance foot by foot, until I'm within reach of his legs.

He spins around and kicks before I can get ahold of him. But he doesn't fire with the Echo Watch—perhaps because it's our mode of transit.

There has to be a way to stop him. As soon as he reaches the other Earth, he'll release the smallpox and thousands could die. If I can't fight him in here …

I glance outside the Transect walls, at the stars, and the forbidding landscape below. I reach out and drag my fingers.

They slip right through, with minimal resistance.

I will the Echo Watch for a final burst of speed. Alternating icy spikes and fiery needles sweep through me, but it's enough. I latch onto Nick's left ankle with both hands.

Then I steer us both out of the Transect.

We burst through, plummeting as gravity takes hold. My stomach's in my throat. This is it. If I have to die, let it be this way—ridding Rampart of evil. The only regret coursing through my heart is I won't be able to tell Jess the truth.

Nick shouts, flailing at me, but I grasp both his legs as we spin. Right before we hit a rocky plateau, he snaps his arm down and hits my Echo Watch with his. Our descent slows in that last foot, then we slam against the stony soil.

Deep violet dirt spatters me. The ground is streaked with black. Gray spiky shrubs spotted with white litter the top of the butte, raised a hundred feet on steep slopes around the rest of the terrain. I scramble to my feet, searching the sky for the Transect. There it is—a shimmering thread far above.

The air's thin, devoid of moisture. Every breath brings in dust. The horizon's filled with mountain silhouettes. Lightning illuminates dazzling neon foliage in purple and blue, which vanish as soon as the strike passes. Thunder rumbles continuously.

There are other sounds, too. Shrieks, like birds-of-prey descending from the sky.

"What have you done?" Nick twists and turns, his eyes wide, hair disheveled. Sweat forms a sheen over his face. "We shouldn't be here."

"You left me no choice." I raise the Echo Watch. "Give me the vials."

He snarls, a guttural, inhuman sound of rage mingled with fear, and lunges for me. His Echo Watch pulsates with such heat I can feel it before he reaches me. Nick swings it up and around, as if wielding a hatchet.

I block his downward strike with the armband.

The impact throws me to my knees. It rings out like the bells of a great cathedral, rolling and echoing across the endless lands. Shrieks stop, lost beneath the majestic, booming song. It penetrates every organ, and pounds at us with such power I'm certain my heart will explode. Ripples shoot out on concentric circles in midair, breezing through our arms as if we're mere apparitions.

Nick shouts at me but the sound flies away, unheard, with the ringing. Miniature lightning crackles between us. Pain lances through every limb, every hair, every cell. I can't stay up. He, on the other hand, shows no signs of faltering.

I force him back, pushing onto my feet again. I can't let him kill me. I won't. But I can't do this alone. The realization strikes me harder than the Echo Watch's blow—when can anything be done alone? Not by my own strength, not as fallible flesh.

Please. Save me. Spare him.

The second thought follows the first. How can I not want Nick dead, after all he's done? Part of me does. But the other part sees a man who calls a ruined world home, a man who's known only war and death and devastation his whole life. And … he's me.

Would I be any different had I been born in his place?

Nick grimaces. The tendons bulge in his neck. "Let—me—go!"

No. Not yet.

He must be stopped.

My Echo Watch increases its cycle of pulses and lightning. The heat has grown so fierce I no longer notice it. I can't feel my arm. It doesn't matter. With a last, raw cry escaping my throat, I shove hard against him.

The Echo Watches shear apart with a tremendous, metallic scrape. Lightning flashes around us. Nick is thrown against the ground, tumbling as a scrap of paper caught in the wind. He sprawls in the dirt. The vials fall from his grasp.

My opening.

I level the Echo Watch and burn the vials into a tiny pile of ash.

There. It's done. I place my hands on my knees and give in to the rising prickles of nausea. When my stomach won't permit anything else to come up, I wipe my mouth with the back of my hand.

Nick moans, his shoes scraping rock. He makes no other motion, still breathing but insensate.

He's finished. But I lean back, squinting into the stormy sky. There's the matter of how to get us back.

Nick's continued groaning concerns me, though not as much as the resumed screeches. I bend near him, and reach for his wrist, to check his pulse.

There's a spark to my touch, when I get a grip, and his Echo Watch expands. It's the same reaction as when Tabitha relinquished her Echo Watch to me. Nick's crawls onto my wrist, adhering, bonding, until it's situated in opposition to the other.

I hold them aloft. Something tangible threads them. Are those whispers I sense? Has to be a trick of the wind.

A new thought occurs: if a single Echo Watch could propel me through the corridor between Earths, perhaps two are strong enough to lift be back into the path.

A tremor destabilizes me. Slithering sounds scrabble at the base of the butte. Whatever's coming up the side moves quickly. Nick's my prisoner, and I'm stuck facing whoever he's planted inside the Interstice.

Whoever, or whatever.

A tentacle slips over the top. Then another. Still more. They're black, shiny with slime, gigantic versions of garden slugs.

The nightmare pulls itself up before me and looms overhead.

Those tentacles lash around a thick, midnight black lump that's speckled as if with diamonds. The spots write in mesmerizing patterns. Three blazing red eyes glare at me, unlike any I've seen or imagined but oozing such malevolence I shrink away. Long, knife-like teeth gnash in a yawning maw.

Terror consumes me. This isn't a soldier shooting at me, or a client berating my work. This is a monstrosity. Darkness incarnate.

I shield myself with the Echo Watches.

They snap together, fusing, seething with heat. Lightning returns, stabbing out in all directions, yet where it strikes me, I don't feel anything but static electricity.

The tentacles hammer away, but they don't touch me. Their impact batters my strength, yet I don't fall. I feel like I could collapse at any moment. I don't. The Echo Watches hold me up, driven to my defense. We're one unit.

The monster withdraws its onslaught. It shrieks at me but doesn't attack. It waits, apparently pondering who or what I am. Tentacles waver.

Come on. I have to get out of here. Whether I'm praying or begging the Echo Watch is of less importance in the frantic moment than the results.

The Echo Watches glow white, with blue traceries illuminating the cryptic designs. My shoes scrape on dirt.

Nick. He has to face his crimes. And I'm not the kind of man to let a person suffer in this hell. I pull away from wherever I'm being dragged. Fingers brush against Nick's arms.

The beast changes direction. Tentacles slash across my field of vision. A breath-taking, piercing cold stabs my guts. I stagger away, latching onto Nick's arm.

I yield to the Echo Watches.

They yank me off the ground, and I lift Nick free. I seize the front of his shirt, drawing him closer. Together we rise into the sky.

The beast's shriek shatters my hearing. Claws rip at my pant leg, but we fly free hurtling into the corridor.

A quick slip through its transparent surface sends us headlong— but which way?

All I can do is picture the loft, with Lark, Jacobs, and Curt.

Then Jess's face fills my view.

Jess.

I have to fix this.

Images flicker across the Transect's inner surface. A bearded man with sword turns a sea to ice—brothers dive from the sky in an antiquated biplane—a family rides the stars in a huge, futuristic ship—a man and a bizarre alien share a car—they all blur into a nonsensical smear of shapes.

We hurtle into light as blinding as the sun.

The world comes to an end.

Unyielding wood halts my flight. Pain shoots through my shoulders and arms. I roll over, slowly, and gasp for breath.

"He's here! He's back!" Curt bends over me. "Hey! Z. Are you okay? You made it!"

I nod weakly. "There's … no more vials. Destroyed them."

"And brought back a prize, I see." Lark nudges Nick with her shoe. "Well done. Well done, indeed."

"You're—all right?"

Jacobs shakes his head. "As if we needed help with those losers once you went after Commander Zein. They're trussed up in the hall, with your Sergeant Ambrose holding them for us."

"Ambrose?" The light's dimming outside. The snowfall's abated. Trembling legs carry me to the frigid air coming through the shattered window. Rampart's turning gold with streetlights igniting the white-coated city.

"You were gone five hours," Curt says. "I thought you were dead."

I glance at Lark. "Not dead, but somewhere unexpected."

CHAPTER TWENTY-NINE

ess needs to know what's happened.

Curt takes Lark's car to get her. If he has any qualms about bringing my wife to meet my double, he doesn't voice them.

I meet Jess at the bottom of the steps. "Hi."

"Hello." Her hands are pushed deep into her coat pockets. "Curt said it was an emergency, but he didn't say it was in this neighborhood. Why aren't you at work?"

Instead of explaining, I lead her upstairs.

Ambrose has Nick and his men trussed up, their arms and legs shackled. His radio buzzes with calls, but he keeps his hands resolutely on his hips. "You sure about this, Zein?"

"I don't have many options." I move aside so Jess can see.

She stares at Nick. He's glowering at the floor. Any pretense of being a more outgoing, charming version of me is lost. There's only the dark persona of Commander Zein.

"This is who's been taking my place since the lunch date at D'Antonio's," I say. "His name is Dominic Zein, like me, and he isn't from here."

"Where is he from, then?" Her voice is calm. It worries me more than a full-out attack.

"He's …well, he's from another version of Earth."

"Okay."

"He came to me weeks ago, offering to take my place at work functions and complete jobs. I did it so we could spend more time together. Things were getting too out of hand, and I was overloaded. His involvement helped me get control of my life, or so I thought."

Jess looks tired, and sad, though there's no sign of tears. "That would mean he's been around since Estes Park."

"Yes. Without him, I would have canceled the weekend."

"What changed?" She gestures.

"Nick isn't who he seems."

"Few of us are, apparently."

"Do you believe me?"

"I don't have much choice. Dominic, he looks *exactly* like you. He acts like you, too, though …" She bites her lip. "I knew something was wrong. You were off. Yes, you were happier and for a few days, so was I, but you went back to being at work all the time. It didn't bother me too much, or at least, I thought it didn't. Until I heard rumors about Anna."

I glare at Nick.

"Don't heap all the blame at his feet. I'd seen you look at her when you took me to company functions, and heard you talk about her. A lot." She holds up a hand, to forestall whatever argument she thinks I'm planning. "If you're going to tell me you didn't cross the line, don't. I believe you."

"Thank you."

"But I think you've come close to that line. That's why this isn't all that crazy, Dominic. A couple more steps, and you could be him." Jess takes a last stare at Nick. "I hope whatever you have planned for him, he'll be locked away."

"He will. His list of crimes includes far worse than impersonation. Jess, I want you to know—"

"Dominic, I can't. Not right now." She hurries down the stairs to the front door.

I catch her at the bottom. "That wasn't me."

"Yes, I know! The problem is I lived with 'Wasn't You' for days! Lived with him like he was you—my husband." She clutches my arm. "I can't process all this. I need time. We both do."

"I'm making this right. I'll fix it."

"I know you will." She gazes out the window, to where Curt is speaking with Loredana. "Does Curt …?"

"Yes. I tried to tell you first, but when I couldn't reach you, it had to be him." Dark thoughts slither in. "Jess … You lived with Nick."

She shakes her head. "Nothing happened between us. You—that man, I mean, who pretended to be you—violated my trust. I was not about to share my bed with him."

The air's gone out of my lungs. Her answer staves off the sickness. And yet, there is my kiss with Tabitha, flashing like a giant electronic billboard in my memories.

"Listen," she says. "All my insisting on having a child … We should probably put that talk on hold. You didn't want to continue it."

I shake my head. "What I wanted then is immaterial. Building our family, rebuilding *us*, that's what I want to make time for."

"Are you sure?"

"No. But I'm sure about us."

"Curt told me about the house." She reaches for my arm. "You're not hurt?"

"No, I'm all right. Jess, I'm sorry."

"I know." She kisses me. This is not Tabitha. This is my wife, the woman I fell in love with all those years ago. "You stay in the house."

"No. You go back there."

"Are you sure? Are you staying with Curt?"

I glance up the stairs. "I'll find somewhere."

Jacobs and I prepare our captives. They're resolutely silent.

Our trip back through the Interstice isn't as eventful as the last one. I keep a watchful eye for the beasts but catch only imagined glimpses on the shrouded terrain.

We explode out the other side, and this time, I stick the landing. Our prisoners wind up in a muttering heap. Can't say I'm heartbroken.

Jacobs kneels, bracing himself with one hand. "Really glad I didn't eat first."

"Yes, I thought the same thing."

Boots pound on the steps. Soldiers swarm the room, weapons drawn. Shouts crisscross, commands to stay down, get out hands up, submit to arrest. It isn't until Jacobs snarls at the Home Guard troops that a semblance of order returns.

"Stand down and take these three into custody," he snaps. "Where's Lark?"

"Headed up now, Sergeant." I recognize the young private from my seizure by Home Guard, seemingly eons ago. "Is that … him?"

"Commander Zein in the flesh. I want six men with him at all time. Lark will make the security arrangements. Move."

Men and women peel off at Jacobs' command. I find myself smiling, albeit wearily.

"What?" Jacobs asks.

"You sounded a great deal like your father."

Lark parts the crowd—this world's Lark, not the one of Earth I just left. It strikes me how little difference between the two there is. "Mr. Zein. Your voyage was fruitful."

I shove Nick forward.

He glares over his shoulder. "No parting words?"

"I could have killed you," I say. "If I hadn't, the thing in the Interstice would have. You're only alive because I spared you."

"Merciful, but not humble, is that it?"

"Stay away from my world, Nick, or the next time we meet, mercy will be the last thing on my mind."

Soldiers drag him away. His face is a study in puzzlement before it vanishes into the hallway shadows.

There's no snow in here, nor is it as cold as I remember. The floor has been roughly patched. Plastic covers holes in the walls and ceiling.

A worn, gray tarp covers the window.

"We've secured the area since your departure," Lark says. "Home Guard has taken possession of the city. The offensive to the west is underway, though slowly, in the winter weather. We're holding our own, thanks to yours and Sergeant Jacobs' efforts. There's no threat of smallpox, either."

I nod. "Nick took some to my world, but it's destroyed."

Lark arches an eyebrow. "Indeed. I would say we're fortunate to have you on our side, Mr. Zein. Sergeant Jacobs?"

"Ma'am?"

"I'm giving you oversight of the prisoners until we return to base. Your superiors have authorized a field commission, Second Lieutenant. Congratulations. Captain Marin's recommendation for OCS was accepted."

Jacobs grins. "Thank you, ma'am."

"Thank you. Captain Marin was quite proud. Please give me a moment with Mr. Zein."

"Yes, ma'am." He extends his hand. "God bless, Dominic. It's been a privilege."

"Thanks for everything you've done, Tyson." It's a strange thing saying the name with such fervent appreciation as we shake. "I hope we meet again."

"Either way, keep this." He digs something metallic from his pocket. Marin's ID tags. "Don't know as the Captain would mind you having these. Take them as a reminder of what we did, and of how things are linked between our worlds."

Jacobs leaves me reading Curt's name emblazoned with Marin's rank and serial number.

"You mentioned what you saw in the Interstice." Lark and I are the only ones up here, yet she's so soft-spoken she could be cooing to a baby. "Perhaps more than just the inside of the Transect."

"I broke us through. We landed in the Interstice itself."

Lark sighs. "That's nothing you were supposed to see."

"And yet I did. What is that place? It must be more than a bridge between two worlds. There are creatures living in it, and I saw …” I slam the brakes on my train of thought.

“You saw, what?”

“Images. People. Places. None of them recognizable. They didn’t make sense.”

She nods. “And the creatures did?”

“No. But I can vouch for their reality.” The weight of the monster’s evil, its sheer hatred, lingers on me, as if I’ve bathed in a polluted river.

“Good. Because they are real. Few know this. The more who do, the more complex our operations become, but I, for one, value new allies. They offer—perspective we as an organization lack.”

“We, being Procyon?”

“Yes. Our role varies depending upon where we exist, but the goal is always the same: To safeguard humanity from evil.”

I shake my head. “I thought you were helping Home Guard with the war here. And where I’m from Procyon is a charitable foundation. One that …”

“Improves the world. It’s a general enough mission statement our founders felt would cover myriad purposes.” Lark reaches for my arms. “And now, you’ve become part of it. The Echo Watch is yours.”

“I didn’t ask for either.”

“Irrelevant. Sometimes, we don’t ask for what life brings us. It does not change whether we accept the new responsibilities.”

I shake loose my sleeves. The Echo Watch—both of them—gleam in the low light. There’s a pulse to them, as if they’re amplifying mine. “I already have a life, and a job. What if I don’t accept?”

Lark smiles. “If you were not going to accept, you would not be here.”

Ambrose agrees to stay quiet. Not without complaining, of course, but what can he do? He’s in the same position I was when I considered going to the police for help. No one will believe him.

Chris's death is treated as a random criminal act by a heavily armed, deranged individual. It's revealed in the media Chris was also responsible for Tyson Jacobs' death. The truth, I suppose, if not a shade of it.

The next morning, I go to work.

Stepping through the back door of Dualpoint, setting my laptop down at my desk, sitting in the chair—all these mundane motions feel strange. Wrong. It's as if my skin is itching to do something, to be someone, and it is not the person I've been all these years.

The light on my phone indicates awaiting voicemail. I reach for the button but can't bring myself to push it.

This isn't right.

I head into the corridor.

Anna's on her way. She sees me and grins. "Hey. There you are."

Her hand drifts down my arm, and she leans in for a kiss.

I stop her, hands braced on her shoulders. "Anna, I'm sorry, but that wasn't me. What we did—it can't be undone, but there isn't anything between us."

Anna's smile fades. "You've got to be kidding. This wasn't some fluke, Dominic. I know how we've been around each other, for a long time. Long before you and I finally made our moves. And they were some moves."

"No. It wasn't what I wanted."

"Why are you doing this?" She folds her arms. "You said you'd leave her."

What a wreck. "I'm not going to say it any plainer. It's over. I've already apologized. Now, please …" I walk around her.

There's a sharp exhale, a sound of deep disgust, and she shoulders by me. The door to her office slams shut.

Kaminsky appears from his open door. "Dominic? What's going on."

"Mr. Kaminsky, I need to talk to you."

He jerks a thumb. "What did I tell you? You two fooling around isn't any of my business as long as it doesn't compromise the work of our firm—"

"I'm resigning."

His lips keep moving with whatever chastisement was coming, but no sound follows. Kaminsky removes his glasses. "No, you're not. You just became part-owner. Tyson's job is yours. We've got Procyon on our plates and a ton of work to finish."

"The designs are all there. Whatever you want me to finish, I'll handle the final details, but then I am done. Consider me a contract employee until then." I extend my hand. "I'm thankful you brought me on board, and glad I've been able to do my finest work here."

Kaminsky stares at my open hand. "Ungrateful …" He mutters. "Tyson was right the whole time. Should've shipped you back on the next flight."

He heads back for his desk. "I need you to finish Procyon, because there's no one else. When you're done, yes, you are through. And I do mean through. You think you'll get a decent recommendation from me? I'll make sure no firm from here to Denver hires you."

Such threats would have terrified me a month ago. Now, though, I smile. "I'm sure you have to do whatever is best for the firm. Keep in mind, Mr. Kaminsky, that both of us could divulge various short-comings to a very interested media—especially when it comes to matters of bias when it comes to young employees. I'm sure the *Post* would love a follow-up story on their favorite immigrant architect."

Kaminsky rolls his eyes.

I gather my things. I've no such plans to betray Dualpoint, how-ever. Tyson would do something similar, I'd imagine. But Kaminsky would neither accept nor believe my reasons for quitting.

On my way out the door for the last time, I flip a business card over in my hand.

Time to give Loredana Lark a call.

The evening crowd at Caerphilly is boisterous. I sit at the same table, far in the back, watching the crowds pass. The aroma of sizzling beef and salty fries drifts by from the kitchen. I trace lines in the glass of water, leaving clean tracks through the mess of condensation.

No one outside shares my face. I've taken care of that. Yet Nick's visage haunts me, when I close my eyes.

There's a deck of cards on the table.

"Got a lot of clients to pass along to the newbies, I take it." Curt leans back in his chair. He hasn't put his beer down. It's draining fast.

"Yes. They're not happy, but they understand, I think."

"About you taking a new job? Probably." Curt grins. "The details, though—"

"Not for public dissemination."

"I get it. I'm just kinda excited."

I frown. "About me quitting? Or living like a bachelor?"

"Well, Part B has appeal, because I get a wingman again."

"I never gave up that job."

"That's sweet, really." Curt makes a face. "Look, I don't get even a quarter of what's going on. Lark thinks there's more of them?"

I tap the deck. "She does. Father Hamra, Chris, those five men …the tip of the iceberg in terms of who Nick had smuggled over here."

"How many?"

"She doesn't know. We'll have to compare notes with the other Lark—not Loredana."

"You call this one Loredana, and the other lady Lark?"

"It's the only way I can keep them straight."

"Man. And I thought keeping track of clients was a pain. All right, Z, this whole thing's crazy but if you're making the change, I'll give you whatever help you need."

"Thanks. I really appreciate it."

"You're welcome." Curt finishes his beer. He sets the glass down with a flourish and lets out a rattling belch. No, he's definitely not searching for companionship tonight. "New question: When do I get to try one out?"

"One what?"

He gestures at my shirtsleeves.

"No. Absolutely not."

"Come on."

"It's not a smartphone, Curt, you don't get to try it out."

"Uh-huh. Sure. I'll wear you down."

"You really won't."

Curt shakes his head. "If we're done here, what's say we hit Bentley's? Not like you have a curfew anymore."

I nudge the wedding band on my ring finger. "I'm not single either."

"You guys are dumb. Kiss and make up already." Curt rises. "You got this one?"

"Yes, it's my turn, I believe."

"Good deal." He pauses in the middle of donning his coat. "Unless—someone's already paid our table."

I very much want to be irritated by him but can't help laughing. It's late by the time I get to the loft.

The bullet holes haven't been covered over, and the broken window's still in need of repair. Loredana assures me the workmen will be here tomorrow morning.

This doesn't faze Sammy. He hurries off to explore every facet of the place, sniffing each corner like a madman.

I lock the door and tip an end table upright. My work things get deposited there.

The plastic sheeting covering the broken window will suffice for tonight. Procyon can afford to splurge one day's worth of the heat being cranked up. Since I'm taking over the lease soon, it's the least they can do.

Sammy settles on the couch next to me. If he's mad about being held at the animal shelter, he doesn't show it. He huffs out a great breath and settles for me scratching his back.

With the other hand, I slide the deck of cards from its box. Dozens of faces look up from the end table.

I extract a Sharpie from my bag. Nick, Tabitha, and four of Nick's enforcers get check marks. Chris, Father Hamra, and the guard Jacobs shot each get an X.

Sammy looks up.

"Not tonight." I set the marker aside and lean back on Nick's couch. "But soon."

I stare at the pale discoloration on the floor, where the Interstice portal appeared, and wait.

Jess reaches into the refrigerator. "Where's the sauce?"

I'm buried in the new floor plans for Procyon Foundation's office complex. Seventh floor. I understand now why Loredana was adamant not to make the contents available. "By the pickles. Middle shelf."

Sammy barks. He nudges the fridge door aside.

"No, I didn't request your help." Jess pushes him from her path. She sets the jar on the counter. "Are you coming?"

"Yes, one second."

"You've let the pasta boil over."

So I did. Water spatters and hisses on the stove. I slap the laptop lid shut and sprint for it. "Thanks. My mind's wandering."

"I noticed. Will your trip take long?"

"Shouldn't be more than a half hour. Loredana has the position marked. All I have to do is wait for her signal—"

My phone buzzes. It's her. <London. Map attached with coordinates and images. Our people in position. Good hunting.>

There it is. My stomach rumbles, and it isn't because I'm hungry.

"Go on. I'll finish up what you started before you got distracted."

I kiss her cheek. She smiles and does likewise. It's as if we're high school sweethearts, even though the ache shadows our life. "Jess, tonight … I thought we'd watch a movie. Together."

"At the house?"

"That was my idea, yes."

"Okay." She winks. "Do you need directions, or do you remember the way?"

"I remember." I turn toward the center of the loft.

She catches my hand. "Be careful. I don't want to lose you, not again."

"You won't. I promise." We kiss.

We're not back to where we were. Closer, yes. There's a lot of steps between here and there.

I step to the familiar spot on the floor. Jess has Sammy by the collar. He whimpers and tries to pace.

Breathe. Pray. I extend my arms. The Echo Watches glow and spin, mirroring each other as pieces separate in anticipation of opening the Interstice portal.

Only, that doesn't happen. Not for this trip.

The pieces spread out and mingle, expanding into a circle. The same translucent shell appears, but it's thinner, like a slim void. Instead of darkness with a bright light at the center, a pinprick of white appears.

Focus. Concentrate. On London, on the coordinates …

On the person Procyon wants me to find. The first doppelgänger I need to apprehend.

The pinprick flashes out, filling the ovoid. A hazy image appears. Trees, manicured lawn, and the edge of a lake. Regent's Park.

I'm not going to the other Earth. I'm going to England, on our ID tag on its chain, feeling the raised letters of Captain Curtis Marin's name.

I glance back at Jess. "I love you."

"I love you, always."

This is me, now. This is what Nick's interference created. I know what's beyond the doorway that I'm staring into.

Purpose.

I step through.

Follow Dominic's adventures in…

Mercury for Hire

Mercury at Risk

Mercury out Cold

Mercury with Style

Interstice Undone
(with J.J. Johnson & Jason Joyner)

www.ingramcontent.com/pod-product-compliance
Lightning Source LLC
Chambersburg PA
CBHW051204190726
48288CB00006B/1809